Stories from Lone Moon Creek

Teresa Millias

*To Roger and Pat ~
Enjoy the stories!
Teresa Millias
3/30/17*

BRIGHTON PUBLISHING LLC
435 N. HARRIS DRIVE
MESA, AZ 85203

Stories from Lone Moon Creek

Teresa Millias

Brighton Publishing LLC
435 N. Harris Drive
Mesa, AZ 85203
www.BrightonPublishing.com

ISBN 13: 978-1-62183-270-6

ISBN 10: 1-62183-270-8

Printed in the United States of America

First Edition

Cover Design by: Tom Rodriguez

Table of Contents

Dedication

TO THE HOLY SPIRIT AND TO YOU, THE READER.

✒Prologue✒

Who are the people of rural America? Are they the forgotten breed? Will they ever matter again?

They don't fit into conventional norms; their backgrounds are as diverse as Edna's quilts hanging over the clothesline on airing day.

Somehow they live and work together as well as do the vibrations of the train whistle which blend with the dewy grass. Newcomers are accepted by the natives as long as they don't incinerate someone's back shed or let their children beat up the little kids on the school bus.

Underneath all the trials and quagmires of life, somewhat like Bert's potato field, is a goodness which emerges as sure as does a thunderstorm on a humid August day. Some say it is God, others don't say it's not.

Rural people all have their histories, but don't we all?

Agnes and Marjory will lead you into each chapter, so meander through Lone Moon Creek and acquaint yourself with some of the folks.

ᚳ᯼Chapter One᯼ᚲ

ON A MISSION

"**Y**es, I saw what's all over the paper and on the news channel, too.

I'm afraid these kids today don't know what they're doing.

She could have stayed home and worked this summer, maybe at that technical house with all the gadgets, or out to the Butcher Shop," Agnes ranted to the wide eyed Marjory.

᯼᯼

"Oh, Kaitlyn, are you sure this is something you need to do?"

"Yes, Mom. This is my last summer of freedom and I promised myself I'd do something nice for other people, not my usual sunbathing on the beach," Kaitlyn answered with determination as she extended her legs onto the deck railing to capture the sunshine.

"But those foreign countries. You know how they are."

"Mom, our group has spent two years researching all of this and we know exactly what we're getting into."

"Well, I hope so. But you know there's plenty of missionary work you could do right here in our own country."

"I know, but we all agreed that going into a third-world country would give us a better picture of the need for God."

"I don't think God expects you young people to put your lives in danger just to spread His word."

"Mother! I can't believe you said that! Ever since I was little you always talked about the brave missionaries who went to dangerous places for God."

"Well, they weren't my daughter."

"Mom, don't cry," Kaitlyn whispered into her mother's soft hair as she hugged her.

"Are we having a sad moment out here?"

"Yes, Dad. Come here and join our crying circle."

"My little girl, being so brave. I'm proud of you, Kaitlyn."

"Thanks, Dad."

"He may be proud, but he's worried, too; he prays for you every single night, Kaitlyn."

"Oh, Dad, that's so sweet. I know I'll be all right. It's such a great opportunity. Besides, when I have my own class in September, I can tell them real stories about real people. Young kids today need to hear that, you know."

"Young kids?" Doug laughed. "You're beginning to sound like one of us old fuddy-duddies. It wasn't that long ago when you were one of the 'young kids.'"

"I know, but college has been good for me; I feel like I have really grown up. I am so thankful that I joined the Global Peace Club. I never knew how aimlessly I was drifting through life."

"You weren't drifting aimlessly," Ruth said defensively. She looked at her daughter not knowing if there was going to be a debate or not.

"Are you sure you have everything? Do you have your ticket, your passport, your visa, your camera, your..."

"Mom!" Kaitlyn laughed. "I know I have everything. We're boarding in one hour—I better have everything!"

Kaitlyn turned one more time to wave and throw kisses. As their group walked the long corridor of the airport in silence, she surprisingly remembered mostly how her little brothers suddenly looked more like a 'Joe' and a 'Jim' instead of Joey and Jimmy. Surprisingly, too, was how tiny and frail Grandma looked. Mom was normal—crying and hanging onto Dad; Dad was normal—standing strong and protective; Kristin was normal—beautiful and quiet.

∽

"Ah," Kaitlyn sighed as she nestled down into her airline seat, "we made it! We're on our way…"

"Was your family all bent out of shape like mine was?" Allie asked, rolling her eyes.

"Oh, yes! I guess it's good to go away. You find out how much they really love you."

"You're right! I couldn't believe my mother! What a nut-case she was becoming."

"Well, I suppose someday we'll have daughters; then we'll know what they're feeling."

"Yeah."

∽

The lone bird flew effortlessly through the sky, as the living beings inside began to feel as though they'd already eaten the sprinkles from the top of the ice cream cone. Gone, too, was the indescribable lusciousness of the first five licks of the confection. Now the dry cone with the disappointing emptiness at the bottom had settled onto the troupe—on the last leg of the long flight.

Kaitlyn took out the tattered and yellowed prayer-card her Grandmother had given her. On it was the prayer that her grandmother asserted she'd said a million times so Grandpa would return home safely from the Second World War.

3

Kaitlyn wondered what her family was doing right now. She'd have lots of stories to tell when she returned home.

∽

"This isn't so bad, is it Kaitlyn?" Allie whispered from her cot to Kaitlyn's cot.

"It really isn't. I'm surprised!" Kaitlyn whispered back.

"We're lucky the other groups paved the way for us; at least we have shelter and food and latrines. I wouldn't have wanted to be in the first group."

"Me neither."

No one talked after that, even though Kaitlyn was sure they were all talking to God each in his or her own way.

∽

The days were spent building and gardening, teaching and nursing. The evenings were spent in singing, and sometimes dancing. The previous volunteers had broken the ice, so now it was relatively easy to develop friendships with the homeland people. They had already learned to trust and knew that the "do-gooders" were there only to help and to display peace. The little children were delightful in their shyness, but never were they fearful. The women were coming forward with their problems and needs. The men worked side by side with the Americans, knowing this was to benefit them and their families. Everyone, young and old, seemed to enjoy the colorful brochures about God.

One night as the visitors and their new friends sat under the stars with the campfire flaming to create a universal, mesmerizing force for all, Kaitlyn leaned toward Allie and said, "Hasn't God given us the most wonderful opportunity in being here?"

"He certainly has," Allie answered. "I will never regret this trip as long as I live."

4

All the cots in the girls' quarters were warmed by thankful bodies that night, happy bodies, American bodies who were proud of themselves for giving up their summer beach houses and parties and cars. In less than two months the village would have three new houses and the produce from the garden would be ripe. Another cow and five goats would have arrived and all the boxes of clothes from their college peers would be there. Two native women would be trained in medical situations, and worshiping God would be a daily practice.

All was well in the sleeping missionary camp for maybe three hours. Four hours? No one knew for sure. Not even the beautiful, intelligent Kaitlyn whose body felt something like steel grips being pressed into her skin and whose mouth and nose were smothered—with what? A rag? A shirt? She didn't know. The others didn't know. Where did her consciousness go? She didn't know. No one knew.

That was when the Global Peace Club went home.

They left, not smiling at the natives; they left not finishing their projects; they left not really convincing the bewildered eyes about God. Everyone went back to his or her family. Everyone except Kaitlyn. They couldn't find Kaitlyn.

Kaitlyn's mother, Ruth, was put on medication; her father, Doug smoked two packs of cigarettes a day; brothers Joe and Jim became "Joseph" and "James"; and her sister, Kristin, never talked.

Government agencies busied themselves; embassies bustled with anger; the media had a prime story; investigators reluctantly postponed their summer vacations; and Kaitlyn still breathed—she knew she was alive, but that's all she knew.

Her body was not her body anymore, it didn't stretch or reach or bend or dance. It was a carousel horse with big beautiful glass eyes that stared into blackness. If it had to be upward, fingers like vices moved it upward. If it had to be moved downward, the vices came again to move it downward. She remembered that the beautiful

5

carousel horses that Mommy and Daddy took her on always had a pole to balance herself with. Kaitlyn couldn't understand why she couldn't find the pole.

She drifted in and out of consciousness wondering why a tight mask was over her eyes.

Were she and Kristin putting on that play again? Maybe. She felt for the fluffy pink, satin costume that she always wore. Kristin would have on the pretty yellow one.

Then came the cloth with the funny smell on it and Kaitlyn slipped into more of her strange world.

She knew Daddy had to get rid of those nasty bees. They had stung her several times in the arm; in fact, always in the same area. She could feel the stinger go right into her skin. Kaitlyn knew Daddy would get rid of them. Daddy could do anything.

Kaitlyn didn't know why her arm didn't come up but then she remembered she was the Palomino Horse, no, the Appaloosa. She would be the Appaloosa today, with the wreath of pink roses around her neck.

She went up, she went down, and sometimes she heard faint voices. A roar? *Why am I hearing a roar? I'm on an airplane/ Oh, no that rag again and...*

...another bee stinging me! Daddy, come!

Oh, I better get up; I have an eight o'clock class today.

Why am I so stiff and sore? I can't even move. No, no, not again.

"I'm sorry, Mrs. Anderson," little Kaitlyn cried. "I'm sorry, I didn't mean to do it in my pants. I couldn't get out of the Monkey Bars; those boys wouldn't let me out."

"It's all right, Kaitlyn, accidents happen. I called your Mom, she'll be right over to take you home and clean you up. Honey, stop crying, it's okay."

"No, it's not okay; I hate this. I hate this smell."

"Mommy, mommy, I'm sorry."

"Honey, it's okay. Let's get you home."

"Mommy, I can't stand this!" The sobbing continued.

They hurried up the stairs to the pristine pink and white bathroom with the matching towels and bubble bath soaps and the ruffled white curtains on the window.

"There, all fresh and clean. Do you feel better?" Ruth cooed as she wrapped her teary daughter in a huge, soft towel.

"Yes," sniffled the little girl as she put her arms around her mother's neck and hugged her tightly. *"I never want this to happen again."*

"Don't worry, Kaitlyn. It won't happen again. I promise."

Kaitlyn tried to bolt upright. The strain she forced upon the cinches, which bound her arms and legs, caused all her muscles to seize-up like something...

...like something when Kaitlyn heard Daddy say to Grandpa that the motor on their boat had seized-up. Grandma and Mommy giggled about the men's shoptalk and never dreamed to ever want to understand it.

"What has happened to me?" Kaitlyn's brain registered the question as a wave of panic spread over her...

...like hot molasses rolling throughout the streets and into the houses.

She began screaming like she had learned to do in a self-defense class in college, "Help! Help! Help me! Help!"

She heard a loud scuffling of feet. She felt the vices with fingernails and the sting. Now she knew it was a needle going into her arm. "Oh, my God, *no!*" she yelled, only to have her last word fade into a crevice of the cell wall.

A little figure in the diagonal corner of the tiny room sat on her mat and counted Kaitlyn's breaths. *Breaths!* thought Bridgett. *Real breaths!*

Bridgett discontinued the counting and let the little breath sounds permeate her ears, as would a virtuoso listen to a symphony of rain. If she could only encapsulate the living sounds and save them to enjoy when she knew she would be alone again for years at a time.

Bridgett didn't know what was going through Kaitlyn's sleeping mind as she periodically expelled mutterings of diverse exclamations. A lot of terror seemed to prevail through the ranting, but occasionally the sweetest little sounds traveled across the dirt floor to the permanent tenant. Bridgett couldn't help but cry when she heard sounds that reminded her of her own childhood, years ago. "Thank you, God," Bridgett whispered. "Thank you for bringing this girl to me."

Bridgett sat and stared at the American, still bound in captivity. As the light from the sole, high window slowly moved across Kaitlyn's face, Bridgett studied every centimeter of it. The delight in seeing a companion was priceless. No museum could hold a more valuable sight to Bridgett. "Thank you, God, for this treasure," she whispered.

The veteran captive knew better than to assist the new girl. She wanted to release her hands and feet, but she knew better. She wanted to remove the tight cloth from around her eyes, but she knew better. All she could do was soak in her presence, bask in her breathing, and thank God for her.

Kaitlyn's consciousness came back ever so slowly, creeping in like a child not wanting to show his mother the grass stains on his new khaki pants. Bridgett sensed the girl was going to scream again, so she risked enunciating an audible, "Shhh."

Immediately Kaitlyn turned toward the sound. "Who's there?" she whispered as she tried to pull to the opposite direction.

The heavy door swung open with a jolt. Bridgett pulled her knees up under her chin, pushing her back into the angle of the corner, and Kaitlyn lay paralyzed.

The man barked orders to Bridgett and then left.

Bridgett crawled across the dirt floor to the trembling woman. "Shhh, don't be afraid. I am Bridgett. I will help you."

A volcano of relief gushed out of Kaitlyn's mouth—so much so that Bridgett put her hand over the soft mouth and said, "Don't make noise, they hate noise."

Kaitlyn curtailed her sobbing sounds, but the volcano came out of her shoulders, which pulsated and heaved with her silent crying.

"Shhh, shhh," Bridgett kept saying as she used her crippled fingers to remove the blinders from Kaitlyn's eyes.

Kaitlyn looked out of her eyes and saw nothing—she was one of the merry-go-round horses with glass eyes. What would her mother think when she learned her daughter had gone blind? Slowly, slowly, however, she noticed first the light from the small window. But that wasn't her focus. Her focus was the person who was helping her. She stared at the figure kneeling beside her. Everything facing her was in blackness; she saw only a profile because the window permitted light only on the person's back.

Bridgett started using her fingers to work out the knots that bound Kaitlyn's hands. The light now allowed itself to spread across Bridgett's hands. Kaitlyn could see huge joints and three missing fingernails and scars and roughness. With the little bit of dexterity Bridgett had, she worked over the knots with the dedication of a surgeon. Kaitlyn was thinking of the monumental hurdle that the knots had compelled the little woman to overtake when she suddenly became very aware of her own stench. A stench permeated from her entire body.

"Bridgett, I'm sorry, I'm sorry," Kaitlyn cried as she hung her head in shame.

"Shhh, they'll hear you."

Kaitlyn pushed her mouth into her own shoulder to stifle the sobs. She mumbled, "God, help me, help me."

Bridgett could not undo the last knot until she used her teeth to pull the rope one way and pull with her fingers the other way.

When the release came, Kaitlyn immediately rubbed her wrists and her arms and her shoulders and her hands. Now she could use her hands to bury her face and cry.

When she realized her liberator was struggling with the foot binding and she wasn't doing a thing to help her, she bent down to use her long, straight fingers to help with the tight knots. As they worked, Kaitlyn exploded with a litany of questions: "Bridgett, why are we here? Where are we? What is going to happen?"

"Shh, I'll talk later after they sleep. Lay down and be quiet."

Kaitlyn buried her face in the crook of her arm and cried. She wanted to be home; she wanted her family; she wanted her quaint little Lone Moon Creek; she wanted her America. She started praying, "God, please help me, please get me out of here, spare me from this demoralization, come to help me, please, please." Something made her pause. She lifted her head to hear the tiniest of sounds. She stared at the blackness of the corner. Out of the opaqueness, came wee little tones. Tones—as from vocal chords, tones coming out of Bridgett. Bridgett was singing a tune in the quietest of voices, much like her sister used to do when she was painting her fingernails or making cookies.

How could she sing? How could anyone in here sing? Anger arose in Kaitlyn almost to the point of scaring herself. How could she sing?

The American returned to her crying.

Suddenly the door boomed open. Kaitlyn jolted to her hands and knees. A huge doorway of light nearly blinded her; she used her hands to shield her eyes, and between the cracks of her fingers she saw the profile of a man, who again yelled commands to Bridgett.

Kaitlyn quickly looked at the singing, corner-lady to see her completely enveloped in lightness.

Oh, my God! Kaitlyn thought as she gasped at the sight of the woman—a tiny figure sat in the corner with...with...no feet.

Kaitlyn remembered seeing all sorts of pretty, sparking, little specks of neon lights, and that's all she remembered.

"Kristin, I'm so glad you came to the beach today as she lay on the sand letting the surf come up upon their feet and legs.

Kaitlyn quickly pulled her feet back and sat up startled.

"It's all right, honey. You're in the washroom."

Washroom? Kait thought as she looked around at the trees. She was in a puddle, a large puddle. She was in brown, muddy water. She jolted to her feet, but went back down when Bridgett said, "Sit."

"I'm not bathing in this smelly, brown water!" Kaitlyn arrogantly said.

"You are the one who made it brown," Bridgett retorted just as arrogantly.

"Oh," came Kait's meek response when she realized what Bridgett meant.

Bridgett mellowed, too, and softly said, "You get the worst off, then we'll move to the cleaner water."

Kaitlyn was thankful for the water and yet she could hardly bear to be in it. She cried as she had to scrape the crusted residue from her body with her fingernails. She thought of her mother's sparkling pink and white bathroom. She lifted her teary eyes to heaven and prayed, "Lord, where are you? Come to my rescue."

Bridgett called out, "I'll be right over there by the cleaner water when you're ready. I'll have a clean pants and shirt for you to change into."

Kaitlyn watched the woman crawl onto a board that had small yellow wheels and then lie on it like a surfboard, using her hands to push against the ground. As the board went forward, she listened to the wheels squeak the entire way. She stared at the ends of the woman's stumps.

Kait used her old shirt to hold in front of her as she used a stick to hurl her pants into the brown puddle. She never wanted to see them again. She ran to the next puddle. She had never been in such a humiliating circumstance in her whole life, she thought.

Kaitlyn felt, maybe, eighty-five per cent cleaner when Bridgett suddenly shouted in a whisper, "Get out now! They're coming!" Kait somehow managed to get her wet body into the cotton uniform when they appeared. Two men in nice uniforms stood facing the American. They looked from her head to her feet, from her feet toher head and down again.

Kait became a terrified statue and Bridgett never moved a muscle on her board, at least the wheels didn't squeak. The men turned and spoke to each other in an Oriental language, unfamiliar to the college graduate. She thought of different countries but she didn't know. She could hear them laughing as they walked through the barricade of trees.

Kaitlyn put her hand to her stomach, her other hand went to her head; she felt every pore in her body begin to spin.

"Mom, is dinner ready yet? I'm starving."

"Give me two more minutes; I've made all your favorites – roast beef, mashed potatoes, gravy, carrot and raisin salad, and warm apple pie with vanilla ice cream."

Kaitlyn opened her eyes wondering why she was watching the dirt move past her face at a distance of about six inches. What was that awful squeaking? She knew she was starving and weak; she couldn't even lift her head until she wondered how the surfboard was moving. With blurred vision she thought she saw the footless woman pulling the board as she crawled along in front.

No, Kaitlyn thought, *that can't be.* She closed her eyes and thought that probably the squeaking noise was Grandma out on the porch swing.

"Come on, dear. Take a little more. That's it. Open your mouth. Swallow, that's it. One more spoonful, one more. Swallow. Good girl. We'll have more after a little while."

Bridgett went back to her corner as the young missionary slept. She was filled with emotion and thanked God for bringing the young girl to her. This was Bridgett's miracle!

Again Kaitlyn awoke to quiet singing in the dark. This time it brought her comfort.

"Bridgett?" Kait called out in a nighttime whisper.

"Yes?"

"I have to go to the bathroom."

"Okay, put your hand on my back and I'll lead you outside."

"Don't you want your board?"

"No, no. It's too noisy."

The two women, one walking stooped over and the other crawling, quietly left the hut.

"Thanks, Bridgett."

"Can you eat a little more soup now?"

"I think so."

"Good. What's your name?"

"Kaitlyn."

"Oh, that's very pretty."

"Why am I here, Bridgett?" Kait asked, starting to cry again.

"I don't really know, Kaitlyn. Maybe it's my fault."

"Your fault?"

"Well, I've prayed so hard and for so long that God would grant me a miracle. I think you are my miracle."

"No, I'm not! That doesn't even make sense," Kait said angrily.

"Kaitlyn, I've been here for almost forty years, by myself, I mean alone from people of my own hemisphere. They chopped off my feet when I tried to run away."

"Eww, I'm going to be sick; I'm going to throw up."

"Grab my back, we're going out!"

❧

"Are you feeling better this morning?"

"I don't know."

"Let's get you outside for awhile."

"We can go out?"

"They know I can't go too far. Of course," Bridgett paused, "they don't know about you, yet."

Both women looked at Kaitlyn's feet. Kait curled her toes under.

Bridgett braced herself against a tree while Kait sat beside her, both looking down into a luscious green valley.

Bridgett let her eyes slowly swoop across the valley. Kait, for the first time, noticed Bridgett's unevenly cut white hair. "It used to be fire red," Bridgett interjected.

"Huh?"

"My hair."

"Oh."

"Ah, yes. A young Irish lassie right from the Emerald Isle, who went out to change the world—but who never made it back home."

"What do you mean?" Kait asked with a sick feeling in her stomach.

"I was a young woman who went out to tell the world about God."

"And God punished you for it?"

"Oh, no! He didn't punish me. He brought me here to find Him! I didn't know God, Kaitlyn. How could I tell other people about someone or something I didn't even know about?"

"He's here? In this place? You're crazy, I mean...I didn't mean to say that Bridgett, you've been so good to me, but maybe your mind has started to go."

Bridgett laughed so hard and so long, she brought the attention of two soldiers. They watched the women for awhile, and then walked away.

"Oh, it's so good to hear opinions from...what country are you from?"

"America."

"...opinions from America!"

After the laughter nestled deep into the green trees of the valley below, Kait leaned toward Bridgett and whispered, "How am I going to get out of this place?"

"I don't know, child. Just don't try escaping the way I tried."

Kaitlyn wanted to control her eyes, but unsuccessfully she looked down at Bridgett's uneven skin. "I've got to lie down," she muttered as her face turned snow white.

As Kaitlyn drifted to sleep, Bridgett wondered if the girl would still be there next winter when the snow would be so cruel.

"Where did all of this come from?" Kait asked as she roused herself and rubbed her eyes focusing in on vegetables and fruit.

"Oh, some of the neighbors saw me sitting up here on the hill and came to visit."

For a minute, Kait thought she was back home, but no, she knew. "What do you mean 'neighbors'?"

"The people who live down there in the valley; I call them my neighbors."

Kait sat staring at the footless woman wondering which of them was losing her mind. "Aren't you a prisoner here?"

"Yes, actually I am," the older woman said with a smile.

"And?"

"And what?"

Kait raised her knees to hold her elbows and used her hands to hold her head. "Okay, let's start with, why did they bring you this food?"

"They like me, I guess."

"The guards don't mind if they visit you?"

"Oh, no. They don't mind at all."

"Why are you a prisoner?"

"As long as I'm here, my family, town, and parish send money to these people."

"What?"

"I guess they don't want me to be killed, so they send money for my protection."

"You mean, like a ransom?"

"I think that's what you would call it. I'm not really sure."

"So the money is supporting these people?"

"Isn't it wonderful?" Bridgett answered as her green eyes sparkled like dew upon shamrocks. "These people are so poor. My people aren't. They can afford to send money here every month."

"But they are doing it for you. They're not doing it to help the needy and the impoverished."

"Exactly! And shame on them!" Bridgett exclaimed loudly as she slammed her hand down upon the ground.

"So if you weren't here, these people wouldn't get the...money," Kaitlyn let her voice trail off into the one lone cloud.

Bridgett didn't affirm Kait's statement; she only thanked God that these people weren't starving.

"Wait a minute!" Kait suddenly broke the silence. "Do you want to be here?"

"Yes, I do! What good could I do for these people back home? I would talk myself blue in the face before I could convince anyone to send a few pennies to the people here. Besides, I have found the peace of God in this place. As much as I thought I had it before, it wasn't even a dollop compared to what I have now."

"But why did you try to escape?"

"Oh, my goodness. When they first brought me here, I was like a wild cat! All I could think of was escaping to get home. I wanted my family and my friends. That's why I said earlier I didn't know God when I, in my pride, went out to teach others about Him. I had no idea of His love or His mercy, to say nothing about His plans for me!"

"Love? Mercy? Why did He let your feet get chopped off?" Kaitlyn asked with tears in her eyes and sweat droplets on her forehead.

"He didn't want that, sweetheart. In my arrogance and defiance I brought that upon myself. I know you can't understand all of this, but it has become my blessing—even though I will always regret my foolishness. I didn't even care, back in those days, if they killed me. Now what good would I have been to anyone then?"

The young college grad put her hands over her face and cried until all of the Far East must have wondered why there seemed to be sadness upon their hearts.

A guard came over, but Bridgett motioned him to leave. She waited for Kaitlyn to get this all out of her system, remembering decades before how she had done the same thing.

Finally the wailing that pierced the air of the East quieted, the birds ventured to chirp again, the mothers in the village below released their children from their arms, the guards tempered their guilt with a strong cigarette, and Kaitlyn looked up. She looked up into the sad eyes of a little boy who had climbed the hill to see the wailing woman.

In those child's dark eyes Kaitlyn could see...Kaitlyn understood.

"This is why you can't leave, right Bridgett?"

"You're right, Kaitlyn. We are all children of God. They are our brothers and sisters."

"Oh, my God!" Kait groaned.

"Shh, honey, shh," Bridgett hushed her friend as she linked their arms and rocked back and forth on the green grass.

The little boy put a wildflower in front of Bridgett and one in front of Kait, and then ran home. Kaitlyn's was pink.

The two women sat for a long time not saying a word.

As before, the woman with the most questions broke the silence, "Why don't they give you a better house and better clothes?"

"Ah, you Americans!" Bridgett giggled. "I don't want anything better than what they have. Why would I?"

"It's just all so strange to me," Kaitlyn said quietly.

"It takes a lot of getting used to, I know. I lived back in the materialistic world at one time, too, you know."

"And God is there, too!" Kaitlyn snapped defensively.

"Indeed He is! But I think His heart is with His children who need the most help."

"Oh, my God; you are so right," Kait uttered as she lay back on the grass, curling up like a child. "How did they choose me? How did they zero in on me? Our group was thousands of miles from here in a different country."

"I'm sure it was just a random pick."

Up bolted the American. "It could have been Allie or Ashley or Lindsey or...why me?"

"Yes? Why you?"

Kaitlyn didn't quite know how to take Bridgett's last comment but she didn't dwell on it, as a sudden rush of emotion crept into her heart as she thought about her friends—they must be worried sick. And her family! Oh, dear God, she couldn't imagine what hell her family was going through.

She twirled at Bridgett and screamed, "How could you do this to your family? This is very selfish of you!"

"They know I'm alive and that I'm well," she said quietly.

"Do they know about your feet?" Kait continued to snarl.

"No. They don't need to know that."

"You don't want these foreigners to suffer, but you make your own family suffer! What's the matter with you?" Kait snapped again.

"Decisions in life are hard, honey. It's taken me years to absolutely know that this is the best place for me to be."

"Daddy," Kaitlyn cried out.

"I know, sweetheart, I know."

"You don't know! I want to go home! If you think I'm here to be your replacement—forget it!" Kaitlyn screamed as she jumped up to run.

Bridgett unsuccessfully lurched forward to grab hold of Kaitlyn, but she fell forward, her face smacking the ground.

"Kaitlyn, No! Don't run!" she screamed.

How could there suddenly be a rock in the well-worn path to trip Kaitlyn just as the bullet whizzed past her ear? How could Bridgett have used her board so quickly and adeptly to get to Kaitlyn? How could she have thrown her body on top of the escapee if a second bullet was to come?

Only God knew.

"How very, very generous my family and friends and town and church have been for the past ten years," Kaitlyn remarked as she fed Bridgett her soup.

"I'm glad." The old woman smiled.

⟪Chapter Two⟫

The Boxcar

"**Y**es, it is still open; Esther works there. I have no idea what she does in Herman's butcher shop.

No, Marjory. We're not driving four miles out of town to buy hot dogs today."

❧

Esther let her finger slide slowly along the shininess of the blade. One millimeter below the honed edge was her thick fingernail—the same one that had been smashed in the boxcar.

"Esther! You're not here to daydream! Get those knives sharpened!"

Esther's dark eyes rolled silently to view the obese, bloodstained apron stretched across the even fatter stomach. She didn't speak. He knew she wouldn't.

Esther let the whetstone sail across the blade graduating into a *clickety-clack* rhythm—the same rhythm of the boxcars.

The obese man let the side of beef slam to the table as he used one of Esther's scalpels to pierce its flesh.

Esther's head bobbed to the motion of her work much as had the eighty or so heads she remembered in the stifling train car. "Where were they going?" her eyes would ask as she stared upon her mother's staid profile. She wondered the same thing with every jolt of the train. The last command of *hush* forced Esther to see deep into her mother's eyes and know she was never to ask again.

Esther picked up the next butcher's knife as the light fleetingly glared from the blade. She remembered how she had to cover her eyes when the huge steel door rolled open to force more people into the sweatbox, or to yank people out. Why? Where was "out"? She did not know.

"How can she sit there every day and sharpen knives?" Russ mumbled to Ethan as they sliced the white fat from the steaks.

"Beats me," Ethan responded. "I think she's crazy anyhow."

"Yeah, those damn eerie songs she gets going on give me the creeps. Doesn't she know any American songs?"

"I doubt it. She doesn't even talk right."

"Shh. She's looking at us," Russ whispered as he threw a hunk of fat into the pail.

"Christ almighty. Don't make eye contact with her. She could stare the warts off a hog!"

Esther remembered staring into the soldiers' eyes, trying to read their minds, trying to find why she and her mother were being herded away. Away from their beautiful home, away from Papa and Rufus. She knew the answer would be in their eyes if she could only look deeply enough. After all, she always knew what her Papa was thinking; of course his eyes were kind like Mama's and Rufus'. But Esther couldn't find the answer in the wild ones, no matter how desperately she stared.

"Psst! She's getting up," whispered Russ wearing a stuffed pig grin.

"Oh God, this is going to be hysterical!" Ethan snickered.

The two young men ceased their fat trimming as they watched with lowered heads and raised eyeballs.

Esther's one leg jutted out first, her good leg. Upon that limb she pushed down with her hands to swirl the not-so-good side around, the side that had been crushed under the rocks as she and her mother had peered out at the black boots. Esther pushed on the tabletop as her body creakily arose. She stood motionless as the ravages of war marched across every bone in her body. She paused and waited for the pain to retreat. The young shoulders silently shook with laughter as old Esther drew step by step to the slaughterhouse. The door closed on the hooting and howling of the younger generation.

"What the hell's the matter with her anyway?" Ethan laughed.

"Probably arthritis or something," Russ chortled as he stabbed the point of the knife into the rump roast.

"Would you two shut up. Just shut up for once," screamed a voice from the corner.

The two pair of eyes looked over at the hair-netted girl with what looked like fire coming from her eyes.

"Yeah, yeah, shut up yourself, Nerdy." Russ scowled as he wielded Esther's exquisitely sharpened knife through the roast as if it was butter.

Esther paused just inside the slaughterhouse door, as she did each and every time. She took deep breaths as she steadied herself with one hand and reached for her large handkerchief with the other. Even with the coldness of the compartment, she wiped the perspiration from her face and continued the process around to the back of her neck.

"I don't know why Herman keeps her," Sharon whispered to Sarah as they walked past the old woman.

"Yeah, I don't either, but she sure can sharpen a knife."

"That's true."

Esther slowly pushed against the inner cold door to expose the dangling carcasses. She hurried along the row the best she could, fearing someday she would lose her footing and brush against the bloody flesh. She knew she never took a breath through the hedgerow of carcasses; it wasn't until she sank into her wooden chair that she inhaled. From there, her mind always saw the unfocused rows of people—rows and rows clinging to barbed wire.

$$\infty$$

"Esther! What are you staring at?"

"Oh, oh, Herman. I am sorry. Nothing, nothing. I am staring at nothing."

"Are you all right?"

"Yes, yes. Thank you," Esther answered slowly.

"How's everything at home? Did the roofer show up to fix the leak?"

"Oh yes. Yes, thank you, but you did not have to do that."

"It was the least I could do," he spoke in a whisper as he touched her shoulder.

Esther began sharpening the knives as she thought about the kindness of Herman.

"Put it in anyway," she heard Ethan say to Russ.

"Do you think I should?"

"Why not, nobody is going to know."

"Somebody might get sick."

"Oh, hell, time they barbecue this meat, all the badness will be cooked out."

"You jerks!" Moriah screamed. "You can't do that!"

"Shut up, Nerdy. You can't tell us what to do."

The hair-netted girl pushed the elastic off her eyebrows and scowled. "I'm going to tell the boss."

"You tell Herman and I'll put this knife to your throat," Russ growled as he pointed the blade toward her neck.

Ester's arm jerked. She winced, and looked at her fingertips. Somehow she thought she hadn't cut herself, but then, out of each invisible slice came a rising ridge of red. She stared at the blood and saw helpless eyes, eyes that protruded beyond the starving gray faces; eyes that saw death all around; the eyes of her mother, which cried for her.

"Esther!" Moriah screamed. "What happened?" The girl ran to the flooded hand of red. "Get Herman!" she shouted to her archenemies as they stared at the unmoving statue.

Moriah quickly wrapped her white handkerchief around Esther's hand.

"Oh," whispered Esther, "oh, I am sorry. I am all right."

Herman called across the rows of carcasses as he ran to her, "Esther! Are you okay?"

"Oh yes, yes; this is nothing, nothing. I am sorry. Everyone go back to work. This is nothing."

"Keep your hand up and press into the handkerchief," Moriah said calmly.

"You sound like a nurse," Esther smiled weakly.

"I have lots of brothers and sisters, that's all."

"Oh, how nice! I had a brother once."

Herman stammered and wiped the sweat from his overheated face. "Moriah, take Esther into the Lone Moon Clinic, would you?"

"Sure."

"No, no, I am fine. This is nothing."

"Yes, Esther you are going. And here, Moriah, use this to buy yourself and Esther some lunch. Russ and Ethan, let's get back to work."

Russ glanced at the tainted meat.

"Did you think Russ was going to hurt me with the knife?"

"The knife? Oh, I remember," Esther said slowly. "I didn't know what he might do. It is very hard to be around you young people. It does not seem that you understand about many things."

"What things?"

"Well, you three are always fighting, always arguing, always disrespectful to each other."

"But Esther, you see how they are; they are pigs."

"They are people; you are all God's people," Esther said with a volume that caused nine people in the waiting room to look.

Moriah quickly grabbed a magazine from the pile. "They laugh at you, Esther. I try to defend you," she whispered behind the pages.

"I know you do, dear, and I thank you, but I think they do it to make you angry."

"Well," Moriah said haughtily as she snapped the magazine, "you might be right, but you see what slobs they are. They don't even care about spoiled pieces of meat."

Esther stopped talking. She swallowed an overabundance of saliva as the room became unfocused, and as clear as day she could hear herself talking to her mother. "Mama, I am so hungry."

"Hush, child, hush. Everyone is hungry, but we can't eat that; it will make us sick."

"Esther, are you all right?" Moriah called out as she sprang to her feet.

"Oh, I am sorry, and yes, maybe, if I could have some water?"

"Why were you telling your mother you were hungry?"

"I was?"

"Well, never mind, when we finish here I'm going to take you for a nice lunch."

Moriah pounded dollops and dollops of catchup onto her French fries, as she asked, "How's your burger, Esther?"

"It is delicious. I did not realize I was so hungry."

"Just hope this beef didn't come from Russ and Ethan," Moriah exclaimed, as she rolled her eyes and peeked under the hamburger bun.

"Oh Moriah, for heaven's sake, set your thoughts on higher things."

"What do you mean, 'higher'?"

Esther lifted her face, and her eyes seemed to stare through the art deco poster hanging over their booth. Moriah looked at the print and wondered why the old woman was transfixed; it didn't look at all like something that would interest Esther. But somehow, for Esther, the bold lines and starkness brought back her mother's directive: *Keep you thoughts on higher things. Think of beautiful mountains and flowers; golden tabernacles and candles; picnics and music boxes; Grandma's pastries and dancing.* And it was with those thoughts that Esther could fall asleep on the wooden floor, as the blanket of death spread over her people.

"Esther?"

"Oh, I'm sorry," Esther uttered as she looked to see that all the niceties from her burger had slipped downward and now sat in a pile on her plate.

"What higher things were you talking about?"

"Well, instead of being annoyed all day, maybe you could think of things that you like."

"Like what?"

"Moriah. You are not a child. Think!"

"Well," said Moriah slowly as she held a French fry much like the soldiers used to hold their cigarettes, "I suppose I like to think about cats."

"Cats? Well then, cats it is," Esther said as she used her hand to try and cover a giggle. "And what else?"

"What? More?"

"Yes. I think more if you are going to get through the entire day."

Moriah's face strained with thought, as Esther watched her make the soda rise in the straw.

"Man, this is hard," the young girl groaned as the brown liquid again sank to the bottom.

"Maybe that could be your goal: to think of pleasant things to dwell upon while you are at work."

"Yeah...maybe it could!" Moriah's face brightened.

Esther wondered if the glimmer of hope she saw in Moriah's eyes was the same glimmer that her mother had seen in hers.

She hoped it was.

⤞Chapter Three⤜

THE PEACE FIELD

"**I** 'm surprised you remembered it, Marjory! That mean old Leon really put a black mark on Lone Moon Creek.

And Abbey? Now she doesn't have anyone to visit with, poor thing."

⤞⤜

Oh my, goodness, Abbey thought as she looked at the gravestone. *This woman and the baby died on the same day... must have been in childbirth.* Abbey's eyes moved to the right of the stone to notice that the man lived fifty-two years beyond his wife and baby. *I wonder if they had other children?* Her head pivoted further to the right. Thomas was there...thirteen years old. Abbey furrowed her brow involuntarily. *I guess Thomas Sr. never remarried.* She bent to pull a few tenacious weeds that had pushed themselves out from under the granite.

Abbey slowly walked on, tossing the weeds to the ground. What had that man been through? What kind of life did he have with no wife and two children who died? "God rest his soul," she murmured as she straightened the flowerpot at the next stone. "Hmm," she uttered as she noticed that the Graysons, Elizabeth and Harold, had lived a long life together. Well, she didn't know about "together," but that they each had long lives. There were no other Graysons nearby...maybe they didn't have any children...maybe their

29

children were married and were going to be buried elsewhere. Families don't get buried in large family plots anymore, Abbey knew. A lot of her friends had no intention of coming back to little Lone Moon Creek to be buried. Some of them weren't even going to be buried, just cremated and scattered to the four winds. Abbey shuddered at the thought, as the cool October breeze sailed against her body at the same time. She pulled her sweater together and held it in front of her chest with her fist.

Oh, look at that beautiful mum plant. Abbey sauntered to the direction of the deep burgundy. She bent to touch the mound of color. *Ethel Harlig...someone must think you're pretty special, Ethel. Hmm...she lived through World War II. Just twenty-one at the start of the war. Died five years ago. I guess she never married. Maybe a niece or a nephew brought the Mums...someone still has her lovingly in their thoughts. That's nice.*

Abbey sighed at the sight of the geraniums and petunias that had been killed by the first frost of autumn. Black, too, were the other annuals that once hailed lavenders and periwinkles, mauves and scarlets; flowers that people had planted last spring. *Oh well, that's how it goes. Some of the people will be back next spring to plant more, and some won't.* Abbey looked over at another mum plant— yellow this time. *It's such a silly thing...everyone knows the souls have gone on and the old bones don't need flowers...Oh, well, mortals just need to do it...it's a good chance to think about life and death, while you're fussing around the gravestone.*

Abbey bent to brush off a few red maple leaves and a curious, small formation of fungi from Mr. Weatherspoon's marble bench. She always sat a few minutes with Mr. Weatherspoon, seeing how he had requested it on his tombstone: "Sit with Me." She never could pass without reflecting upon those words. Why would he have such an epitaph on his stone? Did he like company? Was he a lonely man? Abbey never recalled seeing anyone else sitting on the bench, except children who used it as a waiting spot while their mothers tended to various plots.

This is a nice place, Abbey thought, as she looked up into the October sky. One section glowed bright blue and the rest an ominous "I'm coming to get you" gray.

You take care, now, Mr. Weatherspoon, I'll sit with you another day. Abbey wanted to say it out loud, but she knew better than that—she wasn't crazy.

I wonder where he is? Chamney—Ruth and Henry. Both born in the 1890s. She died in 1946. His death date wasn't engraved into the marble. He must be dead, or he'd be over 110 years old and famous. She knew of every famous person who once lived in Lone Moon Creek and Henry Chamney wasn't one of them. *Where is he, Ruth?*

Ah, the sedums! *A perfect flower for fall!* she thought. Abbey had watched them all summer with their chartreuse heads. In September they had slowly turned into the slightest of pinks. Now the transcendence had brought them to their darkest of maroons. A perennial...a good choice for the Abbot sisters. Five names, all Abbots: Mother—Edna, Father—James. Three girls: Anne, Judith, and Emily. Anne—twenty-seven at death. Judith—sixty-five. Emily—seventy-one. *Hmm*...Emily has only been dead for three years. Could she have planted the sedum? How odd, to plant your own graveside flowers...how odd...*Maybe practical, though. I wonder if one or more of the sisters went back to their maiden name? Did none of them get married?*

Abbey leaned over to pull the grass that wanted to grow in between the three sedum plants. Judith and Emily must have been sad when their older sister died at only twenty-seven.

Abbey veered to the left when she saw an American flag lying horizontally on the ground. "What happened here Lt. William L. Harrigan?" She pushed the spike into the ground, which brought the flag to full attention. "Killed In Action During the Korean Conflict." The flag fluttered, seemingly glad to be returned to its vertical position...*twenty-four years old*...May Perpetual Light Shine Upon Him...*I wonder if his mother had those words inscribed upon his stone...probably...and I say the same thing.*

"Oh, no," Abbey gasped, as she looked at her wristwatch. Her cotton skirt swirled around her legs, as her feet in her black pumps wasted no time in getting to the car.

"Where have you been?" The raspy bass voice came from an unshaven face.

Abbey rushed past the granite form of a man, as she held her breath and spoke at the same time, "Just visiting, Leon. I lost track of time. I'm sorry."

"This visiting business is going to stop," he bellowed as he whacked the wall with a newspaper. "You know I want my lunch before I go to play cards."

"Yes, Leon. I got it all ready before I went to the cem...Cemturrio's house. I just have to heat it up. Sit down, now."

"Why do you associate with that Cemturrio woman? None of them in that house can speak English. How the hell can you carrying on a conversation with them?"

"We do pretty good; they're learning."

"What the hell are you, the teacher?" Leon laughed like a spike splitting through a child's cotton candy, sending it to the ground.

Abbey mumbled, "No," as her spirit sank into the floor, much like her cemetery acquaintances had been lowered into the ground.

The sound of eight cylinders leaving the driveway resounded in the autumn air as Abbey finished her tea. She sat holding the empty cup, looking out the back window at her flower garden. Hers, too, portrayed only a few mums. No more was there a cascade of color, no more a game of anticipation. She knew this was the end until next spring. *Oh, dear God, how am I going to get through the long winter?* she prayed.

Oblivious of the dishes, the same dishes that her girlfriends had given to her when she married Leon forty-five years earlier, Abbey snatched the clippers from the bottom kitchen drawer and hurried outside. She grabbed tall hollyhock stems and cut them within inches of the ground. She grasped peony stems and iris spears, lilies and golden glow—which were already lying flat to the ground, seemingly moaning, "Enough of this life!" Being oblivious to her dainty rose dishes still on the table, and now, to her own shoes, was not like Abbey. She worked feverishly, cutting back the withered and frozen plants, as she wiped tears from her cheeks. Streaks of brown ran perpendicular to the water flow of her tears. She didn't know her skirt was dragging in the dirt or that there were small, hard pieces of grit in her shoes. She didn't feel the pain in her soles, only her soul.

Way into the afternoon, Abbey worked in her garden. Not a garden of beauty, but now a bad crew-cut garden, mimicking the haircut Maggie Polston had given her little brother when they were Abbey's neighbors years ago. The stubble irritated Abbey as she kicked at the three-inch remains of the phlox. Nothing. She knew she'd have nothing until spring.

She didn't know why she didn't hear the big lummox of a car roar into the driveway, but she didn't.

Abbey swung in terror when she heard, "What the hell are you doing?" It wasn't until she dropped the clippers that she saw her dirty skirt and felt the grit under her feet. She dropped to her knees to hide her disgrace. "Get up and get out of that damn dirt. What the hell is the matter with you? And why hasn't the table been cleaned off? I can't take your stupidity. I'm going down to Shanahans."

Abbey stood as a lone scarecrow in her own garden. Her hair was stiff as straw, sticking out to the sides, and there were circles of black around her eyes. Her clothes were those of a vagabond, with shoes someone else would have discarded.

The scarecrow woke up the next morning, however. She knew she could go downstairs to her sparkling kitchen as she'd had the whole evening to do her chores. Once Leon went to Shanahans, he never returned until the wee hours of the morning. She turned to look at him. There he was, snoring through his whiskers, inches from her, emitting fumes of smoke and alcohol.

Hmm, two doctors, Dr. Irving Thetson and Dr. Doris Thetson...that's interesting...no flowers...both died on February 15,

1973. Both? Maybe they were in an accident...how tragic. Maybe suicide? Oh, dear. The wind belted against the Thetson stone and bolted back at Abbey. Her "God rest their souls," sailed on the back of the wind, twirling wildly as if looking for trouble.

Abbey walked to a mass of black cone flowers. She knelt in the grass to break off the dried stems; they would grow again next year. This plant, with the pretty pink flowers, like daisies with their huge coned centers came from her own garden. Abbey planted them for Nell Cauthers, wife of John Cauthers. On her knees, Abbey was careful not to edge too close to John's side of the plot. The flowers were just for Nell, not John. Abbey stayed in that position until the barren stems were snapped and a prayer was said for Nell. She guiltily glanced toward John's side, but did not pray for him. "I'm sorry, Lord," she said, as she left the pile of stalks behind the stone. Abbey shivered and pulled the stretched sweater over her cold fingers. She thought of all the nights Nell had come to her house crying, because of John.

Abbey checked her watch. She didn't have to leave yet. Cassidy—My One True Love. *That's odd...I swore I saw that same inscription up on the hill...maybe not.* Cassidy Spears 1925-1972.

Abbey started up the hill. *Where did I see that stone?* The fluttering of her dress became more evident as she ascended away from the protection of the valley, but Abbey didn't notice. Her black pumps dug a little harder into the trajectory of the land, but Abbey didn't notice that either. Her eyes zoomed from stone to stone. Where had she seen that inscription?

I must have imagined it, Abbey thought. Her shoulders raised to take in a large breath of crisp, cool air and lowered to release a changed phenomenon, one of warmth, carbon dioxide and moisture. The woman never thought about that, of course, she was vacillating between her mind being acute and her mind being—gone.

Abbey looked at her wristwatch again, the same watch that her mother had given her when she graduated from high school. "Oh, no," she gasped as she rushed to the emergency. Abbey quickly put her hands down against the waving material of her dress, just as the smooth leather of her shoes careened off the slickness of a still shady, dewy spot.

Ooof. Abbey groaned as she landed on her back. Did she think the people from the graves were watching her? Her only thought was to get up quickly; she was embarrassed in front of—nobody. As she rolled on her side, her eyes spotted "My One True Love." *There it is!* Her embarrassment prior to the discovery was forgotten, as Abbey let her body crawl closer to the gravestone. Annabelle Rindfell—My One True Love. 1939-1989. *I wonder if this came from the same man? Who was he?*

Abbey drove in terror to her own house. Why couldn't she just keep driving and never go home? She saw Leon standing on the kitchen porch with his arms folded across his chest. *Oh, dear God, no.*

Abbey walked up the path never lifting her eyes to Leon until he said sarcastically, "Ah, my one true love is home." And that was the last time Abbey looked into Leon's eyes, because Leon didn't live at 8 Appleton Avenue anymore. Leon resided at the federal penitentiary from then on.

Abbey, however, began her journey, first trying to think if she had washed her pretty dishes, and then wondering where her wristwatch was.

"Oh, don't worry about that now. Come and sit with me," a kind voice spoke from somewhere, though Abbey didn't know exactly from where. "I'm Mr. Weatherspoon, and I'm so pleased to finally have the opportunity to visit with you."

"Mr. Weatherspoon with the bench?"

"Yes, indeed, the very same! How are you Abigale?"

"How did you know my name?"

"Oh, I've gotten smarter in my old age," he laughed. "I want to thank you so much for taking the time to sit with me at my grave site."

"Well," Abbey said shyly, "it did say *Sit with Me.*"

"Indeed it did and I was absolutely amazed when someone finally took me seriously!" he proclaimed with a jubilant laugh. "So where are you going?"

"I really don't know, sir. I remember looking into Leon's eyes and trying to find my wristwatch, but after that I have no idea what I'm doing or where I'm going."

"Not to worry, not to worry," Mr. Weatherspoon said gently. "I know exactly where you're going, and I shall help you get there."

"Really?" Abbey asked in awe.

"Come along, dear one. I want you to meet Thomas."

"Hello, Abigale, I'm Thomas!"

"Hello, Thomas. But I don't think I know you, do I?

"You always said, 'God rest your soul' when you stopped at my grave—I should say 'our' grave. Abigale, this is my lovely wife and my beautiful, brand-new baby. And this is my namesake, Thomas Jr!"

"Oh, my gosh!" Abbey squealed as she put her hands over her mouth. Thomas, yes, of course I know you. You're all together again. What was it, after fifty-two years apart?"

"Yes, exactly! And Abbey, God did rest my soul. After years of turmoil and loneliness, I finally learned to settle down and let the peace of God come upon me. Thank you, Abigale."

"Oh, my goodness. I never knew I was doing any good."

"More than you know, Abigale," Mr. Weatherspoon interjected. "Shall we continue on, dear?"

"Oh, yes. I'm kind of lost right now, Thomas," Abbey whispered in confidence to the radiant man who was holding the baby in his arms, "but Mr. Weatherspoon said he would direct me."

"To be sure, he will, dear heart. He will."

Abbey turned to wave to the little family.

"Well, aren't they nice," she said and smiled. "I'm so glad I got to meet them."

"At ease, Lieutenant. Abigale, this is Lt. William L. Harrigan."

"Harrigan," Abbey murmured as she tried to think who he was.

"Many times you straightened my flag, ma'am, and prayed for my soul."

"William! Yes, of course! Oh, William, how are you?"

"I'm fine, ma'am, and I want to thank you for your respect."

"Oh, no, everyone respects our soldiers."

"Perhaps our human capabilities, ma'am, but not so many think to care about our souls."

"Really? I didn't know that."

"Come along, Abigale. We have quite a ways to go yet."

As the two sojourners continued their trek, Lt. Harrigan saluted the woman in the cotton dress with the black pumps.

"What's all that giggling up ahead, Mr. Weatherspoon?"

"Oh, that has to be the Abbot sisters. What a trio. Come, you've got to meet them!"

"Abigale! Hello! It's so nice to finally meet you face to face. I'm Anna and these are my sisters, Judith and Emily."

Abbey remained quiet as she tried to picture the names.

"Remember the sedum plants that Emily planted?"

"Oh, yes, of course, the sedum plants! What a great idea that was, Emily. They were beautiful this fall!"

"Thank you for looking after them for me and remembering us in your prayers."

"Land of mercy, that was quite all right. I always had a special place in my heart for you three girls. It must be fun to be back together again, isn't it?"

"It surely is," they all giggled. "We have missed our Anna for so many years," Judith replied as she pulled both sisters close to her side.

"Where are your parents, Edna and James?"

"Oh, they're up ahead someplace; they get tired of us girls laughing and carrying on all the time. They claim they need some peace and quiet once in a while!"

"Well, I think I can understand that!" Mr. Weatherspoon articulated. "Are you ready, Abigale?"

"I think so," Abbey replied dreamily. "It's just so nice to be around people who laugh. But, yes, I need to find out where I am. Bye, girls."

"We'll see you again, Abigale. And thank you."

"I can't believe I'm meeting such wonderful people. It must be my lucky day!"

"It's a lot more than luck, my dear," the older man said quietly.

"Mr. Weatherspoon, wait a minute. I know that woman!" Abbey took off with such a spin that Mr. Weatherspoon almost dropped the pipe from his mouth.

"Nell, Nellie!" Abbey cried out.

"Abbey? Oh my soul, is that you Abbey?"

The two women melted together with hugs and tears, memories and laughs. Mr. Weatherspoon stayed back to relight his pipe.

"Oh, Abbey, thank you so much for all the Masses you had for me and the beautiful cone flowers! I love them so much!"

"You are entirely welcome, my dear friend." Abbey paused, as she looked downward.

"What's the matter, honey?"

"I'm sorry I didn't include John. I just couldn't," Abbey said sadly as she remembered how cruel John used to be to Nellie. "Is...is John here?"

"I haven't seen him."

Mr. Weatherspoon sauntered over to ask, "Are we ready to roll?"

"Give me one more hug, Nellie. I'll see you again."

"Indeed you will!"

"This has been the best and strangest day of my entire life, Mr. Weatherspoon."

"And it just gets better and better!"

"Boy, am I glad I sat on your bench!"

"Mr. Weatherspoon laughed until he almost choked on his pipe smoke. A woman walked over and patted him on the back, "Sam, for goodness sake. When are you going to stop smoking that darn pipe."

Mr. Weatherspoon gave one last cough and said, "Probably when hell freezes over. Ethel, I want you to meet Abigail."

"Abigale! It's me, Ethel Harlig."

Abbey looked embarrassed as a deep furrow delved into her forehead.

"You know, with the beautiful mum plant. Burgundy."

"Yes, yes, of course. Please forgive me."

"Thank you for your concern and your prayers. You were wondering who brought me the nice plants, right?"

"Well, it was none of my business. I'm sorry."

"Don't be sorry. My son remembers me with flowers. You see, as you know, I was a young woman during World War Two and one thing led to another while I was stationed in France and I...I became pregnant. I gave my son to the good sisters and they arranged for him to be adopted. What a surprise when he came to America as a grown man to find me. What a wonderful man he is, too. You know? I prayed every single day for him, and now he prays for me. I can hear him. He's a good man."

"Oh, Ethel, what a beautiful story; I'm so happy for you."

"Oh, no, not more hugging," Mr. Weatherspoon snorted, as he refilled his pipe.

"Come along, Abigale. You women, I don't know," Sam muttered as he walked ahead with his hands clasped behind his back and the pipe commandeering out in front.

"Sam? Sam?" came a voice from the left. "Sam, have you seen Henry today?"

Mr. Weatherspoon removed his pipe and slowly said, "No, Ruth. I haven't seen Henry but I want you to meet Abigale. Abigale this is Ruth Chamney."

"Hello, Ruth. I remember thinking the same thing, believe it or not. I always wondered where your husband was, too. He must have passed away by now."

Sam had a terrible choking spell on that note and it took the women many a harried moment to get him through it. "I'll let you know if I see him, Ruth," Sam called over his shoulder as he quickly pulled Abbey along.

"What's the matter, Mr. Weatherspoon?" Abbey whispered.

"Henry Chamney is living someplace else, but we don't want to tell Ruth. It would break her heart, so we keep it quiet."

"Oh," Abbey concluded. "I certainly wouldn't want Ruth's heart to be broken."

"I knew you wouldn't."

They walked onward until Sam said, "Abigale, would you sit with me for a while?"

She laughed, "You really do like that question, don't you?"

He smiled. "I guess I do. But I want you to look at something."

"Ah," she gasped. "Whose grave site is that? It's beautiful! But how could there be tulips and hyacinths at this time of year? Roses? Pink peonies and iris? That doesn't make sense, how could that be, Sam?"

"Someone very special is buried there, Abigale, and her heavenly friends have a great deal of pull to make just about anything miraculous happen."

"Let me see if I can read what it says from here," she said, as she leaned in front of Mr. Weatherspoon.

"Abigale Lamont —My One True Love."

Chapter Four

A FULL HOUSE

It's *Pearl's daughter.*

Do you remember Pearl? She passed away.

Her daughter Estelle, still lives in that same house.

You know that road that curves to the left and has daffodils on the banks of the road?"

"Things change," Estelle murmured to herself as she pulled in her stomach to squeeze past the boxes. She remembered just plain walking through the pathway, but now it was a sideways stroll. Not the provocative stroll that she once watched the high school girls do at the Friday night gymnasium record hops, but just a side-step, side-step with no sexy moves. Estelle didn't recall that the boys—the boys who dared to dance with those girls—looked particularly provocative, but they did look "cool" with their shirt cuffs turned up.

She wondered how the path could have gotten narrower until she remembered putting in another row of boxes. *Oh, how could I have forgotten? Stupid me. Stupid, stupid me.*

Her thoughts darted to the shed and the cold rain; her sweater wrapped around each box as she ran bent over, using her back as an umbrella. She knew that her mother's glassware had to be saved before the roof collapsed.

"Gunna collapse, gunna collapse one of these days," pelted Lambee's raspy voice through Estelle's memory. The intrusion made Estelle exhale enough to cause her once svelte stomach to touch a box. "Damn him," she muttered as a new breath inward brought no ability to minimize.

Estelle squeezed into the blue and white room. She loved this room, and by swaying her head to the left, and then to the right, she could still see some of the beautiful toile pattern of the wallpaper. She remembered the week her mother and Aunt Mary worked every day to hang the wallpaper. Estelle continued to bob and sway to secure a glimpse in and around the piles of newspapers and boxes. "Oh, my goodness," Estelle giggled at the thought of all the nerdy girls dancing in a group, bobbing and swaying up and down, left and right. But Estelle's brow suddenly furrowed as her eyes rested upon a crate labeled "shoes." She know her old nerdy saddle shoes would be in there, or in that one, or that one or…

"What on earth?" She reached out to feel something scratchy. It was poking out of the grasping hole of a banana box quite as yellow as the tattered label of bananas. "Oh, no!" she gasped as she covered her face with her hands. For a minute she couldn't see the lifetime of stuff she had saved and stored, saved and stored—her things, her mother's, her grandmother's.

There was Lambee standing in front of her asking her to dance. Lambee, the girls' nickname for the darling Lambert Farthington III. *Him* asking *her*? He swirled her on the old, but smooth boards of the gym floor; the gym floor where, earlier that day, her team had lost the game because she, *the giraffe,* had tripped and lost the ball. Now with the music, the floor was golden, until another swirl—and her yellow crinoline fell beneath her full skirt and lay passively on the gym floor.

Estelle pushed the scratchy material back into the crate so quickly that a splinter ripped the skin between her thumb and first finger.

The giraffe knew better than to turn left into the green room, but she did, maybe hoping to get the dance out of her head, or maybe to escape. There they were: the college books, the baby books, the cookbooks, the school yearbooks, the everything books. Boxes and boxes sitting in front of the original walnut selves that her grandmother had lined with exquisite volumes. Oh why did her mother have to buy every novel of the day, every cookbook, every travel book, every Civil War book for Dad, every everything? And why did Estelle have to follow suit knowing there was no room? But, there would be room because Estelle was going to sort through things and get rid of…

∽

"Miss Everett! What is this mess?" Estelle froze as the vice principal pulled her locker door wide open. An avalanche whisked across the floor. "Clean out your locker, right now!"

The red-faced giraffe couldn't hear the tyrant's wing-tipped shoes click against the black and green tiles as he walked away, she only heard the snickering of the girls and Lambee cheering, "Go, Raffee, go!"

For the whole afternoon, there she was, going from page to page, book to book, box to box—her captivating retreat. Gone was her locker and the dances and gym class.

Estelle awoke suddenly wondering how long she had slept on the chaise lounge. She had forgotten about the valentine boxes that had been piled on the foot of the lounge, and a spray of reds, pinks, and lace sailed to the floor when her legs swirled around to let her sit upright. "Oh, good grief," Estelle moaned as she knelt to retrieve the love tokens that her grandpa and dad had given to their women. *"How can anything be so beautiful?"* Estelle wondered. As with hundreds of time before, she fingered the silken flower sprays of lilies of the valley, forget-me-nots, and roses. She read the love poems and studied the attire of the couples on the labels. She held the boxes close, believing she could still smell the chocolates and creams and jellies. And there, the little one was her valentine box, small but pretty with a tag neatly printed by a fourth grader: Happy Valentine's Day, Estelle. From Peggy Sue. Estelle gave a quick flick of her wrist which surprisingly made the red heart land smack-dab on top of the pile. "Peggy Sue, sure. Miss Hotsy Totsy!" Estelle mumbled under her breath.

Memories of Peggy Sue swarmed into the almost fifty years out-of-school alumnus. Pretty shoes, pretty dresses, pretty ribbons. A real thermos in her lunch box lined with real glass, of all things. Cute, extroverted, popular. And in high school a dancer, an athlete, a cheerleader, a singer...

"Enough, enough," Estelle reprimanded herself as she hurried out of the maze.

Into the "desert" room she lumbered. *Much more like a camel rather than a giraffe*, she thought, as she suddenly stood perfectly still. It never failed. Her first reaction to the desert room was always as a marble statue. Immobile. The vastness, the sterility, the starkness—her barren desert. Using the inheritance from her mother, Estelle had added this room onto the back of the house. She carefully selected a couch, a chair, and a coffee table from Baxter's Furniture Store, which were—to this day—the only items in the room. No papers, no boxes, no keepsakes. Nothing else. This room was to be Estelle's turning point, her inspiration to make the rest of the house resemble the orderliness of the desert room. Baxter's Furniture van was last seen at Estelle's house twenty-five years ago.

The camel-giraffe sat on the couch and stared at the fading sunlight across her back yard. She had tried to get her house in order; actually it was in order, she rationalized, as she sat a little straighter. Things were in neat piles, boxes, and rows. Even the buttons had been sorted by color and put into little juice cans. Maybe if the shed hadn't collapsed, she would have been all right, she thought. Or maybe each time the Good Will truck had been around, she could have made a decision as to what she could donate—that would have helped. But Grandma's things? Mother's things? How could she?

She felt a need to have some beautiful books on the bare coffee table; she felt quite alone in her desert. "No," she quipped aloud and looked to the left and right as if embarrassed that someone might have heard. "I won't start," she exclaimed boldly. Estelle's school yearbooks flashed into her mind. Down she slouched into the Baxter couch. "Leave them out so everyone can see them, dear," she remembered her mother pleading. "You should be so proud of your school years."

45

"Proud? And what does Estelle leave to the juniors?"

Estelle Everett leaves fifty tons of papers spewing out of her locker at any given time and a yellow crinoline slip for your dancing pleasure.

Page 56 - Class Prophecy

Estelle Everett will be an Olympian Basketball Star able to dunk without jumping.

Peggy Sue could have stopped that from being printed, Estelle rationalized; she was the editor.

Estelle turned to leave the desert room when there came such a knock on the back door that her feet left the floor. She wanted to crouch behind the chair, but caught a glimpse of Lambee's orange and purple letter-sweater that he always wore. She figured he hadn't taken it off since the day he graduated. That big purple and orange letter *H* with four or five white bars sewn on so everyone could see that he had been in every sport and every club and every everything.

Estelle went to the door. Before she could say a word, Lambee hurled a bundle of mail at her. "What's the matter with you? Can't you get out to get your mail once in a while? The box won't even close anymore."

Estelle stared at her neighbor, his stained sweater, his old-fashioned sneakers, his balding head. *Humph,*" she said to herself, *now he's in no condition to cheer, 'Go, Raffey, go.'*

"Thanks," she muttered.

"Right," he replied as he exited into the darkness.

Estelle quickly turned off the light in the desert room and wound her way strategically to the kitchen. Carrying the bundle was almost as cumbersome as trying to carry a child through the maze at the circus's house of mirrors. She wished that her mother had never taken her in there. She looked like a freak.

Estelle was relieved that Lambee had only seen her orderly room and that she had maintained its décor, even though there really wasn't any décor.

Estelle rearranged the top of her kitchen table with her right hand, hoping to do enough consolidation to put down the bundle of mail. "Oh my, I guess it has been a few days since I went out to the mailbox. I might have known that Lambert Farthington III would have his nosy nose into watching everyone's business—just like at school. I wish he'd never come back here to live; I hate having him next door.'

Estelle couldn't remember if she had even eaten lunch. She grabbed a frozen dinner and tossed it into the microwave. Her thoughts went to the food's container and her need to save it, because in her mind it would be perfect to put under potted plants. She was quite captivated with the duel layers of strainer and bottom dish. Her eyes turned to the already substantial stack of similar containers piled and leaning next to the stove.

The mail sorting began: bill, bill, bill; junk, junk, junk, junk; sale, sale…"Oh, no!" Estelle sank into the wooden chair as she faced the envelope. That penmanship, that neatness—she had witnessed it every five years since graduation.

Let's get the old gang together

For our (50th) anniversary from school!

Let's reminisce about the good old days!

See you at the school gym!

Love,

Peggy Sue

RSVP

Now it was written in gold ink because of their 50th, Estelle surmised.

She mixed the vegetables into the sauce or was she supposed to mix the sauce onto the vegetables? Her thoughts were nowhere near her culinary skills, she only knew where the orifice was that devoured food.

47

Estelle washed the plastic dish and strainer and, like a crown, placed them on the top of the tower, wondering if now with the new "king," the others would notice their demotion as they took their places lower and lower on the society pole. Estelle wondered about her place in her class society pole as her eyes rested upon the bottom plastic dish. And, as with most governments, the pile was dethroned with all the subjects scattering, when the siren of the telephone screeched through the house causing Estelle to accidentally kick over the someday pot-holders.

"Did you get it?" the raspy voice asked.

"Get what?" answered a shaky, breathless voice.

"The invite, Raffy, the invite."

Why does he still call me that? Estelle bristled as she realized it was L.F. III from next door.

"I did."

"Well?"

"Well what?"

"Are you going?"

"No."

Click.

Estelle leaned against her mother's baby grand piano as the piles of music books, boxes of photographs, and LP albums seemed to say, "We'll keep the piano grounded as you lean your troubled soul against it." With more and more things piled on top over the years, Estelle thought it now looked like a dromedary humped up with its four legs ready to march! But not into her desert room. *No!* Not into her desert room.

Estelle let the moonlight be her guide as she lay in bed. There was her own orange and purple school letter sweater. It didn't have any white bars sown onto it, but she did participate enough to earn the basic letter. Underneath was her spelling bee trophy that she'd won in the eighth grade. No big deal, she pondered, she could spell any word

48

with no effort. She did proofread the yearbooks for four years, but was never the editor, like Peggy Sue, however.

The moonlight directed its beam to the playbill, which her dad had framed and hung. She knew she had a pretty important part, but she hated being cast as the straight-laced, middle-aged librarian. She had wanted Peggy Sue's part—Peggy Sue had received a standing ovation. She *was* great, Estelle knew.

The next three days found Estelle thinking more and more about her classmates and imagining what their reunion would be like. "Thank God, thank God, I'm not going," became her mantra.

Squeezing through her tunnels of possessions and touching labeled boxes brought her some sort of comfort. Anyway, it would all be over in four days. Her classmates would have all dispersed, and chances were there wouldn't be another big reunion. Little by little there would be no more…

Estelle was almost in a trance between the sewing baskets which dated back for five generations to the rolls and rolls of ribbon that—if ever unleashed—would flutter clear to China, when suddenly, in that almost comatose state, the back doorbell rang with a shot that could have pierced an iceberg. Estelle's neck cracked as she swung her face toward the direction of the desert room.

"Oh, no" she sighed. "Lambee. What do you want?"

"Hi, Raffy. There's someone here to see you."

Lambert stepped aside, and there was a woman leaning on a walker.

"Hello, Estelle. How are you?"

Estelle looked from the woman to her neighbor.

"You don't know who this is, do you?" Mr. Letter Sweater grinned.

"No, I don't," Estelle answered agitatedly.

"For God's sake. It's Peggy Sue!" L. F. III roared smugly.

49

The giraffe looked down at...at...a humble, quiet...maybe a beautiful llama or a gazelle, but one who had been compromised. She needed help to walk, to stand, to climb the steps.

"Peggy Sue, please, come in. Here, sit here Peggy Sue."

"Oh, Estelle, it's so good to see you!"

And there...there...were the smiling eyes that Estelle remembered, the eyes that everyone loved.

Estelle couldn't remember from her childhood stories if it had been butter that melted and spread through the streets, or porridge, or pudding, or grits. But whatever it was, it felt like the same thing was happening to the two women. Estelle's heart was melting right before God, right in the desert, even in the presence of Lambee.

"Peggy Sue, what has happened to you? I mean...I mean..."

"It's okay Estelle. A lot has happened. And guess what?" she whispered as she leaned closer to Estelle on the Baxter couch, "You can just call me Peggy. Peggy Sue sounds so juvenile!"

"All right Peggy," Estelle said pensively as she sat a little straighter.

"I'm sorry to just show up, but my buddy over here convinced me that we would have to do something drastic to get you to the reunion."

Estelle shot him a quick glare, but quickly reversed it when she realized that the Red Sea had just parted.

"Oh, Peggy S...Peggy, I can't even begin to tell you what has been going on in my mind for the last fifty years. But tell me about your life. What have you been doing?"

For the next hour Estelle and Lambert sat as pillars of salt while they heard of Peggy's marriage, the abusiveness, the divorce, the second marriage, the two children, earning her college degree, and the car accident that killed her husband and two children. Peggy survived.

The giraffe now peered into the eyes of a...a...little lamb. Estelle swaddled her with her long arms and the little lamb cried into her shoulder.

"Damn," exclaimed their male classmate, as he used the bottom of his letter sweater to wipe his eyes. "Things sure change, don't they?"

"They sure do," Peggy interjected, as the beautiful smile that everyone loved spread across her face. "That's why we want you at the reunion, Estelle. Everyone wants you there."

"They do?" Estelle was visibly shocked by the news.

"Of course, silly. We spent years together at school. We're almost like sisters and brothers!"

"Sisters and brothers?"

"That's our Raffey," Lambert said and laughed. "Always over-analyzing everything."

"Over-analyzing?"

"See? There you go again!"

Estelle put her hand over her month and looked from Peggy to Lambert. "Is that what I've done all my life?" she asked timidly through her open fingers.

"Well, I think that is a fair assessment," Peggy replied tenderly. "Remember how you always gave us the correct spelling when we were making posters for the dances, or writing term papers, or...or the yearbook! You were a tremendous asset to us."

"I was?"

"You would set your mind and your eyes straight ahead and spell out any word we'd give you. You were amazing!"

"I was?"

"Oh, stop, you two!" III laughed. "You girls are too much!"

"We were, weren't we?" Peggy replied as she winked at Estelle and tossed her head just as she had when she use to make her ponytail fly. "Well, my dears, I've got to get to my hotel and lie down for a while. I'm exhausted."

The girls hugged and Estelle could feel…she felt…she felt her soul being cleansed.

"Oh, Lambie, be a dear and run out to your car. I have something for Estelle."

Estelle sat on her Baxter Furniture Store couch for a long time that afternoon, staring at the beautiful blooming cactus plant sitting on the coffee table.

"My desert is blooming!" Estelle smiled.

⟨◦Chapter Five◦⟩

COUNTRY ARMS

"**Y**ou know where it is Marjory; you take the road next to the creek.

Remember that road that used to have a big dip in it and you would get carsick?

She lives up that way."

⟨◦⟩

"That damn smell," Betty grumbled as she closed the window to the aroma of the neighboring farm. "Sure enough, I knew it!" She continued her litany of exasperation as she gulped at the sight of the brown stuff flying out the back of the manure spreader.

Betty sank to her knees with her soft, lotioned hands pressed against her teary face. "I hate it here. I hate it," she wailed to the decreasing volume of the tractor chugging on the other side of the white picket fence.

Betty let her legs stretch out across the new carpet, which Andrew had agreed to purchase because she had agreed to move to the country. She stared at the blue roses with the delicate yellow leaves. She thought about the afternoon when Andrew had walked through the new French doors to see the room for the first time. Betty had spent the week alone in the country except for the contractors and Juliet, her decorator. This was the room that Andrew loved best. He would sit in his huge, blue-striped chair with its matching ottoman, while the afternoon sunlight danced upon the floor of roses. He would visit with his darling Betty, who would be curled up in her blue and white gingham chair, only too anxious to lay down her book whenever her husband wanted to visit with her.

Andrew had gone through a long period of retirement contemplation, but Betty somehow never thought of it as actually happening. She envisioned her husband remaining in his retirement-thinking mode for another ten or fifteen years. "He can't leave the company," she would say, laughing to her friends while they planned the next event in their closely knit community.

"Someday we're going to move out into the country," he had said for forty years. *It was just one of those things that men say*, Betty had thought. She never argued with him; she merely said, "That would be nice, dear," and immediately dismissed it.

Betty lay back on the carpet and traced the intricate cove molding on the ceiling with her eyes. Why had she given Andrew such a hard time about moving? And he had been so patient with her, so patient, she reiterated as she rolled to her side and stared at the fringe on the edge of the lampshade that Juliet said they absolutely needed. "Very nice, Betty. I like it," Andrew said lovingly. Betty knew he was building up her resume of country living confidence.

Betty watched the sunlight dance across the three framed mirrors above the couch. Her eyes wandered to the custom-made throw pillows in gingham and stripes. She could distinctly see the dancing maple leaf silhouettes that the sun had catapulted into the mirrors. "The maples," Betty uttered. It had been the huge maple trees in front of the house that had compelled Andrew to come to a full stop on the narrow country road.

"This is it," he had whispered.

"What?"

"This is going to be our new home," he had continued almost inaudibly.

Betty remembered becoming transfixed behind her seatbelt, thinking that he was serious, but then she breathed deeply knowing she could talk him out of it.

She couldn't. She used forty years of married strategy, but Andrew was resolute. In a strange and peaceful sort of way, Andrew led the way, with Betty letting him cajole her with an almost tantalizing love that she found irresistible.

"I need to go back to my roots, Betty. I need to go," was the sentence to which even she had no rebuttal.

Andrew made it more than pleasant for his wife; she was given full reign of the decorating, and he willingly gave up the idea of having an office so Betty could have three guest rooms instead of two. Her mind began filling with wonderful thoughts of the weeks she would play hostess to their long-time friends. The four couples would languish on the huge front porch and take walks into the woods; they would go antiquing and eat at the quaint Lone Moon hotel in town.

Donavon lifted his head from the French roses and looked into Betty's eyes. He emitted a whine that Betty knew was a question. "Yes, you can come over by Mommy. Come on." Donavon slowly pulled himself up and lumbered over to his best friend. "Yes, you can lay down here my me, old buddy." Betty put her arm over top of Donavon and cried into his long auburn hair. His breathing and hers melded into one, as the dancing in the mirror ceased and the light went along to people of other lands.

It was Donavon who jolted first. "What is it?" Betty whispered as her head bounded upward.

Donavon growled. "Shh," Betty cautioned. She could hear something on the porch. "Oh, my God," Betty thought as she realized she had slept through, missing her nightly walk through the house to lock doors and windows. She knew the door to the porch was unlocked. Donavon tried desperately to stifle his growl; he only allowed a low sound that could have been mistaken for a sustained note from the bow of a bass viol.

Betty whispered "shh" again, knowing no dog on earth could have as much self-control as Donavon was having at that time.

Another crash. She knew it was the ceramic pot of geraniums.

Betty crawled on her stomach to the telephone with Donavon following suit. Thoughts of Andrew and the puppy playing on the floor flashed in-between Betty's fears. She reached for the phone. She hated the blackness of the country. Andrew had installed a pole light in front of the house for her, but Betty had slept through her nightly vigil, so now it was standing in the night with no power.

"Speak up, ma'am. Speak up...Okay, but the nearest officer is thirty miles from you; it'll be a while. Can you call a neighbor?"

4040; Betty knew the number. Their last anniversary was a 40; their old address was 4040. Andrew asked her every day if she knew the neighbor's number in case of an emergency. This was an emergency.

Within minutes, Betty heard the distant sound of a tractor. "Oh, my God," she thought, "he's coming to rescue me on a tractor." She buried her head into Donavon's side as she listened to the scuffling on the porch.

The night was pounded by the silence of the deadened tractor engine. Betty heard the farmer's heavy footsteps clomping up onto the porch and the screen door rattling with all its might as knuckles pounded upon its lazy wood.

That was it for Donavon; no longer could the obedient companion contain his voice.

"You all right in there?" the rough voice called out as it sailed through the screen, giving Betty permission to rise up from her stiffened position.

She caught herself tripping over the ottoman, glad that the farmer couldn't see her through the darkened house. Before her hand reached the light switch, the farm smell dallied through the screen.

"You okay?"

"Somebody was on my..."

Betty stepped back when the sudden sight of long, wild, curly hair encircled the person's face. *Who was this wild man?* Betty's mind ranted feverishly.

Again she heard, "You okay?"

"Yeah, I think."

"Oh," the person uttered reaching up to the wild hair, "my hair! Sorry. I was just brushing it out for the night when you called. It's pretty wild, isn't it?"

"No, no," Betty stammered, "I mean, it's just that uh, uh, I guess it surprised me, that's all."

"Yeah, my husband used to tease me about it."

"Your husband? Wait a minute." Betty stopped to remember the situation at hand. "Who was on my porch? Did you see someone running away?"

"I saw them all right," the woman said and laughed. "You had yourself two raccoons up here! I imagine they were after those cookies you have there in the box."

"Raccoons?"

"You shouldn't be leaving food out at night."

"You're right. I forgot to clean up after myself when I had my afternoon tea."

"Well, five o'clock milking time comes early; I best be getting back."

Betty watched the muscular woman stride to her tractor. Betty flipped on the yard light for her. The woman gave a little wave before the mop of hair and the engine roared down the road.

Betty hurried through the house doing her lock-up chores, while promising she would never let this happen again. It was when she looked through the nearly empty refrigerator for some supper that she hesitated long enough to think of her neighbor.

"She's a woman! I can't believe it."

The cool quietness of the belly of the refrigerator suddenly revolted when Donavon yelped through the quiet kitchen. Betty bolted upright and peeked over the top of the refrigerator door toward the well-lit porch.

"Oh officer, I'm sorry; I should have called back. I'm embarrassed to say that my intruders were raccoons. My neighbor scared them away with her tractor."

Later that night, Donavon lay on the little rug beside Betty's bed and listened to her cry. He knew her sorrow; he missed Andrew, too.

By noontime the next day, Betty was waiting on her porch for the mailman. Every day she was there like a latchkey child, waiting for her mother to come home. She listened to the silence of the grass until she heard the distant motor of a car. *No,* she thought, *that wasn't the mailman.* The car didn't stop at her neighbor's. She watched as it went by. They waved, she waved. It seemed to be a country thing to do. She listened as it went far beyond the grove of trees. There, she smiled, she heard the familiar motor stop and start at *4040.*

Betty arose from the white wicker chair with the floral cushion and walked the stone pathway to the mailbox. She knew she would arrive at her destination just as the rural mail carrier stopped.

"You stay there, Donavon. I'll be right back."

He did just as he was told; he knew the daily routine.

"We've got mail Donavon!" Betty sang out as she waved the letters high in the air, lightening her footsteps. Donavon's tail wagged—he liked to see his mistress happy.

"Donavon, this one is from Jeannie. Listen." And Donavon sat on his haunches through all six letters, sitting attentively until he heard Betty say, "Well, that's it for today, old boy." He knew he could then release his position and lie in the shade of the hydrangea bush. Betty reread each and every letter to herself.

"What are we going to do, Donavon?"

The old dog lifted his head in the cool shade.

"My friends want me—us—to move back to Pindar's Point, but I don't think we could live there again without Andrew. What do you think?"

Donavon lifted his aching body to walk to Betty. He rested his chin on her leg and she leaned down to nuzzle into the top of his head. "Daddy's been gone for three months. It seems like an eternity, doesn't it?"

Donavon whined.

"I guess I should have had him buried in Pindar's Point, but he wanted to be here in the country. We have to stay here with him, don't we, boy?"

"Got you some mulberries here!" The farmer's voice shot across the front lawn like a bullet leaving the deer hunter's gun. Betty and Donavon lifted their heads at the same velocity.

"What?" Betty limply questioned.

"Mulberries. Picked you a bucketful."

Betty watched *4040* stride across the lawn in her heavy work boots that seemed to require very few steps. With one bound, the farmer woman stepped up and over the porch rail, handing the gift to Betty. She acknowledged Donavon with a hearty rub behind his ears.

"I'm Mildred, by the way. Mildred Eagan. And I know you're Betty."

"Yes, and this is Donavon," Betty said sheepishly, feeling embarrassed she had never taken the time to find out her neighbor's name.

Betty looked down into the bucket. "I don't think I ever saw a mulberry. Where did you get them?"

"Right off my mulberry tree," Mildred laughed. "Try one."

"Mm, they're good!"

"Thought you might want to make a pie or some jam with them."

"Thank you, that was very kind of you."

"I imagine you've been feeling pretty bad over here since the passing of your husband."

"How did you know all that?" Betty remarked, almost resenting the fact that she had to share her private life.

"Word travels fast up and down the valley. We have all been feeling for you. I lost my husband six years ago, and I'm telling you, if it weren't for some of the neighbors I would have gone stark raving mad."

Betty looked into Mildred's pale blue eyes and didn't see the muscular, manure-spreading farmer, only a gentle pool of compassionate water lilies.

Suddenly Betty lowered her head and Mildred watched the teardrops drip upon the purple mulberries.

∞

"Yo! Come on in!" Mildred's voice trumpeted through the screen door as Betty reached for the dangling door handle. "Well, I'll be. Come on in. Here, let me clear you off a chair. By golly, you did bake a pie!"

"It's just a little thank-you for rescuing me the other night," Betty exclaimed, as she discreetly tried to look at the hundreds of things in the large country kitchen.

"Well, I sure do appreciate it neighbor. I don't have time for no baking anymore. How about you sit right down here and I'll pile a scoop of vanilla ice cream right on the top."

Betty had never met anyone like Mildred. Her friends from Pindar's Point were nothing like this farmwoman. Mildred's flannel-shirted elbows were on the table as she talked to Betty like they had been friends for fifty years. Betty found herself captivated with Mildred's stories. Betty laughed; Betty listened; Betty stepped out of herself and out of her grief for two short hours.

"Oh, my stars; look at the time!" Betty gasped as she looked up at the strange old clock with the filigreed pendulum. "I didn't mean to take up so much of your time, Mildred."

"You know, sometimes we have to take time for life. I'm glad you stayed."

60

"Me, too," Betty whispered, feeling a tear roll along her bottom eyelid.

"No letters today? I guess they're busy. Tell me, Mr. Winston, who lives up the road that way and who lives up there where I can just see the top of a silo?" she asked the mailman.

Then, "Come, Donavon, let's go for a drive!"

Betty lifted Donavon's back quarters into the car and checked that the basket of jam jars was snuggled securely into the seat beside her.

That afternoon Betty didn't stare into her French blue carpet, she met Rachel and Emma, Ruth and Stephanie. They all knew her. Some said they had stopped at the house but no one had answered the door. Betty could believe that. They told Betty that their hearts and their prayers had been with her every single day.

Betty smiled, and was held by loving, country arms.

༄Chapter Six༄

Getting Together

"**M**arjory, I don't know what you are talking about! She never had any sisters.

What do you mean they were in your grade at school? I have no idea what you are trying to tell me."

༄

"Now, Belle, tell us when this first began."

"Why don't you take a flying leap," Belle snarled as she folded her arms under her bosom and looked up at the wall.

"Well, okay," Dr. Eden replied clinically. "Bellarose, why don'you start."

Bellarose felt the tag in the back of her collar, was it showing? She felt the hem of her skirt to be sure it was below her knees. She examined her cowlick with her fingertips to assure herself that it wasn't sticking up. She panicked momentarily. Could there possibly be lipstick on her teeth? Quickly she wiped the front of her teeth with her forefinger as she pretended to cough.

"All right, all ready," Belle yelled as she swung her face towards Bellarose. "Just talk, we all know you look like a nerd. Do you have to advertise it?"

"Belle!" Dr. Eden interjected sharply. "You know the rules; give Bellarose a chance to speak."

"What an insecure little wimp she is. If I were like her, I'd kill myself."

Dr. Eden saw tears come to Bellarose's eyes as her shoulders slumped and her left foot went on top of the right foot. "Do you see how she is?" Bellarose stammered. "She is so mean to me. She makes me feel like an idiot."

"You are an idiot. Face it."

"I am not," came the wailing. "I have a good job."

"Yeah, the same freakin' job you've had since graduation. You've never even gotten a promotion."

"I don't want a promotion. I like it right where I am."

"Of course not, any little change would throw you right into a tailspin."

"I don't need to change things every minute like you do," Bellarose sobbed. "I have security and calmness in my life."

"Ha!" Belle shouted as she flicked her long glossy hair off her shoulder and crossed her long, thin legs. "What you have is boredom and dullness."

Dr. Eden looked from one to the other: Belle with her short skirt, short blouse, and high heels—and Bellarose with her gray skirt, white blouse, and flats. "Tell me how you got so separated?" she asked. "You are the same person, you know."

"Oh, God, don't keep telling me that," Belle whined as she crossed the other leg leaving the underside of her thigh exposed as it usually was.

"I can't be her, I just can't," Bellarose lamented into her tissue. "I would never wear clothes like that or act like she does."

"What's the matter with the way I dress? I look good, not like you: something out of a musty library."

"Girls," Dr. Eden started anew, trying to get at least one solid answer, "were you separate people when you were little?"

Finally Belle didn't have a quick, flippant answer, so she merely replied, "I don't remember."

After some thought and checking to be sure that her blouse was buttoned, Bellarose answered. "I only remember me as being one little girl."

Well, that's a start, the doctor thought to herself. "Were you a happy little girl?"

"Oh, yes!" Bellarose expressed a sense of joy. "I wish I hadn't grown up; my life now is nowhere near its finest like I had back then."

"Why wasn't I there?" Belle interrupted, feeling a great need to put herself somewhere in the childhood. "I don't like not remembering anything about when I was little."

"Do you want to tell us about your childhood, Bellarose?" Dr. Eden asked encouragingly.

"Oh, sure," she answered. "I was the only child, so you know I got a lot of attention. And I loved it! The three of us would go places every weekend, and on school nights my mother and father would help me with anything I needed help with. We even put on plays together and made puppets...and danced...and played games..."

"All right, all right, we get the picture," Belle blurted out with her puckered red, glossy lips.

"Well, there. You're jealous aren't you?" Bellarose asked with an uncommon air of superiority.

"You've got to be kidding me. You would have to be the last human on earth for me to be jealous of you. Besides," she hesitated to point her red manicured fingernail at Bellarose's face; "I must have been there, if you and I are the same person."

"No, no, no," Bellarose screamed as she jumped to her feet and stomped, "you were never in my childhood. It was just Mommy and Daddy and me—not you. Never you!"

"Ladies, ladies," Dr. Eden trumpeted as she stood to maneuver Bellarose back into her seat. "Belle, when do you first remember meeting Bellarose?"

"Oh, God. I'll never forget the day..." Belle rolled her eyes as she looked disgustedly at Bellarose. "I was going to my third period class—that was when I was in the seventh grade—and I tripped over this nerdy, ugly girl who was literally crawling on the floor to pick up her books. I was so grateful that I was not like her—the geek!"

"You were horrible! You didn't even say you were sorry or offer to help me," Bellarose wailed.

Dr. Eden quickly spoke before another onslaught began, "So that was your first encounter with Bellarose?"

"Yeah, that was it."

"How about you, Bellarose? Was that the first time you encountered Belle?"

"No, I had seen her around school, sashaying through the halls with her girlfriends and the boys following close behind."

"Did you want to be like her?"

"Oh, no, it's wrong to be like her," Bellarose said very seriously.

"What do you mean, 'wrong'?"

"My mother taught me about *those girls* and how never, never to be like them," Bellarose said quietly as she leaned closer so Belle wouldn't hear her.

"I heard that, you moron. Do you think you're better off being what you are?"

"What is she?" Dr. Eden jumped on the opportunity.

"She's a useless, boring, piece of..."

"Belle!"

"Well, she is. She never goes out or has any fun. And look how she dresses!"

"It's very apparent that the two of you are very different, but is there something wrong with that?"

The two women looked at Dr. Eden with the same expression; they both slanted their heads in the same direction. The Dr. was surprised she wasn't getting an immediate reaction, especially from Belle.

Consequently, Dr. Eden wasn't surprised when Belle began, "I just don't want any part of knowing that half of me is a weirdo."

"That's just what I was going to say," Bellarose piped in. "I would be humiliated to think that half of me was a pros...pros..."

"What are you trying to say, Bellarose?" the doctor asked.

"Yeah, what are you trying to say?" the irate Belle shouted as she moved forward to the edge of her chair.

The red-faced girl took a deep breath and said, "Prostitute."

"How dare you call me that, you little milk-toast. Take it back!"

Dr. Eden stood again. "All right ladies, calm down. Let's get to the bottom of this. Bellarose, why do you think Belle is a prostitute?"

"Because she has a date almost every night and it's not always with the same person and...and...some nights she doesn't even come home."

"That doesn't make me a prostitute, you jerk."

"Well, what does it make you?" Bellarose said with unexpected forcefulness.

"It makes me someone who knows how to have a good time, that's all!"

"Good time, good time," Bellarose reiterated to herself. "That certainly is not a 'good time.'"

"Tell us what you do for a good time, Bellarose," the doctor continued.

"Oh my God," Belle murmured as she pushed her curved hips back into the seat. "Get ready to be bored to death."

Bellarose gave her other half a scowl, and then directed her answer to the doctor. "I put on my favorite music and read a great book. Or I take a walk in the park. Or I go to the art museum. Or I go down by the ocean. Or I go to a movie. Or I go out to lunch with a friend…"

"All right, all right. Enough of your sentences that start with 'Or.' See what a bore you are?"

"Well," began Dr. Eden, "you both have different social lives to be sure, but isn't that okay? Do you think you should be the same?"

Again the exact expressions and the slant transpired while she waited for an answer. "I wish she was a completely different person, not me. I wouldn't care what she did if she was out of my body."

"Yeah," exclaimed Belle. "That's the first thing you've ever said that I agree with."

"Are we making progress?" Dr. Eden asked.

"Yeah, we would be if I could chop her out of me."

Bellarose turned to scowl at Belle.

"That we can't do," said the doctor, "but hopefully we can learn how to cope with one another."

"But I can't stand her, and she obviously can't stand me."

"Wow, now there are two things you've said that I agree with."

"And," added the doctor, "with work, there will be more things that you both can deal with."

There wasn't a sound when Belle looked at Bellarose and Bellarose looked at Belle.

"Bellarose, what do you do when Belle goes out on one of her dates?"

"Well, what would I do? I worry and fret and stew until she's home."

"Okay, and Belle, what do you do when Bellarose is involved in her activities?"

"She makes me such a nervous wreck by sitting for hours doing nothing that I chain smoke until I have to get out of her sight."

"So, each one of you bothers the other?"

"Duh! What the hell did you spend all that money on your degrees for? Isn't that what we've been telling you?" exploded Belle.

"Sorry, I should have stated that differently."

"It wasn't a statement, it was question," added Bellarose.

"Well, you girls are..."

"What? Smarter than we look?" Belle questioned as she swished back her long hair.

"Good one," Bellarose giggled.

"You mean you girls get along sometimes?" the doctor asked with surprise.

"No!" they both answered.

"Well, where was I?" the doctor asked seriously. "Oh, yes. Bellarose, what could you do instead of worrying and fretting when Belle goes out on a date?"

"Don't tell her to go the hell out with me!" Belle shrieked.

"No, I'm not suggesting that. First of all, do you think Belle is old enough to make her own decisions?"

"Yes," came the shallow answer.

"Do you really need to worry about her?"

"I worry about her soul."

"Ahh," the doctor said as if she had struck gold. "You worry about her 'soul'?"

"What soul? What the hell are you talking about?" Belle questioned.

"See how she is? She doesn't even know she has a soul!"

"Let's leave this for a minute and ask Belle if she thinks you are old enough to make your own choices. Do you, Belle?"

After a long pause came, "Yes. But I just want her to have some fun."

"So, we have someone worried about the other's 'soul' and someone wanting 'fun' for the other. Does it sound like there might be a little caring going on here?"

"I knew better than to come here," Belle screamed as she jumped up to get a cigarette out of her purse.

"Please don't smoke in here, Belle," Dr. Eden dictated.

"I will if I want to," Belle blatantly spouted as she lit her cigarette.

Bellarose leaned over and whispered to the doctor, "See how she is?"

"Are you saying you don't care about Bellarose?"

"What a brilliant deduction, Dr. Five Diplomas on the Wall."

"Why don't you care?"

"Because she took my childhood away from me. She took my mother and father away from me. I don't even remember them."

Belle slammed her cigarette into the dirt of the potted plant and stared out of the window.

"Bellarose, do you care for Belle?"

"Of course I care about her. I don't want her to end up in hell."

"In hell? Is that where you think she's going?"

"Well, yes," the young woman answered innocently. "That's what my mother said would happen to 'bad girls.'"

Belle swung around. "Well I never had a mother to tell me such things. Did you ever think of that, you mother-stealer? Maybe I would have known that, if it wasn't for you!"

That last remark brought silence to the room. "Gosh," a little voice finally uttered. "I never thought of that. What have I done to you, Belle?" the teary-eyed Bellarose asked.

"Oh, hell, it doesn't matter," Belle mumbled as she looked down at her shoes. "I have my life and you have yours."

"But Belle, I do care for you. I love you."

"What do you mean, you love me?"

"I don't know...I've always admired your personality...and how you have so many friends..."

"Oh, brother," Belle moaned as she lit up another cigarette. "Don't get nostalgic on me now."

"Belle," Dr. Eden intercepted, "is there something about Bellarose's personality that you admire?"

"I told you. She drives me crazy."

The three women sat and watched the smoke rise into the air—the once, pristine air that Dr. Eden valued for its purity. Now it didn't seem to matter; it was as if Belle's nicotine fix was more important than purity.

"Well, maybe a couple of things aren't too bad," Belle uttered releasing the accolade along with the smoke.

"And what's that?"

"I kind of like the way she can be content with a book or a walk. It never ceases to amaze me how she can do that."

Bellarose looked over at her with the awe of a hummingbird at an azalea.

"Would you like to join me sometime?" the little hummingbird asked with a shaky voice.

"No thanks. Would you like to go out with me sometime?" Belle laughed.

"No thanks," Bellarose answered.

"Well, ladies, would you say you might be able to develop a little tolerance for each other?" Dr. Eden asked.

"Maybe," they both replied together.

"Now," said Belle looking squarely at the doctor, "why don't you tell us why you were the only one who got to go to college? You weren't the only smart one, you know. Look how smart Bellarose is, reading all the time and everything. And I could have gotten a college education, too, if you didn't use up all the money."

"She's right Dr. Big Shot PhD Bellinda Eden," Bellarose concurred. "We never got the chance because of you."

"Well, some of us got it, and some of us don't!" Bellinda laughed as an attendant came in with her medications.

"How are you today, Bellinda?" the attendant asked.

"Oh, I'm just fine, honey. I should say, all three of us are just fine."

"The three of you today, huh? Oh, uh, well. That's good. I'm glad all three of you are fine," the attendant uttered as she left the room rolling her eyes.

Chapter Seven

A BLANK CANVAS

"*Yes, we perhaps could go to the art class. I hear that Loretta has signed up and maybe that would be a good place for Pearl's daughter—you know, get her out of that house a little.*"

❧

"That's it, Mr. Avery. Try that stroke all across the reflection of the water and see what you think."

"Thanks, Serena. Let me see here," muttered Mr. Avery as he stood hunched over his canvas with the brush full of white, supple paint.

"Dab, dab, pull," she heard him mumbling to himself as she walked on.

"Loretta! I love the gleam of sunshine you've added to your barn roof!"

"Do you, dear? It just came to me that something must be going on up there besides that boring rooftop."

"Excellent reasoning, Loretta. Always use the sun for inspiration; think what it's doing, where its rays are playing."

"Oh, I like that: 'Where its rays are playing,'" Loretta said as she stood back to look at her painting. "'Where its rays are playing.' I'll have to remember that," she added as her head tilted in obvious directions of searching.

"Right there, Serena. Don't you think there would be sunlight on that chicken's back?" Loretta asked excitedly.

"Well, yes I do. You're exactly right!"

As Loretta brought out a gleaming radiance that would have startled the others of a real flock, Serena moved on to Mrs. Illiad.

"Well, this is the damnedest mess I've ever gotten into." Mrs. Illiad scowled as she saw Serena approaching.

"What's the matter, Mrs. Illiad?"

"This damn peacock looks like some kind of bat flying out of hell!" the large, red-faced woman exclaimed explosively. She pushed back wild hair and rolled a sleeve on the huge flannel shirt that hung over her cuffed jeans. Then she rambunctiously dabbed more and more red and yellow spots onto the peacock's feathers.

"Mrs. Illiad, calm down. Here, try this." Serena demonstrated by using her student's paintbrush to blend some of the background colors. "There. I think if you make just the peacock the dominant subject, you'll like it better. Try doing that to subdue your background."

"Oh," Mrs. Illiad said meekly, as the redness dissipated from her face. "I think this is going to work. I didn't crap it up after all, did I?"

"No." Serena laughed as she walked away. "I think you're going to be all right, Mrs. Illiad."

"Vi! What's the matter? Why haven't you started?"

"I can't, Serena. I can't do this!"

"I don't understand, Vi," Serena said gently, "your last painting was beautiful."

"I know," she spoke with a trembling voice, "but now I have to start all over again. I can't do another nice painting. It just won't happen."

"Why do you think that, Vi?"

"Because my heart and soul were in that last painting; I can't muster up those feelings again."

The young woman with the sleek, blonde hair, swooped back by ivory barrettes, was ready to cry.

"Oh, my dear young lady," Serena empathized, "I have a feeling you have a lot more of those wonderful emotions that help you create. They're in you. With your first stroke they'll be awakened and you'll be surprised how anxious they'll be to intermingle with your work!"

With eyes as trusting and sincere as those of the doe Serena had seen from her kitchen window that morning, Vi asked, "Do you really think so?"

"I'm sure of it. It'll only take one stroke of paint."

Serena quietly walked away knowing about the quiet privacy that an artist needs.

"Ahh!" Serena gasped as she looked at the next painting.

Manuel motioned for her to be quiet; then he whispered in her ear, "I don't want Vi to know I'm doing her portrait."

Serena whispered back, "It's beautiful!"

"Thank you, she's a great model. She doesn't move."

"I know," the teacher said worriedly.

Serena gave Manuel the noiseless thumbs-up sign as she meandered on.

"What do you think, Serena?" Harv asked as he stepped back for the two of them to look at the painting.

"Well," said the night-school teacher, taking her time to study it, "it's black."

"Black it is!" he said proudly. "My favorite color."

"As I recall," Serena said contemplatively, even though she could recall exactly, "your last three pictures have all been black."

"You're right!" the yuppie businessman proclaimed excitedly. "You're exactly right! That is why I tell everyone what a great teacher you are!"

Serena stood very still staring into the sea of blackness, not necessarily admiring the painting, but wondering...wondering so many things about Harv. Most recently, his latest comment.

Finally, Serena asked, "Are there other colors underneath the black?"

"Oh, my God, you're a genius!" he said as he slapped his hand on his forehead.

"Why do you cover them over?"

"Everything in life is covered over, or should be covered over," Harv commented seriously.

"What do you mean?"

"All goodness is covered over, and all badness should be covered."

"Hmm," Serena uttered, shaking her head in accordance and deliberation. "Would you ever let another color show?"

"I've tried to, but I always end up hiding it under the blackness."

"Are you afraid to let it show?"

"Afraid?" Harv didn't answer for quite a long moment. "Maybe I am, Serena, maybe I am."

They both stood shoulder to shoulder peering into...what? Eternity? Safety? Asylum? Fear? Hopelessness?

Harv suddenly returned to reality and began packing his supplies. "I have an early meeting tomorrow morning; got to run, but thanks for your input. I feel I can be free in this class."

"Oh, that's good," Serena said with a great deal of bewilderment in her thoughts. "I'm glad you do. I'll see you next week?"

"Absolutely!"

"What a weirdo," Mrs. Illiad proclaimed when Harv closed the door to the studio.

"Mrs. Illiad! That's not nice to say."

"Well, it's the truth! I never saw anything like it! What kind of damn fool paints black all over his painting? I think he should be in the loony bin."

"I think you're the one who's nuts!" Mr. Avery said as he looked up from his hunched position. "Your paintings look like someone went on a rampage in the paint store."

"Oh yeah, you old coot! I hear you talking to yourself over there all the time...'dab, dab, pull' and 'swift, up, swift, up' or whatever the hell you're saying! It's enough to drive the rest of us crazy."

"People, people..."

"Why are you painting my portrait? You have no right to paint me. Who gave you permission to paint me?" Vi screamed at Manuel when she saw her portrait on his canvas.

Manuel was not able to answer; he could only stare at his model. Vi sobbed as she grabbed her sweater and ran out of the studio.

"Now you did it, you stupid bastard," Mrs. Illiad shouted, changing gears quickly to now denounce Manuel. Her wild hair became even more electrified when she continued, "Why are you men dumber than fence posts? What woman would want someone painting her without her knowing it, you stupid dope!"

"You don't need to worry," Mr. Avery piped up again. "It would take a lunatic to want you as a model."

"People, people," Serena called out once more to stop the bantering. "Stop, please. This is terrible. I think we'll call it a night, everybody." Serena skittered from student to student bidding each good night, not wanting anyone to leave on an upsetting note.

"Loretta!" Serena abruptly exclaimed as she looked over to see her still painting the sun's reflections. "The class is over for tonight."

"Oh, it is? Already? I guess I didn't hear you make the announcement. I found so many places that needed a reflection, it had me totally engrossed!"

"Ah, you did find a lot of places." Serena could feel her eyelids expand at the sight of the hundreds of yellow spots over the entire canvas. "If you wouldn't mind staying a little longer, Loretta, I'll show you a trick about reflections."

"Oh, I wouldn't mind at all, dear. I love this class."

Serena looked lovingly at the older woman as she demonstrated how the yellow could be blended into the adjacent colors leaving just a slim highlight on the top with a decrescendo of hues descending from it.

"Well, yes of course! Now that looks much better," Loretta exclaimed as she followed suit with her paintbrush.

"You can keep working while I straighten up if you wish," Serena offered.

Loretta worked in silence as her teacher methodically straightened the room while thinking about her students. *Why are adults so much like children?* Serena wondered as she folded the easels and put them in the corner. *Of course, God loved the children. Maybe that's his way of keeping them close to his heart.*

It was hard to say which woman in the studio was more intent in her thoughts, the artist or the teacher. Either way, they both screamed when the lights went out.

"Loretta? Are you all right?"

"Yes, I'm standing in the same spot that I was a second ago. What do you suppose caused the lights to go out?"

"I have no idea, but you stay right there. I'll work my way over to you."

The ladies tapped into two of their senses: Serena extended her hands to feel her way across the room, and Loretta said, "I can hear you coming."

"I'm glad I already cleared away most of the easels," Serena replied just as she stumbled into a remaining one. The scraping of the legs against the wooden floor made a noise that seemed exceedingly loud for such a customarily mundane noise.

"Are you all right, dear?"

"Oh, yes. Yes, it moved with me. I think I'm almost to you now. Put out your hand."

The black air laced with the scent of oil paint was pierced with little giggles as the two women tried to find each other's hand.

"There!" interjected Serena. "I found you!"

"Ah," sighed Loretta, "the touch of another human being! From babyhood to old age, there's no substitute!"

"Hmm, I guess you're right," Serena answered, letting the thought drift in and around the darkness of her mind—the same darkness that was outside of her thoughts as well.

Serena was awakened out of her thought when the older woman asked, "I don't mean to interrupt your thoughts, but shouldn't we work on a plan of action?"

"Oh, yes! Yes, I'm sorry," Serena sputtered, glad to know that her reddened face wasn't visible. "Let's walk over to the row of chairs and make some plans."

The two women felt themselves pulling apart. "This way, Loretta."

"No, dear, the chairs are to my right."

"Oh," the humbled responder uttered, "I guess I've gotten turned around in my mind."

"That's all right, dear. When you get old like me you start studying directions and locations because the fear of getting lost is more prominent. You probably never worry about getting lost, do you?"

"No, I guess I don't." Another concept of contemplation accompanied Serena on their slow walk to the chairs.

The cold metal chair came to life when the teacher's shin contacted enough to push it into the next metal chair, "Here they are," she exclaimed. Both ladies leaned forward to feel the structures and place themselves upon the seats. Side by side they sat in silence until Loretta laughed, "I feel like we're at the movies only there's no movie."

"Or popcorn."

"It's good to have someone to laugh with." Loretta chuckled as she leaned into Serena's arm. "Thank God I'm not in this situation by myself; I hate being alone when the lights go out."

"Yeah, I know what you mean. I live way out in the country and I certainly feel the isolation without the power to rely upon. I don't know how the pioneers did it."

"They must have been amazing. I always think of them, too."

There was a long pause between the ladies, almost like they were showing their respect for the dead.

"Well, do you think we should try to get out of the building?" Serena asked.

"You could try if you wish, but with my bad leg I know I could never walk down two flights."

"Oh, that's right. We'll stay here together, how does that sound?"

"Sounds good to me!"

They both sighed at the same time, which in the stillness of the world sounded more like the north wind than two stranded ladies.

"You know," said Loretta thoughtfully, "this blackness reminds me of Harv's paintings."

"Hmm," hummed Serena, "you're right. They always start out with objects and colors and then he covers everything in black. I wonder why he does that?"

"I've been thinking about that, too. Do you suppose it's his way of protecting them?"

"What do you mean, 'protecting'?"

"Well, no one can see the painting underneath, I assume it's still there, safe. Maybe everything of significance has been taken out of Harv's life, and that's his way of hiding what's left from the world."

"Well," Serena added after a length of deliberation, "that could very well be it. I don't know. It's interesting though, isn't it?"

"Very."

Both women sat motionless in their 'theater seats,' staring into the black screen with only their thoughts for the movie.

Serena became cognizant of traffic down on the street; she had never noticed the vehicles' engines from the studio before. She thought of the black sidewalks and the blackened stores. She hoped her other students had made it to their cars.

"I wonder what's bothering Vi," Loretta spoke suddenly.

"Gosh, I don't know!" Serena replied as she sat up straighter and looked towards Loretta, even though she didn't need to. "She was really upset when she saw that Manuel had painted her portrait."

"That I can understand, but why couldn't she begin painting?"

"She said her 'heart and soul was in her last painting' and she didn't think she had anything left to put into a new painting."

"Hmm, that's interesting. It reminds me of pregnancy."

"Pregnancy?"

"Yes, sometimes women just don't know if they can love and nurture another child. Of course they always can; the love never ends, and that's something they discover as time goes on."

"Children and paintings...children and creating...I never made the connection before." Serena paused before she added, "But, some paintings don't come out so good."

"And?"

"Well, some kids don't come out so good either, even though their creators had their hearts and souls into the project."

"It's just one of those things…" Loretta's voice paled into the quiet night. Serena thought of her mother telling her she didn't know why she was such a problem child and a rebel compared to her brothers and sisters. Loretta thought of her son who was wandering the country, probably still taking drugs.

More sighs were released to intermingle with the faint smell of turpentine.

"Do you have any candles in the studio?"

"No, I'm afraid not, Loretta. Wait…the last time we did a still life there was a candle in the display. Oh, yeah. Let me make my way over to the cupboard. I know exactly where that box is."

After a few seconds, Serena was back to the chair. "Nuts," she uttered, "even if I do find the candle, I don't have any matches, do you?"

"No."

As a teacher, I'm not very well prepared for emergencies, she thought to herself. *I should have a flashlight here, at least, and maybe Band-Aids and…*"What are you laughing at?"

The sound was so uplifting and joyous it made Serena join in, even though she had no idea why she was laughing.

"Isn't that Mrs. Illiad a hoot?"

"A hoot? That's putting it mildly!" Serena laughed knowingly.

"I just about can't contain myself when I hear her going at it. And the way she and Mr. Avery banter back and forth. It's a stitch!"

"Why do they do that? I'm afraid someday they're going to have a real knock-down, drag-out fight."

"Oh, no. They really like each other."

"What?"

"Yes, seriously! What you're seeing is part of the mating game."

"I never act like that when I find someone I like."

"Maybe you should try it."

Loretta didn't need to say anything more. Serena was thoroughly engrossed in the new "movie," and Loretta was content to be still and watch one of her reruns.

"Why are we faced this way?"

"Huh?"

"The windows are to our back, I just turned and the sky is full of stars. Wouldn't it be nice to look at the stars?"

"Oh, yes. Yes, of course," Serena stammered, still into her mating-game thoughts.

"There, isn't this nice?"

"It certainly is! Wow, look at them all."

The stars then became the backdrop for thoughts that might transpire, and they were much more interesting than the black, blackness.

"Why does God do this to us?" Serena asked.

"Do what, dear?"

"Give us something nice, like stars, and then have something bad happen like the electricity going out."

"Oh, dear one. How old are you? Excuse me, I didn't mean that literally. I was just surprised you would ask a question like that."

"Why?"

"Now, honey, I'm not being critical, but that's something a five-or six-year-old would ask."

"Well, I guess that's about as far as my God education went. So? Why did He?"

"It's true that God gave us the beautiful stars, but I think you'll have to file your complaint about the electricity with the power company."

"But God could step in and get this power back on and He could step in and stop all the heinous things that happen in this world. Couldn't He?"

"He surely could, but He gave all that responsibility to the people."

"But the people aren't doing it."

"I know. It's sad."

"Why are the people doing bad things?"

"They are following their own wishes and desires, not God's."

"Oh. Will God ever step in and take control of the situation?"

"Oh, yes, in His own time…in his own time."

Silence befell the room again. The ladies watched the stars wondering if He had seen the mess that the world was in and wondering when God would say, "Enough."

"What time do you think it is, Loretta?"

"I would think around midnight, but I'm not sure. Look down on the street to see how heavy the traffic is."

"Gosh, there's hardly any traffic. It must be pretty late. Are you tired?"

"Actually I am. It's way past my bedtime." Loretta laughed. "I hope Chuckles isn't too upset that I'm not home."

"Is that your cat?"

"Yes. I've had him for seventeen years now."

"Wow. I hope my animals are okay, too. I fed them all before class, so they should be. Do you want me to drag the pile of tarps over? You could lie down for awhile."

"Oh, no. I don't want to be any trouble."

"It won't be any trouble, Loretta. You must be getting stiff sitting on that metal chair. I know I am."

"Well, if you don't mind, I really need to stretch out; my leg is in a lot of pain."

"Oh, Loretta, why didn't you say so? I'll get you all fixed up in a jiffy."

Loretta listened to the shuffling and the banging. It all sounded so loud—probably similar to a human walking through a quiet forest where the woodland animals find it alarmingly resounding.

"There, give me your hand, Loretta. Your bed is all turned down."

"Oh, my, such service!" Loretta exclaimed and groaned simultaneously as she stiffly lowered herself to the layers of tarp. "Thank you, dear. I desperately needed this. But what about you?"

"I pulled out a roll of burlap; it's going to be my pillow. I'm going to lie right on the floor; it won't bother me a bit. I'm used to roughing it, you know. I've got us lined up with the stars. Pretty cool, huh?"

"Cool."

"Ahhhh," their little duet sang out as they both adjusted to the horizontal position. Their whole world was behind the blackness—much like Harv's paintings.

"Serena?" Loretta whispered in the direction of her roommate, "I hate to say this, but I have to go to the bathroom."

"Guess what? I do too. Good thing it's right across the hall. Here, let me help you up."

Arm-in-arm the two ladies navigated with baby-steps out of the studio and into the hallway, using their free arms as sensors.

"Now why did that seem so easy?" Serena asked on the snail's pace trek back.

"I don't know about you, but I use the bathroom at night quite frequently, and I never turn on the light."

"You're right. Maybe we should do other things in the dark just to get used to it."

"That's an idea," Loretta agreed as she lowered herself to her abnormally substandard bed.

"Loretta, do you have anyone who will be worried about you not being at home?"

"Do you mean other than Chuckles?"

"Yeah." Serena giggled.

"Not really. I always put my car in the garage and the neighbors usually go to bed by ten. Nobody will probably notice until tomorrow morning when we women go to our mailboxes to chat. Even then, they might think I have left early for the day and gone to one of my classes. How about you?"

"No, I'm pretty well isolated and self-sufficient."

"Hmm," Loretta responded, "maybe we shouldn't be so much that way."

The little voice in the dark uttered, "Yeah, maybe."

The two women ever so gradually came to the end of conversation and in the transitional period between consciousness and sleep, thought of things past, present, and future. Loretta prayed to her God, and Serena wondered about God. Serena listened to Loretta's deeper breaths as hers, too, slowed into the phenomenon called sleep.

What happens under blackness? We don't usually know, like Harv knows. Serena and Loretta didn't know. They were unaware, until Loretta suddenly grabbed for Serena in a panic, loudly whispering her name.

Unaccustomed to being awakened in such a manner, Serena jolted upright, mumbling, "What's the matter?"

"Shh, there's someone in the building," Loretta whispered again.

Loretta never released her hold on the other woman and Serena's muscles tensed. They heard a crash in the next classroom, and men's voices laughing. More banging, crashing, and laughing came through the wall and down the hallway.

"They're ransacking the place," Serena whispered to Loretta. "Oh, no, John's original blown glass collection," she moaned as she listened to a million pieces of glass falling to the floor after they had been thundered into the wall. "Quick, Loretta, roll off this tarp. I'm going to cover us with it."

The two women lay side by side with their hard breaths beating up against the covering. The heat emanating from their petrified bodies caused a thick air that made Loretta wonder if there would be enough oxygen.

She grabbed Serena's hand when she heard the voices and the footsteps coming into the studio. They both saw a sudden flash of light streak up and under a corner of the canvas that apparently hadn't lain flat.

"Put the shirt over that light, you stupid jerk," a voice rang out, "and open those cupboards."

"Ain't nothing great in here," the second one said, "just some tubes of paint and shit."

"Hey, throw me out some, I'll show you something cool. See what you do? Line them all up then stomp hard as hell!"

The unmoving women jumped when the stomping began, but the laughter and preoccupation deterred any notice of them as the squirting pattern continued. "Damn, that's the last one."

"Okay let's get out of here."

"Okay, okay, just let me check what's under this pile of canvas."

One set of footsteps went out the door while the other set quickly walked to the tarp.

"Pray, Serena, pray!"

As their lives unfolded before their very eyes, the two women looked up into the dim light of the muffled flashlight and into the face of the intruder. Three pair of eyes looked at each other, all startled, all human. No one spoke; no one moved. At least two of the hearts beat as the timpani in a Sousa march.

"Hey, you coming?" came the voice from the hallway.

"Yeah," the second voice responded as he threw the canvas back over their heads and ran from the studio.

Was it another hour, or maybe two, that the women remained under the canvas? They didn't know, but when they dared, they looked out to see daylight.

Chapter Eight

DIZZY TIZZY

"No, *I never heard of an Eleanor Windham. Are you sure it says she lived in Lone Moon Creek?*

Maybe it was up past where Betty lives."

"Well, I'll be darned; Eleanor Windham died."

"Who?"

"Dizzy Tizzy."

"She died? How do you know?"

"It says right here in the paper."

"Let me see."

"Eleanor Windham of Lone Moon Creek...I'll be. I guess I never heard her real name."

"Morning, Earl. Did you hear old Dizzy Tizzy died?"

"You mean Tizzy Dizzy from up on the hill?"

"Yeah, her obituary is in today's paper. Look."

"Eleanor Windham? That was her name? I guess I never heard it said."

"Morning, Lou. Coffee?"

"Sure enough. What's new?"

"Tizzy Dizzy died."

"The old hermit woman, Lizzy Tizzy?"

"Yeah."

"When did that happen?"

"It says here a week ago. I didn't notice any hearse going through town, did you Bart?"

"No, can't say as I did. But I did see something strange about a week ago, now that you got me thinking. I saw two police cars coming out of Tizzy Lizzy's driveway. 'Course, you know how you can't see into her property because of all the trees in front. Damned old hermit, she sure didn't want anyone looking in at her."

"I'd have trees in front of my house, too, if you drove past everyday!"

"Hey, don't get sassy and pass the sugar, will you?"

"Did she have any kinfolk?"

"Yeah, it says here she had a nephew."

"Well, she sure didn't contribute anything to this world; nobody is going to miss her."

"To the world? She didn't even contribute anything to this town! Did you ever see her at a church social or the fireman's carnival or...well, anything? You have any donuts this morning?"

"Powdered or cinnamon, pick your poison. I saw her go into the grocery store every once in a while, but I never saw that she talked to anyone except the cashier. She sure kept to herself."

"Morning, everybody. My wife told me to find out who Eleanor Windham was. Anybody know?"

"Yeah, it was the old coot up on the hill, Frizzy Dizzy."

"You're kidding? Who the heck found her?"

"Beats me. She could have been dead up there for years. Who would have known?"

"Oh, nowadays they can tell pretty well how long it's been. If they say one week…"

"Okay, mister authority, shove that cream pitcher down here. My wife said she went to call on her one day to join some club or another and she thought Dizzy Frizzy was very inhospitable and cold. She didn't even ask my wife to go in and sit down. I'll have to tell you, though, my wife said that beyond that jungle out front, it was beautiful with gardens, flowers, trees, and walkways. My wife asked her if she would be willing to be on the roster for the summer House and Garden Tour. Of course, she said, 'no.' She sure wasn't very friendly."

"I saw her in the bank a few times. The manager seemed to make a big deal out of her, but I couldn't figure why. They went into one of the conference rooms."

"You're just jealous that you didn't get asked into the conference room! Where's the refill on the coffee today?"

"Barbara said about ten years ago Tizzy would go to one church, then to another church the next week, and round and round. I guess she never settled into just one."

"Well, that figures; those hermits are too strange to respect anything heavenly. They're only interested in themselves."

"You're right. Look how we help everybody—the Girl Scouts come around, we buy a box of cookies; the Boy Scouts collecting bottles—we give them our recyclables; we go down and get the pancakes from the firemen."

"Morning, folks. I hear we got a funeral to go to! Hey, what are you laughing at? Aren't you going to Frizzy's funeral?"

"Is she having one?"

"Jeez, how many times do I have to open this paper to read the obituary? No, no funeral. A private family service."

"Well, that figures. Why would a hermit want people at her funeral? Can't you just see her rising right out of the casket?"

"That's a good one. I'd like to see that! Crazy old fool would probably have a stroke if she saw all of us there!"

"How could she have a stroke when she's already dead?"

"Hey, what's all the laughing about this morning?"

"Hi, Len. Coffee?"

"We're all disappointed we didn't get invited to the Lizzy Dizzy funeral."

"Oh my God, did she die? She'll probably come back to haunt me now."

"Why?"

"This was back in high school, but we used to torment that woman. I feel bad about it now, but we used to think it was funny."

"Why? What did you do?"

"Us guys would drive past her house and honk the horn. We'd call her late at night. Jimmy Tillson had a tape of wolves howling and we sneaked up by her house one night and Jimmy played the tape at full blast!"

"What did she do?"

"Jesus, when we saw a double barreled shotgun come out of an upstairs window, we ran like hell!"

"What's going on in here? I could hear you guys laughing way out on the street."

"We're doing our reminiscing about old lady Tiz-Liz."

"Oh, good Lord. Wasn't she a character? We girls used to sit up in the balcony of the theater and wait for her to come in."

"She went to the movies?"

"Oh yeah, that must have been her only entertainment. She was there every Saturday night."

"By herself?"

"Of course by herself."

"What did she do?"

"She didn't do anything, she just sat there, watched the movie, and took notes."

"Took notes?"

"Yeah, it was like she was studying it or something. We'd be dropping popcorn down on her and she never even moved. Not that our aim was very accurate, but it entertained us. One night she walked out with a bunch of popcorn in the hood of her sweatshirt. We laughed until we couldn't stand straight!"

"I wonder how old she was?"

"I know—I know. Look in the paper. It doesn't say when she was born, but it does say she was born in France."

"France? Well no wonder she was so damn strange. We let those foreigners come into our country, they don't know how to act."

"As if you do?"

"All right, all right. I'm bringing the pot around. Who wants a refill?"

"WZOL?"

"What's WZOL?"

"That truck that just went by, it said WZOL on the side."

"Probably heading for Siena. There's supposed to be a big rally going on over there."

"I wonder if Tizzy's house will be up for sale now?"

"I would imagine. I'm sure that nephew wouldn't want to move here from Arizona."

"How do you know he's from Arizona?"

"That's what it says in the obituary."

"I think I'll drive up in there today. I'm curious about that house. You say it's nice?"

"Yeah, that's what my wife said. 'Course, that was several years ago. It could be a junk heap by now. I don't know."

"Well, Lizzy Dizzy never worked, so where would she get any money to keep it fixed up?"

"That's true. I think I'll drive up there, too. My son is looking for a cheap place. Maybe we can get a good deal on it, seeing how we live in this town, and all."

"WBON? There goes another one. I'll have to watch the news tonight. My aunt and two cousins live in Siena. Maybe I'll see them on TV!"

"Hang on, hang on, let me get the door unlocked, would you?"

"Did you watch the news?"

"It's all over the front page of today's paper, too. I was just reading it."

"I can't believe it!"

"Morning folks. I hope you have the coffee made. I can't believe it!"

"You got the coffee perked in here? I'm about ready to burst at the seams."

"Calm down, you guys. I'm going as fast as I can!"

"Hey, neighbor, sit here by me. Can you believe it?"

"I am in total shock!"

"Can you believe it? Old Frizzy Dizzy had me fooled."

"She had us all fooled!"

"Why did she live like she did?"

"Why did she drive that old car around?"

"So that's why she took notes at the movies?"

"I thought she lived here year round, didn't you?"

"Yeah, but how can you keep track of a hermit?"

"Right, a hermit who only lived here maybe six months out of the year. No wonder she didn't associate with the town that much: she wasn't here!"

"I guess the TV crews were up there most of the morning yesterday."

"Until two in the afternoon, according to Jed."

"How would he know?"

"He sat out by the road and waited. They've got the driveway chained off, and some kind of security guards are walking around the property."

"You're kidding me?"

"Nope, that's what he said."

"Did you see the inside of that house on TV?"

"Did I ever!"

"I couldn't believe the grounds. My Lord! It's beautiful, inside and out."

"What's the paper say?"

Famous Movie Producer's Identity Disclosed

Nephew retaliates against aunt for leaving him nil in the will —discloses her identity in little town.

"How could Dizzy Tizzy have been a movie producer?"

"Well, I don't know, but apparently she was."

"Why didn't we know it?"

"She didn't want us to know?"

"Well, why the hell not?"

"So she was Gabrielle Lisieux. God, I love her movies!"

"I thought the paper yesterday said her name was Eleanor Windham?"

"That was her real name. Her pseudonym was Gabrielle Lisieux. She used that to be anonymous."

"Well, this is all beyond me."

"Doesn't take much, does it?"

"Okay, okay, refills coming. Pass the creamers around will you?"

"Jeez, look at that limo going by."

"Who do you think she left her money to?"

"Don't worry, it wasn't you Bradley!"

"Ha, ha. Very funny."

"That's a good question. I suppose she had her friends, maybe even over there in France. You never know."

"Sure, that's our government, all right. They'd let our American money leave this country to be sent to foreigners. They don't care."

"That damn thick 'jungle' she had, it was no wonder we couldn't keep track of her."

"There goes another TV station."

"You'd better get some nice pies and sandwiches in here. Maybe you'd get some of those high class mucky-mucks to come in."

"Yeah, if I could get rid of you guys. Just kidding...just kidding!"

"I guess your son won't be buying that place."

"I guess not. That'll go for some big bucks."

"You know, that nephew must be a real demon. All those

years Tizzy, I mean Eleanor, I mean Gabrielle—whoever she was—all those years of keeping a quiet, private life, now ruined. Everything she ever owned or cherished is now exposed to the whole world."

"But it doesn't matter now. She's dead. She doesn't care."

"I know…I guess I suddenly feel sorry for her."

"Yeah."

"The media is going to have a field day with this—they don't care either."

"Be careful what you say. I hear they're coming around today to interview people. Oh, shhh, I think this is one."

"Breakfast is on me, everybody. Serve up whatever they want."

"Well, all we got is coffee and donuts, powdered or cinnamon."

"Coffee and donuts it is then! Tell me, folks, what was it like having the famous Gabrielle Lisieux living in your hometown?"

◦◦◦

"Well, what's the matter with you this morning?"

"Did you see us on the news last night? We sounded like fools."

"Good morning, Len. You look like you've lost your dog, too. Coffee?"

"Yeah, you might as well pour it over my head."

"Well you weren't as bad as you-know-who."

"Coffee, gentlemen?"

"Why did you have to mention that stupid story about your high school escapades in scaring Lizzy?"

"You thought it was funny the other day!"

"No this stool isn't taken. Join the sad-sacks."

"Did you have to say she walked around town like an old beggar-woman?"

"I didn't mean it that way. But you know how she used to come across to us—never saying hello or anything."

"Listen to this: my sister called from New Orleans. She's furious with me for saying I thought Gabrielle was an old witch of a hermit. Isn't that what we used to think of Friz Diz?"

"My best friend who used to toss popcorn down on her called last night, too. She screamed at me for revealing that story on national TV. We really did make fools of ourselves."

"We weren't very nice to her, were we?"

"Well, did she ever try to join in with us?"

"What did the paper say?"

Townspeople Give Colorful Report on Famous Movie Producer.

"Well, that's nice, at least."

"Let me go on."

The late Gabrielle Lisieux seemed to have totally hoodwinked the people of Lone Moon Creek. In their eyes she was a "hermit"; "witch"; "disgrace"; "anti-social"; "loser"; "poor"; " useless"; "non-caring"; "odd" woman. Lisieux, who produced twelve-award winning films known for their emotionalism, compassion, and empathy for humanity, lived neighbor-to-neighbor with the locals who never had a clue of her strengths and or talents.

"So what? We only picked up on what she wanted to portray."

"Well, I admit, she did stop at the garage once to have me work on her car, and I told her I wouldn't be able to get the parts. I just didn't think she'd pay me."

"I suppose I could have plowed her driveway that winter, but I didn't know her."

"My wife is so mad at herself right now. And don't tell her I told you this, but when Liz, I mean Gabrielle Lisieux, first moved here, she invited a group of women for tea and nobody went."

"What's the matter with you this morning? You look like someone scared the daylights out of you."

"Something has. I got a letter from some lawyer; I'm supposed to be present for the reading of Eleanor Windham's will."

"Why?"

"I don't know, it just says 'to represent the townspeople' of Lone Moon Creek."

"Oh, no."

"Morning, Bill. Coffee?"

"I think I need something stronger than coffee, but I guess I'll have to settle for that."

"What's the matter with you?"

"Look at this. I'm to appear at the reading of Miss Windham's will to represent the school. I don't have anything to do with the school."

"No, not since your senior year and the 'double barreled shot gun.'"

"Oh, no. She's retaliating, isn't she?"

"You're kidding? Where do you have to go for this?"

"To Siena."

"I guess she's going to get her revenge now."

"Morning all. Guess where I have to drive my wife to?"

"Siena."

"How did you know?"

"Oh, brother, I'm afraid we're in for it now."

"You heard that all the clergy have gotten letters, too, didn't you?"

"There. You can hide behind them!"

"Very funny."

"The firemen, too? She can't be mad at them, can she?"

"For God's sake, she's dead!" What are you worried about?"

"Well, I'm not worried. She wanted to rent this whole diner once and I told her 'no' and I didn't get any letter!"

"Me neither. And I told her I didn't service appliances that far out of town!"

"But why would I get a letter? I don't have anything to do with the theater."

"Just dropping popcorn down from the balcony, huh?"

"Oh, no."

"My husband has to go because he's the road supervisor. He thinks she's mad because the plow knocked down her mailbox five times last winter."

"Drink up, folks."

❦

Miss Eleanor Windham's Last Will and Testament:

To the people of Lone Moon Creek:

Here we are together, all in the same room. A rarity, you would have to agree.

By now, I imagine you know who I am or should I say who I was. It was very important to me that I kept my anonymity over the years. You people helped me to do that, and I thank you. We kept our distance, didn't we? You actually were much better at it than I. I'm afraid if you had accepted me I would have created friendships and spilled the beans.

As you probably surmised, I loved my peace and quiet in Lone Moon Creek. I told everyone about the little spot of heaven I had found, up on the hilltop. I probably should have shared my utopia, but I just couldn't. When I returned from the grueling reality of my job, my little spot was like receiving the peace of God. It would take me weeks to unwind and I apologize for walking around like a zombie. There were times when I couldn't have said if anyone spoke to me or not—it seemed I was either trying to get a completed movie out of my mind or starting fresh with another one.

I look back now and wish I had joined in on some of the fun you townspeople were always having. I missed out on a lot, didn't I? Work was always so important to me.

Growing up as a pauper in France always reminded me to never revert to that state of life. But now I wonder about it all.

I guess it's bringing me to do a lot of soul searching. At the end, people start looking at their lives. Once they have sifted out all the garbage, what's left is the good, the holy, and the just. It's my hunch that those few chunks that didn't sift through the wired screen are all we have to present to God. Imagine that, after all He has given to us, we go home with a mere pittance nestled in one hand.

I hope you have seen my movies and will watch them again, now that we know each other better. You will actually see bits and pieces of Lone Moon Creek if you look carefully. But best of all, in my opinion, I hope you'll appreciate the goodness and beauty and caring which is depicted in each one. I can't begin to tell you how I had to fight to keep value and dignity a priority. That was why I often came home to heal and nurture my soul again. You don't know how blessed you are to live in your little sheltered domain. People out there can be so evil-minded, almost demonic.

Because you have shared your heaven on earth with me, it's now time for me to reciprocate.

My house and grounds will be converted into an assisted living facility for those who are in need of such a place.

All of your beautiful churches will receive a remembrance from me.

The town square everyone has wanted for years is to be constructed.

I have noticed that the children need more playground equipment at the school and the town library needs more computers.

The theater and other organizations will be able to apply for grants through the local bank.

Please, avail yourselves of these, as need arises.

So, good people, take care and au revoir!

ᴄᵍⱽChapter Nineᴄ᷌

CORPORATE HOME CARE

"Let's drive up Harpur Road next Sunday, Marjory; I want to see the house that runs all technically; that's what Edna says anyway.

No, it's not where Dizzy Tizzy lived; it's on the hill on the other side of the creek."

Natalie groaned as she turned over in bed, remembering it was Wednesday. She heard Irene bidding Kiki hello and good-bye at the front door, along with some who-knows-what details about the nighttime. Natalie wondered what they actually said about her. What on earth did she do during the night that they sometimes spent fifteen to twenty minutes discussing?

Why did her daughter have to set up her home care just as she ran her corporation? She hated this. Granted, her daughter's business needed meticulous attention, of which Gwen was so capable, but really, this system for her—the mother of the corporate genius—was way overboard.

"Good morning, Natalie!" chirped Kiki.

"It's Mrs. Pengin to you," Natalie uttered, quite embarrassed with herself for being rude to the young worker. This wasn't her persona. She was a well-mannered and gracious lady, she reminded herself. She watched Kiki throw her jacket into a chair, followed by a lassoed flourish of her purse.

"Sorry, Mrs. Pengin," Kiki mumbled. "I'll do better."

"I'm sorry, too, Kiki. I'm just so out of sorts. I've never had to live like this. I could always handle my affairs just fine. I've always been independent and..."

"Affairs?" Kiki interrupted the stately woman.

"Yes, of course. Oh, just help me to swing my legs over to the side, would you please?"

"Yes, ma'am," Kiki answered obediently. Again Natalie berated herself for treating Kiki unprofessionally. "You sit right still now, Mrs. Pengin, while I run in to get your bath water adjusted. You are sure lucky to have that new walk-in tub that your daughter..."

"Ah, yes. That my daughter insisted I have."

"I think she just wants you to be comfortable and to make your life a...a...happy!"

"Go. Go do what you have to do. I'm not going anywhere," Natalie directed. She remembered how before all of this, she would have bathed, dressed, eaten and been on her way to a committee meeting of some sort, or perhaps a date with the girls, to do something mind-stimulating.

"Ready!" Kiki called out, like a child preparing for hide-and-seek, as she rushed into the beautiful bedroom of roses.

"Mind stimulating this ain't," Natalie mumbled facetiously.

"Oh, oh, oh," Kiki sang out. "Don't say 'ain't' or your mother will faint, and your father will fall into a bucket of paint!"

"Oh, my dear Lord," Natalie sighed. "We can't have that."

"You're so lucky to have all this nice stuff, Mrs. Pengin. Your daughter sure knows what you need."

"Well, she does have a mind for business, and I guess helping me out is business to her."

"I guess it is," Kiki replied as she stared into some sort of outer space. "Too bad we didn't know about this business when we were taking care of my grandmother."

"You helped take care of your grandmother?" Natalie inquired with a gush of curiosity.

"Yeah, for years and years. I think that's why I took this job; my Grandma said I was a 'real peach.' A peach is a good thing, right Mrs. Pengin?"

"Oh, I'm sure it is, Kiki," the patient commented, not having any idea what "a peach" meant.

"Well, you just get your old body into that walk-in tub and I'll shut the door for you."

Natalie tilted her head back as she let the water jets massage her "old body."

She finally gave her daughter credit for insisting on this luxury.

"Isn't it amazing how the water doesn't leak out of there?" Natalie heard Kiki speaking over the gushing water. "Who do you think invented this thing? Some people must be really smart. We use to take a big bowl of water in by grandma's bed and give her a sponge bath."

Natalie lifted her head off of the soft cushion and suddenly felt very guilty for having this elaborate sponge bath thing.

"There. All clean and ready for your breakfast," Kiki almost sang with joy. Do you want to sit on this long chair?"

"It's called a 'chaise lounge,' dear."

"Really? I've never heard of a *chaise lounge dear.*"

"Ah, Kiki, you *are* a peach." Natalie was glad that she was figuring out the definition of the word.

"Here's your new remote for the TV, and the one for your computer, and the one to control the thermostat, and the one to Skype with your daughter. I'll give you the others when I bring up your breakfast."

"Dear, Lord, how will I ever figure all this out?"

"Don't worry, Mrs. P. I'm a whiz at all this stuff." Kiki laughed as she ran from the room.

"Terrific," sighed Natalie. "Now I have a 'peachy' whiz."

Kiki came back with the breakfast tray to see the stately Mrs. Pengin relaxing on her bed of roses—her chaise lounge dear surrounded by floor-length draperies and ruffled poofs suspended over her bed. Kiki secretly glanced across all the dressers at the sparkling perfume bottles and intriguing little boxes. Each day that she worked, she did the same glancing—unable to stop looking at the beautiful things.

"Here's your breakfast, ma'am."

"Oh!" Natalie seemed startled as her eyes flashed open. "I didn't hear you come in."

"Were you off in dreamland?"

"No, I was just thinking about how things used to be."

"Well, never you-a-mind, Mrs. P. Better days, they're a-comin'!"

Ah, Natalie thought, *if my little* peachy-whiz *says it, it must be so.* She sadly let her spoon sink into the oatmeal.

"Quick, the remote," Kiki hailed as she jumped up. "It's your daughter."

Natalie's hand immediately reached upward to feel her hair; was she presentable? How could she keep forgetting that it was now impossible to reach that high? She sighed as she took the next step in good grooming—wiping her mouth with the napkin. The napkin slipped from her fingers.

"Mom what are you doing? Your head is almost in your food. Where is your aide?"

"Gwen, for heaven's sake. I merely bent down to retrieve my napkin. Why are you always calling me just as I'm in a precarious position?"

"Sorry, Mom, but I knew this would be the only five minutes of the entire day that I would be able to check in on you. Let me take a look at your aide."

Kiki bent into the range of view and waved. Gwen didn't say anything but her mother knew that her executive daughter was scrutinizing Kiki's wild hair, multi-pierced ears, and tattooed forearms.

"Hello," Gwen finally spoke.

Natalie held her breath but Kiki only answered, "Hello."

The mother's sigh of relief came just as Gwen called out her goodbyes.

"Well, she seems nice," Kiki remarked as she flattened down some of her fly-away hair.

"Oh, yes, she is very nice, but always busy."

"That's not always a good thing," Kiki commented with the Wisdom of Solomon on her shoulders.

"Who comes in tonight?" Natalie asked as she tried to find her notepad.

"Well, let me see," Kiki replied as she quickly brought up the schedule on the computer while continuing to fan her nail polish dry. "It will be Barbara. And Mrs. P., you don't have to have handwritten notes. Gwen has set up everything right here on the screen."

"Screen, bean," Natalie retorted. "By the time I get that thing figured out, three days could pass. I can still trust my notepad if I can just find it. There, you see? Right here it says 'Barbara.'"

"Do you like Barbara?"

"Well of course I like Barbara; I like everyone who comes in to help me. I don't get to talk much to the night people, however. I wonder what they do all night."

"I hope they never ask me to do the night shift. I would hate it," Kiki exclaimed as she blew on her dark purple nails.

"Why?"

Kiki put her soap opera magazine in front of her face.

"What on earth are you doing back there?" Natalie asked in total puzzlement.

Slowly Kiki's face emerged, actually half of her reddened face. The hidden half was equally as red.

"So, why wouldn't you want the night shift?"

"That's when Billy and I get together," Kiki answered while sliding the magazine a little more over her face.

"Now stop that! You have a right to have a boyfriend."

"Oh, thank you, Mrs. Pengin. Thank you. Does Gwen have a boyfriend?"

"Gwen? I really don't know. I don't think she has time for one, to tell you the truth."

"Good morning, Mrs. Pengin!" Kiki called out. "How was your night?"

"Didn't Barbara tell you?" Natalie retorted.

"No! She just ran past me like a bullet; I figured she had to get home in a hurry. What happened?"

"Oh, dear God. Dear God," Natalie moaned as she rocked her head back and forth with each "dear God."

"Tell me," Kiki implored as she stared down at an unstately woman with bags under her eyes and her hair—well, with hair much like her own.

"Barbara woke me up by almost shaking my arm out of the socket and said she heard the locks all click downstairs. She said it was robbers coming in!"

"Robbers? Oh my gosh. What did you do?"

"I called the police, but I couldn't use the fast way that Gwen had set up for me, because I couldn't remember what she had said.

And Barbara didn't know a thing about all these contraptions, so I dialed the old fashioned way."

"And?"

"And nothing. I was so embarrassed."

"Why?" Kiki kept digging for information.

"Come to find out that my daughter checked the locks on my house from a gadget in her house—which is a thousand miles away—and pushed a button to lock my doors, and at the same time contacted the police department to check my house. Can you believe it?" Natalie ended looking totally exhausted.

"Wow! You had quite a night!"

"Oh, it continues," Natalie added as she rolled her eyes. "I could see the lights blinking and the *beep, beep, beeps* were going off like fury. I knew Gwen wanted to talk to me on that Skype thing, but I forgot which remote to activate, and Barbara had no idea, so here we sat waiting for the phone to ring. But I, in all my excitement, had left it off the hook!"

"Jeez Louise," Kiki gulped.

"It was 'Jeez Louise' all right. The police were banging on the door and Barbara had to go downstairs to tell them I was all right. And somehow they knew that my phone was off the hook and the minute I hung it up, guess who was calling me?"

"Was she mad?"

"She was so controlled I think there must have been icicles running through the telephone wires—that is if there are such things as wires anymore."

"And?" Kiki pursued, as she twisted another lock of hair into a ringlet.

"She wanted to know why the night aide had not locked the doors when she came to work. And why, at two a.m. when she checked my house, they were unlocked."

"She must have a boyfriend," Kiki answered nonchalantly.

"What? What are you talking about?"

"Sounds like she just got home from a date at two a.m. and decided to check on you. Don't you think?"

"I can't think about such things as that. Barbara is going to be fired today, and I feel just horrible. Poor Barbara."

"I'm sorry, too, Mrs. P." Kiki was hoping against hope that she wouldn't be transferred to nights. "Let me pull up the schedule to see who is going to replace Barbara."

Kiki swirled her hand into her tote bag and began pulling out her cell phone, her makeup bag, her iPad, her mittens, gadgets of mystery in Natalie's world, and Billy's photograph. "Here, this is Billy," Kiki announced with a definite amount of pleasure on her face.

"Ah, so this is your beau."

"My what? Here, here is the new schedule." Kiki dashed over to Natalie's bedside to share the screen with her. "Irene will be in tonight and tomorrow night, and then on the weekend...oh, it's me."

"Oh, I'm sorry Kiki," Natalie said softly as she glanced over at the photograph of Billy.

"It's okay, Mrs. P. I need the job to buy all this new technology," she said as she pointed at the menagerie of gadgets she had heaped in a pile.

"I imagine it must be pretty expensive."

"Probably nothing compared to what your daughter has spent on all of this," Kiki commented as she pointed to the wall of equipment in the rose room.

"Oh, yes, the mother board."

"That's pretty funny, Mrs. Pengin: the 'mother board.' I'll have to tell Billy that one!"

Beep, beep.

"Oh my God," Natalie gasped. "What's that one beeping for?"

As quick as a wink, Kiki responded to the signal. "Yes. Yes. We'll be expecting you."

"What? What? What was it? Who is coming?"

"Calm down, Mrs. Pengin. Your blood pressure is registering high so a nurse is coming right over."

"How on earth does anyone know about my blood pressure?"

Kiki was sure it was going higher by the minute.

"Gwen also had this health monitor installed for you. It's all a part of that necklace you wear."

"What? I thought that was something for my falling?"

"That, too. Pretty neat, right?"

Natalie flopped back onto the pillow. "How on earth do you know all about this stuff?"

"It's just pretty easy for me. Most people don't think I know very...*Oops*, there's a message for you." Kiki quickly set up the Skype monitor for Natalie.

"Mother? Are you all right? I was in a meeting when my beeper went off. I got out right away. Are you okay? What's the matter?"

"Gwen, I don't know what's going on."

"Where's your aide? Let me talk to her."

"Hello, it's Kiki here."

"What is that pile of stuff on my mother's bed? How dare you put your junk all over? I'm going to call the agency about you, too!"

"Now you wait just a minute, young lady," Natalie commandeered as she sat up in bed, "this girl here, Kiki, is the only aide who knows how to operate all this high-highfalutin' stuff you have planted in my room. A few of the others have an inkling of how some of it works, but Kiki just plain knows what everything is and can control the whole 'mother board.'"

"Mother board"? Oh, mother, that's a good one!"

"Well, that's what Kiki said, too. Anyhow, a nurse will be here any minute to take my blood pressure. And Gwen, this is getting ridiculous!"

"Ridiculous or not, this is how it's going to be. I want to know what's going on in your life. I'll check in on you later. Bye."

"She thinks I'm part of her corporation! Has she forgotten that I'm a person?" Natalie cried.

"She's probably handling this the only way that she knows how," answered Kiki as she quickly stuffed everything back into her bag. "Anyway that blinking light there means there is someone at the door. I'll go down and see if it's the nurse."

Natalie slept for the rest of the day. Kiki did the laundry, some dusting, took three calls from Gwen, made pudding, and watched her soap opera. Natalie woke up with the changing of the shift.

"I'll see you Friday night, Mrs. P."

"Okay, Kiki. And dear, would you call me Natalie?"

"Well, it's you and me, kid." Natalie smiled as Kiki walked into the rose room on her first, not-so-wanted, night shift.

"Hi, Mrs....Natalie."

"I'm sorry you have to work this shift. I know you don't prefer it," Natalie said sincerely.

"It's okay; Billy has taken on a second job, so he's busy at night, too."

"Good!" I feel better. What shall we do after dinner? Do you like to play cards?"

"Oh sure, but—and we don't have to if you don't want to—but I was wondering if we could make a little notebook of instructions for all your new gadgets."

"Oh Kiki! Not only would that help me, but my various aides could use it too. What a brilliant idea, Kiki."

The young girl grinned from ear to ear and said, "And Natalie, you can call me 'Kateri' sometimes."

"Kateri? Is that your real name?"

"Yes. I was named after the 'Lily of the Mohawks,' but my twin sisters could only say 'Kiki,' so that stuck."

"What a lovely name, Kateri!"

The written and illustrated instruction manual began that evening.

"Kateri, you have a way of making everything so clear and easy. I'm not feeling like such a...a...stupid-head anymore," Natalie said with a laugh.

"You're no stupid-head Mrs. P. You raised a real brilliant daughter."

"In some ways she is brilliant but in others—I don't know."

Kiki closed the notebook. "Let's not start another page tonight. Let's play cards."

"All right! You're on. What'll it be? Poker?"

"Poker?" Kiki laughed. "You know how to play poker?"

"Sure. My husband and I used to play it all the time after Gwen left the nest."

"Mother! What on earth are you doing?" Gwen asked as she checked in through the airwaves. "Oh for heaven's sake. Can't you two put your minds to something more useful?" the daughter whined.

Natalie glanced quickly at the operator's manual but merely said, "Yes we could, but we're...we're...bonding by playing cards."

"Well, that's about as funny as when you said 'mother board.'" Gwen laughed.

Kiki didn't laugh, but felt a special twinge in her heart towards Natalie.

"Just wanted to tell you that a company named Central Star will be there tomorrow to install your new stair lift. You'll be able to ride up and down the stairs on a chair. Won't that be nice?"

"Chair lift? How? Where would…will I be? When will…"

"Hi Gwen, it's Kiki. Do you mind if I ask you some of the details that I know your Mom is worried about?"

"Oh, I suppose not, but I don't know how you think you know what my mother is thinking."

By the time Natalie was ready to sleep for the night, she was quite at ease with Kiki's explanation of how the chair lift would work and what a wonderful advantage it would bring to her life. "I think I'm going to like it," Natalie said with a yawn. "I've been missing my downstairs.

Turn my nightlight on, dear and I'll see you in the morning, or sooner."

The darkness of the rose room with the nightlight glowing softly on Natalie's altar was shockingly beautiful to Kiki. Because she had never worked at this hour, Kiki stood in front of the altar for a considerable length of time.

Her eyes went from the man with his heart showing, to the beautiful woman with her heart showing, to a heart-breaking man with blood streaming down his face as he dragged a wooden cross. Kiki didn't know what this was all about, but she was captivated by it. Then there was a little girl dressed up like a bride—that must be Gwen, Kiki surmised—and an old photo of a man, a woman, and a girl who maybe was Natalie with her mother and father.

Kiki didn't know that Natalie always fell asleep with her eyes directed at the soft light, but when she moved away, she heard Natalie quietly sigh, "Ah, there." She turned to see Natalie smile and close her eyes.

Kiki cleaned the kitchen and did the laundry before she settled down with her knitting. It didn't seem long before the silence was broken when she heard Natalie calling out for Gwen.

"Natalie, it's okay, you were dreaming," soothed Kiki, as she held her hand.

"Oh, yes, I was looking for Gwen; I couldn't find her."

"It was just a dream. Everything is okay. Would you like me to sit up here with you until you go back to sleep?"

"Would you?"

"Sure. Just let me run down for my knitting."

Natalie felt strangely content as she looked over to see Kiki on the chaise lounge with her knitting and the light from her altar shining on everything that was good.

Their bonding occurred more often than just through playing cards. They felt it develop through the writing of their instructional manual, through their practice of using the chair-stair, eating dinners together, stories of their pasts, and working on their knitting.

"Kiki, why do you knit so many baby clothes? Don't tell me that your twin sisters are both expecting?"

"Well, not exactly," Kiki said softly.

"Who are they for?"

"For me. I mean for my baby."

Natalie's hands stopped their knit-one-purl-two motion as she stared at Kiki.

"I hope you won't be mad at me, Natalie," Kiki cried as tears welled in her eyes.

"Well, no. I'm not mad. I'm just...just...shocked!"

"Yeah, my mother was a little more than just shocked. She told me to get out and not to come back until I got rid of the baby."

"What? Where have you been staying?"

"At the Empress."

"Where's Billy?"

"I don't know." And this time Kateri cried an ocean while Natalie tried to comfort her.

Natalie looked at the man showing his heart of mercy and the lady showing her heart of love directing their eyes to Kateri, as she sobbed on the rose chaise lounge dear chair.

"Mother, have you lost your mind?"

"I don't think I have, and I think this would be a wonderful solution to having so many different people coming in and out all the time. Plus, I certainly don't need all the help anymore. You got the doctor's report."

"Yes I did and I'm very happy for you, but you're going to have a pregnant girl move in with you? Do you know what you're getting into?"

"I think I do, Gwen. I think I do."

"Well, be prepared; I'm taking the next flight out. I'll be home tonight."

"Kiki quick. We've got to get in front of my altar pictures!" exclaimed Natalie as soon as Kiki reported to work.

"Why? What's the matter?" Kiki questioned as she saw the startled look on her employer's face.

"Hurry, we've got to send up some prayers right away!"

FIVE YEARS LATER:

You are invited to the kindergarten graduation of
Rose Natalie, with the reception to follow at her house.
Hosted by:
Mommy, Grandma Natalie, and Aunt Gwen

See you there!

⳻Chapter Ten⳼

CHARMS

"**N**o, not that church; it's the one past all those pine trees with the cemetery on the other side.

No, not Cemetery Lane."

"I thought I told you to throw that voodoo doll away," Father Tim snapped as he and the north wind howled into the kitchen.

"I will not! Never, never, never," Maya retorted, using each 'never' as another chance to thrust an assault into the tattered, pin-holed doll.

Each one of Maya's jabs was accompanied by her brother's stomping on the immaculately clean floor to rid his boots of the snow that had not been on the sidewalk before he went to the church to hear confessions.

"What's going on out here?" demanded Mrs. Schmitt, as she marched into the kitchen. She gasped at the sight of her floor. "Look at this mess!" she shrieked as she ran for the mop.

"I'm sorry, I'm sorry, Mrs. Schmitt," Father Timothy whined much as he had done as a boy—when his hair was redder and his freckles stood out like cereal accidentally scattered across a pink tablecloth.

"He's not sorry, Mrs. Schmitt," Maya interjected. Her huge, black, neon eyes flashed from the housekeeper to her brother. "He expects women to clean up after him, just like his father did."

Maya thrust her voodoo doll into the pocket of her flowery circular skirt, and then overtly put her hand over the pocket as a sign to her brother that he would never take it from her.

"That's not true. I loved Mother. I never made her wait on me," Timothy had exploded on his first word, but was almost relegated to tears by his last word.

Maya knew her strength in the moment, and stood to set her skirt twirling, then her long shiny black hair to follow suit, as she readied herself for the pinnacle of her delight. "You and your father were just alike. Mama and I waited on you both—hand and foot."

Just as she said, "foot," Maya stomped hers, making her plethora of ankle bracelets jingle like bells.

By this time, the snow had become a melted puddle, and her exuberant stomp sent the water flying up against the refrigerator and the stove.

Mrs. Schmitt screamed in a shrill crescendo much like a child's bicycle siren and ran back to the utility cupboard for a cleaning rag.

With her head still in the cupboard, she yelled, "Stop it! Stop it you two! Jesus, Mary, and Joseph! I can't stand much more of this!"

Father Tim's blue eyes filled with remorse, and Maya's filled with fire as she sashayed out of the room with her long necklaces swaying heartily in front of her scoop-neck Jamaican blouse.

"I'm sorry, Mrs. Schmitt," Timothy moaned as he took the mop from her hand and began cleaning.

"I know you are, Father Timothy, but I wish you would think before you came tramping into this house with your boots on. You know I like to keep this rectory spotless," she expounded with each swipe across the refrigerator door. "It has to be clean, clean, clean. I don't work eight, ten, sometimes twelve hours a day cleaning this house for you to dirty it up."

"I know, Mrs. Schmitt," Tim replied with a gentleness that he had used just minutes ago, before he had walked through the snow, when he had waited in the confessional for an hour and only one person had come in.

As the last droplet was removed from existence, a peaceful joy spread over Mrs. Schmitt; not only across her face but also across her entire being. Father O'Rourke knew it would; it always did when the chores were completed.

Timothy never remembered his dear mother going through these states of trauma, as did Mrs. Schmitt. Of all the adjusting he had to do being a priest in this northern, frozen parish, adjusting to Mrs. Schmitt was indeed the major feat. Not that he wanted to get along without her. He knew she was invaluable, but how to get along *with* her was a continual puzzle.

Mrs. Schmitt came with the house; she had been there through Fathers Rockwell, Ganlin, and Chabot. Now she was with O'Rourke, the redheaded, freckle-faced island boy who had an Irish father and a Jamaican mother with a young daughter—Maya.

Maya was seven years old when baby Timothey Patrick O'Rourke was born. As far as Maya was concerned, the two men had entered her world and she had to share her beautiful mother. This was a great concern to the young girl, but not at all to Timothy Patrick. He had entered a paradise on earth. He had a dear, sweet, loving mother and a devoted father. He never was given any reason for concern about Maya—in fact he never knew quite what to make of her. She just was there, with Mother and Father as his queen and king.

Island life was a free world for them all: there were no time limits, no pressures, and no unbearable constrictors. Father Tim looked back wondering, *How did I learn? How did I know things? When did Mother do her housework? Why was no one ever upset?* Well, except for Maya. She did become a great curiosity to him.

118

Maybe Mother should have displayed some of Mrs. Schmitt's qualities so that he wouldn't have been so unaccustomed to the general's ways.

"God rest your soul, Mum," Tim said to himself.

"Are you hungry?"

"Uh, no, I don't think so," he stammered.

"Yes you are," the housekeeper quipped assertively. "You are way too skinny. Supper will be ready in one hour. Come back then."

The young frame of a man sank into the desk chair that revolved, rotated. and rocked. Tim had yet to be disenchanted with the American mechanism. He made it sway, that is, as much as it could sway, so he could feel the rhythm and the motion of a hammock. Sometimes when he closed his eyes, he could feel the ocean breeze and the azalea peacefulness. He extended his hands and stared at them. Never had he had such white skin; it was almost as pale as the snow. "Snow," he groaned.

He looked out the window. Snow.

Overhead he heard Maya's reggae music and occasional dance steps. Tim was certain that his sister bounded to her feet every little while to dance, since she had done that since she was a child. For no rhyme or reason, she would begin to dance, leaving behind what had preoccupied her before. Of course, his mother did that, too. Sometimes she and Maya would dance together, so free, so gracefully. He and his father would watch. Father tried to dance a few times upon Mother's insistence, but he certainly wasn't the lithesome, statuesque beauty that Mother was, or Maya, Father Tim realized now.

Tim thought of his study as a sanctuary—that is, when it wasn't occupied with parishioners. The empty, quiet church was often his refuge, also, when he couldn't bear the sound of the vacuum cleaner or Maya's music any longer.

Timothy needed his quiet time with God. On the island, God was so easy to tap into, but...well, he knew God was just as much here in the frozen north. They would find each other.

Father Timothy undid his collar and tipped his chair back. He put his feet up on the blue chair and closed his eyes. Maya's music had tempered itself; it had a nice serenity about it now, the young priest thought.

Somewhere between his thoughts of swaying fronds and the melon-colored sunset, came the belting beat of, "Supper!"

The blue chair went east, the hammock chair went west, and Father Tim went south.

"Judas Priest, what's going on in there?" bellowed Mrs. Schmitt as her black oxfords clopped to the study.

Tim was on his feet by the time the inquirer arrived at the door.

"Nothing...nothing. I'm just trying to rearrange the furniture," he muttered weakly, knowing his face was no longer white but red.

Mrs. Schmitt gave the room a quick once-over with her steel gray eyes and went to the blue chair to give it a brushing off with her hand. Tim surmised she had detected an indentation from his socked feet.

He walked into the dining room with as much awe as he did each evening. Mrs. Schmitt had worked her magic again, preparing and presenting a meal fit for a king. She really was a genius at presentation. The large woman waited with much anticipation for Father Tim to give her his gratitude and appreciation. He had learned to do that from his father. Even when Mum had prepared a simple meal of rice and beans, Father made his wife feel like a princess. Mrs. Schmitt cooked for a crowd every evening, even though there were just the two of them—now three. The presentation always included the best china, silver, and glassware. Fresh linens were always on the table, with stacks more ironed, pressed, and waiting in the sideboard.

Why does she do all this? Father Tim thought again.

"Can you go up and get your sister?" Mrs. Schmitt asked indignantly. He knew she disdained latecomers for meals.

"Maya, come on," Tim said urgently as he rapped on her door. "Maya!"

The music went off.

"Maya, supper. Come on!"

Only silence came out from around the door of Maya's quarters. But then, on that silence drifted a faint odor of marijuana.

Tim opened the door.

"Where did you get this?" he yelled as he ran over to her.

"It's none of your business where I got it. Nobody asked you to come in. Now, get out!" she screamed.

Tim knew he couldn't talk to her when she was in this mood.

"I thought she'd quit," he mumbled to himself as he went downstairs.

"Well! Where is she?" demanded Mrs. Schmitt as she incessantly stirred, lifted, and checked every dish.

"Maya is resting; she won't be joining us tonight," Father Tim said softly as he looked down onto his plate.

Father Tim heard Mrs. Schmitt cluck her tongue. He knew that was a bad sign and wasn't surprised to hear her ask if she could say the grace. *Oh no,* he thought, *grace in German.*

Timothy had never gotten around to telling Mrs. Schmitt that he understood German very well. None of the other resident priests had understood it, and she apparently assumed he didn't either. After the first time of her saying grace in front of him, he was so shocked by what she had said that he was embarrassed to tell her he knew. Tonight was no exception. With his head bowed, Father Tim listened to Mrs. Schmitt telling God that he was a jerk and how having Maya in the rectory was inviting in the devil.

With her "Amen," she smiled politely at Father Tim while he uttered "Amen" and thanked her for saying grace.

"Oh, you're very welcome," she said smugly as she passed the platter.

The telephone rang four times during supper and, just as customarily as Tim pushed back his chair, Mrs. Schmitt dictated, "Your contraption can take the message. People don't need to bother you at mealtime."

"They are no bother, Mrs. Schmitt. I am here for them," Father reminded her.

"I've worked in rectories all my life, and I know how parishioners can wear a priest right down to the bone. Believe me, you keep your distance from them and you might survive." She accented the word "might" as she slammed another piece of Brockwurst down on her plate.

Needless to say, Tim always listened to the messages with one ear just to be certain it wasn't a real emergency. He knew Mrs. Schmitt couldn't hear the messages or she would have expounded upon each and every one of them. She had been in the parish through generations of people, deeming herself an authority on everyone.

Timothy finished the meal with his silent blessing and returned to his study. He pushed the button.

Janet wanted to set up a schedule for Christmas choir practice; Bob Lawson wanted to discuss the homilies; Mrs. Pearseson wanted to discuss her child's reactions to Mrs. Noonan's religious education classes; Sandra needed to talk about her failing marriage.

There was going to be one easy return phone call and three that were already making Mrs. Schmitt's heavy German meal turn in his stomach.

"Okay, the hardest one first." He forced himself into action as he looked at the crucifix. "Yes, Sandra, tomorrow at ten will work.

"Bob, yes, tomorrow at two will be fine.

"Oh, you want to wait until school is over, so you can bring Jimmy with you? That sounds like a good idea, Mrs. Pearseson.

"Hi Janet. Yes, I'll be anxious to hear your ideas for Christmas. Does the congregation do quite an elaborate ceremony for Christmas? Yes, tomorrow evening at seven o'clock. See you then."

Father Timothy stretched back in his chair and looked at tomorrow's schedule.

"What on earth is that?" he said aloud as he sat upright in his chair.

He went to the kitchen to look out the side door. Someone was in an old noisy pick-up truck, plowing the driveway.

"Who's that?" he asked Mrs. Schmitt while keeping his face pressed to the windowpane.

"Oh, that's just Charlie. Charlie plows around here during the winter," Mrs. Schmitt answered nonchalantly while scraping the leftover sauerkraut into a bowl.

"Oh, that's good," Tim remarked as he went back to his scheduling. He wondered if Charlie also shoveled the walks, but dismissed the notion of going back into the kitchen to ask the general. He decided to get up early and shovel them before Mass since he needed the exercise anyway.

Tim awoke at 3:00 a.m. to the rattling of dishes downstairs in the kitchen.

"Oh, no," he groaned. He knew there was going to be a big hullabaloo tomorrow when Mrs. Schmitt confronted Maya about messing up her kitchen.

He pulled the pillow over his head and recited the *Anima Christi*.

Mrs. Schmitt had already begun her tirade when Father Tim went down in the morning. The pots on the stove and the dishes on the counter were playing host to her vengeance. As he mustered his courage to enter the kitchen, he gave a word of thanks that the general was clanking around only inanimate objects with no nerve endings or brain cells.

"Good morning, Mrs. Schmitt," he called out as trepidly as would a sinner greeting St. Peter.

"Don't you 'Good morning' me!" she snarled as she scraped at the dried food.

"I'll straighten the kitchen after Mass, Mrs. Schmitt."

"No, no, no. This is my job and I must do it," she feigned trying to be a martyr.

"Well, I'm sorry for Maya's mess. I'll speak to her later. I'm going out to shovel the walks."

"What about your coffee? It's all ready."

"I'll have it later."

Father Tim wasted no time in exiting the kitchen. As he closed the door, he was glad he was out of earshot of the German exclamations that Mrs. Schmitt had begun to utter. For a few moments, he felt sorry for Maya having to begin her day with the altercation that was brewing. But on the other hand, he knew Maya could take care of herself. He was beginning to realize that he and Maya had been brought up very differently. Maya was right—he had been pampered and prized.

Tim was ready to atone for his sins by shoveling until his muscles ached. He then could offer it up for Maya's childhood. He hadn't meant to take her mother away from her.

"My goodness!" he exclaimed as he peered at the well-groomed sidewalks. "When did Charlie do all this? He must have shoveled last night after he plowed the driveways."

Tim took the shovel and walked to each sidewalk to see that they all had been cleaned. He felt guilty that he had been in the warm house while Charlie had been working, probably for hours.

Father Tim opted to go into the church instead of back to the kitchen. He looked again at the front door just as he had done every morning knowing it was getting more and more askew each day. The screws in the top hinge had protruded another millimeter since yesterday, he reckoned. He had tightened them several times but knew they required further work. He needed to ask Mrs. Schmitt if the church had a maintenance man.

Timothy Patrick O'Rourke grabbed his book of *Morning Office* and became thoroughly entrenched in the prayers and meditations for the day. Slowly, slowly, he could feel every pore of his body become saturated, rinsed, and visited by God. He could feel his soul embracing that of Jesus. Jesus hugged him with tenderness and comfort—oh, such comfort. "If only I could stay in this hour forever," Timothy pined. "Never permit me to be separated from you, dear Jesus," he prayed.

Swoosh, bang! The first parishioner noisily entered the church for daily Mass.

Father could hear her footsteps approaching him.

"Whew, what a morning! I guess it has started; our good old-fashioned winters that we're so famous for. Wait until you experience our winters," she went on almost gleefully. "You haven't seen anything yet! You'll wish you were back on that tropical island; that's for sure. I spent one hour cleaning off my car and getting out of the driveway this morning. I see you're all plowed out here. Just wait until you see our winters!" When Father Tim made no remark, she indignantly added, "Well, you better get ready for Mass."

Father Tim walked back for his vestments trying to reconnect his thoughts with God. All he could think of was, *In Thy wounds, hide me.*

During Mass, one of the kneeling benches collapsed with a huge bang and Lucretia Banks, who happened to be kneeling on the bench at the time, released a yelp of fright. *Poor old lady,* thought Tim, *it's a wonder she didn't have a heart attack.* Suddenly he felt a fit of laughter coming on and he tried to hide his face behind the chalice he was lifting. *Please, God, don't let me laugh out loud,* he prayed.

It was hunger that pulled Father Tim back to the rectory; he could face anything just to get some food. His plan was to distract the fighting hens by exaggerating his immediate need to find a maintenance man.

As he took his boots off on the porch, he peered through the kitchen window. There sat the two women seemingly chatting and having a peaceful breakfast.

"Praise God," he said, as he looked upward.

He had assessed the situation correctly. As he slid onto his chair, he released a smile to accompany those already at the table.

"Father, look!" Mrs. Schmitt said immediately. "Maya gave this to me. Isn't it beautiful, and it really works!"

Tim looked down at the little cloth figure with the big, disproportionate eyes and the wild hair.

He looked over at his sister who wisely chose to avert her eyes.

"Maya?" he inquired.

"Yes, it's true. I gave Mrs. Schmitt a very prized possession of mine, because she is so good to me and I love her like a mother."

Tim knew Maya's ways of getting out of trouble.

"And what did you tell Mrs. Schmitt this doll could do?"

Maya didn't have a chance to answer. Mrs. Schmitt squealed with delight, almost looking radiant as she tenderly held the doll and explained how it would bring her good luck at bingo, it would help her find money, and it could even bring bad luck to the people she didn't like.

"I've needed something like this all my life, Maya! I'll forever be indebted to you, dear. What can I get for you? Another piece of toast?"

"Well, yes, my new mother. Toast would be wonderful!"

"Maya, I want to see you—right now—in my study," Tim ordered.

"She is not going anywhere right now," the general commanded. "You are both going to sit here and eat."

"I'll see you after breakfast," Tim said as he leaned over to glare at his sister.

Mrs. Schmitt twittered and giggled all through breakfast. Tim had never seen her like this. "You know," she said as she wriggled in her chair, "I feel lucky already!"

Maya crossed her long, brown leg and twittered, too. "Guess what, Mrs. Schmitt, I'm feeling that way also!"

The two of them bonded like schoolgirls. Father Tim shook his head.

Oh, no. Is it ten o'clock already?

The doorbell meant Sandra was here for her appointment. Father liked to be mentally prepared for his parishioners and right then, he wasn't. As he jumped up, he quickly remembered to ask Mrs. Schmitt if there was a handyman.

"Yes. It's Charlie," she responded.

That was all she could say, as Father Tim was then in the living room opening the front door.

It wasn't until 10:00 in the evening that Tim realized Mrs. Schmitt was still in a good mood. He really hadn't seen her all day, because he had missed lunch to search the Internet for support groups and literature for Sandra. Later, he'd eaten supper in the study, after Mrs. Pearseson and Jimmy left, in order to quiet his nerves. After bidding the choir director goodnight, he turned away from the door as the clock struck ten.

"Dear Lord," he exhaled as he walked into the kitchen.

"Hard day?" Mrs. Schmitt asked as she walked past him with a cup of warm milk. "I'm going off to bed. See you in the morning. And Father, the little box by the big holy water font is where the priest can put maintenance concerns for Charlie."

"Oh! I wondered what that box was for. Thanks. See you in the morning."

The general started to giggle. "I'm going to bingo tomorrow night! I can't wait."

"Oh, no," Tim sighed after Mrs. Schmitt was out of earshot. "I forgot about that mess."

❦

Tim returned to his study with a dish of ice cream. He listened to Maya's music as the coolness of his late night snack meandered down his parched throat. He wondered what Maya was doing. Unfortunately, he thought he knew. Where is she getting that stuff? He needed to get to the bottom of this.

His thoughts went round and round from Sandra's marital problems to Bob's insults about the homilies, to Jimmy's obnoxious behavior, to the Christmas season, to the two new "best friends" in the house.

He wrote a short list of to-dos for Charlie before delving into his evening prayers.

❦

St. Sebastian's parish awoke to fourteen inches of new snow.

"Good glory be!" Timothy voiced as he looked out of the second story window at the new onslaught. "I've got to get out there and clear the walkways for Mass; nobody will make it up the driveway, and they'll have to park down by the road. Poor Lucretia. I don't think she can walk from the road up to the church."

He flew into his clothes and ran out onto the porch to jump into his boots. Oh, why hadn't he remembered to take his boots in last night? With three wraps of the scarf around his neck, Tim grabbed the shovel.

What? When was Charlie here? Again, everything was precisely cleared with squared corners of white. *I must have been sleeping like a log. He is unbelievable!* thought Father Tim.

The young priest returned inside with his boots in hand. Mrs. Schmitt was standing by the door like a centurion with a small rug to place his boots upon.

"Did you hear Charlie out there early this morning?" Tim inquired.

"Land sakes, no" answered the housekeeper laughing raucously. "I was dreaming I had won the jackpot at bingo!"

"Mrs. Schmitt...about that charm doll you have... Excuse me, I'll answer it."

Tim ran back into the kitchen and pulled on his boots. "Where do the Brownites live? The grandfather is dying and calling for a priest."

"Well, well, well," she drawled as she crossed her arms across her chest, "don't tell me he's finally going to confess his sins after all these years. That figures."

"Mrs. Schmitt! I'm appalled at you; don't ever speak that way about anyone."

"Well, it's true. Everyone knows what a devil he has been."

"Stop it! Just tell me how to get to his house. And if I'm not back in time for Mass, please go over to the church and tell them I've had an emergency."

As Father was closing the door, he heard her mumbling in German about how she thought he was a fool to rush to that dastardly old man.

Tim backed the car down the driveway thanking Charlie with every breath he took.

As the town highway department's big plow pulled Father out of the snow bank, and as Fred Peterson used his tractor to pull Father out of the ditch, and as the sand truck pulled Father Tim out of the culvert, Tim couldn't help but think of the docility of life on the island. *These Northerners play a whole different ball game*, he thought to himself. *God bless them, I guess they do have a lot to deal with.*

He did get to the old grandfather before he died. As he thanked God for that, he made a mental note to send letters of appreciation to all those who helped him get and keep his car on the road. He knew that natural disasters, such as his hurricanes back home, brought out the best in people. No one had indicated that this snowstorm was anywhere near a disaster, however. Just a typical morning in our neck of the woods.

"Did anyone show up for Mass?" Tim questioned as he entered the kitchen.

"Just Lucretia. She stayed for a while and said the rosary, I guess."

"She's a tough old lady, isn't she?"

"She sure is. Been through a lot, too. I noticed that the front door works a lot better. It doesn't drag on the carpet anymore."

"The front door? But I haven't given Charlie my memo about it yet!"

"Well, I don't know when it got fixed, but it's fixed," Mrs. Schmitt said as she dashed around her domain getting breakfast for the frazzled-looking young man.

"Well, you look terrible," Maya mumbled as she shuffled into the kitchen.

"As do you," he answered looking at the puffiness in her face and the blackness under her eyes.

"Did you hear Charlie plowing early this morning?"

"Who?"

"Never mind."

"You know," Mrs. Schmitt interrupted with a noticeable constraint in her voice, "your laundry, Maya, has begun to pile up in the washroom and is causing me to be a little—what should I say— *nervous?*"

Maya tipped her head to the right and stared at Mrs. Schmitt and then to the left, with more staring.

"Wait here. I'll be right back," Maya finally said as she left the room.

"I guess she took that pretty well, didn't she?" the staunch figure exalted as she served a plate of heavy breakfast to Tim.

"I guess she did!" Tim answered as he ate ravenously.

In a few minutes Maya's huge black eyes seemed to beacon her way into the kitchen well before her body entered. Her voice sounded out like an island melody. "Sit here, Mrs. Schmitt, sit. I have something for you."

Mrs. Schmitt blushed and started to giggle.

"Oh, no," thought Father Tim as he cut into his fourth sausage.

Maya took a glittering amethyst bottle out of her gathered skirt pocket. She held it up to let the light dance upon it as she caressed the smooth curves of the glass with her fingertips. Slowly she unwound the golden top.

Maya let the fragrance escalate to her nostrils, and when it had, she inhaled deeply letting her head loll backward and forwards. Mrs. Schmitt's little gray eyes were transfixed upon the Jamaican beauty.

Slowly Maya dipped a finger into the liquid and place the oil on the palm of Mrs. Schmitt's right hand. Maya rubbed the oil seven times to the right and seven times to the left as she chanted an exotic, haunting melody. The same ritual was accomplished on the forehead.

When Maya finished, she took Mrs. Schmitt's hands in hers and asked the older woman if she was still nervous.

Mrs. Schmitt didn't answer right away; she seemed to be in a deep contemplative state. Maya patiently waited; Tim stopped chewing.

Finally Mrs. Schmitt inhaled deeply and said, "No, why no. I'm not nervous at all!"

She seemed to beam with radiance, Father Timothy thought, knowing exactly the ploy Maya used on her.

"You know what I'm going to do right now, my little dumpling? Because you have helped me so much, I am going to go right into the washroom and do your laundry!"

"Oh, no, Mrs. Schmitt, I would not permit such a thing!" exclaimed Maya.

"Yes, yes, you have taken away my nervousness. It is a miracle," she cried and almost ran from the kitchen.

"Are you happy now?" Tim asked as he leaned toward his sister and scowled.

"Of course," she retorted, "why shouldn't I be?"

"You are promoting falsehoods and witchcraft. It's evil."

"It is not! I'm giving that woman some peace of mind and hope for the future. They're the same things that you try to give in your crazy religion!"

"That does it!" Timothy yelled and jumped up causing the chair to tip over and the bottle of elixir to rock. Maya grabbed it quickly and hugged it to her bosom.

The general ran in and Maya darted to her side, slipping her arm around Mrs. Schmitt's ample waist.

Maya began yelling at Tim in Creole while Mrs. Schmitt shouted in German. As he watched the two animated women, he forced himself to think of Grandpa Brownnite receiving the Last Rites in peace, and of his kind snow bank rescuers, and of the goodness of Charlie.

When the tirade finally ended, both women stalked off—even more furious that Timothy Patrick O'Rourke hadn't retaliated.

Tim sighed; he needed to be in the church. He grabbed his list for Charlie and left the house. The new inch of snow on the walkway made him think of his white sand and the promise to his dying mother that he would watch over Maya.

He slipped the list into the maintenance man's box after crossing out the message about the door. The door! He went back to examine the front door. Sure enough, it swung open and closed like a charm. He groaned, wishing he hadn't thought of the word "charm"; it wasn't one of Maya's charms. It was Charlie's hard work.

"Enough of these thoughts," Tim reprimanded himself as he hastened to be with his Lord.

The church felt cold, but he knew better than to turn up the thermostat—he had been given his orders about saving on fuel oil and saving on money during the first meeting with the parish council. *I better get used to it*, he thought. *It's only November and winters last until May.* May? He sighed as he looked up at the sad eyes of Jesus on the cross.

"I need help, Lord," he whispered as he buried his face in his hands.

Father Tim had a long talk with God. It wasn't until he shifted his weight back and forth on his knees to alleviate the stiffness, that he remembered he was on Lucretia's broken kneeling bench. He sat back in the pew and lifted and lowered the bench. Sure enough, it worked perfectly. When did Charlie fix this?

He retrieved the obsolete memo from Charlie's box and started home.

Well, well, he thought as he saw Maya hurrying up the sidewalk, *she's coming to apologize.* He smiled as he watched his tanned sister dressed in a flowery dress, with only a scarf and a shawl for protection from the cold. The white snow looked even more like sand with her gracing its granules. He paused to speak with her, but she hurried by sputtering in her native dialect about the weather.

Maybe she needs to spend a little while in the quiet church, too, he thought. *That would be good!* Maya had been very remiss about attending services.

Mrs. Schmitt was folding Maya's laundry when Tim returned.

"I cannot get her to put on a coat and boots," she whined as soon as she saw Tim.

"Well, this is the first day she's been out of the house. I guess it won't kill her just once."

"First day? Every afternoon she runs over to the church. She's going to catch her death of pneumonia, poor baby."

"Every day?" Father Tim reiterated with great surprise.

He walked into his study feeling like he had just heard the best of news. He had no idea Maya was seeking the Lord! Or wait— oh, no, no. She's not using the church as her pick-up spot! Tim's forehead broke out with beads of fright. *No*, he comforted himself, *she'd never do that.*

Tim tipped back in his chair and looked at the photograph of his mother. "You'd be proud of me, Mum, I'm getting Maya straightened out!"

Before Father Tim left for choir rehearsal, Mrs. Schmitt pushed a piece of paper at him and told him to make a list of three people who should be in invited for Thanksgiving dinner. "It's tradition," she said hurriedly. "We always ask those less fortunate than ourselves, you know. I'll need your reply in two days so I can decide if they're worthy or not. Got to go! I'm going to win *big* at bingo tonight. Bye."

"Oh dear God, have mercy on us," Father prayed as Mrs. Schmitt shut the kitchen door.

Tim could hear the strains of the organ music piercing through the cold air as he walked up the front steps. He thought of the beautiful Christmases he had grown up with. The church services were always important to his father. Consequently the whole family attended, even Maya, until she was about seventeen. His father was very distressed when she rebelled, but Mother pacified him with, "She'll return in her own time."

Tim took heart when he realized that maybe this was her time.

"Do you mind if I sit in with you?" Tim asked the choir members.

The few people who were there made him feel welcome. Janet distributed the music and basically explained the program.

"Now, Teara and Joan," she directed her attention to the young girls, "this is your first time joining us and we're so pleased you're here! You both did a fine job in the school's spring concert when you were only juniors, and now that you're seniors, we'll feel like we're working with professionals."

The two girls giggled and sat a little straighter.

Father hoped that more men were going to join; he sang the tenor part and Steve Swenson was the only bass.

After rehearsal, Father Tim asked Janet if she knew of anyone he could invite for Thanksgiving dinner. She thought as she piled up her music. "Well, there's always Lucretia. How about old Mr. Ericson and Mr. Turnball?

"Could I invite Charlie?"

"Charlie? Well, you could try," she answered.

He scribbled off a note to Charlie and put it in the box and left Mrs. Schmitt's list on the kitchen table.

Father was deep into his evening prayers when he heard such a bang, he thought something had exploded in the house! He ran to the source of the explosion and found the cause. Mrs. Schmitt had not won big at bingo; Mrs. Schmitt had not even won little at bingo.

Oh, boy, he thought, *this is going to be a bad scene.*

He ran to the foot of the stairs and shouted, "Maya. Maya! Come down here. Mrs. Schmitt needs you."

Tim could hear the general's shoes stomping on the kitchen floor. He was afraid every one of his statues would fall to the floor.

"Maya, please!" he called again.

And there, almost floating, came a scarved and bejeweled woman who slowly descended the stairs. Little tinkling bells could be heard from her fingertips and silver bracelets chimed from her wrists. Barefooted and obviously high on something, Maya skimmed past Tim and went directly to Mrs. Schmitt.

Maya took off one of her scarves, kissed it and draped it around Mrs. Schmitt's neck.

"Such sorrow you are in," she cooed to the older woman. "Come, sit with me. I'll make you a special tea."

The stiff bulwark of a woman seemed to melt before Tim's eyes. Like putty, Maya led her to the table.

Father Tim went to his bedroom and closed the door.

∞

"What is this?" Tim wondered as he walked over to what appeared to be a wooden box in the vestibule of the church. He took the piece of paper that had been placed on the cover and read:

I thought we needed something nice in the church for the food donations. I hope you like it. Thank you for the Thanksgiving invitation, but I'm going to have a full house. —Charlie

Tim switched on the light and looked at the box. It was beautiful. He touched the wood. It had been sanded and stained, the edges were beveled, the lid fit perfectly, and even the hinges were beautiful. Tim closed the lid to see carved in the top, *You do it unto me.*

Something took hold of Tim's heartstrings and lifted him far beyond the household squabbles, the grumbly parishioners, and the cold weather. He was reminded of the joy he felt on his Ordination Day.

∞

"I'm not having those two men in this house!" spattered Mrs. Schmitt like water on grease.

Tim hadn't even taken his coat off before the guest list became the news flash of the morning.

"Why, what's the matter with them?" Maya asked hoarsely, not looking at all like the floating veil-girl that she had been the night before.

"Did you ever see how those two men come dressed for church? No, I guess you haven't. Well anyway, it's a disgrace. And that Bob Turnball's old truck backfires every time he leaves the church parking lot. It's gotten so the children stand out there and wait so they can all laugh. And I don't think Alfred Ericson has had a new jacket in thirty years. I called Lucretia, now she's all right. Unfortunately, she promised her neighbors that she'd go there for Thanksgiving. I called some other folks, too, but it seems that they all have plans."

"Then it's settled. Bob Turnball and Alfred Ericson it is," announced Father Tim, as he sat down. He watched Maya's hands shake as she held her coffee cup.

As the days went on, Father Tim deduced that Charlie only worked at night. Morning after morning he went outside to see that he had been there. Every task that Tim requested to be done apparently was done at nighttime. Tim wished he could meet Charlie and talk to him personally.

Once Father asked Mrs. Schmitt why Charlie worked at night and she replied, "How do I know? I have enough of my own work. I don't have time to keep track of other people."

Father also asked if Charlie went to church. "Of course," she answered, "Charlie is there every Sunday."

"Well," thought Tim, "I'll get to meet him one of these days."

On the day before Thanksgiving Father saw a note on the wooden box from Charlie:

I hope you don't mind but I know a bunch of kids who volunteered to deliver food baskets to the needy. I told them I'd drive them around. Some of the families live way out in the countryside. I know where they live so it'll be a lot easier for me. I understand you have a little trouble on the snowy, icy roads! You'll get better after your first winter. —Charlie

Father Tim immediately folded his hands and said, "Thank you God, thank you, thank you." He had been dreading that trip almost to the point of being sick. He vowed that next summer he would explore the countryside and find out where all the roads were and where the parishioners lived.

On Thanksgiving morning Tim said to Maya, "You better do something with the general. She is downright hostile."

"I know, I know. I already have a plan."

He didn't ask.

When Mr. Turnball and Mr. Ericson arrived, Tim kept them in the living room. Maya was the perfect hostess, keeping everyone happy serving hors d'oeuvres and delighting the two guests with her funny stories. Tim admired her ease with strangers; she was a real hostess just like their mother had been.

As Maya passed by, Tim whispered, "how are things going in the kitchen with the cook?"

"Terrific! Everything is great!"

Tim didn't know what Maya had done to calm Mrs. Schmitt, but he knew she had done something. Through the laughter in the living room, Tim could hear singing from the kitchen. *This is how Thanksgiving should be,* he thought.

As Mrs. Schmitt readied the table in the dining room, the singing became louder. Tim shot a look at Maya and Maya merely hunched her shoulders as if to say she didn't know what all the singing was about.

Suddenly Mrs. Schmitt appeared in the living room giving a swooping bow to her guests. She proclaimed as a Frenchman, "Dinner is served." She then laughed hysterically and, grabbing Mr. Ericson's right arm and Mr. Turnball's left arm, she pulled them along saying, "Shall we go in to dine?" The two stumbled along like two little boys being dragged to the dentist by their mother.

Tim grabbed hold of Maya's arm and whispered irately, "She's drunk! You got her drunk."

"I did not," Maya whispered back sharply. "I told her to just have a little."

"Where'd you get it?"

"From the church. Where'd you think I got it?"

They heard a crash; Mrs. Schmitt had fallen onto the table. "Maya," Tim shouted, "help me get her up to her room."

Mr. Turnball and Mr. Ericson sat on either side of the big table with their hands folded in their laps.

"Well, Alfred, this has been quite a day so far."

"Sure has, Bob. Sure has."

The choir rehearsals progressed at an even pace. Teara and Joan practiced dutifully for their duet and Janet was surprised to hear Father Tim whistling the tune of their song. "Oh, sure. My mother used to sing this song all the time," he remarked.

He learned little by little what was expected for the holidays.

"Maybe Charlie will have more of the nativity statues done by this Christmas," Janet said to Father Tim. "I think it was about a year and a half ago that Sean had that terrible accident and most of Charlie's time, of course, was devoted to taking care of him."

"Who is Sean?"

"He's Charlie's husband."

"Husband?"

"Yes."

"Charlie is a woman?"

"Yes! Didn't you know that?"

"I had no idea!" uttered Father Tim in absolute amazement.

"Charlie is the woman who comes to church with the six children. They usually sit toward the middle, on the right."

"That's Charlie?"

"Father, I've never seen anyone look as surprised as you do right now." Janet laughed.

"I'm surprised all right! Why does she work at night?"

"I guess she takes care of Sean and the little one during the day. When everyone is sleeping she says she can get out and get some work done. She has two very reliable teenagers at home."

"How does she know how to fix things and construct and plow?"

"Sean was a carpenter. I think he tells her how to do things and she does it. She's a pretty smart and industrious woman."

"I guess so," sighed Tim as he stared out across the church.

"Do you want me to go around and turn off the lights?"

"No, I think I'll stay here for awhile. Good night, Janet."

"Well, Lord," Tim started to pray, "life is full of surprises, isn't it? Who are these people who stay hidden from all public acknowledgment to work your ways so unobtrusively? They must be very special to you. You, who can see everything; you who knows what's going on down here. I wish Maya were one of your little saints. I'll try to help her, Lord. And Mrs. Schmitt, what am I ever going to do about her? Wait a minute..." Tim paused and straightened his back "... I'd better take a look at myself, shouldn't I? I can't even compare to the sacrifices and generosity of Charlie. From now on, Lord, she is going to be a role model for me. Thank you for bringing her into my life. Maybe there was a reason for me being sent to this God forsaken...it's not God forsaken, is it?"

Tim fell to his knees to apologize.

The nativity scene that was nestled serenely around the altar became a beautiful focal point of the church. The children from the religious education classes used it as a part of their program. Charlie had added the shepherds and the sheep, an angel and the donkey. She said the three wise men would be ready by Epiphany.

People of all ages came forward to admire Charlie's workmanship. She had carved them all out of blocks of wood. The detail was phenomenal, but she swished a lot of the credit to her children who helped with the sanding and painting. Tim could see tears in her eyes when she explained how Sean could still use one hand and, by placing the statue on his lap, he could carve. He was the one who carved the faces.

The Christmas Midnight Mass had been changed to 7:00 due to the years and years of snowfalls that traditionally raised havoc with the parishioners traveling to and from church at that late hour.

Charlie had brought in fresh Christmas trees from their property and the church looked enchanting with the little lights and candles. Someone had donated fifteen poinsettia plants. Everything was ready.

Tim could hear Janet explaining to Teara that Joan's throat had gotten much worse and she wasn't coming in. Teara was going to sing the special number by herself, as a solo.

Charlie wheeled Sean in; the little one was asleep on her husband's lap.

The church was full to overflowing, just as every church around the world was, Tim imagined. He thought of his church on the island. He looked out upon his people as he began the Mass. He really did hope they would have peace, mercy, and joy.

❧

The organ sounded out the introduction to Teara's solo but Teara didn't begin singing. The organist played the introduction again, no singing voice was heard. Janet started for the third time and Teara sat down, succumbing to tears of stage fright. Father Tim stood up ready to fill in for Teara. He sang the first note but stopped when he heard a voice from the back of the church, a voice that filled the entire periphery of the building with melodious tones of gold and silver and angel wings. Everyone turned to see who it was.

Joy welled in Tim's eyes as he listened to Maya's singing.

"Merry Christmas, Maya," Tim whispered.

Father Tim came to the closing line of his well-rehearsed homily and looked toward the back of the church to see a man quietly entering. He handed Maya a small bag.

With the last word of his homily, Father Tim immediately knelt, causing his parishioners great confusion with some standing, some kneeling, and some still sitting. He folded his hands and said, "Have mercy on us, Oh Lord."

"Humph," Mrs. Schmitt snorted as she whispered to Lucretia, "now he's making up his own parts of the Mass."

Lucretia whispered back, "Leave him alone. He knows what he's doing."

ᴄᴈ᠂Chapter Eleven᠂ᴈᴏ

NIGHT WITHOUT END. AMEN

"**C**an we visit at the kid's day care center today"?

"No, Marjory. They're not taking any more volunteers."

"Why?"

"They say it's too crowded."

᠂ᴈᴏ

Phoebe (fee .bi) 1. A feminine personal name. 2. In Greek mythology, a Titaness, mother of Leto, and, before Apollo, occupant of the Delphic oracle. 3. A nickname of Artemis as goddess of the moon; hence, the moon. 4. Saturn's ninth satellite.

Phoebe (fee bi) An American flycatcher (Sayornes phoebe) with grayish-brown plumage and slightly crested head: common throughout the eastern United States.

᠂ᴈᴏ

Phoebe rolled over again, this time looking squarely at the moon nestled between the flounces of the white, eyelet curtain. *There I am*, thought Phoebe as she pictured her grandmother sneaking through the house calling, "Where's the moon? Where's my little moon?"

Phoebe liked being thought of as the moon; the moon according to her grandmother was magical and free. *I think she was right*, Phoebe thought as she stared at the illuminated sphere in the night sky. The moon didn't have to lie awake wondering why it couldn't sleep. It could sail through the sky in total serenity. It didn't have to hear the banging and rattling, the moaning and groaning from next door.

But the serendipitous illusions of the moon faded as her brother Bobby's words came to the forefront of her mind:

Phoebe, Phoebe overbite

Oh what a fright.

Too bad Saturn

You lost your satellite.

Number nine, we've got her here

Have no fear.

She's with us,

But we'll ship her out

On the first bus!

Phoebe rolled onto her back wishing her brother's voice from their childhood hadn't penetrated her night.

She channeled her concentration, instead, upon the distinct trill of her namesake bird, that which her mother had named her for. Every so often she and her mother would sit in the backyard listening for their "Phoebes." When the first proclamation pierced the air, they would look at each other in absolute surprise and delight. Phoebe never had a partner who could share the delight quite like her mother. Sometimes her mentor would trick the bird into answering with her precise imitation of the inverted third. She taught Phoebe how to whistle the distinct call, and the little girl became the envy of her older brother and his friends.

Suddenly Phoebe had the greatest desire to whistle, to whistle the call of *phoe—bee*. She puckered her lips and inhaled, but released only the air. She couldn't whistle in the wee hours of the morning, she thought, as she felt her face smile. *Why can't I whistle? There is no one else in the house. I can whistle!* But she couldn't, and she didn't. *I'm so inhibited*, she sighed as she nestled in on the clock side of the bed.

Phoebe stared into the light of the clock recalling the article about women having less cancer if they slept in total darkness, even eliminating the tiny lights of clocks, night-lights, and electric blanket controls. Phoebe was glad she loved the blackness since she had become an adult. How could she survive without the clock, however? She felt her brow wrinkle. *I've got to stop doing that*, she mused, as she lifted her hand to feel the furrow in her brow. *I'm going to be an old lady with a permanently worried look.* Phoebe worked at smoothing her forehead.

Her hand jumped when the wind took control of the night. "Oh, no," she groaned as she listened to the old building next door begin its unmelodious repertoire.

Which board might that be? she wondered. During the daytime she studied the dilapidated structure, with its collapsed roof and missing sideboards, to use at night in making an educated guess as to where the consternation was coming. She listened. She knew that the sharp slappings were from the loosened, rusted sheets of metal siding. The groaning she thought came from the huge beam that had fallen into the sidewall. The beam and the remains of the wall were apparently stimulated just enough by the wind to rub against each other, causing a desperate, groaning sound. But what was causing the sharp knock, knock, knocking as if someone's knuckles were rapping purposefully against the kitchen door? Somehow she thought two boards must have arranged themselves to act as a large version of castanets. The wind became their force, and now the clappers were clicking out their steady rhythm. The wind, the mighty conductor, led its orchestra through the night like a maestro. There were the dynamics of the percussion intertwined with the howling oboes and the violins that cried. A sudden stillness, too, became an integral part in the maestro's manuscript, when it left Phoebe in anticipation of the next movement. The overture tonight led into a wailing, sorrowful cry that Phoebe had heard before. She wondered about the velocity that could create just that sound. She had named it the *Mea Culpa Overture* because she envisioned the building as a holding pen with people crying and moaning to escape. After an unceasing repetition, Phoebe called out, "Escape, escape! Leave! There is no roof; there are gaps in the walls—get out!" But they didn't; they didn't even seem to make the effort. It was as if they had no brains left to think logically.

Phoebe pulled the blanket up onto her ear; she was surprised to feel that it was cold. *It's a wonder I have any ears left*, she thought as she left her hand and the blanket there. *Oh what fools we were when we were teenagers—no hats, no boots, no brains, but stylish, yes, frost-bitten high-stylers!*

Phoebe watched the digital numbers change from one to the other, every numeral being made from one basic shape. *How does that clock know how to do that?* she wondered. *Why is that light confusing my melanoma? What about the moon? Is that light causing cancer, too? Oh,* she thought nervously, *it is actually the light from the sun.* "Oh, my," she sighed.

Phoebe took the coverings from her ear and turned to the other side just as she thought the top story of her house was going to be blown away. She felt her body tense as she waited for the gale to subside. *Why am I worried about that stupid dilapidated building next door with those moronic souls inside when my own house could be blown away?* She thought she heard another beam, or maybe even a wall, crash to the ground—but she didn't care. What if her roof flew off? What if the high tree fell into her house? What if? What if?

Stop! Okay God, it's true, people wait until the last desperate minute to think about you. Okay, it's in your hands now. I'm going to stop worrying now. Take over.

All right, here we go. A: St. Anthony; St. Anna; St. Aloysious; St. Augustine, B: St. Benedict; St. Bernard; St. Bernadette; St. ?, C: St. Cecilia; St. Christopher, St. ?, C, D: St. Damion; E: …There must be some E saints, what's the matter with me? F: St. Francis, St.…Oh no, this is a bad one, the litanist thought as she looked up at the black ceiling and listened to the timpani roll and the cymbals clash next door. *E, F, G,* her mind scampered. *G: St. Gregory, St. Gertrude, H: St. Helen, St. ...*

Phoebe suddenly peered toward the window; the silence had scared her. She half-grinned at her own fear.

⌒

"Good morning, Phoebe."

"Good morning, Neptune."

"Phoebe, three more kids have been enrolled and they're coming in today."

"Three more?" Phoebe asked worriedly.

"I know, I know. We really shouldn't take in any more kids until we get more help, but business is business you know. Besides, the ad for help has been in the paper for a week; we should get some responses any day now."

"How old are they?" Phoebe asked as she hung her coat on a red peg at: *It's a Life Saver—Day Care Center.*

"Three, almost two, and three weeks," Neptune mumbled guiltily, knowing Phoebe would not be pleased.

"Three weeks! What on earth are you thinking of?" Phoebe spoke, forgetting for a moment that Neptune was the boss and she was only an aide.

Neptune capitalized on the caste system just as Phoebe knew she would and replied, "I don't need to discuss this with you."

The tall, svelte entrepreneur picked up the folders and walked to her office. Her tailored, eggplant suit and white cuffed blouse marched with an aura of determination and relentlessness.

Phoebe began her morning ritual of mixing paints and displaying toys different from yesterday's. She made up another crib with fresh sheets and blankets. *Dear God,* she thought as she ran her hand over the tiny print of teddy bears and flowers, *that baby should be home with its mother, not dumped here with strangers.*

"Morning, Phoebe," Estra sang out as she entered the building quite like the storm that had crashed against the world during the night.

"Good morning, Estra," Phoebe said seriously.

"Land sakes, woman, what are you down in the mouth about?"

Before Phoebe could answer, Estra's voluptuous frame sailed across the room to the green peg exclaiming as she went, "Did you hear that wind last night? Why, I thought my roof was going to end up in the Swanson's pool. I poked Harry and told him he'd better get up and do something quick. Course he said, 'What do you think I can do? Hold the roof down?'

"Damned old fool!" Estra continued. "He wouldn't budge if the house fell in on him. So, what are you making up another crib for?"

"We're getting a new baby today—three weeks old."

"Land of mercy!" Estra squealed as she plopped her hand against her chest. "A real baby. I love babies!"

Phoebe knew that the new baby would spend a great deal of time nestled on Estra's voluptuous bosom, the bosom that instinctively welcomed all children for comfort.

"I do too, Es, but why do these new mothers have to rush back to work? Why can't they stay home for awhile?"

"I don't know, honey. Maybe they need the money," she added, as she bustled through the room, adding her touch to the pseudo home environment. Her plump hands fluffed the pillows in the story center as she finally looked at Phoebe long enough to say, "You look beat. You aren't sick are you?"

"No. I guess I didn't sleep too much last night."

"Um," Estra empathized.

"Oh, to continue with the baby, we're getting another three, and an almost two-year-old also."

Estra stopped her fluffing while her big, brown eyes widened. "What?" She half whispered as she darted a look at Neptune's closed door. "How can we handle..."

"Morning, Estra," sang the business-like alto voice of Neptune. "I suppose Phoebe has told you about our three new clients?"

"Yes, ma'am."

"I figured," Neptune's mascara-lined eyes darted to Phoebe's. Phoebe looked to the floor. "You'll be able to manage, won't you Es?" Neptune crooned letting her sugar drip over the day-care aide.

"Well, sure, ma'am. We can do it," Es replied with a half-smile.

"I knew you could," Neptune said as she lathered another sweet cake upon Estra as she raised an eyebrow to Phoebe. "Well, my dears, I have an appointment, but I'll be back before the newcomers arrive. I told them not to come until ten o'clock today." Phoebe watched Neptune slip into her white cashmere coat. Her long fingernails, painted in matching eggplant, sparkled as she tied the sash.

The four students from the college whisked past Neptune just as the big clock clicked upward to 7:00 a.m.

"We're here!" Cheryl called out as she and the other education majors used the remaining adult pegs.

"Thank the Lord!" Estra laughed, reminding Phoebe of a dozen children bouncing on a trampoline. "We couldn't handle this without you." Phoebe knew that was the truth—seven youngsters and now ten.

"Good morning, Phoebe," the beautiful Cheryl offered.

"Hello, Cheryl," Phoebe answered nervously.

"What's the matter, Phoebe?"

"Oh," said Phoebe slowly as she brushed the hair away from her tired eyes, "I guess I'm just a little worried about taking in three more children."

"Three?" the young early-education major asked. Her sparkling blue eyes weren't daunted for more than five seconds, however, when she resounded with, "We can do it, Phoebe, we can handle anything!"

Phoebe smiled a slow smile as she looked into the eyes of youth, vitality, and eternal goodness. "God bless you, child," Phoebe said softly, as she approached Cheryl to hug her.

Estra stopped chattering to look at her old friend enveloped in Cheryl's arms like a child—a little child who rested her head on her protector's shoulder. Estra had never seen her coworker look so dependent.

Then there was no more time to analyze Phoebe's vulnerability; the door sprang open with the whirlwind of a new day. One after another came the children with the bags and the clothes and the blankies and the Teddy bears and the special snacks and the harried moms and the often-bewildered dads. The orders came fast and furious about medication, naps, runny noses, potty training, food, friends, manners, discipline, dentist appointments, and pacifiers. Eight to ten hours of living were encapsulated into two minutes of instructions. Phoebe absorbed the orders, hoping she wouldn't forget anything. Fast kisses were given as parents scampered out of the door to earn enough money to keep their children in the expensive *It's a Life Saver—Day Care Center.*

The three- and four-year-olds darted to the toys, as Michael and Michelle toddled directly to Phoebe and Estra. The two-year-old twins always needed the first twenty minutes in the arms of the two noticeably older women. The nannies nestled into the oaken rocking chairs as the small bodies clung like parasites, trying to somehow make sense of the absence of their mothers' touches to the touches of the substitutes. Phoebe and Estra knew about their confusion and their sadness; they knew, so they rocked, cuddled, and let comfort travel to the little ones by osmosis.

Cheryl and Joe became immersed in construction while Casey and Evan helped their group with the intricacies of grocery shopping.

Phoebe pulled the corner of the afghan over Michelle's bare legs, wondering why her mother hadn't dressed her in warm clothing. As she watched the college students, she whispered to Michelle, "Thank God we have them." She felt the little child beginning to get warm.

The chair rocked to and fro with the older woman permeating solace and comfort to the child, and the child grasping onto Phoebe, trying to understand the wiles of the world.

Phoebe awoke to Estra's hand on her shoulder. "Phoebe, it's almost ten o'clock. Neptune will be here any minute."

"What?" Phoebe mumbled as she tried to focus on where she was.

"You fell asleep, girl, and we've been as quiet as church mice around here so we wouldn't wake you." Es giggled as the little ones peeked around her large frame to giggle, too.

"I can't believe I fell asleep. I've never done that before."

Phoebe suddenly looked down into her empty lap. "Where's Michelle?" She panicked as she flung back the afghan and lurched forward.

"Me here," came a little voice around the side of Es. Michelle bent forward by putting her hands on her knees, to peek around.

Phoebe smiled as she uttered, "Oh my, oh my."

"Actually," added Estra as she folded the afghan with five majestic folds that caused a breeze, "the two of you drifted off and the rest of us turned into little quiet mice. I think we should do this more often." Estra's voluptuous laugher rang though the room causing all folks, big and small, to look her way. "Michelle only took a catnap, however, and when she awoke, she went right to Casey's outstretched hands. Those college students are good; they really like kids, as far as I can see."

"Hello all. I'm back!" chirped Neptune as she sailed through the doorway as gracefully as a deer silently bounding over a stonewall. "Our new people should be here any minute."

And it was that very next minute that Phoebe watched a young woman come through the door maneuvering two young children over the threshold, while carrying a baby in one arm and three bags in the other.

"Hello," the mother said almost inaudibly. "I'm Christa. Christa Gregory."

"Yes, yes. We've been expecting you. Come in," voiced the confident entrepreneur. "And who do we have here?" she asked, looking at the three-year-old.

"That's Kenneth III, and Marissa, and our baby, Travis." Marissa held onto her mother's leg as the other children gathered to stare at the newcomers.

"Didn't your father-in-law come with you?" Neptune inquired with business in mind.

"Oh, yes," Christa answered as she looked down at the floor. "He's parking the car."

"Well! We'll wait right here for him," Neptune remarked cheerfully. Phoebe thought she could hear the calculator running in her boss's head.

All eyes were on Mr. Gregory when he presented himself at the door as a "captain," or a "king," or a "Prince Charming." Phoebe saw the education students glance sideways at each other. Estra's eyes widened, and she smoothed and straightened her blouse. Neptune's hand floated directly into his manicured, pinkie-ringed hand as they exchanged greetings.

"Very nice, very nice," he uttered as he canvassed the room with his pale blue eyes. "I can see why this center comes so highly recommended."

"Let's conduct our business in my office, while the children get acclimated, shall we?" Neptune purred to Mr. Gregory, as she directed him to her office.

Evan was able to entice Ken III to the puppet stage, but Marissa would not relinquish her mother's leg. Phoebe said softly, "Let's sit over here."

Phoebe looked at the young mother's pale face and tired eyes. She guiltily thought about her own nap. Marissa laid her head on her mother's knee, as she got a better hold on her leg. Christa stroked her daughter's head as she looked down at the baby.

"Do you really have to go to work?" Phoebe asked abruptly, knowing Neptune would be furious with her meddling.

Christa's pale face blushed. "My father-in-law says I have to," she uttered as a tear rolled down her cheek.

"There, there," Phoebe whispered as she used a tissue to wipe the tear, just as she did with the children. "Why would he tell you that?"

"My husband...my husband left us even before Travis was born. He told me he didn't want any more children, but I wouldn't get an abortion. So he's gone," she said as another tear escaped.

"But why do you have to go to work?" Phoebe whispered.

"My father-in-law said he would support the children but he wouldn't support me—he thinks it's my fault that his son left the marriage."

"No cry. No cry," the little voice from the knee implored.

"It's all right, honey," the mother said bravely.

The whispering ceased when the "captain's" voice made the two women jump. "Are you ready?"

Phoebe couldn't recall ever seeing a look more of horror than that which spread across Christa Gregory's face. "I-I have to explain the schedule and their routines and-and..."

"I'll wait for you in the car."

Christa looked pleadingly into Phoebe's eyes. Phoebe wished she could become the magical moon or her namesake bird that could release its call to make everything bad disappear for Christa. But she couldn't. She couldn't do a thing.

"Come, staff! Mrs. Gregory has a few things to tell you!" Neptune twittered.

A few things? Phoebe wondered how a mother, in a few minutes, could explain the entire history of her children, plus all that she has harbored in her heart and mind and soul.

When the door closed, the almost two-year-old Marissa screamed and cried. She pulled on the doorknob and hollered until Phoebe was sure every saint in heaven was on their knees crying with her. The baby awoke and cried. Casey and Cheryl ran to the kitchen to warm the bottle, while Estra laid Travis upon her abundant chest and cooed like a mother dove. Ken III slid off Evan's lap and, without saying a word, took a tissue from his shirt pocket and wiped away the tears his mother had left on the floor.

G, H, I – St. Ignatius; St. Isadora; J – St. John; St. James; St. Jude: Yes! St. Jude, the Saint of the impossible! Dear St. Jude, implore God to help the children, Phoebe prayed.

She lifted her head when she heard sleet against the window. *I didn't know it was going to storm tonight.* She sighed as her eyes stared at the black window with the punctuating staccatos. She remembered the afternoon when she sobbed at the window worrying over the birds. "The sleet is going to hurt them," she had cried to her mother. "It will hurt them!" Phoebe's mother gently held the little girl and reassured her about the instincts of birds and all animals. Phoebe also remembered Bobby and his friends teasing her about seeing dead birds fall from the sky.

Phoebe snickered as she thought of them always trying to get her upset about something.

"Oh, no," Phoebe moaned. She released a lung full of used oxygen while the wind lashed the sleet against the agonizing building next door. She could hear the boards bend and twist against each other, somewhat as a tooth being pulled out of a jawbone. She thought of baby Travis, when he would be teething. His mama would walk the floor with him at night and the center would get him through the pain of the day. Christa would become more and more exhausted, until she dropped right to the floor and died.

"Stop it!" Phoebe said to herself as she yanked her body over onto the opposite side of the bed. She reprimanded herself for permitting her imagination to run wild.

K – St. Kismet; St. Kenneth. Kenny, help Ken III, Lord. L – St. Lawrence; St....

Phoebe jolted upright when she heard glass break. The black night gave her no clues, even though she looked toward the sound. Had a flying projectile hurled itself at her car? No, she didn't think it was quite that sound. Probably just the last of the windows in the old building giving up the ghost...

"Giving up the ghost." She paused on that phrase as she laid back to look upward. "To let your spirit leave the body," she rephrased the words, as a teacher would do and began to analyze the moaning. *I wonder if there is moaning when the spirit...*

Stop, stop, stop, you've got to get some sleep. M – St. Monica; St. Martin; St. Mary Magdalene; St. M...

***

"Morning Phoebe! Did you have to scrape your windshield this morning?" Estra called out with the exuberance of a kid calling her friend about the news of a snow day.

"As a matter of fact, I did." Phoebe wondered aloud, "How did you know?"

"Land of mercy," Es laughed like a bubbling volcano, "do you think sleet only happens over your house?"

"Oh, yeah. I guess the storm was all over town, huh?"

"Girlfriend, you are so funny!"

"I am?"

"You know, I think you're in a fog today."

"I do feel like I'm in a fog, believe me," Phoebe said wearily.

"Well, buck up girl. All the kids come in early today, no ten o'clockers."

"Good morning, ladies," Neptune crooned as she looked down at her high heeled boots inspecting them for salt. "I won't come in. I just want to tell you I'll be at a conference all day. Here's the number if you need to call me. Oh, I'll have an interview tomorrow with a prospective teacher. Good news, right?"

"Right!" Estra quipped.

It's about time, Phoebe thought as she avoided Neptune's eyes.

Phoebe and Estra spent most of the day trying to comfort Marissa and caring for the baby. The twins didn't receive their usual attention from the older women and had a weepy, insecure day. During the last hour of the broken-hearted day, Phoebe wasn't startled when she felt a little hand tapping on her knee. Kenny III was holding up a tissue for Marissa, Travis, Michael, Michelle, and Phoebe.

That night Phoebe didn't know if it hailed, snowed, or even if the house had blown down. She had reached a point of tiredness whereby her mind and body finally shut down.

If Phoebe's mother had told her that someday she would thank God for a good night's sleep, the little girl would have found it incomprehensible. Now she understood.

In between Marissa's sobbing and Travis' crying and the whimpering twins, Neptune led the new candidate through the luxurious day care center. The prospective candidate didn't seem to mind when Clayton accidentally threw the ball into her arm or when Jeffrey leaped at her from behind the easel and growled like a lion. Neither did she discourage Amanda from holding her hand as she took the tour. The interview continued in Neptune's office for more than two hours. When they transcended back into the swing of things, Neptune announced with great joy that Ellie would be the new senior teacher. All the adults clapped for her and the children followed suit. It was a good day, Phoebe thought.

Ellie spent the rest of the day effortlessly meandering from child to child and adult to adult giving each one personal attention. She encouraged spontaneous replies and garnered much information about the existing program and the development of the children.

After the last child had left for the day, Ellie called a meeting for the staff. *How professional*, thought Phoebe. Ellie told everyone how pleased she was to be "on deck" and hoped they would have a rewarding work situation together. *How nice*, Phoebe beamed.

Ellie continued as the staff hung on to her every word. "In my observations, I have come to a few conclusions that I want to share with you. These conclusions are all derived from my extensive education in this field. I'll never mention this again, but I have a PhD in early childhood education and have written three books on the subject."

The college students looked at each other as if to say, "Now, we're going to learn something about children." Phoebe and Estelle looked at each other as if to say, "I see trouble up on the north ridge."

"That being said," Ellie continued, "we will make a few changes in the program. First of all, there is way too much mothering done here. For example, Marissa needs to accept the fact that her mother leaves her here every day, and that crying is not going to be tolerated by anyone. The baby is being picked up way too often. Babies need to learn that they have to rely on themselves and not others for comfort. The twins, too, have to stop their whining; they aren't going to get anywhere in this world by whining."

Ellie's audience was, by this time, in a trance. No one even looked sideways at another.

"Also..."

Oh no, an 'also,' Phoebe thought.

"Also, you're giving too much time to your snack time, nap time, and lunch time. The children could be learning more if you cut back on those three meaningless times. After all, the parents are paying big bucks expecting their children to be learning something— not dilly-dallying around."

Out of the corner of her eye, Phoebe saw some movement. She knew it wasn't from any of the staff, they were still statues. It was Neptune who sat off to the side taking copious notes. With a jubilant smile on her face, she undoubtedly thought she was being educated.

"I am going to work up a program whereby there is much more structure. I am also seeing too much playtime here. We're going to run classes all day, involving every type of subject matter, including child abduction and sex education. I think the parents will be impressed when they hear we are teaching classes!"

Neptune nodded as she wrote feverishly.

"Well, everyone, I am going home to write up all these wonderful changes and I will have hand-outs for you in the morning! *Smile!* The new era for *It's a Life Saver—Day Care Center* has just begun!"

"Wait Ellie! I'll walk out with you," Neptune effervesced, as she ran to grab her coat.

Estra began washing the finger-paint table; Phoebe mixed a new batch of salt-clay, Cheryl sat with the sewing kit to repair the clown costume, Evan sorted and organized the carpenter's bench, Casey hung today's artwork on the bulletin board, and Joe cleaned the gerbil cage.

No one spoke; only an occasional sigh could be heard. Their goodnights were uttered not expecting anyone to have one.

For Phoebe, it came to fruition. Even with no deafening sound caused by the elements, the stoic silence of the night would not lead her into the escape of sleep. She was awake—awake to the coldness of this generation; awake to the insensitivities of the educated; awake to the god of materialism that forces children into sterile camps.

Chapter Twelve

THREE OLD SOULS

"*Isn't Marian related to Esther somehow?*"

"*Yes. The butcher-shop Esther.*

I heard she's going to be over on Dovetail Road. You know, where that little bridge goes up to the apple orchard."

"...and Ma, how's Great Uncle Louie?"

"Oh, you know. He's the crossword puzzle impresario."

"Still doing those crossword puzzles?"

"I guess you could say that," Odelia chuckled.

"And Grandma CeeCee?"

"She's doing well."

"Still saying lots of prayers?"

"Oh yes. Lots and lots of prayers." Odelia half-chuckled.

"They're lucky you've been so kind to take them in."

"Monica! They're family!"

"I know, I know, but..."

"My cousin Marian is here now, too, honey," Odelia relayed the news rather reluctantly.

"What? Why?"

"Well, she's getting on in age you know, and her kids can't seem to manage her-her-uh...artwork."

"What kind of artwork?"

"It's sculpture. Yes, it is. Sculpture! She's very creative," Odelia answered supportively.

"Gee, Mom. I know you like to help people, but it must be a lot more work for you."

"It doesn't seem like much more work. In fact, when the seven of you were growing up, it was much more work than this!"

"Thanks a lot, Ma!"

"Oh, you know what I mean."

"I guess I do, but Ma, take life a little easy will you?"

"Monica, don't worry about me. I'm fine."

Odelia passed away so unexpectedly that spring, not one of her seven children had a chance to say goodbye. It was the youngest, Monica, who received the phone call:

"Réquiem ateérnam dona eis, Dômine; et lux perpétua lúceat eis."

"Excuse me?" Monica inquired of the person on the other end of the line.

"Réquiem aetérnam dona eis, Dômine; et lux perpetua lúceat eis."

"Oh! Grandma CeeCee? It's you!"

Monica called her mother's neighbor, who called the ambulance, who called the coroner, who called the priest.

"John, quick, pack a bag. We're flying home tonight."

"It's our home now, John; Mama left it to me."

John and Monica moved out of their studio apartment and both applied for teaching jobs in the Lone Moon Creek school district. Maybe it was because the other six of Odelia's children all had houses and families that she left the house to Monica.

"My little *Babina!*" Grandma Cecelia cried and hugged her "baby."

"Anima Christi, sanctifica me,

Corpus Christi, salva me.

Sanguis Christi, inébria me,

Aqua láteris Christi, lava me..."

"What is she saying?" John whispered to his wife.

"She's praying."

"Oh."

"Uncle Louie, are you hungry?"

"Eight letters, m, m, m, esurient, famished, indigent, m, m, fourth letter I, m, m, last letter T."

"What is he saying?" John whispered.

"He's just thinking about words."

"Oh. Do you think he's hungry?"

"He usually is."

Monica and John pulled dish after dish of funeral and condolence food from the refrigerator. The five inhabitants sat to eat.

161

Grandma CeeCee began grace, while Uncle Louie stared at the cold chicken, and began his deliberation of five letters: "Biddy, capon, chick, fryer, poult. Third letter Y, fourth letter E, wait no, six letters pullet."

"What is he doing?" John mouthed the words to his new wife.

"He's eating his chicken."

"Oh!" John replied with a look more quizzical than Uncle Louie.

"Cousin Marian, sweetheart! That salt shaker on top of the fork balanced on top of the water glass might fall!"

"Fall?" asked the tiny little lady with the lace collar.

"Yes dear, it might fall," Monica guided just as she had heard her mother do.

❧

John ate in silence as he listened to the prayers, in what language, he didn't even know, to some sort of imaginary crossword puzzle deliberations from the old Uncle with the wild hair, to the clattering and banging of tableware objects Marian tried to erect into her sculptures. His forehead wrinkled as he watched her, ever so delicately, try to place peas on the lid of the sugar bowl.

"Monica, we have to talk."

"Talk," Uncle Louie mimicked as he ran his hand through his startled hair. "Address, blabber, chatter, declaim, discuss, seven letters, three Bs, two Ts. Which?"

❧

"Honey, we can't live this way," John whispered to Monica as they settled back in a much-needed quiet house.

"John! We're fine; we're all fine."

Monica knew what he was implying. She knew that John had come from a completely different background than she—a small family, a sane family, all proper. *Oh no!* She caught herself thinking of synonyms for "proper."

"Monica, Monica, wake up!" John shouted as he shook her arm violently.

"What's the matter? John, what's the matter?"

"I smell smoke!"

The two newlyweds dashed to the hallway and immediately Monica knew what it was.

"John, it's okay. It's Grandma. She's lighting candles and praying."

"What do you mean lighting candles? Do you want her to burn the house down?"

"They're votives; they're in glass cups and—shh—you'll wake the others."

"I don't care. I won't allow this!

"Cecelia!" John exploded as he pushed open the door to her sanctuary. Two steps into her space and John stopped. There was the little Grandmother on her knees, praying with such fervor that she never heard her grandson-in-law enter her room.

"Sancte Michael Archángele, defénde nos in proelio,

Contra nequitiam et insidias diáboli esto praesidium,

Imperet illi Deus, súpplices deprecámur; tuque,

Princeps militiae coeléstis, Sátanam aliósque spiritus

Malignos, qui ad perditiónem animárum pervagántur

In mundo divina virtúte, in inférnum detrúde. "

John blew out the candles and swung around to Monica. With fire in his eyes much like the flames that previously had burned on CeeCee's altar, he ordered, "Handle this!"

The next day all the candles were replaced with battery operated candles. Grandma CeeCee wasn't upset at all; Monica was grateful.

"Monica," John whispered as he helped his wife with the dishes, "how can you stand this?"

"Stand what?"

"The three people in this house. How can you stand it? Do you know that Marian got into my toolbox and concocted some God-awful thing. It's going to take me days to unwrap all that wire and duct tape."

"I did see it, honey, and I thought it was one of her best."

"Well, two more weeks of this and we'll be out of here, thank God," John sighed.

"You mean: *Deo Grátias?*"

"Don't you start that now," John half-laughed, even though he was serious. "We desperately need at least two weeks of vacation with my parents."

"Vacation," Uncle Louie piped in as he walked to the refrigerator. "*Mmm*, respite, recreation, intermission, leave of absence. Okay that will fit."

"You do have it all set up with your sister to come here and stay with them. Right?"

"Right." Monica laughed as she saluted.

"That's it!" Marian called out as she caught sight of the salute. "Patriotic. I'll make my next sculpture patriotic!"

"Ah, 'patriotic.' That's it. That's the word I've been searching for." Uncle Louie howled as the light from the refrigerator shone through his wild hair.

"*Glória in excélsis Deo!*" Grandma CeeCee's prayer could be heard from the living room.

"Oh," John groaned. "Good Lord. I'm going upstairs to pack," he murmured, wishing he hadn't said the words "Lord" or "pack."

"Are you kidding me?" John exploded after Monica explained the phone call from her sister. Monica, froze; the sculptor's hands halted in mid-air; no words jettisoned out of Lou, and Grandma CeeCee had no prayer.

"Well, I'm going anyway!"

The gloom of the newlyweds' first separation settled over the house. Monica tried to hide her tears, but the others knew. Maybe Cecelia prayed a little harder; maybe Marian silently took more supplies out of the cupboards, and probably Uncle Louie still mentally worked through his crossword puzzles, but Monica was in her own little world of sadness and didn't know.

Several days later...

"He's sorry! He said he was sorry!" Monica cried out as her spirits rose as high a Gram CeeCee's prayers. "He'll be home tonight!" Once again the house came back to life.

Five days later...

"Thank you for staying with them again, Mrs. Pearsall. I really appreciate it."

"You're very welcome, dear. And remember, I'm right next door if you need any help over here."

"Thanks." Monica sighed as she half-smiled. She looked at the hospital bed in the living room and knew John would be placed in there as he recuperated from the car accident on Fishtail Road. She was sure of his recovery, but she worried if he would be able to tolerate the menagerie of old souls who lived in the house.

Their teaching jobs were to begin in two weeks—that is, Monica's teaching job. John now had to give up his until November 1st or later.

Monica hired an aide to come in while she was at work, and John became more and more disgruntled.

"How was your day, honey?" Monica would sing out every afternoon, and every response was…not kind.

"Why do they have to hover around me? They're always in the living room with me. Why can't they do their stupid stuff in their rooms?"

"John! They worry about you. They care about you."

As Monica passed by Grandma CeeCee she whispered, "Pray, Grandma. Pray."

John tried to keep his eyes closed, but for how long could he do that? He peered over at Marian. Now her card-table workbench was three feet from his bed. There she was, hunched over her sculpture, trying to glue on some asinine thing.

Uncle Louie also had an old rickety card table that he was hunched over. John could see him using a ruler.

"At least they're quiet," John sighed with gratitude.

Even Grandma CeeCee merely sat in her big wing back chair, where her feet didn't touch the floor, and prayed to herself. John could see her lips moving in silence. He laboriously turned so he could face the wall.

Day after day passed, when finally John could sit up in bed. He found himself watching Marian's progress more and more. She surely was persistent, he chuckled to himself. He discovered that she would work for hours until she got one piece or another to fit and meet her approval.

One day Uncle Louie slowly walked over to John's hospital bed and handed him a clipboard with a crossword puzzle attached to it.

"What's this?"

"I made it for you," the old man uttered. John could see his face redden up into his spiked hair.

"Well, thank you," John mumbled as his eyes scrutinized the ruler drawn lines, the darkened blocks, and the tiny, little numbers.

Marian watched, and CeeCee watched with her lips moving.

"Oh! Wait a minute," the old man said while he lumbered back to his card table. After one glance, he immediately navigated to Marian and, without saying a word, she handed him a pencil with an eraser.

"Thank you, Uncle Louie." This time John smiled at the old man.

"Where did you get that?" Monica inquired that afternoon.

"Uncle Louie made it for me. Hand-made it. Can you believe it?"

"Wow! But you haven't finished it."

"I know; this thing's very difficult."

Marian and Cecilia could see the corners of Lou's mouth turn up in a smile.

Over and over John watched as Marian tried to insert a red fingernail-polished washer onto a conglomeration of wooden toothpicks. "Marian," John implored, "try putting it on that piece of chain first."

Marian did…and it worked. "Oh, thank you, John. Thank you so much!"

"You're very welcome, Marian. You know, that's quite an interesting sculpture you have there. Very ingenious!"

"It's going to be for your first wedding anniversary. Oops, don't tell Monica." Marian gasped as she put her hand over her mouth.

John laughed, "I won't Marian. It's our little secret."

<hr />

"How was your day, honey?"

"Good. Really good." John smiled as he stretched up to kiss his wife.

"Day after tomorrow will be your big consult with Dr. Brenner."

"I know," John replied as his whole demeanor sank, body, mind, and spirit.

"Maybe you won't have to have the operation, John," Monica cooed softly.

"I hope not."

The next day John couldn't muster any interest for his crossword puzzle nor was he curious in watching Marian's progress. He turned to the wall and went to sleep.

<hr />

Had he gone on to eternity? Was he in the funeral parlor? John turned to see rows and rows of chairs and candles burning, real candles, and soft music playing and words, people saying words together. The only people he recognized were Grandma CeeCee, Marian, Uncle Louie, Mrs. Pearshall from next door, and his aide. What was going on?

Suddenly Monica burst through the door and rushed to John.

"Monica, what's happening here?"

"I have no idea." Her eyes scanned the audience. "Grandma! Aren't these your friends from church?"

"Indeed they are."

"Why?"

"Because John needs prayers for tomorrow."

"Oh."

"Memoráre, o plissima Virgo Maria, non esse auditum a sacculo quemquam ad tua curréntem precsidia, tua implorántem auxiliary, tua peténtem suffrágia, esse derelictum. Ego tali animátus confidéntial, ad te, Virgo virginum, mater, curro, ad ye vénio, coram ye gemens peccátor assisto; noli, Mater Verbi, verba mea despicere, sed audi propitia et exáudi. Amen."

John grasped Monica's hand as the doctor sat down.

"John, I've gone over and over all your tests and x-rays. I can't explain the change, but there has been a change. John, you're in the clear. You won't need the operation."

"Deo Grátias!" the young couple uttered together.

"I think that was a good way to put it." Dr. Brenner laughed.

Chapter Thirteen

STITCHED HISTORY

"Yes, Marjory, maybe we should get back into quilting, but you know they don't meet in Lone Moon Creek anymore.

I think we would have to take that steep road up behind the old Creamery."

◆

Ooohs and *ahhs* rose from the group as Gretchen humbly held up her finished quilt.

Gretchen had been one of the original members of the quilt club, and now, almost twenty years later, no one even knew how many times she had been in front featuring a quilt. She was now the last member to totally sew the entire masterpiece by hand. The others used their computerized sewing machines, or at least simple electric machines. So it wasn't uncommon that the chatter over Gretchen's quilt went on and on with questions and comments, especially after all the ladies left their seats to hover around the kaleidoscope of colors.

"Gretchen, could we lay this over the tables so we can really look at it?" Sharon requested.

"Oh, yes," Gretchen replied in her demure and diminutive way.

The women were brought happiness—the way only women know how to do. They could hover the same way over a new baby or a jewelry counter, or a kiosk of arts and crafts. Today they raved over the perfect stitches, the millions and billions of perfect stitches, and the perfect placement of the pieces so that the points would exactly meet. As the buzzing of the honeybees continued, Gretchen's thoughts sailed back to her mother and grandmother. The three of them would sit together every evening to make their quilts, all by hand, all with patience. Even as a little girl, Gretchen learned that a needle and thread were mere appendages of her own hand. "Oh, she's such a good girl," her grandmother would say in her broken English as she patted Gretchen's head.

"That she is, Ma. She's our shining little star," her mother would say adoringly.

The little student quickly learned more about the art of quilt making, precision, and creativity. And as she sat in the family circle, she also learned more about the war and the reasons why Papa was away for so long. The three quilters missed having their man around the house. Missed him so much. Papa was Grandma's son, and Papa was Mama's husband, and Papa was Gretchen's *sweetheart*. That's what he would tell her, as he winked at Mama.

For several years the quilts were stitched with hope and laughter as they talked about their wonderful future when Papa would come home. But as the time passed, month after month after month, the pieces were quilted together with fear and anxiety, loneliness and depression. And after the day when Mama stepped out onto the porch to talk to some man in a uniform, Mama never quilted again. Only Grandma and Gretchen let their needles go up and down as they listened to Mama crying upstairs in her bedroom.

"Where did you ever find a pattern like this, Gretchen?"

"Gretchen? Gretchen?"

"Oh, what did you say?"

"Where did you find a pattern like this?"

"It was one that my Grandmother created," Gretchen replied, still trying to shake her thoughts back to the present.

"Gretchen, do you think you could sit with some of us and show us how to hand stitch?" Sandra asked.

"Of course I could. I'd be glad to."

Sandra squeezed Kate's arm. "She'll do it! She'll help us."

Sandra and Kate were the newcomers, young, enthusiastic, and making great progress.

Sandra had come into the club with experience about the sewing machine because her mother had taught her how to use it as a little girl, but had never shown her quilting. Sandra's mother could have won honoree of the year, the way she taught her daughter how to cook, sew, paint, garden, and care for pets—plus making sure she had her dance and piano lessons, while learning how to swim and camp and…

"Sandra?" Kate laughed. "What are you thinking about? Claudia wants to know how many people want Gretchen to do a teaching session next month on the fifteenth."

Sandra's hand shot up as did several others.

On the drive home, Sandra again went to thoughts of her mother. *I was so lucky*, she reminisced as she inhaled deeply. *So lucky that I was chosen out of all the other babies waiting to be adopted. My mother and father picked me over all the others!* Finally the huge exhale came and Sandra began to tap the steering wheel in sheer jubilation.

"Hi, Mom, I'm home. Mom? Why are you lying on the couch right before dinnertime?"

"Oh, I'm just a little tired today," her mother answered with the same smile she always showed when Sandra entered the room. "But I'm better now." She laughed as she bounded off the couch and nearly pranced to the kitchen.

"Oh, Mom, you are too much." Sandra fawned as the two hugged. "Too much" was exactly how Sandra thought of her Mom's abilities and her desires to pass along everything she knew to her daughter.

"How was quilting today?"

"Great! Those women are unbelievable. You should have seen that one quilt that Gretchen made; it was all hand stitched, just like she always does. It was unbelievable."

"Well, I am so sorry that I never learned how to quilt, Honey, I could have taught you that."

"Mom, it's okay! Look how many things you did teach me. Plus, just by knowing how to use the sewing machine," she said as she drew closer to her mother and whispered in her ear, "—which you taught me—quilting is pretty easy for me."

"I always promised the good Lord that if he'd send me a daughter, I'd bring her up right and teach her everything I could. Now, help me with this dinner. Your father will be home from his card game any minute."

"Mom? What are the tears all about?" Sandra asked heartstricken as she reached to wipe away a tear from her mother's cheek.

"Oh, I'm just being sentimental," Maria giggled. "Don't mind me."

"Ma, do you remember Dad trying to teach us different card games?"

"Teach? You, yes. Me, no," she laughed. "I never could catch on quickly like you did. I don't know where you got all your brains from. Oh! I'm sorry; I didn't mean to say that Sandra." Maria's face displayed the tribulations of the world.

"Mom, don't be silly," her daughter said heart-warmingly as she hugged her. "I know I probably got some of my traits from by biological parents, but it's from you and Daddy that I got—"

She suddenly stopped.

"Got what?" Maria asked as she froze with one fork halfway to the left side of the plate.

"Hmm., I'm trying to think of something...you must have given me...something," Sandra spoke as she furrowed her brow.

And just as fast as two squirrels attacking a full bird feeder, the women shrieked out their laughter as Maria chased Sandra around the kitchen table.

"Good glorious day!" Bill cried out. "What's going on here?" He knew exactly what they were doing; they'd been doing this hot pursuit game since Sandra was two years old or so.

"Whew," Maria howled as she collapsed into a chair, "I'm getting too old for this!"

"Sit still, dear. Sandra and I will wait on you tonight."

"Oh Daddy, you mean the card game didn't tire you all out?" Sandra teasingly asked.

"Hey, you young whipper-snapper," Bill teased right back as he threw a towel at her head.

Finally, in between the passing of the mashed potatoes and the peas, Sandra answered the *got what?* question. "Mom, this is what I got from you and Daddy: the fun, the teasing, the closeness the...Mom! You're tearing up again. What's the matter?"

"I'm just all in today. I don't know why. If you two don't mind, I think I'm going to go to bed early tonight."

"Mom? It's only six o'clock."

"I know," Maria said, then chuckled, "but I have a big day planned for tomorrow."

Father and daughter cleaned the kitchen just as Mom would have done. She'd taught them well.

"Did the school call you to teach tomorrow?"

"No, not yet, but as you know, most of the calls come in the early morning hours. I was actually glad that I didn't get called in today—even though I need the money— because I was able to go to my quilt club."

"You like that, don't you?"

"I really do. One of the older ladies is going to teach us how to hand quilt."

"Wow, you're going back to the old days," Bill teased.

"There's something captivating about it, Dad, and something comforting. You know, I think I'm going to start drawing some plans for a quilt."

"Well have fun. I think I'm going in to watch the captivating, comforting news."

"Yeah, right Dad. Good luck."

Sandra stared at her blank paper. She remembered Gretchen saying that her grandmother would design her own quilts. Sandra started penciling in diamond shapes and triangles and rectangles. It didn't look very creative. *Wait a minute,* she thought, *I could make something for my mother. Her birthday is in six months. Yes! In every square I'll hand sew something that she has taught me. Gretchen can show me how to do it.*

Meanwhile, across town, Gretchen sat in her big overstuffed chair and switched on her sewing lamp. She pulled her quilt into her lap and started the stitch directly after last evening's stitch. No discerning eye could ever tell where one day ended and the next day began.

Her mind began formulating plans for the 15th. *Maybe they'd like to watch me appliqué,* she thought. She remembered the quilt that she, her mother, and her grandmother had made with the deer, trees, flowers, and the path. They each had their own little verses they would recite about Papa coming home from the war. Sometimes they even put the verses to song as they appliquéd and dreamed of the future.

Gretchen's nerves suddenly tightened in the back of her neck as she remembered how she and Grandma had finished the quilt in silence after Mama took to her room.

∞

The 15th came with twelve people wanting to learn how to appliqué. Gretchen seemed like a mother hen with all her little chicks sitting around her; Sandra and Kate were as close as they could get. To begin, Gretchen carefully unrolled the "Pathway" quilt. All eyes and mouths opened widely as they took in the intricacies of the landscape. Even those who were working around the edges of the room hurried over when they heard the fluctuating drone of the bees.

"Do you see the blossoms on that cherry tree?"

"Look at the birds!"

"Notice how the deer are behind the trees. How did she do that?"

"There's something significant about that path. I wonder what it is?"

Gretchen felt tears in her eyes as the ladies were in complete adulation of her work. "Wait ladies, I can't take much credit for this one. My grandmother, my mother, and I worked on it together." She didn't tell them the whole story.

"This is appliqué; are you sure you want to try it?

After an overwhelming *yes*, she continued.

"You are going to need something to sew onto your background," she said simply.

"Excuse me, Gretchen, would these be okay?" Sandra reached into her bag for the sixteen pieces, which she had carefully cut out.

"Oh, Sandra, tell us about them."

"Well, I want to make a special quilt for my mother, and I thought I would depict some of the greatest things she has taught me over the years."

"Great idea," chirped Kate.

"Definitely," agreed Gretchen. "I wish I had thought of this for my mother."

"Well, my mother is so special! I don't know if you all know this, but I was adopted, and I couldn't have had better parents."

A swirl of love seemed to blow in upon the quilt ladies as Sandra laid out her depictions.

"I came up with about a hundred ideas, but I settled on sixteen," she explained.

"That one shows you cooking," squealed Kate, "And gardening there, and dancing!"

Others piped in with the swimming, church, painting, and camping out.

"That's music and that's traveling, I think," Claudia interjected.

"Are these your pets? Here's an ABC book and then this must be your college."

Sandra laughed as she said, "I guess I'd better make the last four a little clearer. No one said what they were. I'll work on them and maybe next time you'll be able to identify them."

"This is a wonderful start, Sandra," Gretchen uttered kindly. "I'm sure this will inspire everyone to begin developing their ideas. Now let's get on to the nitty-gritty."

❧

Sandra could barely wait to settle in after dinner with her project.

"How was your doctor's appointment today, Mom?"

"Oh, you know, more tests, more tests. How was your quilting club?"

"It was good. We've started something new."

"Oh, that's nice. I wish I could help you, but that's one thing I never learned."

"That's okay, Mom. You taught me plenty of other things." Sandra watched across the room wondering why her Mom was so tired a lot of the time.

❧

Gretchen sat after dinner with needle in hand, appliquéing more samples for her students. She wanted this to be a nice experience for them, just as the women in her life strived to convey to her. Such a divide, she remembered, so happy and then so sad. Papa did that to them by not returning from the war. His wife withered up inside of herself. His mother died shortly after. And Gretchen? Maybe because she had had a strong and stable beginning, Gretchen more or less got herself through school. She excelled even without a parent in the audience, at the games, or even at graduation. Her guidance counselor helped her get into a good college, and she was fine. She was okay. Besides she knew she was in Papa's, Mama's, and Grandma's hearts.

And then it happened. A brilliant shining star came into her life. He was her beautiful professor, and they formed a bond immediately. He dated and charmed her, and called her *sweetheart* just like her father had done. She loved him with all her heart. She felt alive again; she hadn't realized how she longed to be cherished and adored.

❧

Gretchen, invisible to the world, sat weeping into her hands. She couldn't stop herself from wailing into the empty room. She remembered his quick goodbye and the news of the sabbatical he was

178

going to take in England. She would have waited for him— she knew how to wait. A week later she picked up the college newsletter to read that he, his wife, and two children were in England.

A needle pierced Gretchen's finger that night.

***

"Anyone want to guess what these four pieces are?" laughed Sandra.

"That's the different suits of cards, right?"

"Right."

"And those are birds flying with baskets of hearts?"

"Very good!"

"Hmm," pondered Kate. "Are those ripples on the lake?"

"Yes, our vacation spot."

No one came up with the correct answer for the last one. "Give up?" piped Sandra just like her third graders cried out yesterday when she played a game with them. And amazingly, since women remember the sounds of childhood, they all replied just as the third graders had.

"Okay, I tried and tried to think how I could create something that would depict my biological mother. You know, I've never given much thought of her, because I've been so happy with my adopted mother. But, there must have been something good about her. At least she didn't have me killed!"

"Sandra stop. You're giving me the willies," Kate interjected.

"But what is it?" Sharon implored.

"Well, that star is me on the left hand side of the huge teardrop, and that star is my biological mother on the other side."

"Oh," they all mumbled in puzzlement.

"You just had to be there." Sandra laughed as she tried to portray Groucho Marx, bent over with his cigar, just like her Dad had done every so often.

"Let's get started, group," Gretchen said quickly, obviously anxious to see what the others had designed, also.

Sandra's mother spent her birthday in the hospital, but from that day to her last, her daughter's quilt lay proudly and impressively on top of her sheets. Even when she couldn't speak anymore, she would lift a corner of the quilt to direct everyone's eyes to her joy.

The quilt ladies cried together with Sandra. It was those tears, they knew, that would bind their hearts together just like the stitches and patterns of a quilt can do.

"Girls," Claudia called out, "at our next meeting, which will be in a month because of the holiday, "the executive committee thought it might be nice to reminisce over some old quilts. So please bring in something that you've had for years and we hope you'll have a story to go along with it."

The group rejoined after the holidays. Sandra's eyes were not red and swollen anymore, and everyone held tightly to their treasures in great anticipation of sharing.

Oh, the stories, the stories. The ladies were captivated by what they saw and heard. From the underground quilts to the fire disaster-relief quilts, to those which came with the immigrants, to the bridal heirlooms. The women held history in their hands.

"Sandra, do you have something?"

"Yes," the motherless quilter replied, as she carefully placed a box on the table. "You all have been so kind to me since my mother passed away. I wanted to share these treasures with you. Mom had left instructions with my father to wait for two weeks and then give me this box." Sandra stroked the top of the box gently.

"Look," she almost whispered as she drew out a gold crucifix with a gold chain. "I don't know why my mother never showed me this before. "And look at this," she uttered excitedly, "A quilt block! Can you believe it? But I don't know who made it, maybe her mother?"

"Oh my dear God," they heard Gretchen saying as she put her hand on her chest.

"Gretchen, what's the matter?" Claudia called out as she ran to her. Gretchen was ashen. "Gretchen, do you need an ambulance? Quick somebody get her some water."

Suddenly Gretchen stood, and looking only at Sandra, unfolded her heirloom quilt that her grandmother had made. She held it up. In all its splendor, it was immediately evident that a corner block was missing.

"Why is there a block missing, Gretchen?" piped the anxious Kate.

"It's-it's-not m-missing," she whispered.

Gretchen pointed to Sandra's box.

"Years ago I had to give up my baby girl for adoption." Gretchen started to cry. "I packed a box for her. That box," she sobbed. "I removed one block out of this quilt that my grandmother had given me. I wanted my baby girl to know that I loved her."

Chapter Fourteen

WILD STRAWBERRIES

"**Y**ou remember Clara and Joseph from the grange meetings?

Yes, that's right. We all went there for a picnic.

No, they didn't die."

"I don't want to go!" screamed Claire.

"I don't!

"I don't!

"I don't!

"I don't!

"I don't!

"I don't!"

"What's going on in there? Joe asked his wife as they passed each other in the upstairs hallway.

"She's having a temper tantrum," replied Justine while trying to juggle several pieces of luggage.

"Oh."

"Why did I say 'yes'?" cried Clara. "I can't have a teenager here all summer.

"I can't

"I can't

"I can't

"I can't

"I can't

"I can't"

"What's going on in there?" Joseph asked his wife as he walked past their bedroom door.

"I'm having a temper tantrum."

"Oh."

And so the summer was about to begin for Claire and Clara.

Claire was "Claire" because of "Clara."

My name was "Clara" because my mother liked the name.

Claire was the last of Joseph's and my grandchildren—the youngest. After a succession of six grandsons, a girl. Fifteen grandchildren in all. Four were girls, so I knew about granddaughters who came a-visiting. Been a long time, though, a long time. Jennifer must have been the last when she stayed for July the summer her twin brothers were born.

She and I had lots of fun, I recalled, but that was when I had two spry legs and could play hide and seek half the night.

Jennifer, she'd follow me around like a shadow. I'd say, "Jennifer, are you attached to your Grandma?"

She'd say, "Yes, 'um."

Don't know where she got that, "Yes, 'um" expression, but she sure had it for everything.

I remember most the first three nights when she cried for her mama. She was so homesick; I worried maybe Joseph and I would have to drive her home. But she got through it. About broke my heart to hear her crying. I'd go in and read to her until she fell asleep.

I think it helped too, when I let her sleep with Dolly. Dolly was her mama's doll when she was a little girl. Dolly was well worn, but I reckon she still held all the loving that Elizabeth put into her.

Lots of visits with grandsons, but they took to Joseph and tagged along with him out in the barn or in the field. Didn't see much of them except at mealtime. They'd get all tanned and strong muscled before they went back to their parents.

They were all fun. Each one had a personality, kept Joseph and me laughing way into the winters. Wasn't odd for neighbors to drop by and Joseph and I get telling some story or another about one of the grandchildren. Most of the grandkids didn't live on a farm, so this was an adventure to them; they loved spending part of the summer here with us. I think their folks thought it'd be good for their young ones to experience nature and work—hard work like they remembered from when they were kids.

Course, those days we had what you'd call a prosperous farm. We were good competitors to our neighbors; what with the six kids working we were producing high quantities of milk from our herd.

Now, it's nothing compared to then, but Joseph and I, we still keep on farming in our own little way—a few of this animal, a few of that animal. We like a nice variety. Then there's always the big garden, the berries, and the fruit trees. Joseph, he's good about helping me, now, with some of the "woman's work." I remember when he wouldn't be caught dead slicing apples or washing out jars for the strawberry jam. Men change over the years. "Get more docile," Sadie says. Sadie lives down the road about a mile on the next farm. She and John got a farm like us now —just "a puttering around farm" with a lot of big memories.

I admit, I got kind of set in my ways the last six, seven, eight years or so. So has Joseph, except he'd never tell to it. I think it sort of came to us like an old barn cat, creeping up on a rat. We like to have the liberties to do as we please for a change; farming was always so demanding. I'm telling you, when those cows needed milking, you did it, or when the crop needed getting in, the whole world stopped until it was done. Now, when that old Mr. Sunshine comes peeking over the hill there isn't anything so important that we have to jump up like two jackrabbits. Joseph, he can be a lot more leisure-like when he goes out to the barn, and me, I can leaf through old cookbooks until ten o'clock in the morning, if I'd a mind to.

I've got books and magazines I'd been putting aside to read, for years. All those years of, "Yup, that's a good one. I'm, going to read that someday," have finally arrived! Just the other day, the rice boiled all over the stove when I got so engrossed in an article about the first lady, Mrs. Carter. Doesn't that just prove how far behind I am?

So, I'm not set in my ways about things I want to do, or when I want to do them, I guess you could say. Joseph, he doesn't care much about what time a meal gets on the table, as long as he has an inkling that it's coming sometime or another. Not like it was once; you could set your clock to our mealtimes. The milking and the meals better sure be on time. It was a good lesson for my girls to know how to judge when to start peeling potatoes and when to put the roast in—and that you better be making the pies in the morning if you knew what was good for you. They all turned out to be pretty good cooks, except now I bet they aren't making things from scratch.

My boys, however, I can't be a bragging about their cooking abilities. I never knew boys and men ever had a place in the kitchen, except to eat. Never even dreamed that they could have been helping with the dishes or stirring the soup. No, they had their outdoor work. Kind of funny though, how us girls always pitched in with the barn chores and bringing in the crops. Maybe we weren't too smart, or maybe we knew that without the selling of the milk we'd have no money at all. Those cows were our livelihood, and we knew it.

Got into looking through a big box of quilt pieces the other day. Land sakes, I was hours at it. Some my mother had started and some my aunts. I called Sadie and she came over. We went through every piece. Some I could remember where the fabric came from, and some reminded Sadie of history in her family. Joseph, he finally went on down to chaw with John. I asked him if he'd eaten anything. He said he and John made some sandwiches. That they can do, I know.

I've got picture albums to go through, too. Must have five shoeboxes full of photos I never got around to put in the books. That'll take me all summer I'm sure.

And the piano…I want to get back to playing again. I used to be pretty good, way back when Joseph came a-courting to the house. The way he would look at me, I knew I would play the piano forever. But after that first year, the concerts got less and less until there were none. I think Joseph would like to hear the music again, too.

I know that this year we're going to the county fair every day; we just cannot get around to see everything in a big hurry. We love the farm animals and the new machinery. Joseph can't get over some of the new equipment they have now days. Once we thought we were pretty hot stuff with two tractors and a baler. I get a big kick out of seeing who won the first prize ribbons for the pickles and the jams and the garden vegetables. Joseph, he goes right along with me; doesn't seem to mind looking at the foodstuff. I don't think he's too interested in the flower arrangements or the handiwork, but he doesn't complain none. He goes right along, walking with his hands held behind his back and nodding at most everything I say.

I don't know, sometimes I like to work in my garden during the cool of the evening; sometimes I go in the early morning. Whatever suites me—that's how I do things now days.

Want to have the neighbors in some nights to play cards and want to be free on the first Tuesday night to go to a grange meeting. Lord knows how many things we missed when we were bringing up our family and always plum tired out most nights.

Joseph isn't getting any younger either. It's not surprising to look over and see him taking a little nap—don't blame him one bit. He dang near scared me to death the other morning when I walked up into the haymow to see if the hens had laid any eggs. I saw his big old feet sticking out behind some bales. Sweet Lord a Jesus, I thought he'd died. "Just taking a little siesta," he said.

I can't believe Joe wants Claire to fly all the way from California to spend the summer with us. I hardly know the girl—they've been out here only twice since Claire was born. I know Justine has to be in Spain for almost two months taking pictures of something they've discovered underground, but Joe could get someone handy to stay at the house, you would think. This business of "She needs to get out of L.A. and away from her friends" and "She should experience nature and a farm" sounds fishy to me. I don't think Joe can handle her anymore. Does he think we can? I don't have anything in common with a teenage girl anymore, especially a very—does a grandmother dare to say—"spoiled" girl?

Oh, Lord, forgive me. I know I was there for all the others and I realize every child should know their grandparents, but Lord, I just don't know if I'm up to it. Maybe I'm plain being selfish. I know I'm going to need your strength, Lord.

I thought about the storeroom that I was going to put a dent into this summer.

"You sure you know how to get there?"

"I do."

No sense to keep on asking him. If he says he knows, then he knows. It's been years since I've been to the airport. Lord a mighty, I think it was when Ray first came out of the service. I told Joseph that if I didn't get to go along to the airport, I would walk to town and take the first train going through and never come back home. He didn't put up any fuss. Guess he knew how my heart had been breaking to see Ray.

I sure don't remember all these buildings along the highway; I suppose everybody is moving upstate to get out of the city. Some good and some bad to that whole process. I've seen some beautiful houses going up and real nice kept property, but you can't see a country mile anymore without somebody settling in. If it gets too crowded, it's not going to be good. What we have up here is precious. Hate to lose it.

"You sure you know how to get there?"

"I do."

Well, I suppose he does. He gets out more than I do—goes to talk with the men down at the feed mill or at the convenience center. Doesn't come home with much information except maybe who bought a new car or who's going fishing over at Chandler Lake. He's surprising sometimes, though. Out of the blue he'll come out with some news that makes you think: *Now, how does he know that?* Never brings me home any gossip, though—not that I think gossip is proper, but once and awhile I'd like to know something first. Always everybody else telling who had the baby or who's getting married.

I hope Claire likes the bedroom. It's on the east side, so she'll get the sunshine first thing in the morning. I always love that. It makes you happy before you even know what day it is. Has the same wallpaper as it's had for years, but it's still my favorite. The little pink roses seem capable of taking you right into dreamland, too. Everything's nice and clean for her, with fresh spanking sheets right off the line smelling heavenly.

I'll bet Claire doesn't even know you can hang clothes outside to dry.

My Lord, the clothes that used to go through this house in one week! It's a wonder that old wringer washer didn't blow a gasket or whatever they blow. Every Monday: bring in the two metal washtubs, set them in the kitchen with the washing machine, hook up the hose to fill the rinse tubs and the washer, squeeze out the water through the wringer, rinse twice, and hang the clothes outside. For eight people, it makes me tired just thinking about it.

With every girl, same instructions: don't get your fingers or your hair caught in the wringer. Be careful. Sometimes the boys would hang around; they seemed to be fascinated with the wringer. Course that made the girls pretty proud that they were allowed to operate such a dangerous machine. All day it took us. When the girls were in school, I had to use Tuesdays, too. What a feeling to take frozen clothes off the line and set them up in front of the wood stove. The boys' work jeans could stand for quite a while before they melted.

Still only one bathroom; we were always planning on putting another one in, but didn't get around to it. Seemed kind of senseless with everyone leaving and going off on their own.

Our old outhouse is still standing. Looks kind of nice with the clematis growing up the trellis. Everyone who comes visiting always gets a chuckle out of it.

Sure as shooting, having a bathroom upstairs would be nice. I know those winter nights of having to go downstairs are not pleasant.

"Do you think we should put a bathroom upstairs, Joseph?"

"Might be nice."

I smoothed out the wrinkles the seat belt was making in my good dress. Darn old seat belts; they always make you look like you missed spots in your ironing. At least they got this better fabric now that doesn't wrinkle so bad. I can't imagine wearing those starched outfits we used to wear and going under the seat belt!

I suppose wrinkles don't matter much these days though. Last time I was in the bank, the teller looked like she'd slept in her clothes. Our ironing went on for days. Just 'cause my kids were farmers didn't mean they went to school with wrinkled clothes.

"Sure are a lot of cars out this way."

"Sure are."

"When did they put in all these roads?"

"Oh, a while back."

Good Thunder and Blitzen. Thank heavens I'm not driving. Give me those old country roads any day. It wasn't until five years ago that our road was paved; cuts down on the dust a lot but now everybody's like a streak of lightning going up and down the road. Used to be people would stop when they saw me working in the garden. Now there's hardly time enough to wave as they go streaming by. I don't know about this progress thing.

Maybe I'll get into that quilting class. They brought in their work down to the grange; it was beautiful. I know how to sew; I would like to do that.

"There's the sign for the airport, Joseph!"

"Yup, there it is."

Jumping junipers, look how this place has changed! It's a good thing Joseph knows where he's going. Where in land sakes are all these people going to? Course, I've got a granddaughter coming clear from California. Joseph and I never even been to California. I think the farthest west we've gotten to is Columbus, Ohio, when we went out for Joseph's brother's funeral. That was a trip, to be sure. I was never so glad to be pulling up into our driveway as I was on that Friday morning. I almost kissed the ground—probably would have if I didn't have to help carry four sleeping kids into the house. I recall, too, I was expecting.

❧

Joseph and I sat in the waiting area at the airport. We were just fascinated watching the people. At least, I think Joseph was.

That one there, if she isn't the spitting image of my cousin Irma. My Lord, how does that happen?

How could she be traveling with three little kids all by herself like that? You wouldn't think she'd even want to leave home.

He sure looks like a cowboy with that hat and boots!

I see Joseph looking at him, too. He would, he always got a charge out of a western movie. I remember the boys teasing and teasing until their pa would do his John Wayne impressions for them.

Then they'd try, and everyone would laugh. I remember one night, Grandma stomping up the stairs muttering how she might as well go to bed as to sit and watch such nonsense.

When Joseph and I went to the barn dances, lots of men had on cowboy boots and hats. Pa said he didn't need to be spending money on luxuries, but I think he would have liked to own a set. Those dances were fun, getting to see all the folks for miles around. One social gathering like that could last you for a month of Sundays.

It was at a barn dance when I first seen Joseph. All the girls were a chasing after him. When he walked in with his six brothers, heads turned, I'll tell you. It was a sight to behold. I didn't figure I had much chance, me being so shy and all, but Land of Goshen, if he didn't spot me and ask me to dance. We knew we were right for each other first thing, and been right all these years.

I looked at Joseph, he was still watching the cowboy.

Seems people don't get so dressed up anymore. I remember when we picked up Ray, I wore a hat, gloves, nylons, high heels, and my best dress. All the women did, I think. Seems I'm the only woman here in a dress today. I wanted to make a good impression on Claire. I wonder when she's coming in from the airplane.

"Are you sure we're at the right gate?"

"I'm sure."

People were dwindling down now; a young couple over there; a sailor; a young boy and an old man wearing plaid shorts and one of those colorful Hawaiian shirts.

Joseph checked his watch and looked up at the board with all the numbers on it. He walked over and talked to the lady in a uniform. I saw her shaking her head. Do you suppose Claire missed her airplane and will come in later? Oh, no, it will be so late by the time we get back home.

"I don't know," Joseph said as he sat back down. "She says everybody got off the plane."

As we were figuring what to do, the boy across the way took off his baseball cap and hair tumbled down way past his shoulders. It wasn't a boy, it was a girl. Claire?

I walked over to her and asked, "Claire, is that you?"

She looked up with blank eyes and said, "Yeah."

"Claire, I'm your Grandma."

"You are? You're old."

"I sure am, honey. Your Grandpa and me," I pointed to Joseph, "we're older than the hills!"

By that time Joseph had come over.

"Howdy, Claire, I'm your Grandpa."

"You are?" she asked with no emotion.

"Yup. I hear you're staying out on the farm with us."

"Yeah, that's what I've been told." She sort of rolled her eyes.

Pa carried Claire's bags while she and I walked behind him.

"How was your trip, honey?"

"I don't know. I slept."

"Are you hungry? We can get something."

"No."

"How's your dad and mom?"

"Busy, I guess."

"Do you want to sit up in the front seat with Grandpa so you can get acquainted?"

"No, that's okay. I'll sit back here and take a nap. I'm very tired."

192

Oh, blessed God of the Universe, S-O-S, S-O-S! We need help down here!

How am I going to survive the summer with a girl like this? My granddaughter? What have Joe and Justine done to fashion a child who...calm down, calm down, you don't know about this girl. Give her a chance. Poor thing, being shipped out here like a crate of pineapples. She knows she has two months without her friends, her folks, her things. At seventeen I sure wasn't sent away from home; my mother needed me too much.

Oh, dear, Claire doesn't think anybody needs her. Poor baby, look at her, all curled up back there like a child. She's so thin; I'm going to have to put some meat and potatoes on her bones.

I wonder why she'd wear those old clothes while traveling. I hope she brought some nice outfits for church; I'm intending to show her off on Sundays.

She is very pretty with big eyes like our bossy cows, except they're such sad eyes. Oh, that'll change after she gets some rest.

Her hair is beautiful and shiny, that's a good sign. At least it is with the animals. I suppose it's the same with people. My hair used to be like that. My sisters and I all had thick, shiny hair that we—sure as clockwork—brushed every night. We always had a pretty ribbon to wear. Mama saw to little things about us girls that really were special, when I think about it now. She could have let us go shabby, but she didn't. I wonder who was at Claire's house to see her off?

I couldn't help but look back at Claire every little while, like checking on new baby kittens.

"Is she all right?" Joseph asked.

"Better days are coming," I replied with shaky confidence.

"Claire, wake up, honey, we're home!"

"Oh, goody, can I go out and milk the cows and slop the pigs?"

"We've got ourselves a worker here, Joseph! We'll hitch her up to the plow tomorrow morning."

"Yeah, right," Claire said with no laughter.

She followed her Grandpa up the back steps and stopped short just inside the doorway.

"Oh, my God! Is this your house?"

"We sure aren't busting into the neighbor's house!" I laughed. Then I knew what she was referring to.

"This is just the back shed; used to be called the 'Old Kitchen'. It's good to have, so we don't have to wear our old manure boots into the main house; we can leave them out here."

"Oh, goody." Her nose wrinkled.

"Would you like to see your room first or eat first?"

"Whatever."

"I have a notion Grandpa might be hungry. Right Grandpa?"

"You hit it right on the head, Clara."

"I really would like to lie down; I have a splitting headache."

"Oh, sure, Claire. Let me show you where it is. There's nothing worse than a headache. Come, follow me. I remember one time Betsy Casdid had a headache for nine days. Can you imagine? Nine days? Well, come to find out she was pregnant! After she resigned herself to the idea, her headache went away. Funny how that works, isn't it?

"Here we are; you've got the prettiest room in the whole house. If I was bedridden I'd stay right in here to my dying day. Isn't it pretty, Claire?"

"Uh, where's the computer?"

"Computer?" I howled like a Banshee. "I'm afraid we're not up to date on that, honey. We got a set of encyclopedias if you want to look something up. Salesman came around one day when your dad was still in school and none of us could believe it, but your Grandpa up and bought the whole set! Salesman left here strutting prouder than a rooster."

"I wanted it for e-mail," Claire said as she massaged her temples.

"Oh, we get just the regular mail outside in the mailbox. Herm, he comes by just about noontime everyday except Sundays. You probably already know this, but if you want to mail something out, you put up the little red flag so Herm will see it. It's a cute way to signal him, don't you think?"

"I told my friends I'd e-mail them as soon as I got here," Claire whined.

"I put a new box of real pretty stationery in you dresser drawer, dear. I was figuring you'd want to keep in touch with your pals back home."

"How about a phone?"

Claire started howling again. "A telephone! Everybody has a telephone now days! You would have died laughing if you'd ever heard Silvia Batesman. She was our telephone operator for years and years. If there was anything you wanted to know, you could just ask Silvia. She was a busy-body all right."

"I don't see it," Claire interrupted the story.

"Oh, Claire, the phone's not up here; we got it downstairs in the living room."

"You only have one phone?"

"Well, I reckon I can only talk to one person at a time." I chuckled. "Course Joseph might disagree with that.

"Say, the way you keep rubbing your head, I'd better get you a couple of aspirin."

"I've got some in my suitcase. Is my bathroom through that door?"

"Oh, no, that's a storeroom. I keep my collections of projects that I'm going to get to someday in there. Used to be a playroom when the kids were little. They would put on plays, and Joseph and I would go and watch and clap. Oh, what fun."

"Where is my bathroom?"

"It's downstairs, same place as our bathroom; we all use the same one."

"Oh, my God," groaned Claire as she fell back on the bed.

"Honey, honey, you all right?

Joseph, get up here."

"What's the matter?" Joseph hollered up the stairway.

"I think Claire has fainted!"

"I haven't fainted," Claire spoke from underneath the hand she had over her face.

"That's good! I hate to think you need more rest, but maybe you do. Grandpa will get you a glass of water, and I'll start supper. You lay there for awhile and keep your eyes closed. I'll call you for supper."

❦

After delivering the water, Joseph went out to tend to the animals. I didn't have to think about cooking, I could just do it. Maybe that's why I like it so much, I can concentrate on other things and not even have to think about mixing and chopping and peeling. Right now, I'm thinking about that poor, sickly, girl upstairs. She doesn't seem healthy to me. No life, no talking, just wanting to sleep all the time.

She's way too thin to suit me. I haven't seen anybody that thin since Florence and Harry's daughter, Rosalie, had consumption and went to the TB hospital over there in Big Oaks. I hope Joseph and I won't be put up to some big decision like that. 'Course, during our day with all the kids and the animals we had major decisions all the time. It's different when you got other people's children to decide for, however.

Oh, shucks, I'm just worrying for nothing. Claire will be fine in a few days.

There, everything looks ready.

⌇

"Joseph! Claire!" I hollered to both of them.

"Could you go up and rap on her door? Try go get her to come down."

I felt like an old woman listening to his slow footsteps, hearing years of experience punctuate each board.

"Claire, it's Grandpa. Supper's ready."

"I'm not hungry."

"You haven't eaten all day."

"I don't care. I'm not hungry."

"I would suggest that you come out now," he said sternly.

Claire opened the door. "You sound just like Dad," she said disgruntled as a polecat.

"There's probably a reason for that," Joseph said matter-of-factly as he followed her down the stairs.

"Now, isn't this nice?" I twittered, trying to give mirth to the occasion as I had heard the birds do. "I'll say the grace."

Heavenly Father, thank you for this food. Thank you for this day having Claire with us. We are grateful for her safe trip across our big country. Watch over our entire family and help Marie, down there on the four-corners, to have a successful operation. Amen.

⌇

Claire took a serving of everything that was passed around the table.

Hallelujah! I knew she'd come around! I exalted to myself as I gave myself an extra dollop of potatoes for success.

"What grade are you going into, Claire?"

"Twelfth."

"Twelfth grade? Why, I can hardly believe it. Joseph did you hear that? I bet you're excited to be a senior?"

"Not really," she said tearing off a piece of bread with no butter.

"Oh, honey, your senior year is one you'll remember for the rest of your life; I know I do mine: the senior trip; our senior play in the auditorium; the senior dance; the senior picnic. We really were treated special. Some of our teachers even invited us to their homes for socials. Of course graduation was unforgettable. That whole year was something to remember. I still get Christmas cards from some of my friends from school. What special things does your school do for the seniors?"

"I don't know."

She ate a tomato wedge.

"How are your mom and dad?"

"Okay."

She ate two macaronis, one sticking out of the right-sided tine and the other out of the left.

"They'll be so far apart for the summer. How are they going to be able to stand it?"

"They like to be apart. They'll probably get a divorce anyway. All my friends' parents are divorced."

Joseph stopped eating and looked up.

I stopped talking.

Claire started pushing the food around on her plate.

"May I be excused?" Claire asked.

"Honey, you've hardly eaten a thing."

"I'm not a big eater."

"After you eat half of what's on your plate," Joseph interjected with no frills attached.

"Oh," she groaned, "you sound just like Dad."

"I'm not surprised," he replied getting back to his meal.

She ate the half.

No sooner had she gone upstairs than she was back down again.

"Where's my TV?"

"In the living room. Would you like to watch it?"

"No thanks."

She turned on her heel and ascended the stairs with stomps loud enough to camouflage her words. I was glad for that.

"After only one day, I'm exhausted," I admitted to the bottom of my teacup.

"Well, the dishes aren't going to get up and wash themselves. Here goes nothing," I said out loud, as I did every night.

Joseph didn't go in to watch the news.

"We'll get through this, Clara. No person can be around you all summer and not come out a better person."

I just about melted to the floor. I was so overwhelmed with the compliment that I had to wipe the tears out of my eyes.

Joseph doesn't say much in the romantic department, but when he does, watch out, your heart will be a-fluttering for the next six months. He knows how to swoop me right off my feet!

After the dishes, he and I sat at the card table working on the jigsaw puzzle. It was going be a beauty.

I could work on puzzles for hours; I don't know what's so intriguing about them. Joseph doesn't usually sit for too long, but he did tonight. It was like we were giving each other strength, passing it silently back and forth between us. Strength for the summer.

⌇

"Claire, I'm going up on the side hill to pick strawberries, you want to go?"

"No."

"Okay, your breakfast is on the back of the stove keeping warm. Are you going to get up pretty soon?"

"I don't know."

"I think I better turn the stove off but you can turn it back on. I'll be back in a couple of hours."

Berries are just the nicest treat farmers can have; most just grow wild. I don't know how they ever got started but I'm sure grateful they did. When the work is a drudgery, or you're in a sad spell with the weather, berries can brighten your day. It's such a joy not only to eat them but to feel them between your thumb and fingers and to study their incredible little delicacies.

Who could sit down and make a berry? Anybody? No, they're miracles! Picking them is like gathering gold. I imagine there are people in some parts of the world never seen our kind of berries. My, wouldn't they be excited to see these little strawberries, so tiny and so sweet just a-hiding under the leaves, growing in with the grass. Next winter when the wind is howling and the snow is up to the bottom of the windows, we'll stay in where it's warm and have strawberry jam on our pancakes.

"Joseph, look!" I beamed as I hurried off the last slope of the side hill holding my buckets out like trophies.

"Mmm." Joseph smiled as he reached in for a berry.

"Why don't you come in now, Pa; according to the sun it's nearly lunch time. We'll have a small bowl of these with sugar and milk for dessert."

"Well, good morning, sunshine! I'm glad to see you're up. How is breakfast?"

"It's okay."

"Would you like some fresh strawberries?"

"What's the matter with them?" Claire asked as she looked into a bucket.

"There's nothing the matter with them." I couldn't stifle a laugh. "They're supposed to be small. They're wild berries. Best tasting little devils you'll ever know."

"You sure?" Claire looked doubtful.

"Sure as preaching! Go on."

"Mmm, it is good."

"Sure, have some more, eat all you want, we can pick more tomorrow!"

"I've never picked berries before," Claire exclaimed popping another one into her mouth.

"Well, there's nothing hard about it." I laughed again.

"We'll have a combination breakfast-lunch here at the table. It'll be fun."

"So, what are you going to do this afternoon, Claire?"

"I have no idea; there isn't anything to do."

"Would you help me make the strawberry jam?"

"Make jam?" she looked totally perplexed. "Jam can be made at home? I thought it had to be made in a factory."

Well, that was it for Joseph! He ran out into the old kitchen pretending to be sneezing and blowing his nose, but I knew he was in fits of laughter.

It was only by the grace of God that I kept a straight face.

This'll be one to tell the neighbors when they come to play cards next winter!

After breakfast-lunch, we got started.

I asked Claire to wash out the jars while I measured out the sugar and got the big pot on the stove. I saw she was opening a lot of cupboards and drawers, so I said, "Honey, what are you looking for?"

"The dishwasher," she answered innocently.

Joseph jumped up with his handkerchief over his mouth running for the door. I called after him, "I think you can find some work to do outside for awhile. We women need to get our work done. Men," I scoffed.

"You can just put them in the sink and wash them; we don't have one of those electric kind."

She gave me a funny look but she didn't say anything.

"Wow, how did you get it so red?" Claire asked as she pushed her hair behind her ear and bent down to see the jars being filled.

"That's just the natural color. Isn't it beautiful?"

"What did you do with the rest of it? There's only six jars here?"

"That's all it made. We can pick more tomorrow."

"Good God, what are you pouring on the top, Grandma?"

Oh, no, don't tell me she uses the Lord's name in vain?

Grandma! She'd finally said, "Grandma!"

"It's wax," I tried to say nonchalantly not wanting to deal with the Lord's name right then, just wanting to savor the fact that she called me "Grandma." I didn't want this moment of matronly ecstasy broken. "It will seal the jars so no air or moisture can get in to spoil our delicious jam." I didn't know if I was even breathing.

"Cool. My friends would just die if they heard about me making jam."

"Why don't you start a letter, or even better, a journal. Keep track of the 'cool' things you do."

"Maybe I will. That'll help pass the time away."

My bubble broke and I floated down to earth not nearly as graceful as had the spider who came off the flour bin earlier that morning.

Oh, Claire, don't pass time away, I thought to myself. *There's not that much left for any of us.*

"Thanks for helping me," I called after Claire as she started for her room, "and honey, do you think you could get out of your pajamas and get dressed?"

"Oh, yeah, I forgot," she said looking downward as if to review what she was wearing. "I usually don't get dressed until five, right before Mom gets home from work."

"That's okay," I muttered as I tried to recreate the bubble.

Thank you, God, for strawberries! They brought out a glimpse of humanity in that girl, and she called me "Grandma!"

Joseph and I were working on the puzzle when Claire came downstairs.

"Hi there, sweetie, what have you been doing?" I asked, not looking up, but fitting in a piece that I'd been searching two days for.

"I started my journal and took a nap. Making jam tired me right out."

I kicked Joseph under the table. He managed to contain himself with only a small squeak of laughter.

"I was about to walk down to the road for the mail. Want to go with me?"

"Sure."

"Cool."

Joseph looked up at me.

"Let's go this way so I can show you my garden. Grandpa got it all plowed up on Memorial Day weekend. They say you never want to put your plants out before Memorial Day or they're apt to freeze. We get some hardy frosts around here clear up to June. Did get my peas in early, though, they won't freeze."

"What are those strings doing in the garden?"

"Those are my straight lines. When I planted my seeds those kept my rows straight."

"Cool."

"Here, try some peas," I said as I handed her a few pods.

"Where are they?"

Oh, are we going to howl this winter!

"They're in the pods. Let me show you."

"These are good!"

"Sure are, I could stand here all day and eat peas. Later, would you like to pick a bowlful for supper?"

"Yeah, but we don't have to cook them, do we?"

"Not if you don't want them cooked."

"How did those plants over there get so big all ready?"

"Those are the tomato, pepper, and cabbage plants. They can be started by seed in the house, but I just buy them already started and put the plants out. Last time, the two cats knocked over all my little pots, so I've given up on that."

"What two cats?"

"Oh, haven't you seen them? They're around, probably spending more time outdoors now that it's warm. You'll see them soon; they don't stay away for long. Do you have any pets?"

"No, Mom is allergic to them."

"How about we take the tour tomorrow?"

"The tour?"

"We'll see all the animals Grandpa has."

"Yeah, I guess."

❧

"Ah! The *Times* is here!"

"The *New York Times*?"

"No, it's our Lone Moon paper."

"Oh, that figures."

"Now I can see who went to whose house for dinner and who's traveling and who's on what committee and when all the social functions are." I chattered aimlessly, trying to remove the hurtfulness of those beautiful eyes being rolled in disgust of her grandmother's ways.

"Anything for me?" Claire asked sharply.

I was hoping there was something for her, Claire's spirits sure needed to be rinsed in lavender water.

"Gosh, I don't think so, sweetie. Wait a minute. What's this? A flyer on the annual arts festival that's held in town every summer. Would you like to enter?"

"Me? What could I enter?"

"Well, do you do any kind of drawing or painting or clay work or things like that?"

"No."

"Maybe Grandpa can show you how to whittle."

"Whistle?"

"No, whittle."

My bubble flew over just in time to shower me with a silent belly laugh.

Claire and I sat on the back steps shelling peas. I gave up talking for a spell; just wanted to listen to the clicks the pods made when you pressed just right against their spines. To me, the sound meant success; sometimes you got it and sometimes you didn't.

"I guess this is tradition—sitting out here," I finally said after feeling fulfilled with my successes. "Do it every time there are peas or beans to snap."

"Why?"

"To tell you the truth, I don't know. It's just something I've always done. I'm kind of a stick in the mud, you know. When I enjoy doing something, I do it over and over. Can't improve on perfection, you know. Every once and again I try to change the routine, but it usually doesn't suit me.

"It's nice to look down the valley, don't you think, Claire? Sometimes, I have to admit, I stop my work and just stare through the pathway between the two hills. I sometimes wonder how far some people travel looking for happiness, whereas me, I stay right here. Your dad traveled the farthest of any of my kids. Did he find happiness, Claire?"

"I don't think so."

"That's too bad."

"What are you girls cooking up in here?" Joseph asked as he came into the kitchen.

"Well, we're having raw peas, prepared by Miss Claire and Southern fried chicken, by Mrs. Clara."

"Sounds good to me!" Joseph replied.

"What do you have behind your back there, Mr. Joseph?"

Joseph brought a small pail forward. "Just happened to be up on the side hill and picked a few strawberries for my favorite ladies."

"Yummy," Claire exclaimed, reaching in for a berry.

"Claire! Your dad is on the phone."

"Hi, Dad."

"Yeah."

"Yeah."

"Yeah."

"No. I hate it here."

I looked at Joseph; Joseph looked at me.

"Would you like another piece of chicken, Claire?"

"Sure, our chicken in California comes out of a bucket. I like this kind better."

"Joseph, I told Claire you could teach her how to whittle."

"To whistle?"

"Whittle!" both grandmother and granddaughter, said together.

"I think you two fell out of the same coconut tree."

I laughed.

The next morning we got ready for the "tour."

"Here, Claire, I think you better slip on these barn boots."

"Why?"

"Just in case we have to walk through some rough spots."

I slipped mine on with defensiveness rising up in me thicker than manure on a winter heifer.

Thoughts started entering my mind just like the preacher said they would if you let the devil walk through the door.

"If this girl tears down all of Joseph's hard work and pride I'm going to send her right back to that damn father of hers."

∾

Dear God, forgive me. Give me patience with Claire, she doesn't know any better.

∾

"Grandma! Are you going to answer me? Don't those chickens have to be in a cage or something?"

"Oh! No, we let them run around loose out here. They don't do any harm."

"Why are they swarming around us?"

"They know I'll throw some cracked corn down for them. Here, you want to do it?

"You don't need to throw it down piece by piece." I couldn't help but giggle. "Sling three or four handfuls right on the ground, like this."

"Oh, look at them eat!" squealed Claire as she bent down to pet the white one.

I'd never seen a chicken being petted before, oh wait, I guess some of my girls used to play "baby" with some of the chickens. Gosh, I hadn't thought of that in years.

"We'll collect their eggs later."

The way my thin, little waif looked at me, I couldn't even imagine what she was thinking.

This girl who is almost in her last year of school is such a child; it's hard to believe she has experienced so little. She has basically nothing stored in her brain to draw from. Both her parents are so educated it would make your head spin. Did they think Claire was going to learn by osmosis, or whatever the word is?

All through the morning, Grandpa became engaged in the "tour" and showed Claire the animals; he steadied them so she wouldn't be frightened; he let her give them handfuls of grass or grain.

This was the husband I'd watched for so many years teaching the children with his mild mannered ways. Now to Claire—the last of the grandchildren and the neediest.

"How would you like to help me every day with the feeding and the cleaning?" asked Joseph.

"That would be fun!" beamed Claire. "How do you clean animals?"

"Well," thought Joseph, "I didn't actually mean we'd clean the animals; we'd clean out the barn."

I know Joseph was regaling with laughter inside his head.

"Oh," Claire said weakly.

After some thought, she replied, "Well, that would make quite an entry in my journal, wouldn't it Grandma?"

"It sure would, kid, it sure would."

"Miss Popularity, you got three letters today!" I hollered from outside the house.

"I did?"

Claire ran out to retrieve her treasures and then off she went to read them upstairs.

I'm that way, too. I love to read my personal mail in a special spot. I remember when my best friend, Luanne, moved away with her new husband; once a week I would write to her and the next week I would get a letter back. We had the most wonderful things to tell each other so it was no wonder my reading her letter was an event. It was the best we could do, being miles apart from each other. I think we shared the most heartfelt news during our pregnancy days; we somehow knew how to bring each other comfort and courage. Friends and words. Each needs the other.

Miss Popularity came down with a sad, almost ashen face.

"No good news?" I asked.

"Good news for them, not for me," she said slumping into a chair.

"What's the matter, honey?" I asked as I sat down, too.

"All my friends are having a good time this summer, and I'm stuck here on this old farm. I'm not going to have any fun, and they get to go to the beach and the mall every day. I hate it here! I wish I had never come!"

Claire ran out of the house.

I stayed in my chair like a limp dishrag. The tick of the old clock didn't halt like I did. I sat listening to its thunderous marching feet—not stopping, not giving itself time to feel sorry, not taking in hurts, giving no hurts out.

Well, God, come and inspire me, please.

I fixed an extra special supper, bringing up from the cellar my last jar of homemade dill pickles and a jar of applesauce; made a pot roast with potatoes, carrots and onions; made biscuits for strawberry shortcake, and shelled the peas leaving them raw.

Around 5:30 p.m., Joseph came in.

"She's gone, Joseph."

All the peeling, cutting, mixing, stirring, and snapping had kept the tears at bay until then.

"Clara, Clara," Joseph cooed as he came to me, "she's right outside getting her surprise ready. She's not gone. I spotted her going down to the creek. We had a long talk."

The corner of my apron came up to my eyes just as my mother's had for hers.

Claire walked in.

"What have you two been doing?" I asked, conjuring up a smile just as I did when Jimmy walked in with his homemade present for me after I had called all the neighbors searching for my "missing boy."

"Grandpa showed me how to catch a fish with my bare hands, Grandma!"

"He did? That's quite a trick; he's the only one in this neck of the woods who can do it."

"But now I can do it, too!"

There was no, "I'm sorry I yelled and ran out of the house," or "I do like it here," or "I hope I didn't make you worry."

But the fish…maybe the fish was her peace offering.

"Well, I'll be jiggered," I heard myself saying. "Guess we better get skinning those fish for supper."

"Oh, no, Grandma," Claire said as her beautiful bossy-cow eyes became as wide as the saltshaker half filled with rice. "They're going to be my pets!"

"Oh, then we don't have to throw out the pot roast?"

"No way," Joseph piped up.

"Let's take a survey, gang," I announced as we spooned into our shortcake. "Who thinks catching fish bare handed is more fun than going to the mall?"

"Me," Joseph said immediately.

"Me," I voted.

"Well, maybe," said Claire slowly.

"Now, next question: Who thinks going to the beach is more fun than shoveling manure?"

"Me."

"Me."

"Me."

"And it's unanimous!" Joseph laughed.

⁂

"Did you bring something pretty to wear to church tomorrow, Claire?"

"Church?"

"We go every Sunday, unless we're sick."

"I never go to church."

"How come?"

"I don't know. We just never go."

"Your dad grew up on church."

"He did? I didn't know that. What do you do in church?"

This time, Joseph wasn't laughing. Neither was I.

"Well, honey, it's a real nice place to get together with your neighbors and thank God for all your blessings," I said.

"I didn't bring anything fancy," Claire said. "I didn't think I would be going anywhere nice."

"Where'd you think you were going to, a penitentiary?" Joseph laughed giving her a poke in the arm.

"I'm sure whatever you wear will be fine," I retorted with a sincerity that lands most people in purgatory.

***

I lay in bed that night wondering what happened to our oldest son, Joe Jr. It's true, when you have kids you never stop worrying about them. Joe did well in everything he set his mind to. Got all that education; took a long time finding the "perfect wife;" had only one child later on in life—and this? Didn't have enough sense to teach her anything of a practical nature; didn't even tell her about God.

I'm so mad right now I could just scream. Gave her every material thing in the world, but didn't spend any time with her. Justine, too. I'm so mad I could spit nickels.

Joseph raised up on his elbow, "What's the matter with you tonight?"

"I'm madder than a wet hen, that's what."

"Maybe it was us, Clara."

He knew what I had been thinking. "Maybe we didn't give him enough attention. Splitting up our time between six kids and the farm. Maybe none of them got enough attention. Maybe I drove him too hard with all the farm work and schoolwork and all. Who knows?"

"I guess you're right, Joseph. I shouldn't be passing any judgments. I'll pray for the situation."

"Me, too, Clara. Me, too."

***

Claire came down in a nice pair of pants and a blouse.

"That's such soft material," I told her as I felt a smidgen of it. "It looks swell."

"Mom brought it back from Italy, I think."

"Let's go before we're late."

I pray that one little thing will happen this morning, Lord that will inspire her—just one tiny miracle for Claire, God.

"Your great-great-grandparents and some of their neighbors helped get our church built out here in the wilderness, Claire. They saw a real need to get a house of God for the country folks. Our church is one of the oldest in the county."

"Uh, huh," she mumbled.

"Here we are," I said excitedly, as Joseph pulled into the tire-trodden driveway with the strip of grass running down the middle.

"This little thing is it?" Claire asked in that voice, that voice connected to her heart which seems tighter than the wire on my cheese cutter.

"Good things sometimes come in small packages, honey." I smiled as I doubled up on my prayers.

Our friends were pleased to meet Claire and made her feel more than welcome. She seemed to respond nicely, I was happy for that. Ann Marie's girl was there, about the same age as Claire, so I introduced the two and some younger girls, also. I saw Claire looking over at Fred and Renee's son; if I can catch up with them, I'll introduce her to him.

The church still has the original floorboards, with the wide old planks the men hewed by hand, I'm sure. The same squeaks that have been heard for years.

There have been renovations, of course. We saw a new heating system go in; no more wood stoves with black stove pipes; nice bathroom added on. A new organ—the old pump organ Gladys Shiller played for years finally gave up the ghost. New front steps…things like that. Mostly all done by volunteer workers.

The scent of lilacs filled the church. Big bouquets of fluffy whites and lavenders adorned the altar. Madge and Ned donated the flowers; my turn usually comes around gladiola time.

The windows were open, bringing in June's sweet air to help folks find a place to settle and listen.

There we sat in our usual pew, old Joseph and old Clara, with a pretty, young girl between us. We were special this Sunday.

Years ago it used to be a scramble to get us all ready and on time for church, but we did it. We made the effort to honor God. We could have done it at home, but I figured it was important to show God we really cared. I don't think He'll forget it when Joseph and I "go home."

Whatever happened to our son, Joe, I don't know. I don't know.

Every once in a while I'd look at Claire, trying to guess what she was thinking. She just was staring straight ahead at the only stained glass window in the whole church. It sure was one to stare at, such color. When old man Averyston died, he left a bundle of money stipulating it be used for a stained glass window.

The pastor, I thought, gave a very touching sermon on why people gather in a church community instead of staying home to worship God. The reason being that when you're down and out and don't have the presence to pray, or even think straight, your church family will do the praying for you. They will ask God to send his blessings to you, his strength. That is how people get better, heal, and restore their souls.

After the last hymn, we filed out shaking the pastor's hand like we always do and thanking him for his words.

Joseph introduced our special guest to Rev. James Pierceson. He enveloped her little, thin hand in both of his and spoke so quietly I was a little peeved that Florence wouldn't stop talking about her bum leg so I could hear what he was saying to her.

Oh, well, there was Anna and Iris, Renee and Fred with Ryan.

"Renee, good morning, morning Fred. This is my beautiful granddaughter from California. Claire, pleased to have you meet Renee and Fred and Ryan."

Claire said hello to each of them, looking longest at Ryan, of course.

Maybe I could have some of the young people come out to the farm for Claire to have some company with. Poor child, only having me and Joseph to jaw with. I'll do it; I'll fix up a little social gathering for her.

On the way home, I asked Claire what she thought about going to church.

"I don't really know," she said, seeming to be thinking intently, like she was deep into figuring it out.

I was hoping that was a good sign. She was so quiet; I took it to mean she had been touched by something blessed.

After dinner we took our Sunday drive. I sure was glad Claire wanted to go with us. Joseph got a big kick out of explaining the different places along the road and how things have changed.

We stopped at his little one room schoolhouse where he and his brothers started out. He sounded like the teacher the way he gave us the tour all the way around the building. He told stories about the devilish things he did to get into trouble. I think he was embellishing a bit to make it funnier, but that was okay. Claire was laughing.

He showed her where the bell used to hang out front and the field where they played ball at recess, and where the woodpile was and the water well. Everything was overgrown but he knew how to bring the memories back to life.

We walked up the road to the waterfalls. This had always been a special spot for our family. When there was no money to be spending on entertainment, we'd take a picnic lunch and all go to the falls. We'd sit on the huge flat rock to just barely feel the mist; it was the most refreshing feeling on a hot day that you'd ever want to experience. The kids sure would have fun in the old swimming hole perfectly formed by the waterfalls and nature.

Claire seemed to be quite taken when Joseph told her about how his teacher would take all the students to the falls for writing class—if they'd been good. For five days in June, they would go there to write stories and poems "to get inspired," the teacher told them. They were allowed to illustrate their works in pencil.

Then, up the dirt road we walked farther to Joseph's old homestead. This was where he was born and grew up with all those strong, handsome brothers.

His eyes welled up a few times as he pointed out different things about the farm, 'course somebody else lives there now and things are different.

He told Claire more about what was gone then what was there. Gone was the chicken coop, the outhouse, the icehouse, the smoke house, the milk house, the hop house, the heifer barn, the snow apple trees, the gooseberry bushes. Several times I saw his eyes misting up a bit; can't blame him, those things were part of his life.

He told Claire he'd show her some old photographs of how it used to look. I was surprised on how many questions she asked. I think that maybe she does have a natural curiosity about things. That's good.

"Well," said Joseph as the face of his watch seemed to draw him back to the present, "we'll have to continue our Sunday drive next week. It's getting time to take care of our animals."

Old farmers never change, thank goodness.

After supper, as we were doing up the dishes, Claire asked, "Grandma, what do you do when you have to make a decision?"

"Well, I think about it."

I was so overwhelmed with what she might be thinking, that I couldn't even think what else to say. What was she deciding? Was she going to leave? I could tell she wanted more information than, "I think about it," so I tried to think of more words.

"Then I weigh each side to see what would be best for me and to those that would be affected by it."

"Is that all?"

"Then I ask God to direct me in making the right decision."

"Good! I'll see you in the morning. Good night!"

"Good night."

What on earth is on her mind? I know her mother is going to call her tomorrow; maybe it's something related to that. Maybe Claire wants to go to Spain with her mother. Well, I wouldn't blame her; a girl should be with her mother.

"Joseph, tell me to calm down."

"Calm down, Clara."

Claire was up bright and early the next morning.

"I've made my decision," she announced confidently to Joseph and to me.

"I've decided that I will help Grandpa with the animals in the morning and help you, Grandma, to make supper in the afternoon!

I don't know why it took us several seconds to respond, but finally it kicked in and we both uttered, "Oh! Wonderful!"

"Let's go Gramps," she called as she hurried outside.

"Lord," I said as I looked upwards, "you sure got some way about you."

I laughed all the way to the garden.

"Hi, Mom!"

"Yeah, great."

"Yeah."

"I think the animals like me!"

"Uh, huh."

"Yeah."

"Uh, huh."

"Guess what? I met this great guy. You would love him!"

"Yeah."

"How is Spain?"

"Okay."

"Love you, too."

"Bye."

Oh, my.

"How's your mother?"

"Great! She says she'd like to live there someday."

"It must be nice," I said with a worrying spell coming on.

"Must be. Now, what do you put in after the cinnamon?"

"Claire, I feel like going up into the storeroom and poking around. Want to go with me? Maybe we can work off that big supper."

"Sure."

"Joseph, you want to go with us?"

"No, thanks. I'll sit here and go through this farm journal. Oh,

Claire, the baked apples were delicious, thanks."

"Grandma said they were one of your favorites."

"She was right, and you're getting to be a good cook."

"Thanks, Grandpa."

"My journal is filling right up, Gram," Claire announced as we walked through her room to the storeroom.

"I'll bet it is…"

Claire looked around the storeroom.

"Good grief." Claire gasped. "This is a lot of stuff."

"It sure is, honey, a lifetime of stuff."

We started opening lids and looking into boxes.

"Oh, my goodness." I laughed. "Claire, look, it's all the old report cards and papers from school. Do you want to see how your dad did in school?"

"Yeah! I can't wait to see this…" she proclaimed as she dug right into the papers.

I meandered around the boxes wondering what I was saving all the ribbon for and trying to think of what I was going to make with the seashells and baler twine. Oh, mercy, here's all the strips of fabric I was going to crochet a rag rug with. My mother's and her mother's button box; I would never in a million years throw that out. Broken pieces of a mirror from the day Ken slugged the ball through the open window to hit my big mirror over the dresser. Hard to believe, but here's the evidence. I saw how to make a mosaic tabletop using broken mirror pieces in one of my magazines; I thought it was so unique. Well, I'll just have to get at it one of these days.

"Didn't he ever get any Cs or Ds?" Claire piped up.

"Not that I remember."

Dolls, the girl's dolls.

"Claire, want to see your aunt's dolls?"

"In a minute, Gram."

Oh, my, here are the marionettes that Joseph's brother sent all the way from Ohio.

What's this?

Written by Emily. Age eleven.

The Marionettes

"Please take your foot out of my mouth!" yelled Gabriella.

"I'm sorry," replied Gretchen, "I can't see a thing in this dark, smelly trunk."

"I know," apologized Gabriella, "It's such a heap we have to lay in until the next show."

"Show!" mumbled Anthony. "Did someone say it was time for the show?"

"No, Anthony, go back to sleep," the girls replied.

"Sleep?" grumbled Anthony. "How can anyone sleep with their parts laying here and there and down there and over there with loose string all over the place?" He didn't wait for an answer but was soon snoring again.

Gab and Gret sighed. They waited in darkness with their painted-on-eyes staring up at the closed lid. They knew it would be another long wait in the darkness of their old trunk. They longed for the children who would clap and smile to see them at the next show.

Emily always had a good imagination.

"Oh my. I think there's every wallpaper I ever used in this house. I was always going to do something with these leftovers.

"Claire, here's some of your bedroom wallpaper! Do you want to make something with it?"

"Yeah, maybe. Did you know Dad was sometimes moody in school?"

"No, not that I recall, why?"

"I've read it two or three times now."

"No. I don't remember that at all. Come and look at this stuff with me. Here's something funny."

"What are they?"

"They're the boys' fishing lures. They'd sit for hours trying to concoct a lure that would catch the most fish. How do you like this one with feathers and fake pearls?"

"Neat! Did they catch any fish with them?"

"I suppose they did; I don't really remember."

"Oh, this doll is beautiful!"

"That actually was mine. I never let the girls play with it; that's why it looks so good. I never got to play with it either when I was little."

"Mom and Dad are getting into antiques now," Claire said.

"They are?" I was flabbergasted.

"I've got loads of antiques around here just wishing someone would take them, especially family. Tell your parents to come out here and get some."

"I will."

"Look at the little tea set, Claire."

"Oh, how adorable!"

"I bet you had all kinds of nice things to play with."

"I did, but Mom didn't save anything," Claire said distantly. "I actually had a tea set to die for."

"Well, if you see anything up here you want, you just tell me."

"What are all these plastic lids for, Grandma?"

"I have no idea." I laughed.

"You two spending the night up there?" Joseph hollered from downstairs.

"Be down soon," I hollered back.

"Seen enough for one night, Claire?"

"I don't think so. This is fun! Can I stay longer?"

"Sure, I'll go down and have a cup of tea with Grandpa, I know that's what he's thinking of."

"See you later."

"What would you like with your tea, Joseph?

"How about some good old baking powder biscuits with honey and butter, or syrup?"

Joseph must be in a talking mood tonight.

Those baking powder biscuits soaked up many a thing...why Aunt Mae's son's wife's cousin went to visit her grandmother... all of Grandpa's stories about covered wagons, prairies and horses...all the news from school and how they might send the school bus up our road now that we had neighbors with seven kids...and they soaked up all the reasons why Sarah couldn't go get a job in the city

We never had a good talk without baking powder biscuits.

"You're doing a mighty fine job with her, Clara."

"Why, Joseph, thank you," I fawned. "You're not doing so bad yourself. Don't forget to get out those picture albums so she can see how your farm used to look. She seemed real interested."

"You got me thinking, Clara, about how maybe we didn't do enough with Joe, or any of them. I never thought about it before, but something must have been missing to not have him bring up his girl better than he did."

"I don't know, Joseph. Did you ever think of Joe as moody?"

"I don't recall that in him. Quiet maybe."

"On his reports from school, some of the teachers said he was moody."

Claire came running down the stairs, "Grandma can I have this?"

She held up a terribly wrinkled dress.

"Land of mercy, Claire, that's a costume. The girls used to dress up in it. You don't want that!"

"But the material is beautiful with the cobalt blue background and the delicate pink flowers. I tried it on. It fits perfectly. Well, maybe it's a little big, but that's okay."

"You want to hear something funny? That's the dress I left on my honeymoon in. To me it was the prettiest dress in the world. After, it hung in the closet for years. I finally gave in to my girls and let them use it for dress up. I, too, was very thin in those days.

Joseph, dig out our wedding pictures so Claire can see me leaving on our honeymoon. Get you farm pictures, too, while you're in there."

Ah, it's going be a great night for baking powder biscuits!

"Why on earth do you want that dress?"

"Well, if we can clean it and press it nice, I can wear it to church on Sunday."

I heard Joseph drop the album in the other room.

I forgot to stop pouring. Had to eat two more biscuits in order to soak up the extra maple syrup.

The next morning after chores, Claire and I drove into town to buy a cleaning solution for the dress. She was anxious to see our little town. I warned her not to expect any malls. In fact we only had three stores: grocery, hardware, and drug. Most times you didn't need anything more than what you could find there. Course, what's most fun is never knowing who you're going to run into at the store. Never gone when I didn't return home with bits of yarns about who I saw.

"Maybe we'll see some of your friends from church, Claire."

"That would be nice," she said cheerfully, sitting up a little straighter.

"How would you like to have some friends over for a July Fourth celebration?"

"Could I? I would love that. I'm good at planning parties."

She immediately got out her pen and note pad and started making notations of some sort.

"Do you think we should invite Ryan?" I asked. I had to find out how much she was taken with him.

"Ryan? Oh sure. He's nice."

She didn't sound as enthused about him as when she was talking to her mother. But that's good; I don't want her to get anything started. I'm not up to that.

"Here we are, at the market!"

Go into the little town market on a day blistering from the heat outside...but refreshingly cool inside.

With a breeze blowing through from the back screen door to the front screen door...with no hot lights...and there'll be people dawdling along ready for a bit of conversation...carrying little baskets or handsful of supper, over the old wooden oiled floor with a few curious knotholes.

In an old, ornate cupboard you'll see huge jars of fixins...probably waiting for the fireman's carnival or the grange picnic.

A little meat counter conversation as you watch pieces being customized...and a little friendly chat here and there in the little town grocery store will end your stay as you go again to the heat of the outdoors.

"Well, this certainly is going into my journal!" Claire laughed. "This town is like something out of a movie."

"But it's not!" I said theatrically, "It's *re-e-e-e-a-l*. Ann Marie's daughter, Amy, works in the drug store. Do you want to stop in and say hi?"

"Sure."

Now this is like a general store; it has a little bit of everything. We saw Amy move the ladder along its track and ascend to reach what the customer wanted. There were shelves up to the ceiling, Claire was fascinated.

"I wish my friends could see this. This is hysterical."

"Don't you mean 'historical'?"

"No way. I hope my English teacher has us write a *What I Did Over the Summer* essay. I used to dread that topic, but not now. They won't believe it!"

I wanted to believe Claire wasn't poking fun at all she saw. I slowly released the tension in my hands after I realized I had been digging into my palms with my nails.

I knew I had to change my line of thinking.

"What kind of party would you like to have?" I asked weakly.

"How about food and music?" she asked.

"Food and music? Is that something new out on the west coast? I don't think I've ever heard of such a thing around here. Food and music at a party?"

"Grandma! Stop teasing!"

We both laughed.

"Claire, you wouldn't mind if I invited some of our friends, too, would you?"

"Of course not. That's what Mom and Dad do, then everybody has someone to talk to."

"Swell. We'll plan the menu after lunch."

"So, did you get your dress cleaner solution?" Joseph asked.

He had been sitting on the shady back steps waiting for lunch, no doubt.

"Yes," I said, waving the bottle at him. "I think this'll bring the old dress back to life."

"I'd like to see that dress come back to life..." he blushed.

"Simmer down, mister, simmer down." I smiled as we went through the old kitchen.

You know, it's funny –

In the summertime...No one pays much attention to the drone of the tractor in the field...No one pays much attention to the water pump going on and off...No one notices much as dishes clink and drawers open and close when the gingerbread is being made...No one's attention is drawn to the squeak and squeal of the clothesline being pulled out...No one but the dog attends to the milk truck driving up into the yard...The banging of the screen door from the cat going in and out isn't the sound of any consequence.

But after lunch when no one moves and nothing moves...the sole buzzing of a fly becomes the master of sound.

◈◈

"Well, I better get some work done today," Joseph suddenly said, moving his chair back.

"Us, too. We have to plan our party. Let's put the dress to soaking and begin."

"We'll start with the food; I'll get out the cook books."

"Aren't we going to have it catered?" Claire asked without blinking an eyelash.

"Yes. We'll use the Claire and Clara Catering Company!" I laughed.

"Well! What shall the CCCC prepare?" Claire asked, imitating Julia Child.

"How about this: Southern barbecued chicken?"

"Great, but we have to have hot dogs and hamburgers, too."

"Okay."

"And watermelon."

"And potato chips."

"Sounds like a plan."

"Everyone will bring a dish to share, too, even though we would never ask them to. We'll have plenty. I'll make up a milk can full of lemonade."

"Now for the music. Shall we hire a DJ?"

"I don't think so, honey," I replied, trying not to laugh. "Maybe I can get Len to bring his guitar and I hear the reverend plays the violin. Maybe he'd like to come. Shall we ask him?"

"Sure," Claire answered.

I could have sworn Claire just blushed.

"Would you like to be in charge of decorations?"

"Oh, yeah, cool; I love to decorate," Claire answered jubilantly.

"So, we have food, music, and decorations covered," I pondered. "What else do the four C's have to do?"

"Just the invitations, I think."

"We'll start our list tonight; we can't be sitting around much longer."

"That's for sure," Claire exclaimed jumping up to grab the broom.

I hung the honeymoon dress in the bathroom to drip dry and Claire dumped the mop water out by the hollyhocks, when Joseph bolted through the screen door.

"The calf is ready to be born! Come on! I need your help!"

"Are you sure you want to go?" I asked Claire as the three of us scurried faster than the chickens getting out of our way.

"Yes! Grandpa and I have been waiting for this baby and I'm going to name it," she proclaimed excitedly.

I can tell you about animals being born and I can tell you how some deliveries are difficult. This was a hard one.

I kept eying Claire worrying about her more than the cow, but she stayed right with us, by golly. I wasn't sure she was going to make it, but she did. She was a real trooper.

She stayed in the barn with Joseph to put new bedding down for the mama and baby, while I went back to wash up and start supper.

You wouldn't think we could go from birthing to eating, but farmers can. Just like doctors can.

Before she even opened the screen door I heard, "Her name is *Arianna*."

"How nice. Congratulations!"

"Go in and wash. I'll fix you a cup of tea; you can take it easy for a few minutes before I send you out to the back steps to husk the corn,"

"Is that the corn-husking place?" She laughed.

"It is." I grinned and shot her a pirate's-eye look.

I couldn't resist picking up some corn at the market. Bert said it came clear from California, I guess they ship anything from out there. Pineapples, corn, children.

After supper, Joseph and Claire went to the barn to check on Arianna one last time.

When they returned, I thought we could start on the invitations.

"You know, Gram, I've never been too tired to work on party plans, but I'm exhausted. I've got to go to bed."

"I'm so glad you said that; I'm tired, too."

"Good night, my dear, see you in the morning."

"Joseph, are you ready?"

Joseph opened his tired eyes, "I'm beyond ready."

The next morning we all stood around Arianna like three gawking pedestrians. "You know what, Grandma? Claire asked. "If you know how to take pictures, I'd like to start a scrapbook of my new baby and me. My camera is still in the suitcase."

"Well, I'm no genius, but I think I can push a button."

I could hear Joseph laughing from clear over by the grain bin.

"Go run and get it; I'll stay here. Isn't she something—Arianna? She'll be a good second mother to you."

"Okay, Grandma, just look through here and push this button."

"Right on, chief."

So that was the beginning of visual memories for Claire: Arianna and Claire; Claire feeding the chickens; Claire gathering eggs; picking berries; hoeing weeds in the garden; cooking at the stove; sitting by the waterfalls; holding baby lambs; Claire and Grandpa; Claire and Grandma—it nearly brought tears to my eyes. And there would be more picture taking to come, I was sure.

"Claire, look how the fabric brightened right up! All you'll have to do is iron it."

"Grandma, I don't know how to iron," Claire said desperately.

"Oh dear. Would you like to learn?"

"Sure."

"I'll tell you what, I'll show you how to iron Grandpa's handkerchiefs. You can practice on them."

While the steam iron was warming up, I pointed to a set of old flat irons and asked, "Do you know what those are, Claire?"

"Yeah, book ends."

I shouldn't be sucking on hard candy when I ask that girl a question. The candy flew out and hit the cat right in the ear. Poor thing yowled and ran upstairs. I hollered up to him, "I'm sorry. I didn't mean it."

My mother used to iron with them. She'd heat them up on the old type stove they had back then, wrap a rag around the handle in order to hold on to it and press clothes."

"It's so heavy," Claire exclaimed as she gave it a hoist.

"Number one rule, be careful; keep your hands out of the way of the hot part. Slide it back and forth like this."

"Great. Let me try."

While Claire ironed in the kitchen, I started making pie dough.

"Now, even though I want you to concentrate on your ironing, sort of watch this dough process a little, just so you get a wee notion of it, okay?"

"Okay."

After Claire had a nice, neat pile of Joseph's hankies done, I graduated her to pillowcases. Not that I am in a habit of ironing pillowcases, but it was a good step up, I thought.

"That looks like fun to roll out the dough," she spoke up.

"Well, I guess it is kind of fun, now that I think of it," I said, pondering the thought.

"What kind of pie is it going to be?" she asked, easily able to keep the iron moving as she looked up.

"Strawberry rhubarb."

"Is rhubarb a berry, too?"

Oh, Lord, where's the cat?

"No, it's a stalk with huge elephant ear leaves. I'll take you out to the rhubarb patch in a few minutes."

"Say, what's going on in here?" Joseph asked coming in the back door.

Claire picked up her pile of handkerchiefs. "Grandpa, look what I did for you!"

She hurried over to Joseph, catching her foot on the cord and pulling the iron to the floor.

She let out a scream.

"Oh my dear God," I moaned as I ran over.

"Did it burn you?"

"No," she cried, "but it scared me."

"Well, thank God you're okay. This is how we learn though; next time you'll be more careful. I know I had to learn the same thing when I was young."

"I didn't know you knew how to iron," Joseph interjected wisely to calm her down.

"I just learned today," she said weakly.

"You're doing a mighty fine job."

"Thanks, Grandpa."

"What's going to be after pillowcases, Gran?"

"How about, tablecloths? But why don't you turn the iron off now so we can get some rhubarb?"

"Better take the sugar bowl with you," Grandpa laughed.

"Oh, I did see this out here, I just didn't know what it was," Claire stated.

"That's understandable. It always looks like a weed to me, too. What we'll use are just the stalks, we'll cut the leaves off—heard people say they're poisonous. Don't know for sure, but am not about to find out either. I'll give you a little chunk to taste, but beware, it'll be sour."

"Eeee," Claire squealed. I could see the veins in her neck being pulled.

"This *is* sour! Are you sure you want to put it in the pie?"

"Oh, we'll put lots of sugar on it. Do you want to cut up the rhubarb or go back to you ironing?"

"I think I'll iron. I've got to get good so I can iron the dress for church. I want to look nice."

"Okay, I'm going to get the stew simmering for supper."

"Well," Joseph said as he slapped his thighs getting up, "if you're going to be doing all this slow cooking, I'll be outside waiting for the delicious smells to drift out on the breeze."

Clear down to the hop house you could smell the cabbage frying in the pork fat. Half way over to the neighbors you could smell pot roast a-simmering in garden fresh garlic.

On a good day you could come off the hill and smell peppers and onions a-sizzling in the old iron frying pan. Way into the hay mow you could smell fresh corn relish, or green tomato preserves being readied for the winter.

What a treat, when you were down-wind from the just-picked berry pies.

The food she made...cooked for a long while and the smells had time to meander in and out and over and around the whole farm.

"Maybe Grandpa will teach me how to whittle tonight?" Claire asked as she ironed.

"Maybe."

"We need to get our list ready, too."

"You know, I think I'll just mention it to people I see at church, and those I don't, I'll give them a jingle on the phone. We don't need to be so formal."

"Can I ask Amy and the reverend?"

"Sure."

This talk is so typical of women in the kitchen, working and talking—a great combination, in my book. I had forgotten how much I missed it.

"Tablecloth is done. What's next?"

"How about aprons?"

"Will do."

"Oh," I half screamed, "Land of mercy!"

"Grandma, what's the matter?"

"I need to take your picture! You'll definitely want you friends to see this. Smile!"

"Oh, wait a minute, let me get a flat iron. That'll really get them."

"Now you're getting the old farm humor."

"Let me run out quick to say good-night to Arianna and I'll be back to help you with the dishes."

"Thanks, hon. I'll be sitting right here until you get back."

"Very good supper, Clara, thank you for it," Joseph said kindly.

"You're very welcome. It was fun cooking while I visited with Claire."

"You know what I've been thinking?" Joseph asked as he stirred his coffee.

"What's that?"

"What would you think if I asked Joe, Jr. to spend some of his vacation out here with us while Claire is here?"

I sat utterly staring at my husband. In fact, I stared and said nothing for so long he leaned over and touched my arm. "Are you all right?"

"Sometimes I think you are brilliant. And this is one of those times."

"We'll ask Claire what she thinks, too."

∞

"So, I hear you want to learn how to whittle?"

"Yeah, what is it?"

"Did you see the wooden animals up on the buffet?"

"Yeah, they're neat."

"I carved them out of wood."

"What? You're kidding!"

"We're going to start very basic, just learning how to swipe the knife across the wood and take off little slivers."

There they sat with newspapers on the floor to catch the shavings and she looking over at his skilled hands so she could do it too.

Flash: "Gotcha!"

"Geez, Clara. That's not the smartest thing to do when we've got knives in our hands." Joseph looked startled.

"Oh, sorry, I didn't think about that!"

Without lifting her eyes, Claire said, "Oh, gee, maybe Grandma could take a picture of the ambulance crew when they come in to get us."

Joseph roared, "That's a good one, Claire."

"Oh, you two. I'm going to go and get my quilt pieces."

"When did you start whittling, Grandpa?"

"Actually, I got into big trouble the first time I did any carving."

"You mean you carved your initials in the top of a school desk?"

"Are you joking? That would have meant death at sunset! No, I carved mine and Grandma's initials into a tree out in the woods."

"What's so bad about that?" Claire asked innocently.

"Well, my Pa didn't go in for that kind of thing and that tree was the first to go when he needed to sell a load of fence posts."

Their names were carved on a tree always to be together forevermorer...until the tree was cut down and severed into fence posts...Across someone's field runs a fence of many posts which stands not so erect anymore...through every day and night.

On one chipped post...quite leaning to the right...you can see left sided letters...On the crippled post next to it...leaning quite to the left...are letters to fit the left sided love.

"Somewhere out there Joseph and I are still together," I sighed as I sat with the box in my lap.

"Have I done enough practicing, Grandpa? Can I get to something real now?"

"You'll never have enough practicing, but I know what you're saying."

"What do you intend on carving?"

"I think I'll do Arianna."

"Ouch!" I screamed when I pricked my finger.

"Sounds like Grandma needs more practicing over there," Joseph winked knowing why the needle slipped.

"How should I start?"

"Well," Joseph pondered, "whittle out everything that isn't Arianna and you'll have it."

"Yeah," said Claire thoroughly engrossed in the idea.

"I did pretty good on Grandpa's shirts, didn't I Grandma?"

"You sure did. I never saw anyone learn so fast, and today's Saturday. D-Day for the dress."

"Here goes."

Heads turned when we three walked in. I didn't need to show off my granddaughter, she was doing it all by herself. What a dress does for a young lady is what the first autumn tree does to the forest. I think, anyway.

Her thinness was almost statuesque; her thick dark hair met the cobalt blue with the compatibility of two friends. She seemed to be standing straighter these days, not so slouched as when we first saw her at the airport.

I didn't know she brought white sandals with her; they were pretty.

Oh, my goodness! She'd polished her toenails!

"Oh, good morning, Reverend. You remember my—"

"Claire." He extended his hand without me having to finish, "I'm so glad you're here."

"Clara, Clara," Ruth Ann called out.

I couldn't hear a darn thing again, and now he had both his hands enveloped around hers.

He marched up to the pulpit and we filed into our pew.

I looked at Claire. She, of course, was looking forward—at the reverend.

Is this why she wanted to come to church? Is *he* the reason for the dress?

Oh, dear God, batten down the hatches! I need you now. Please don't let there arise a situation of—of you know. I don't need a lovesick girl pining over the reverend.

Sure was hard keeping my mind on the sermon. Why the painted toenails? Why did Joe send her out here, anyway? I wonder if she was getting into trouble back home. What kind of friends does she have anyway?

What? Church is over all ready?

We waited our turn to shake the pastor's hand.

"Thank you, Reverend Pierceson. Wonderful sermon," I said, hoping he didn't know I wasn't listening much to the sermon.

Claire said softly, "Thank you, Jim."

He took her hand again. "I'm glad you enjoyed it. God Bless."

Jim? She called him Jim?

"Would you like to come to our Fourth of July party and bring your violin?"

239

"I would love to, what time?"

Claire looked at me.

"Uh-uh-uh-one. One is it," I stuttered and stammered.

"Thanks for inviting me, Claire."

He let go of her hand.

"For a young man, the pastor seems to have a lot of wisdom and compassion. I thought 'unfounded suspicions' was a good topic for the sermon, didn't you, Clara?" Joseph asked on the drive home.

"Unfounded suspicions? Oh, yes, yes, that's something we all have to be careful about."

"What did you think, Claire?"

"Oh, sorry, Gram. I guess I was daydreaming. What did you say?"

"That's okay. We'll talk later."

"So," Joseph asked as he pulled up our road, "who's going on the Sunday drive with me after dinner?"

"Me."

"Me," I said weakly.

"Claire, after you change, could you run down to the garden for some lettuce? And some chives, too?"

"Sure. I'll check if there are any more peas, too."

"Joseph, sit for a minute. We need to talk."

"What's the matter?"

"I think Claire has eyes for the reverend."

"What?"

"Yes. I'm serious, the dress, the hair, the—well, everything—and just the fact that she's so anxious to go to church."

"I don't know where you women come up with this stuff."

"I just know," I insisted.

"He's probably fifteen, eighteen years older than she is. Why would she be attracted to him?"

"Don't you see how kind and inviting he is? The poor child is starving for a father figure, or male attention, or something. She's a teenager who doesn't know how to sort out her feelings. He, in all his compassion, wisdom, gentleness, love, whatever, is just what Claire needs to fill her void. In her mind, she probably would want to be with him forever so he could take care of all her troubles and watch over her. Apparently those longings weren't fulfilled as a child. She's going into adult thoughts with the ways of a child still to be tended to."

"I never knew you were such a psychiatrist."

"I know I'm not a psychiatrist, this is only my true feeling."

"We need to get Joe, Jr. out here," Joseph proclaimed quietly.

"Grandma! Grandma, you have purple orchids blooming out by the house." Claire came running through the "old kitchen" to the screen door.

Joseph and I looked at each other. He grabbed for his handkerchief.

I love her innocence, I thought to myself.

"Honey, those are iris. They're the 'East Coast orchids.'"

"When did you plant them?" she asked starting to rinse the lettuce leaves in the sink.

"Gosh, I don't know. They've been there for years. They come up every year all by themselves."

"You mean all those green plants out there are going to have flowers?"

"That's right; they're all perennials except for my gladiola bulbs that I put in every year. You weren't here yet when the crocus and daffodils were blooming. Then we had the hyacinths and tulips and the silver dollar plants. Let's see, blooming now are the wild bleeding hearts out by the cellar door and the lilies of the valley under the hawthorn tree. I saw a mass of blue around the base of the front porch—those would be the forget-me-nots.

"What else, Joseph?"

"Our lilacs didn't make it this year; the buds all froze during the last frost. I think next we'll have the peonies."

"Wait until you see those, Claire. All summer something will be opening up. I love the hollyhocks and the black eyed Susans."

"My favorites would be the roses and the lilies," Joseph said thoughtfully.

"I can't believe it." Claire looked astonished. "I wish I had a perennial garden."

"Oh, the delphiniums," Joseph interjected. "I like them, too."

"How about the sedum? Oh, that's more for fall, but we'll have daisies and outhouse golden glow.

"Jeepers, we'll never have dinner if I don't get a-moving here," I said quickly, as I grabbed my apron.

"Joseph can you help Claire with the corn? You can do it out on the back steps so you don't get the hair on the floor."

"Hair?" I heard Claire say on the way out.

"How about we go to Chandler Lake?" Joseph asked during dinner. "Let's take our whittling with us, Claire."

"I'll get the camera and my writing pad," I said.

"Oh, I'll take my mail with me, too," Claire said. "I haven't gotten around to reading it yet."

"Can't be too interesting?" Joseph said inquisitively.

"No, those guys do the same thing every day—go the beach and go to the mall."

"Wow," announced Claire. "This is beautiful."

"Isn't it though?"

The lake was smack dab in the middle of a wood. The outer edge was in shade, that is, depending on where the sun was and we entered on the shady side. We sat on our familiar log, the one that looked like it had been there for years, probably having succumbed to a storm.

I stared out at the sparkling water, Joseph started his whittling, adding clean litter to the soil, and Claire read her mail.

A bullfrog croaked and Claire jumped.

"Just a bullfrog," Joseph answered before she could ask.

"Just a fish jumping," I inserted.

"I can't believe it!" Claire said looking up from one of her letters.

"My friend, Miranda, wants to know if she can vacation out here with me."

Joseph's wood went flying one way and the knife went flying the other.

"Holy Cow, that's never happened to me before." He sounded apologetic.

"Do you think you'd want her here?" I asked.

"No way; she's a bore."

She went back to her reading and I got out my writing pad.

"What are you writing, Grandma?"

"Oh, just a little story. The coolness of the woods is making me think of the last patch of snow."

"Your Grandma has been writing stories ever since our kids were small. Remember that one year when you wrote each one a story for Christmas? That was the year when money was real scarce, and each year after that they wanted their story present."

"Yes, I remember, but even better was when they got up and read their stories to all in the household. That was entertaining, wasn't it?"

"Sure was."

"Oh, brother," Claire exhaled, "Bill's been grounded for two weeks. Oh, well, grounded or not, he'll be stoned for the entire time."

"Just a blue jay screeching."

Stoned?

"Claire," Grandpa whispered.

Claire looked at him and Joseph pointed. A doe and a fawn walked out of the thicket; we humans didn't move. The two walked to the lake for a drink, walked along the edge and out of sight.

"Oh, I wish I had taken a picture," Claire lamented.

"That would have scared them. You have your best picture in your mind, right?"

"Right."

Claire started her work on "Arianna."

I scribbled out some words and put in other words.

"How would you like your Dad to fly out and spend a couple of weeks with us?" Joseph asked.

"Dad? Why?"

"I thought maybe he'd enjoy it, getting back on the farm again."

"No. He's no fun to be around. He'll spoil everything," she said very emphatically. "Plus, he's not the farming type."

"He was for eighteen years," I reminded her.

"Well, maybe then, but he sure isn't now. He wouldn't like it, believe me." She tried desperately to drive the point home.

"We don't need to talk about it now. How about we walk around the lake?"

"Can we hear Grandma's story first?"

"Of course."

The snow escaped down into the earth; fleeing from the spring sun, it sought shelter underground.

Determined to stay snow, it held on to every root and rock.

It waited many months in darkness, sometimes pushing itself down further, as the heat seemed to be descending to capture it.

In such blackness, it couldn't see itself, but hoped it was still white and beautiful, and full of unique flakes.

One day, a sudden force came over Snow and it knew it was time to emerge. Snow was anxious to lay on top of the earth again.

Up and out it came, finding to its great dismay, that it was nothing.

"I told you she was good."

"Where are all your stories?"

"Upstairs in a box."

"Can I read them sometime?"

"Of course."

"I found out that I kind of like to write. Before I go back to California, I'll show you my journal."

I turned to see her squarely. Just a trace of sunlight peeked through the thickness of the woods to illuminate her face. I thought, *What is in that beautiful head of yours? You are so capable; the possibilities are obviously endless. Why are you just beginning to learn?*

"I would be honored," I admitted freely.

"Come on slow pokes," Joseph called back for us to catch up.

Every step brought something new to the eye. I reckon beaches are nice, but I can't imagine them having all that a wood can hold.

"Claire, look at the toad stools," Joseph said and pointed with his walking stick—a branch he had picked up from the ground.

"Are they a plant?"

"Yes, a type of fungus, like that on the side of the tree. Kind of unique, isn't it? Ever eat mushrooms?"

"Sure."

"They grow in cool, damp areas like this. But you better be knowing your mushrooms: some are poisonous."

"Ah, Jack-in-the-pulpit," I exclaimed, bending over to pick some.

"This grows wild?" Claire asked as she examined it closely.

"Oh, sure, we'll see lots of beautiful flowers today. They're perennials; by next month you'll see a whole different set."

"Neat. What did you say this is called?"

"Jack-in-the-pulpit."

"Should be 'Jim-in-the-pulpit'!" Claire said with her eyes sparkling.

I kept walking.

Lord, let me be aware of the opportunity of setting things straight. Please be with me at that time.

Pointing again, Joseph indicated a huge patch of blackberry bushes that would be loaded with berries in August.

"We've got the same thing up in our north woods, Claire. We'll pick lots of them before you leave. You have to wear protective clothing remember."

"Why?"

"The bushes are full of stiff prickers. If you don't wear long sleeves and long pants, you'll come out looking like you been in a cat fight with fifteen cats."

"Oh, my," Claire replied looking up high at something that caught her eye.

"What's that?"

"Oh, my Lord, Joseph. Is that the eagle I read about in the paper? It said bird watchers all over the Northeast are tracking it."

"I don't know," he whispered, trying to get a better look. "I don't think so. I think it's just a very big hawk."

"Is this like a rain forest we studied about?"

"Well," said Joseph, "it's not a rain forest, but its characteristics are similar; all these plants and animals depend on each other. The lake, too, is in connection with the whole region around it and what's in it. Sure is interesting how it all works."

"Yeah, kind of makes sense now," Claire stated as she gazed all around with knowledge just a-soaking through her eyeballs.

"When my sisters and I were young, we used to play wedding," I explained. "We were always running into the woods for something."

～

We went into the wood for the lushness of green ferns…

And into the wood for the softness of Princess Pine…

Into the wood for the gentleness of moss and the coolness of mint…

And there we picked violets and jack-in-the-pulpits and Lady-Slippers…

We gathered white birch bark and pine boughs and huge Oak leaves…

Then on to our big, shady front porch…we decorated for the grandest wedding ever held in the summertime.

～

"I always wished I had a sister," Claire lamented.

"Why don't you get into that Big Sister program?" asked Joseph as he pointed out a rabbit.

"I never thought of that!"

"Somebody's out in a canoe," I said looking out across the lake.

"Nice day for it," Joseph remarked.

We walked on, stepping over limbs that had come down and going around this bush or that bush. We named the different kinds of trees we came upon and collected leaves so Claire could compare the differences, that is, if she was interested.

We came to a half-shady, half-sunny clearing and sat looking out at the canoeist. His paddles never made a sound in the water. He was coming our way.

"I think that's Jim!" Claire said standing up and waving.

It wasn't long before the person was waving back. It *was* him.

He approached closer and closer until he called out, "Hello, over there."

"Hello," Claire chirped, grabbing her camera. "Smile!"

The canoe slid up onto the shore and he stepped out.

"Afternoon, Claire, Clara, Joseph. Beautiful day."

"Come and sit with us," Claire said invitingly.

"Well, thanks, but I can't stay; I still have to paddle back across the lake to my truck, then I have a supper engagement at the Thomas's."

"Could I go in the canoe with you?" Claire asked boldly.

"Sure. Joseph, where's your car?"

"It's on the other end of the lake, too."

"I'll get Claire over safe and sound."

"I know you will. See you there."

As they started off, we began our trek back to the car.

"Why did you let her go, Joseph?"

"Why not?"

"I told you, I think she likes him."

"She should like him."

"You know what I mean."

"Clara, who has that girl spoken to since she arrived here?"

"Only us."

"Let her have a little freedom. Jim isn't going to steer her wrong."

"Oh, Lord, I hope not."

The walk back wasn't anything like our walk with Claire. We didn't stop to enjoy anything; there was no teaching and learning. I missed that.

"You know what my problem is, Joseph?"

He stopped and looked at me.

"I want Claire just to enjoy us and not anybody else."

"Oh, honey," he whispered as he put his arm around me and held me close. "That's just your motherly nature; it's a wonderful quality but flowers have to bloom, you know."

"I know…" I sniffled into his shoulder.

Joseph held my hand the rest of the way through the woods.

On the drive home, Claire rested her head back on the seat and said, "This has been the best day of my whole life."

"Your whole life?" I reiterated.

"My whole life."

A few nervous seconds went by until she said, "My mother is just going to love Jim."

"Are you planning on introducing Reverend Pierceson to your mother?" I asked hopelessly.

"Oh, yes, he's a perfect catch for Mom."

"Joseph, watch out for the bridge!" I screamed.

"Oh, I'm sorry. I guess I wasn't thinking," he said.

"Sorry, Claire, what did you say?"

"I think Mom would be very happy with Jim. He's kind, smart, good looking, you know, all that stuff."

"Isn't your mom still married to your dad?"

"Oh, yeah, but I think she ought to dump him."

That was it for the questions, I was totally exhausted physically, mentally, and emotionally. Spiritually, all I could pray was: "Help!"

I think Joseph must have felt the same way—all through supper and the rest of the evening we sat like two lumps on a log.

Claire, on the other hand, was working in her scrapbook; writing in her journal; whittling Arianna; leafing through Cook Books; tracing out leaves; playing with the cats; looking up flowers in the seed catalog; and making a new cover for her journal with the extra wallpaper that matched her bedroom walls.

"You guys look tired," Claire said looking over at us.

"I reckon we are. Maybe we'll get to bed now. See you in the morning."

"Okay Gram.

"Grandma, I love you.

"Grandpa, I love you."

"We love you, too, honey."

The two lumps went upstairs and stared at the dark ceiling. Restlessness took over during the night.

When Joseph and Claire went out to do the morning chores, I went to the storeroom for my box of stories. I needed to find Joe.

Here's one of his stories:

My Island

by Joe, Age 9

An island came up out of the water just for me.

When I went to my creek, it rose right before my eyes.

I would wade out to my island and be the captain all afternoon.

I had my palm trees and parrot, colorful flowers and beaches.

Many dangerous ships went by, knowing better than to stop.

When it was time to go home to supper.

I waded back to the shore, turned to my island and watched as it lowered itself down into the water and out of sight until my return.

Was he looking for power?

Was he feeling powerless?

I think this next was when his best friend, Pete, moved away, maybe age 11 or 12.

Separated Pirates

Do you have your looking glass

Up to your eye?

Are you turned towards me

As I am to you?

On a clear day

I know I see you

Standing on the beach of Calais,

Wearing your ratty old pirate suit

As am I.

Why must this Strait of Dover

Keep us apart?

Dover just isn't the same

Without you.

My pirating days

Are as dull as Sara Jane's stories,

Remember her?
I salute you
across the water, Matey!

Feeling abandonment?
Feelings of loneliness?

In the Depths of the Sea
Way under the sea,
where you must be brave,
you'll go with me
through coral and cave.
What will it be,
in the depths of black,
with things that flee
but stay on track?
Tail fins we'll see
with ripples that'll tell
you're there with me
in that watery carousel.
While alone with thee,
as creatures swim by
in the depths of the sea,
take my hand, 'tis I.

His first love?

Who was she?

What happened?

A Musical Flight

Eng. Comp. 102

The black notes upon the page

Skipped and jumped to set the stage.

Notes of music which hailed from thee,

Flew off the paper and grabbed hold of me.

They swept me up and sailed me away;

The notes together led me out of the day.

I sailed on my venture as the overture lasted

Then back to earth as a ship unmasted.

I shall never forget the voyage of delight

Upon the musical notes floating into the night.

A college love?

Here's the story I wrote for Joe when he was so sick. He was probably five years old at the time.

Magic Medicine

The little angel

whisked across the lawn,

flitting and darting to every flower petal

and dew-dropped spider web.

Into her silvery pouch

I could see her putting droplets

of the shiny liquid.

Sometimes she disappeared

so far into a flower

I could only see two tiny feet

sticking out of the top.

She scurried around

even faster than the Hummingbird,

who quite knew by now,

to stay out of her way.

While the whole house slept,

and before Mama

would come in with my medicine,

I spent each new dawn

watching my angel

out on the just awakened lawn.

When her pouch was full,

I would raise myself on my elbow

to reach out onto the windowsill

where she left the magic drops,

which she and I knew

would make me better.

"Clara, you up there?" Joseph yelled up the stairs.

"I'll be right there."

"Let's have a cup of coffee, shall we?"

"Okay," I said as I came down the steps. "I was just reading through some of Joe's stories; trying to find out what escaped us."

"Here, Clara, sit down. I'll fix it."

Suddenly he said, "Clara, I'm going out to California to see Joe."

"What?"

"I have to," said Joseph pensively, "then I'll bring him back here for a week or so, if he'll come. You and Claire can manage things around here, can't you?"

"Well, yes. We'll be able to manage. How long will you be gone?"

"I'd say three or four days.

You haven't said what you think of the idea."

"I think you're a good father for trying to help, but keep in mind, it's their life. We can't tell them what to do."

John took Joseph to the airport while Claire, Sadie, and I waved from the yard.

"Bye, old man. Be safe," I whispered.

"When's the last time Joseph went away on a trip, Clara?" Sadie asked.

"Never."

"Well, you girls will be all right. John and I are right next door, you know. You can call on us any time, day or night."

"Thanks, Sadie,"

We stood looking down the road long after the car had disappeared out of sight.

Finally Claire broke the silence. "Can I serve you ladies pie and coffee now? I made the pie."

"Oh, yes."

We older ladies sat at the table while Claire bustled around the kitchen.

"This is kind of fun having the men gone so we girls can just visit, isn't it?" Sadie asked.

"Well, I miss Joseph already, but I know what you mean," I consented.

"Maybe that's how my mom felt when she went to Spain," Claire thoughtfully said, as she poured our coffee. "Maybe she just needed a little time away from Dad."

"Yes, that's important every once in awhile," Sadie spoke, looking over the top of her glasses.

I was going to deny it, but the point was exactly what Claire needed to hear.

"Claire, this is delicious! You know, I have a granddaughter who doesn't even know how to make a pie or anything else."

"Well, I didn't know either until my grandma taught me," Claire said as she looked lovingly over at me.

"You're a quick learner, honey; it makes it easy for the teacher."

Sadie said emphatically, "Now there's a thought! How are these kids going to know how to do anything, if nobody teaches them?"

She started nodding her head with a faraway look and continued, "You know, when women get together we learn from each other, don't we?"

"We sure do," Claire spoke like a woman of many more years than she was.

"Sometimes fathers need their sons and sons need their fathers, too," I said distinctly, trying to get my subtle point across.

"You mean men get together and talk like women do?" Claire asked with an utterly surprised tone.

"They sure do! Maybe not as often as we do, but they need that male companionship as well. Those of them who deny it end up suffering in the end. People need people. If you don't talk out your problems, your problems will eat you up," I confirmed the point.

"Oh, my gosh," Claire said almost in a whisper," Dad never talks to anybody; I don't think he has any male friends. And he has stopped talking to Mom and me. Maybe that's what's the matter with him. Now I'm glad Grandpa is going out to see him; Grandpa will be good for him. Poor Dad."

Sadie and I wiped tears from our eyes while Sadie said, "What a mature young lady you are Claire. Such compassion. I wish my granddaughter knew you."

"Thank you, Sadie, but somehow this farm is bringing something out of me that I never felt before."

Sadie looked lovingly over at me. "This farm has good roots, child."

"You and Grandpa were right, Gran. Dad needs to come home for a while," Claire said as she wept into her napkin.

And so it was, Claire and I on the old homestead, doing the outdoor work, the indoor work, and all the work in between.

We helped birth a new calf—a cousin to Arianna, Claire said.

Retrieved the sheep heading for the neighbors and fixed the

fence.

Canned up fifteen jars of dill pickles, eight of sweet, and five bread and butter.

Picked thirteen quarts of raspberries, made two pies and put up seven jars of raspberry jam.

Cleaned out Joe's bedroom in case he came home.

Had the vet come for old Babe; got the medicine for her.

Made Joe's favorite bread in case he came home.

Weeded the garden.

Mowed the lawn.

Joe and Joseph came home on the fifth day. Joe rented a car at the airport.

I knew where I was when I felt the dip in the road...I knew I was close when my stomach went up and my head went down.

Close to the mint patch and the mulberry tree...when five red barns in a row whizzed by...close to the blackberries and the puff-balls...when an abandoned hay loader seemed to lift its head at me/

When the sky went a long ways over and there were ups and downs to run upon...I was close.

Once past the dip...I knew I'd feed chickens and remember driving the old blue Chevy that still sits in the yard.

Yes, very soon I would want to get up at dawn and be entertained all day...until the stars in the sky winked me off to sleep.

We were in the barn doing chores when the car pulled up the driveway.

Both of us women went running out wearing our tall barn boots.

"Joseph! Joe!"

"Dad! Grandpa!"

"Clara! Claire!"

"Mom! Claire!"

Joe met his brand new daughter and Claire looked at her father with different thoughts.

Joseph and I disappeared deep into the farm in order for Joe and Claire to get reacquainted.

The Fourth of July party was a success, with Len playing the guitar and Rev. Jim serenading us on his violin.

After a time, Joe returned to L.A., and Claire stayed for the rest of the summer.

⟨∂Chapter Fifteen⟩⟩

THE RAP SHEET

"**I**t was so good seeing you again, Liz," Agnes said softly as she hugged the retired policewoman from the County Sheriff's Department.

"You, too, Agnes, but I'll always be sorry we couldn't solve the case."

"Me, too, dear," Agnes cooed softly. She darted a glance at Marjory who never ventured out of her corner chair. "And Liz, please stop again."

"Why couldn't Liz find my mother and father?" Marjory asked just as she had for the past forty-three years.

"We don't know Marjory, but we've gotten along just fine, haven't we?"

"Yes, Grandma," Marjory replied slowly, and then with a sudden burst of joy exclaimed, "The soaps! The soaps! We're missing our soaps!"

❧

The retired cop sat with her feet up on the adjacent kitchen chair and laughed, "This is what I should do." She picked up the pen and circled:

Want to divorce your grown children? Why not, they don't appreciate you. They have their own lives. *Right*? Join us in Montana for a month. Believe me, they won't care if you go. Call today: 333-333-3333

Liz half-laughed again, but left the circled page face up while she went to the gym.

"Liz, slow down," Jeff commanded as he switched off her machine.

"Why, what's the matter?" she responded, suddenly startled that maybe something was wrong in the building.

"Look at your count on this dial—it's way too high."

"Whoa, I guess so, I wasn't paying any attention. Sorry."

"Well, wrap up and sit out for awhile," Jeff snarled, meaning he could be held responsible if something happened to one of the patrons.

As Liz sat out like the bad little girl from gym class, she knew exactly what had taken her mind away from the business at hand. Last week's conversation with her daughter had been as bad as taking a bullet, maybe worse.

"You thought us kids had a good life? You must be kidding. It was horrible!"

Liz felt a cold chill careen across her sweaty body just as she had felt during many situations on the job when the cops were in a cold sweat. She lifted the robe's sleeve and looked at her arm. How can the body do that?

"Get over it," she told herself as she yanked the sleeve back into place. "Get over it" had been her partner's favorite expression on the job. She learned never to complain and especially never to express any emotion around him. The phrase rang in her ears.

"All right, get on that machine and kick ass, but watch those numbers," the arrogant Jeff said as he released his power to let the delinquent back into "gym class."

38, 39, 40, 41...

❧

"What do you mean it was horrible?"

"It was. You never had any compassion for us; you were always yelling; nothing was ever good enough for you."

"I just wanted you to do better for your own sakes! Do you think I raised you to end up with some mediocre job making minimum wage?"

"So what if we had? We had feelings that you never cared about. You never lightened-up long enough to know that!"

"Oh, sure, now you can say that after every one of you is successful and making lots of money. Do you ever thank me for pushing you and pounding it into your heads that studying was important? No. Of course not."

☙

"That's it!" Jeff shouted. "You're out of here for the day."

Liz slammed her locker door three times before she leaned her forehead against the coolness of the metal.

"What's the matter, Liz?" a voice echoed along the row of lockers.

"Oh, sorry, Carmella. I didn't think anyone was in here."

"Is everything okay?" the stocky woman asked with sympathetic brown eyes that looked ready to absorb the woes of the world.

"Yeah. I just couldn't concentrate, and you know how Jeff is—the tyrant."

"Guess what?" Carmella asked as she inched herself closer to Liz as if Jeff was going to hear their conversation through the walls of the women's locker room. "I read in one of my magazines that men who use those power tactics are really very insecure."

Liz looked at Carmella's absolutely sincere face. *God love ya, Carmella*, Liz thought to herself. *Everything is so plain and simple with you—a good way to be I guess.* Liz recapitulated all the insecure men she had dealt with on the job. Why hadn't she been smart enough to realize that they were "just insecure"?

She didn't laugh at Carmella but told her, instead, that she had made a very interesting statement.

Carmella seemed to be pleased with the compliment and suggested they go somewhere for lunch.

"Gee, I don't know, Carmella. I was just going to have a juice and crackers."

"Oh, please, Liz. I really need someone to talk to."

"Okay, Carm, let's do it."

As they walked past Jeff with his muscles bulging like caution signs on a slippery bridge, Liz leaned down to Carmella's ear and whispered, "Insecure."

Carmella's perfectly round, wrinkle-free face immediately turned red as Liz's laughter shot through the front door of the gym.

"So what's the problem?" Liz asked abruptly. Carmella rolled her eyes just like the little tugboat in a storybook that Liz had read every night at the insistence of one of her kids—she couldn't remember which one.

"Gee whiz, you don't have to act like I'm under investigation," Carmella retorted with those teary tugboat eyes.

"Oh, Carm, I'm sorry," Liz submitted with total honesty. She patted the pudgy hand across the table and said, "I'm so accustomed to using power tactics."

The two women quickly looked at each other with those words.

"Insecure," whispered Liz weakly.

"No, not you, Liz. Not you."

Liz sat silently and blinked, just blinked. Carmella couldn't tell what she was looking at or what she was looking through.

"We need food," Carmella uttered as she desperately motioned for a waitress.

Liz did seem to focus better after a few bites of her sandwich, and Carmella's worrying dissipated, too, knowing full well that it's food that settles all problems.

Carmella didn't wait for Liz to begin her questioning. She initiated the saga with a low moan and a high roll of her harbor eyes. "Do you think my children have forgotten that I am their mother?"

Liz swallowed and looked intently at Carmella. "I wouldn't think that children could actually forget they have a mother," she said as though she had thought long and hard about the question. "Why? What's going on?"

"They don't call, sometimes for weeks at a time, so I call and no one is home. I leave a message and wait sometimes for days before they call back."

Liz noticed that Carmella stirred her coffee on every fifth word.

Carmella laid the spoon on the saucer and waited for a response.

"That seems to be the norm these days. I think we just have to acknowledge and accept that it's the way it's going to be."

"I can't imagine not calling my mother right back. She would have had the French Foreign Legion on my doorstep!"

"Yeah, I know what you mean, but times have changed."

The two women sat posed with expressionless faces, each glaring into the past.

The crunch of Carmella's potato chip brought Liz back to reality. "It's always, *there's nothing wrong, nothing is wrong, Mom.* Well, I think there is something wrong. They just don't want to tell me."

Liz watched Carmella's short, stubby index finger press into the chip crumbs and bring them to her mouth. She was quite proficient at it, Liz thought.

"They're in their own world, Carmella; they have their own lives now. We are not part of it, that's all."

"Well, why not? They were the center of our lives, weren't they?"

Liz could see the lieutenant drawing a circle on the blackboard. He always pounded the center until it was riddled with dots. The victim was always in the center and the cops were always somewhere on the arc of the curve. *Where were my children?* Liz thought as she pushed her plate forward. *Maybe my job was the center of my life; maybe my kids did feel left out.*

"Weren't they the center?" Liz could hear Carmella's question somewhere outside of the arc.

"Well, I can't say that mine were. I mean, sometimes they were, but there seemed to be several centers that rolled in and out."

"Sometimes, I just don't know what you're talking about," Carmella dauntlessly uttered as she reached for the dessert menu.

So, Liz thought as she analyzed the unaccustomed boldness of her friend's voice, *she does have a little bit of a backbone; that's a good thing.*

After lunch, the two waved goodbye—Carmella not satisfied that she had gotten any solutions and Liz wondering why she had so many centers to her life.

Carmella suddenly called out, "You going to the gym tomorrow?"

"Oh, sure. That young punk doesn't intimidate me."

Carmella gave her the thumbs-up sign, as she twirled around to assume her power-walking maneuvers.

Liz began thinking about the "intimidate" word she had just used.

"Get over it!" rang out her deceased partner's voice.

Liz picked up her rate of speed as she thought about burning off the calories from lunch.

"Hey, stranger!" blared a voice three feet from her left ear. Liz swung to see Drew sweeping out the doorway of The Corner Bar.

"Hey, yourself Drew. How are you?"

"Better than nothing," the familiar face answered with his customary reply. "Where've you been?"

"Haven't you heard? I don't drink anymore."

"What? What the hell happened to you?"

"Drew, I haven't been here in over a year."

"Yeah, I just figured you found another Friday night joint."

"No, it was cold turkey for me."

"Damn, you getting any help?"

"Yeah, I go to AA."

"I bet you know half the people there. Like all the people you arrested for DWI!" Drew laughed.

"Yeah, it started out being kind of a funny situation, but we all accept each other. In there, no one is any better than anyone else; AA has been a big help."

"Well, we'll miss you at The Corner Bar."

"No, you won't, and that's okay. See you, Drew."

"Yeah, take care of yourself."

As Liz walked away she could smell the day-after stench of cigarette smoke and spilled beer drift out of the front door that Drew had propped open.

Had drinking been one of the centers of her life? Liz asked herself as she picked up speed through the park. She never thought of it as a problem—she'd worked, she'd raised her kids, and done everything normal people did. She merely had a few drinks every day after work. So what?

Liz started jogging.

"Do you think we liked being home alone every Friday night while you were out with your friends?" Her daughter's question sounded as clear as if she were there saying it.

"You guys were all right; you were teenagers. I wouldn't have left you if there was any danger."

"Well, we didn't like it! Why didn't you stay home with us?"

"You were happy to have me out of the house. Are you kidding me?"

"What was the sense. We couldn't do anything; you watched us like a hawk. You even had Mrs. Janus spy on us from next door."

"She wasn't spying. I merely asked her to keep an eye on the house."

"It was like a prison! We couldn't have kids over and you called every hour."

"I was just looking after your welfare."

"Well, you ruined our lives!"

The ground came up to meet Liz. The stones arrogantly absconded with some of her flesh, and in return, Liz gave some of her blood to the cause.

"Damn!" Liz expounded as she stretched her knee to survey the extent of the abducted skin.

"Are you all right, ma'am?"

"Oh, sure," Liz lied. "I just wish I had remembered to tuck and roll."

"Sounds like you've had a course on falling," the good Samaritan smiled.

"That I have, but as you can see, falling sometimes sneaks up when we least expect it."

"Ah, well said. Can I help you to get home or to your car?"

"Thanks, but no. I only live a short distance from here."

"Well, take care."

As Liz hobbled home, she wondered how many times she had fallen in the eyes of her children.

"Mother of Mercy, Elizabeth! What happened to you?" Mrs. Janus exclaimed as she hurried through her rose arbor to the sidewalk.

"Oh, it's nothing, Mrs. Janus. I took a little tumble, that's all."

"You should have had your long pants on, not shorts. Long pants would have protected you. Now you come right up to my steps and sit down. I'll clean you up."

"Mrs. Janus, please…"

"Not another word. Wait right here."

For the first time, Liz thought she might have an inkling of how her kids thought of Mrs. Janus as their prison guard with—oh, no! She slouched and put her hand to her cheek—with herself as the warden.

She knew of lots of prisoners who hated their warden even though they had never seen him.

"Did you scrape your cheek, too, Elizabeth? You be still now. I'll get you all fixed up. Why would you wear those good socks for exercising? You should save them for something special."

Why is she treating me like this? Liz wondered as she grimaced every little while.

"How are the children?" Mrs. Janus asked as she bandaged.

"I don't know. They all hate me," Liz said dryly.

"What?" The angel of mercy brought her amateur nursing skills to a halt.

"They say that their life with me was horrible."

"Horrible? After all you did for them?" Mrs. Janus remained a bandaging statue.

"I thought I gave them everything, but apparently not," Liz sighed.

"Well, you know how kids are; they have the funniest notions." Mrs. Janus rocketed herself back into action as she continued, "Look at my son, fifty-some years old, and to this day he swears up hill and down that his brother was favored over himself. Now why in God's name would I favor one over the other?"

"I don't know," Liz replied half-heartedly, not really giving accreditation to her neighbor's problem. "Thanks, Mrs. Janus, for doing this, but I really need to be at home now."

"I understand. You call me if you need anything. I'll be right over."

"I'm sure you will," Liz called out while limping across the lawn and ducking through the arbor. She never flinched as she felt a thorn tear another gouge out of her skin. She hid her bloody arm from her neighbor.

As Liz let the cold water run over her arm, she glanced at the newspaper still open to the article on "how to divorce your grown children."

She looked at the refrigerator door. *Oh, no! No not that. God—I need you! God quickly! I don't need alcohol. Calm me down, Lord. Having a drink won't help matters.*

Liz soaked in the tub full of bubbles; bubbles that she had only discovered since retirement, indeed an unknown luxury of time. As she leaned back and closed her eyes she said, "God, you are amazing; every time I ask for help, you help me. I guess you are bound and determined to get me off alcohol. That stuff never did me any good, did it? I didn't realize the kids resented it so much; I was pretty self-centered, wasn't I? Why did I think I was doing the best I could do? Until I got into AA, I didn't realize how many character defects I had. And God, you really came to life in AA. I used to drag those kids to church every Sunday but I never taught them about your mercy and kindness and compassion or that you were always there for them. I don't think they even know they can ask you for help; you are waiting to be asked. What was I doing, Lord? You should have been one of my centers of life, and where did I put you?"

Liz scooped up a handful of bubbles and gently blew them into the air.

"Do you know what happens when I bring up your name and tell them how I'm longing for your peace? They think I'm nuts! They know you only as a stranger. What have I done?" Liz shouted and stood so quickly the water splashed over the side of the tub.

"Hi, Libby. Do you want to go to the movies tonight? Oh, you're babysitting your grandchildren again? I thought you were going to speak to your daughter about that? I know, I know, you don't want them mad at you. It seems that's all grown children know how to be. Oh nothing, I was just talking to myself. Call when you're free. Bye."

"Hi, Gina. Do you want to catch a movie? You are? How long are you going to be housesitting? Wow, it's their fifth cruise? When are they going to take you? They don't think you'd fit in with their friends? Well, I'd better let you pack. Call when you're back. Bye."

Liz looked over at the telephone number listed in the newspaper just as the phone rang.

"Loren! What a surprise! Oh, that's okay, I know you're busy. How's everybody?"

"Great, Mom, just wanted to tell you we've changed our vacation plans and we're heading out west instead of coming home. John has researched some wonderful places to visit, so we're going to give it a shot."

"Oh? When will you make it home?"

"It probably won't be until Christmas, but we're not sure."

"Loren, before I forget to ask, will Johnny be making his First Communion this year? He's seven now."

"Well—well, no he won't. John and I have found another religion now and everything is different."

"Oh, I see."

"Mom, please don't start with me. I'm not a kid anymore; you can't force your ideas on me anymore."

"I know I can't, Loren. Karen told me it was pretty horrible growing up here with me. Is that true?"

"Well, kind of. I mean, you were always on us for something. Did you ever just relax and enjoy us?"

"I don't know. Didn't I?"

"No. You were always stressed out or mellowed out or something that didn't include enjoying us."

"Being a single parent isn't easy, you know?"

"I can't imagine it is, Mom, but if you'd been smart, you would have known how to hang onto Dad."

"What?"

"Well, it seems to me you brought on your own misery and we had to suffer through it."

"I think we'd better hang up for now."

Liz put her hands over her face and sobbed. *Why, why, did I even bother with those kids?* She felt like the sculptor whose work had been smashed to the floor. "I can't go back, I can't fix it," she wailed.

"Didn't you hear me knocking out there? Elizabeth! My Lord! Does your knee hurt that much?" Mrs. Janus compassionately asked as she rushed over to Liz.

"No," Liz said embarrassed, "I was just thinking about something sad."

"Well, here is some soup for you, and cookies, too."

"Thanks, that was nice of you," Liz replied half-heartedly. "Here, Mrs. Janus. Sit with me for a minute."

The older lady looked at Liz with suspicion as she inched toward the chair.

"What's the matter?"

"Just the way you said, 'sit with me for a minute' reminded me of how you'd tell one of your kids to sit down before they were to catch 'what for.'"

"What do you mean?"

"Well," Mrs. Janus began with a great deal of trepidation, "you'd always start out quite hospitable, but—and I don't know if I should say this—but, it wasn't long before you were interrogating and lecturing and passing out the sentence."

"What?"

"Well, I don't mean anything bad by it, but you were a tough cookie."

"I just wanted them to do what was right, Mrs. Janus."

"I know you did, but kids are kids. They aren't adults when they're kids."

There was a long silence, until—

"Oh, my God," Liz whispered as she stared at the hanging light fixture over the table.

"What? What is it Elizabeth? Is your neck stiff?"

"No, what you said. I didn't let them be kids."

"Honey, I think maybe you should lie down, you look awfully pale."

"No, I want to ask you what went on here. Did my kids think I was a good mother?"

"Of course they did. All kids want to think that their mother is the best."

"But did I show them?"

"I suppose you did. They always had nice bicycles and toys and good clothes. They never looked like poor kids."

"No, I wasn't going to let them grow up poor like I did, but what did I show them?"

"I think you were more of a, 'do as I say' not 'do as I do' person."

Liz leaned closer to Mrs. Janus and almost tenderly, like she had been taught on the job to do, said, "Tell me what you mean by that, Mrs. Janus."

"Well," said her neighbor as she took her folded tissue out of her apron pocket and dabbed her forehead.

Was she sweating? Liz wondered, as she looked at her neighbor's seemingly dry forehead.

"I don't really know, you always talked a good talk to your children, but I suppose as they got older they may have noticed a few things that didn't exactly correspond to your preachings."

"Preachings?" Liz reiterated as her eyebrows raised.

"Well, maybe not preachings, maybe lectures."

"Lectures?"

"Would you stop that? I'm trying to explain the best I can. Anyway, why am I talking about this anyhow?"

"I'm sorry, Mrs. Janus," Liz apologized with the ulterior motive to keep her talking. Liz took the older woman's hand in hers and gently asked, "What might my kids have noticed about me that was contrary to my 'preachings'?"

"Well," she started slowly, "maybe all the time you used to spend trying to rehabilitate those juvenile delinquents from the street—maybe your own kids resented your time with them."

Staying very calm, Liz nodded and gently said, "Yes, that could be true. What else?"

"Maybe, and I know you couldn't help the extra hours you had to work, but maybe they resented being with the baby sitter an extra two or three hours when they were expecting you at a certain time."

Again Liz nodded and responded sanely, encouraging Mrs. Janus to continue.

"You never did get them another father, not that I was looking over here all the time, but I noticed certain men on occasion. I thought you must be getting pretty serious, but then they'd be gone and I never saw them again. Maybe your kids would get sort of attached thinking they'd be getting a new father. But it never happened."

"That's very true. Mrs. Janus, you certainly are a very perceptive person." Liz smiled as she dug her fingernails into the palms of her own hands. "You really are giving me some wonderful information this evening, good neighbor. You go right on, you're doing a great job..."

"Well!" remarked Mrs. Janus as she wriggled in her chair as a contestant on a game show. "I would think that your late Friday nights out would mean you needed to sleep lots on Saturday. Right?"

"Oh, yes, yes, right."

"You know how kids like to go places on Saturday and do things as a family. Well, they probably didn't get to do things."

"So, do you think that's all, Mrs. Janus?" Liz asked with such sugar, she was afraid the ants would begin coming into the house.

"It might not be, but I am getting very tired. It's almost my bedtime."

"If you think of anything else, you can tell me tomorrow. How would that be?"

"Oh, wait! Church! I might be wrong but having a shouting match before church might not be interpreted as spiritual."

"Great!" Liz smiled with her teeth clenched. "See you!"

Liz waited until she saw Mrs. Janus close her side door before she threw the first saucepan. The clutter from the kitchen table was relegated to the floor. The knickknacks from the shelf sailed across the room in one full sweep. She hurled the soup and cookies into the garbage can and slammed the lid nine times.

All of this happened before the once-honored cop collapsed to the floor in a mourning frenzy.

"Hey, Drew!"

"Liz! I haven't seen you in over a year and now it's twice in one day. Well, one day and one night. You made it under the wire, kiddo; I just announced last call. You want the usual?"

"Yeah, the usual," Liz said grimly as she slid onto the barstool.

"Liz! How the hell are you?" slurped Phyllis. "Damnation. I haven't seen you in a dog's age."

Liz knew it was coming—Phyllis wrapped her arms around her neck and started singing, "You Are My Sunshine."

Drew yelled out, "Phyllis, Stan is looking for you."

"Ooo, Stan, I'm coming, honey. Here I am!"

"Thanks, Drew."

"No problem. So, you're going off the wagon are you?"

"Yeah, I might as well. I've got to get some relief somewhere."

"Well, I'll tell you what," Drew said as he slid the drink back towards himself, "if you'll think about this for twenty-four hours and still want to drink, I'll let you drink free for a week."

Liz stared at him.

"I know what just happened, Drew," Liz said in awe.

"And what's that?"

I didn't ask God for help. Truthfully, I didn't think of it. Anyhow, He put you in my path Drew. Jimmy could have waited on me—he wouldn't have held my drink back."

"Maybe you're right, Liz. I've heard odder things than that happening in this bar."

"Thanks, Drew," Liz called out as she went back out across the threshold.

Liz looked up through the summer night sky and literally sang, "Thank you, God, thank you, thank you, thank you!"

"Yoo hoo! How are you this morning?" Mrs. Janus asked as she hollered across the hedge. "I thought of something else wrong with your household. Can I come over?"

"Of course. I need to hear more," Liz answered facetiously. She couldn't believe how seriously her neighbor had taken this assignment.

"Do you want coffee on the patio?"

"Sure. You can serve the cookies, too."

"Oh, oh...I ate them last night," Liz fibbed.

"I thought you had. You were never any hand to bake sweet treats for your kids or yourself."

"Was that what you were going to tell me?"

"Oh, no, I just thought of that one. I wanted to discuss your drinking."

"My drinking?" The stream of coffee that Liz was pouring stopped halfway between the carafe and the mug as if it, too, wanted to hear "this one."

"Well..." she wriggled in the chair again and straightened her house dress, "I would notice that you would come home from work like a bear, and as soon as you fixed yourself a drink you'd be joking around with the kids, laughing, talking, running around, playing ball, whatever."

277

"What was the matter with that?"

"That's not good for children. They need consistency. They can't always be wondering and worrying what kind of mood you're going to be in next."

"You know," Liz said very slowly, "you are absolutely right. Too bad you didn't tell me this years ago."

"I never thought it was any of my business to interfere. Plus, would you have listened?"

"No, probably not," Liz admitted truthfully.

"Let's talk about something else," Mrs. Janus proclaimed, bringing a little relief from the advanced class of Motherhood 404.

"You were out a little late last night, weren't you?"

Liz choked on her coffee and Mrs. Janus jumped up to pull the victim's arms straight up into the air.

"I'm okay, I'm okay," she said in between coughs.

"Yeah, I went out for a little while and I met an angel! Mrs. Janus, with all the things I did wrong, did you notice that no man ever was invited here to live with me?"

"Well, I would hope not!"

"It's been a very common thing to do, you know, but somehow, I knew better than to ever do that to my children. That's a plus for me, isn't it?" Liz asked with pleading eyes, sounding like a child begging for mercy.

"It sure is, honey, it sure is."

❧

Carmella looked up from tying her sneaker to Liz's bandaged leg.

"Oh, my! What happened to you?"

"Just a little fall."

"Are you going to be able to exercise?"

"I'll be able to use some of the machines."

"That's good. Oh, by the way, congratulations."

"Congratulations? For what?"

"Didn't you watch the news this morning?"

"No."

"Karen unveiled a statue out there in Seattle."

"My Karen?"

"Yes. It was gorgeous—her own creation. The city park committee commissioned her to do it for their new park. You didn't know about it?"

"Not a word."

"Oh, sorry."

"Don't be sorry. I'm glad you told me."

"She sure is a creative person."

"Yeah, she always was," Liz said nostalgically. "You know what Carmella? I was the only mother in the neighborhood who would let their children make mud pies."

"Well, that's probably where her sculpting abilities began."

"Hooray!" Liz said with a smile. "That's 'two' for me!"

"Huh?"

"Oh, nothing. What was the subject of the statue?"

"It was a mother with three children, two girls and a boy."

"A mother with three children? Two girls and a boy?" Liz reiterated almost reverently, seemingly awestruck.

Then Liz whispered as her hand went up by her lips, "Were they happy?"

"Oh, yes, very. There's just one thing I didn't understand. She entitled it, 'A Fantasy Life.'"

The cop who was awarded a medal for saving her partner's life with bravery, stamina, ingenuity, and determination collapsed onto the bench and cried like a baby.

"Liz, Liz," Carmella consoled as she knelt by her friend in the locker room.

"I'm sorry, Carmella," Liz uttered as she pulled herself up. "I'm just a little stressed right now."

"I understand, honey. Being retired isn't what it's cracked up to be."

"Retired? I don't think retirement is doing this to me, but I'm okay now. I'm going to skip exercising today; I'm pretty sore anyway. I'll see you tomorrow. Don't let Jeff yell at you."

Five people stopped her on the walk home to offer congratulations on Karen's achievement.

"You must be so proud of her," became the comment of the norm and "Oh, yes," became the pat answer.

∽

Why wouldn't she tell me about this? Liz asked herself as she walked past The Corner Bar.

The angel! How many times has God helped me when I hadn't even thought that He was around? Liz realized now how many miracles she had witnessed on the job, in her home, in her car...

Liz stopped and bowed her head. "God, I didn't know I was such a screw-up as a mother. Please help me."

As Liz approached the rose arbor, she heard, "Elizabeth, Elizabeth! Run home and turn on your TV for the noon news. Hurry! But don't run, don't run."

With the same steady hand that once shot an attacker, Liz held the remote with a hand that shook.

Oh, Karen is so beautiful, Liz thought as she sank into her recliner. *There it is! There's the statue! Oh my gosh, how did she make it, it's so big? It's so, so perfect. The mother, the children, they're perfect.* Tears streamed down Liz's cheeks.

The camera panned in on the faces. They were beautiful, lovely, and charming, but they weren't Liz's family. *I guess they were Karen's "Fantasy Family." Her happy family.*

"Tell us Karen," the announcer asked, "did you have certain people in mind when you created them?"

"Oh, yes. The woman here, is my beautiful mother Elizabeth, with my sister Loren, my brother Vincent, and me."

"Well, your family will always be together in this statue. Thank you, Karen."

Liz pushed the off button and stared at the blackness as if it were her tunnel to eternity. She didn't even hear the pitter-patter of Mrs. Janus' feet running through the house.

"Wasn't that wonderful? Wasn't that just something? Elizabeth? Elizabeth?"

❧

It wasn't long before the phone rang.

"Hi, Mom, did you see it?"

"Vincent! Yes, I saw it."

"Were you surprised?"

"Surprised? I was flabbergasted! But why didn't she tell me? I know nothing about her life anymore."

"Well, first of all, she wanted to surprise you for your birthday, and secondly, she's an artist! You know how temperamental they are—especially Karen."

"You mean, you've noticed, too?"

"Noticed? I don't know how you and I survived those two girls. They were always plotting something against you and me. I think they were trying to drive you crazy for being so strict with them. But you did good, Ma. I know what their friends were like and thank God you didn't buckle to their whining and complaining."

"Vincent, why didn't you tell me all this before?"

"Tell you what?"

"Oh, never mind. Then you didn't think our life was so bad?"

"Not at all! I learned to do my own stuff and stayed clear of Karen and Loren. When I ignored them, they stopped tormenting me."

"They were something, weren't they?" Liz laughed with a relief that she thought could only come from a prisoner who was being exonerated. "You don't think I was too strict and too demanding and too moody and too judgmental?"

"Hell, yes. You were all those things. But now I can look back and see that you saved your two daughters from—well, you know what lurked out in the world for them and me. Remember when I ran for office and my opponent set out to find something on me? He finally said, 'What the hell's the matter with you? I can't find anything in your closet.' And I said, 'If you had a mother like mine, there'd be nothing in your closet either. I'd rather be sent to Devil's Island than face my mother!'"

"Vincent!"

"No offense Mom. You know, we all turned out pretty good. My sisters are still nuts, but that's okay. They're getting better."

"I hope so."

"Well, Mom, here comes some really big news. I've asked Ashley to marry me."

"Vince, congratulations!"

"Your airline confirmation should get to you in a few days. I'm calling the 'two stooges' right after I hang up from you. Are you up to having a family reunion at the reception?"

"Of course, Vincent. I hope we can all be together. By the way...where will the wedding be?

In Ashley's hometown. In the great state of Montana."

"Montana!"

"Mom, why are you laughing?"

"Oh, Vincent, I'll tell you some day!"

↬Chapter Sixteen↫

A STITCH IN TIME

"**A**re you looking at those old photographs again, Marjory? I'm surprised you haven't worn holes right through them.

Yes, you were cute dressed up in all those costumes that Aunty Anna made for you! It was too bad she moved to the city; she helped me a lot when you were little. But I suppose, just like other people who left Lone Moon Creek, they were all hoping to find their dream job in the city."

↬↫

"Celeste! Hush!" the older woman ordered as she leaned deeper into her hand-stitching, while Celeste pressed harder upon the foot pedal of her sewing machine.

By the industrious whir of her partner's machine, Anna knew it was going much too fast for the curve of the armhole that Celeste was navigating. The senior seamstress didn't call out a warning to the young girl, however, because Claudette was coming into the back room.

"Where is that dress?" Claudette demanded. She tried to tuck her silk blouse inside her snug skirt, the skirt that used to hang beautifully on her.

"It's hanging right there, ma'am," Anna indicated with the tip of her needle.

"Why didn't you bring it out to me? Mrs. Leonard has been waiting for ten minutes."

"You don't like it when I go into the shop," Anna answered quietly.

"Well, that's true," she added and clucked her tongue as she stormed over to the dress. As she reached up, Anna stole a glance at the shopkeeper's spiked heels. She could see that her feet were swollen with protrusions of flesh bunched higher than the sides of her shoes.

It's no wonder she's so cantankerous; her feet probably hurt, thought Anna. She stitched on another gold sequin, maybe her millionth, she didn't know.

As Claudette left through the curtained doorway, they could hear her say to Mrs. Leonard, "You know how the help is nowadays; so sorry you had to wait."

Celeste's machine went faster.

"Celeste," Anna called out in a loud whisper, "slow that machine down!"

The warning came too late. "Damn it, damn it, damn it!" exploded the young novice. "Now I've got to rip out all these stitches! I hate this job."

"Shhh, Claudette will hear you," whispered Anna as she hurried over to Celeste.

"I don't care," the hostile girl exclaimed as she yanked at the material.

"Yes, you do care. Now slide over and let me see if I can get you back on track."

Anna leaned into the sewing machine, looking much like an integral part of the mechanism—as important as the bobbin, the pressure foot, or the thread.

"See if you can sew on some of those sequins while I'm doing this, would you please?" Anna asked, not looking up from the tight, teeny stitches. It was obvious that Celeste had used the wrong setting on the stitches-per-inch regulator.

The young girl groaned as she threw her fingernail file down and walked over to Anna's station of hand stitching.

"Just follow the pattern that I have going there," Anna uttered, again not looking up.

Anna heard the bell of the shop door ring several times as she spent precious time on the results of Celeste's act of rage. She knew Claudette had a successful business; she had worked in the back room for eighteen years. Many ladies had relied on Claudette's good business sense and ability to feature the latest fabrics and patterns. Claudette also offered customized sewing, which of course Anna did. That is, Anna and one of her young coworkers, of whom there had been many over the years. It seemed they all loved being the model when Claudette would wrap and drape heavenly materials around their statuesque, thin bodies, but when they had to return to the back room to help assemble the outfit, they became disenchanted very quickly. Often, many of them had exaggerated greatly about their sewing abilities in order to get the modeling position.

Ladies would spend hours in the shop browsing through the pattern books and the fabrics. Sometimes they would ask to see a certain dress on the rack modeled for them. All the dresses on the rack were made to fit the model, and the model was carefully chosen by Claudette to make the ensemble look sensational. The customers could select and customize to their heart's desire. Claudette was a genius at measuring and making recommendations to enhance the figure of any woman. She knew what would flatter them—that's why she kept her clientele for years.

Anna was the genius in the back room. She could take a flat piece of material, along with a pattern and Claudette's meticulous measurements, and create a work of art. This she could do at remarkable speed. Only if there was hand stitching would the progress seem slow. Every stitch had to be in place; every bead or sequin or button perfectly positioned. She knew how to decorate with French knots, daisy stitches, blind stitches, and so many others. She was an expert at smocking, gathering, and pleating.

Anna laboriously finished taking out the last stitch of the seam that had gone awry, and looked over at Celeste to ease the strain that she felt in her eyes. Anna couldn't help but smile. There sat the five foot eleven inch beauty, hunched over the sequined gown, with her knees pressed together and her toes pointed inward as though she were pigeon-toed. The bowl of sequins rested in her lap and her tongue stuck out ever so slightly from the corner of her mouth as she intently placed a tiny gold sequin over the sharp point of the needle. "There," she muttered, "that's five."

Celeste had just reached into the bowl for number six, when the air was pierced with, "Where's the green sheath?"

Anna stretched her arm in the direction of Celeste thinking that maybe she could catch the millions of tiny golden specks that, for a second, brought sparkle to the drab back room.

Celeste stretched her arm also to the cascading golden display that rocketed away from her. The two women caught not one sequin, just as Anna remembered as a child, catching not one pretty color from her first fireworks show.

Suddenly the old, dark linoleum was the highlight of the room; it had never held such glory. Customarily it was adorned only with stray pieces of thread and snippets of material.

"Don't just sit there! Pick them up; they cost me an arm and a leg!" Claudette commanded sharply as she stormed out with the green sheath.

Anna got on her knees to help Celeste. The short, scar-embellished woman knelt across from Celeste, who towered above the older woman.

"I hate this job. I hate it, I hate it!" Celeste uttered with every sequin she threw into the bowl.

"No, you don't hate it," Anna commented, not lifting her head to peer into the beautiful face that ascended so much higher than her own.

"Yes, I..."

"Celeste, we need you out here," Claudette sang out in her "I'm in front of a customer" voice.

"Sorry. Got to go," Celeste said in a tone that had nothing to do with sorrow. She lifted herself lithely.

Anna remained amidst the gold, thinking of God retrieving souls who had gone astray: kindly, delicately He brought them home.

⁂

"Sorry you had to pick them all up by yourself," Celeste said sheepishly as she later sat down at the sewing machine.

"It was all right," Anna said serenely. "I had a wonderful thought as I did it."

Celeste didn't ask; she wasn't in the mood to hear one of Anna's weird thoughts.

⁂

"I'll be taking a long lunch with a-a client," Claudette announced hurriedly as she fluffed her hair and used the tiny mirror over the yellowed sink to apply her lipstick. She pulled in her stomach, which was a new development for her, and pressed her hands against it as if by doing so it would stay in. "This basket contains everything you'll need for Elaine's gown, and this basket—which I forgot to give you last week—has everything for Charlotte's suit."

She left with a little wave and a "Later."

Claudette always seemed cheerful just before she went out for a long lunch with one of her "clients."

"Yea!" cheered Celeste as soon as she heard the front door close. "I'll have a chance to run to Xavier's for their great sale."

She, too, used the mirror and then turned to say, "Later!"

Why not, thought Anna. "Later," she responded. Celeste laughed.

Ah, thought Anna, *the nice part of the day*! She leaned forward to turn on the radio; she liked the station with the old music. She and her husband used to dance to that music, before she had scars. She made the coffee and got her lunch bag out of the tiny refrigerator. The smell of fresh coffee always made the room seem more homelike, Anna thought. When her husband used to come home for lunch, they always had coffee together. In fact, he would say, "Anna, when I'm still on the first floor I can smell the coffee perking, and by the time I've climbed the stairs to the third floor, I have a wild desire for you and your coffee!" They used to laugh.

Anna turned up the volume to Nat King Cole's "I Love You For Sentimental Reasons." She raised her cup and thought, *Here's to you, Jimmy.*

Anna stuck her head out of the back door to test the weather; it was warm and sunny. She loaded everything onto a tray and went out into the alleyway to the wooden bench. She returned to place the radio up by the little window and let her melodies drift out upon the soft air.

If there were such a thing as a perfect, noontime alleyway in this city, it was this one. Because of the location of the surrounding buildings, there was never sunshine permitted on Back Alley Boulevard, except for this time of day. Anna figured that the height of the sun and its location around 12:00 p.m. gave the sunrays clear sailing down onto her "B. A. Boulevard."

About five years ago, the kids had knocked down all the partitions that used to section off the shopkeepers' private domains, allowing even more sunlight to roll on through. Anna liked it better that way. Now she could sit on her bench and look left down the alleyway clear to the Chinese restaurant, and right past the shoe and jewelry stores to the pastry shop. Quite often the workers would holler out greetings to one another, and Anna enjoyed seeing them.

The seamstress rested her back against the boards of the building and lifted her face toward the sunshine. She closed her eyes and thought of Jimmy and herself spending Sunday afternoons at the beach. How young they were and how much in love. She thought about Lone Moon Creek with Agnes and Margie. She let the music play with her thoughts, her wonderful thoughts.

It wasn't until the last of her coffee had turned cold, that she roused herself enough to go back inside. She left the back door open to entice the last few rays to enter. Anna knew the precious sun time on Back Alley Boulevard was limited. The drone of a saxophone from the radio caused her to do a few dance-turns on the old, dark linoleum before she walked to the sink to wash her hands.

She looked at the baskets. Her expertise dictated the necessity of starting Charlotte's suit before beginning work on Elaine's gown. Anna could see from the patterns that the suit with its piping, besom pockets, scalloped front edges, and fitted bodice was going to be much more intricate to construct than the basically simple, flowing gown. The seamstress could tell from Claudette's notes that the added two inches on the jacket's length and the elimination of the collar were to benefit the stature of the patron. She knew exactly what Claudette's notations meant.

Anna touched the material—very nice. Stunning buttons. She wondered how many successful business meetings Charlotte would conduct wearing this suit. Many, she hoped.

Anna laid out the material with the pattern pieces on the huge table and began cutting.

Just before 2:00 p.m., the tardy Celeste came through the back door with two shopping bags from Xavier's.

"Is she back yet?" whispered Celeste.

"No, not yet," Anna answered as she moved to turn off the radio and close the door. She looked out at the dark, shaded alley and didn't look again.

"Thank God," the young girl grinned. Anna wondered if Celeste ever did thank God for anything.

"You should see the bargains I got!" Celeste exclaimed excitedly as she pulled article after article of clothing from the bags.

"What do you do with all the clothes you buy?" Anna asked in amazement at the seemingly never-ending clothesline of materialism.

"I wear them, of course. Isn't that what most people do with their clothes?"

"I suppose they do—those who have them."

"Oh, no, don't start again on 'those poor people who have only one change of clothes' or whatever. It's their own fault, not mine."

"We, who have so much, need to share with those who have next to nothing."

"We? Your wardrobe is nothing to brag about!"

"Ah, thank you, that's the best compliment I've had all week," Anna said sincerely.

"I don't get you at all," Celeste said angrily as she shoved her short-lived excitement into the bag.

"Someday you will, Celeste. Someday you will."

The two worked in silence until they heard Claudette unlocking the front door and banging over the Open sign, and then banging it back again. As the smell of coffee drifts through an apartment building, so does liquor. Anna and Celeste looked at each other.

Claudette staggered through the curtain, holding onto it way longer than was necessary. Anna hoped she wasn't going to pull it down.

"Girls," she began, "girls, I just stopped to tell you something has transpired and I need to be away for the rest of the day. You two stay here and work. I'll see you tomorrow. Keep the door locked."

Claudette looked very disheveled with her blouse hanging completely out of her skirt with the waistband wrinkle-marks in the silk material. It looked like she had spilled some food on her shoe. All those years of being impeccable were quickly dissolving. Anna wondered why.

Claudette left and Celeste dashed into the shop.

"Just as I thought," she said as she returned to the back room. "There was a man waiting out front for her."

"A man?"

"Well, even Claudette must have needs, you know?"

"Needs?"

"Maybe she'll be more civil to us if she gets her needs taken care of."

"Needs?"

"Would you get into the twenty-first century? How do you think we women survive this cruel world? If we didn't hook up with a man every once in awhile we'd go crazy."

"Life isn't supposed to be like that, Celeste."

"Well, maybe it isn't supposed to be, but that's the way it is. And I'm taking off, she'll never know I left."

"But, you'll know."

Celeste laughed, "But, I'll never tell! Bye."

Anna didn't mind if she was left to work alone, even though she had planned that Celeste could sew on more of the gold sequins. She immersed herself in Charlotte's suit as she waited for her radio program.

Every afternoon at 3:05 p.m. came her "Miss Sophie Speaks." To Anna, Miss Sophie was one of the smartest people she had ever heard. Men and women both called in to ask Sophie how they should handle their problems. Celeste and Claudette couldn't stand the show; Claudette would never dawdle in the back room if she heard Sophie's voice, and Celeste would moan, groan, and make derogatory comments throughout the entire show. Celeste and Sophie were *au contraire* on everything. Over the months, Anna came to the conclusion that Celeste looked forward to 3:05 p.m., because it gave her a chance to voice her *avant garde* opinion, which she loved to do. So, today, Anna could listen without the glares from Claudette and the denigrating remarks from Celeste. Only twice did Anna stop her work momentarily, due to the utter shock of a question posed to Sophie. Usually, Anna could work through an earthquake and never be distracted.

"What is happening to this generation?" she asked out loud during one of those distracted moments. She knew if Celeste had been there, it wouldn't have shocked her. *How can these modern women be so accepting of evil?* she wondered.

"Way to go, Miss Sophie," Anna grinned at the radio hostess's answer. "God will bless you, Sophie!" declared Anna after another answer.

The seamstress held up the jacket. She was pleased with how well and how quickly it was coming along. She had just started to set in the remaining sleeve, when there came a wild knocking at the back door. She could hear Ju Ming's voice hollering desperately.

"Good Lord above, what has happened?" she muttered to herself as she hurried to the door.

Ju Ming was telling her something in Chinese, something that along with his gesturing definitely indicated he needed help. Together, hand in hand, with Ju Ming pulling Anna along, they half-ran through Back Alley Boulevard to the Chinese restaurant.

"Oh, dear God," Anna gasped as she saw Loo Ni on her knees holding her bloody, gashed hand.

"Shhh, dear, I'll help you," Anna said as she got her to the sink. "Ju Ming, call 9-1-1."

"No, no. Fired. Loo Ni will be fired," he spoke with tears in his eyes.

"You have to Ju Ming; she needs stitches. Hurry!"

Anna pushed the gaping slash together and bound it with a wet, cold towel. She held Loo Ni's arm up for her.

❦

Anna walked alone back through the alley asking God to be with Loo Ni and Ju Ming who were so far away from their homeland and their parents.

She wondered what the young alley-gangsters would think if they saw her now—the blood-soaked, scar-ridden woman.

Anna washed the best she could using the little sink. She straightened up for the night, taking the basket with the unfinished suit and the dress with the sequins home to work on.

The next morning, Claudette was not in the shop, and Celeste had not arrived either. Anna did not flip the sign to *Open*, nor did she leave the door unlocked. She turned on the lights only in the back room.

Anna hung the sparkling dress on the rack, each and every sequin in place, like rows and rows of centurions ready to defend their empress.

She set up the ironing board and adjusted the temperature gauge on the iron. Anna dampened the pressing cloth and lifted the suit out of the basket. She read again the tag that she hand-stitched into the garment: a Claudette Fashion.

That's a nice looking suit, Anna thought to herself as she finished pressing and carefully placing it on one of their designer hangers. She slid a clear plastic casing over top. "I hope Charlotte likes it."

Anna started looking over the pattern of Elaine's gown when someone knocked lightly at the back door. She knew it would be Celeste.

This girl really is stunning, thought Anna when she opened the door to the tall, trench-coated girl. Her collar was pulled up sharply in the back, accentuating her long, thin neck, and the belt was tied in a perfect square knot accenting her tiny waist. She wore huge sunglasses and a swooping hairdo that dramatically covered her left cheekbone.

"Good morning, Celeste," Anna said cheerfully.

"I see Claudette isn't here yet," she uttered weakly.

"No, just me and the angels."

"Angels? I wish I had some angels."

"Why?" Anna asked in great surprise to ever think she'd hear Celeste mentioning anything spiritual.

"Oh, never mind."

Anna watched her as she removed her coat. The girl appeared to labor with it as if each muscle and joint was stiff as cardboard. "Are you all right, Celeste?"

"Yeah, just a little sore," she answered with no conviction.

She couldn't lift her arm high enough to put the coat on the peg.

"Dear God," Anna exclaimed as she hurried over to Celeste. "What's the matter?"

Celeste screamed when Anna touched her shoulder, then she started to cry.

"Child, child, come over here, sit down. What happened to you?"

Celeste cried and cried. Every time she lifted her head to speak, she had a new deluge of tears.

My goodness, thought Anna, *what's the matter with this modern woman?*

"Oh, no," said Anna quietly as she heard Claudette opening the front door. Apparently Celeste hadn't heard her, however, since she kept sobbing.

Sure enough, there stood Claudette between the spreading curtains. She was wearing the same clothes that she had on yesterday. Anna immediately lowered her eyes to the floor; she was embarrassed to see Claudette looking like that. Her skirt and blouse were a mass of wrinkles and stains; she had no makeup; her hair was straight and stringy; she didn't even have her shoes on.

"What's the matter with her?" Claudette asked with a thick, gravelly voice.

"I don't know," Anna replied as she finally looked up, "she just started crying."

Celeste took off her dark glasses. Anna gasped and Claudette snorted. "Who corked you?"

"My boyfriend," Celeste said as she started sobbing again.

Claudette shuffled over to the sink in her bare feet and let the cold water run over two washcloths. The shuffling then continued to Celeste; she handed her a washcloth, the other she folded in fourths the long way and placed it upon her own forehead.

The women sat in a small circle like three busted up tricycles that little children had abandoned. Anna looked from one wash clothed woman to the other.

Finally Celeste finished dabbing her tears and asked, "What happened to you?"

"God only knows, I don't. I hope I had a good time though." Claudette tried to laugh, but held her head instead.

Anna quietly said to Claudette, "God *does* know. He knows everything we do."

"Don't start on me," Claudette moaned as she ran to the sink, having dry heaves.

"I'm going home," the hung-over shopkeeper groaned. "Celeste, you better go home, too. You'll be no good to anyone today either."

Well, thought Anna, as the two good-for-nothings left, *it must be awful to realize you are good for nothing*. She couldn't imagine anyone being that way—didn't God make each and every person? He absolutely wouldn't make a good for nothing.

She sat thinking about that concept when Loo Ni popped into her thoughts.

Anna hurried down the alley to the Chinese restaurant. She peeked in the back window to see if the boss was there. Not seeing him, she tapped on the glass when she saw Ju Ling walking through the kitchen. He came to the back door in a very anxious state; she knew he couldn't talk for long. He said Loo Ni was home, but fired. Anna told him she was sorry.

"I know you are," he said as he reached out for her hand.

Anna slowly walked through the cold, shadowed passageway thinking of the world's injustices when she stumbled over something and fell to the ground. Still on her hands and knees she turned around to see what had tripped her.

"God Almighty," growled a man as they looked each other squarely in the face, "what kind of scar-faced demon are you? Get the hell away from me!" He jerked himself back away from her. Anna struggled to get up, then ran the best she could.

She shut the back door and leaned against it, panting heavily. Anna needed her Jimmy and her coffee and her music. The tears ran crazily down her cheeks trying to stay in the ruts of her scars. They couldn't careen smoothly and predictably as most women's tears; they had to take treacherous rides. Just as after the fire in the apartment building that had killed her Jimmy, Anna lost her confidence, her dignity, and her self-worth.

But this time, after years of rehabilitation, she needed only a few minutes to remember that she was a child of God and to Him she was very, very special. As she knew it would, a beautiful peacefulness settled upon her soul and she thanked God for that. She knew it was an overt blessing directly from Him.

As she drank her coffee, Anna heard someone knocking at the front door. She ignored it; she knew Claudette wouldn't want her opening the door for customers. It continued and continued and continued. *Maybe it's an emergency*, Anna thought as she listened to the unrelenting persistence.

She set her coffee cup down and listened some more. It led her to look through the curtain. She didn't recognize the woman; she had never seen any of the clients. The woman looked desperate going back and forth from the door to the window, rapping on both. Anna realized that the woman could see the light in the back room and knew someone was inside. Anna took two steps into the shop. The woman saw her and vehemently gestured for her to come over and let her in. For the second time that morning, fear crept onto each vertebrae of her spine and used its tentacles to slowly creep onto the skin of her neck.

Anna opened the door.

"Hello!" The woman extended her hand to Anna. "I'm Charlotte. Am I ever happy to see you! We've had a big change of plans, and our cruise ship is departing this afternoon. Can you believe it? There's never a dull moment, right? We're still going to be able to have our executive board meeting on the ship, thank goodness, but when that's over we plan to party the rest of the way. Are you the cleaning woman, honey?"

"Uh, cleaning lady?" Anna had been so engrossed with Charlotte's story that it surprised her to have the lady stop to ask her a question.

"No, no ma'am, I'm not the cleaning lady."

"Well, maybe you can help me find a suit and a gold sequin ball gown. I don't know if Claudette has had a chance to even start them say nothing about finish them. I told her I wouldn't need them for two weeks. So, I'm here on a wing and a prayer, that's all, just a wing and a prayer."

Anna smiled. She knew about prayer and, on the outside chance, maybe Charlotte did, too.

"I do know where they are, and they're both finished!"

"What?" squealed Charlotte, "Oh, I could just cry!"

"Come back with me," gestured Anna.

"Oh, that Claudette is a genius, a master seamstress, a creative marvel!" exhorted Charlotte as she examined each piece. "When did she find the time to finish them? Finished! I can't believe it.

"Tell Claudette I was here and this is a check for her excellent work. Thanks for letting me in."

"You're welcome. Have a nice trip."

"Oh, I will! Bye."

"My goodness, look at the time," Anna said to herself. "I better get busy on that gown over there."

Anna looked with dismay at the clock and at the material. She hated to miss her limited sunshine in the alleyway, but she didn't want to stop working—she felt very behind with all the happenings of the morning.

Wait a minute, she thought. *I have an idea!*

She walked next door to the shoe store. Ed was out back cutting up cardboard. "Hi, Ed, could you lift something for me?"

"Sure, Anna what's going on?"

Ed moved Anna's sewing machine in front of the opened back door just as the sun's rays reached the door casing.

"That's great, Ed, thanks! Can you come back around two o'clock and move it back?"

"Anything for you. Anna, and thanks for the applesauce cookies the other day. My kids loved them."

"I'm glad."

And there sat Anna sewing in the sunshine, praising God for her health, her hands, her feet, her eyesight, her hearing, her apartment, her job, her faith, her everything.

299

At 3:05 p.m., Anna decided to eat her lunch with Miss Sophie. *She's always good company.* Anna chuckled to herself, as she laid out her sandwich.

Oh, I wish Celeste could hear this, Anna thought. A woman had called in with the same problem that Celeste had—a domineering, abusive, boyfriend. Wow! If Celeste could just hear what Sophie is saying, she'd dump that guy in a hurry.

Anna swung around when she heard Claudette's voice. Where was she? Anna waited for the curtain to open. *Wait a minute, that's Claudette on the radio!* Anna tiptoed over to the radio so as not to miss a word.

She never gave her name, and she didn't divulge anything about the business. Oh, my goodness, she's crying. She doesn't know what's the matter with herself anymore. She hates everyone; she hates herself? She can't stop drinking? She has no dignity left?

What's Sophie going to say?

"Dear Lady, you need help; you need professional help. You've taken the first step by calling me, and I want to commend you for doing that—it took courage. I'm going to switch you over to Linda, and Linda is going to set up some appointments for you. God will be with you every step of the way, too. How does that sound? Here's Linda. And remember, we're all pulling for you."

Anna's hand reached up to turn off the radio. She went to her chair and sat. Sat for maybe forty-five minutes before returning to reality.

Anna went back to her sewing, but she didn't remember sewing.

At 5:00 p.m., she stood up and stared at the gown as if to say, "Where did this come from?"

As she hung the gown on the rack, she heard two little raps at the backdoor, when Celeste walked in.

"Celeste! I was thinking about you this afternoon!"

"I bet you were. I listened to Miss Sophie, too. I couldn't believe it. That woman who called in could have been me."

"I know," Anna said softly.

"You probably won't believe this, but I listened to Sophie's answer, really listened to it I mean, and she's right. As soon as that call was over, I turned off the radio and called Steve. It's over, Anna. He has no right to treat me like that."

"Oh, blessings to you, child. Blessings to you," Anna whispered as she took Celeste's hand.

Anna was glad Celeste hadn't heard Claudette on the radio. Claudette needed to regain her dignity with dignity.

"I need to do one more thing before I go home," Anna said to Celeste.

She sat at her chair, held the gown, and stitched in the label: a Claudette Fashion.

Chapter Seventeen

The Highway

"The big road, Marjory, the big road; not around here.

Yes, our cousin Lorraine works over there.

No, we're not driving way over there to see her."

❦

"That'll be a dollar thirty-five, sir," Lorraine said, as she looked at the dollar twenty-five in her hand.

Through the open window, Lorraine could hear the man shout at his wife, "You said it was a dollar twenty-five."

"Well, excuse me. I thought it said a dollar twenty-five," a shrill voice darted out of the window and into Lorraine's ear.

"Damn it. Where's there another dime?"

"Just give her another dollar, for God's sake. She'll give you back the change."

"Thank you, sir, and thank you for traveling the thruway," Lorraine uttered calmly as she placed the change in his hand.

"Yeah, right," he grumbled.

The car jolted forward as the fumes spiraled upward, ready to invade her domain. Lorraine quickly pushed the window closed just in time to save herself from the poisons of progress. The thruway attendant leaned back to let her fan have full access to clear the remaining residue from the air as she reopened her window.

"Thank you, sir. I hope you enjoyed the thruway."

"Enjoyed? What was to enjoy? Just one long, stupid road."

Lorraine thought back several years to her first week on the job when everyone who went through had nothing but compliments for the brand new road that had saved countless hours of travel time.

"Excuse me, ma'am," declared Lorraine as she peered into the next car that pulled forward, "but that child has to be in a car seat."

"Don't tell me what to do," snarled the woman, "just take the money."

"I'm sorry, ma'am, it's the law."

"Well, he's sick of sitting in that seat. How would you like to ride a hundred fifty miles in a car seat?"

"Pull over and put the child in the seat," Lorraine said as she picked up her telephone. "An officer will meet you right over there," Lorraine continued as she pointed to the designated area.

The woman flung the money to the ground and swung the car to the side of the highway. Lorraine could see the little boy fall against the back seat.

"Thank you, ma'am," Lorraine said to her next paying customer."

"Miss, can you tell me how to get to Printsville?"

"It's right off this exit and fifteen miles south."

"So, when I get to the end of this exit do I go left or right?"

"Printsville will be to your right, but there is a sign to direct you."

"Do you know where the shopping center is in Printsville?"

"No, I don't, ma'am."

303

"Do you know if it's anywhere near the old A and P Store?"

"I'm sorry, I can't help you. Please move along."

"Was that a left or a right off this exit?"

Lorraine used her hand to motion the inquisitor forward as the driver in-waiting began blasting his horn.

"You're not getting paid to stand here and socialize!" the irate man exploded as he thrust his handful of money at Lorraine.

"Sorry you had to wait, sir."

"Yeah, I bet you are," he hissed. "This is why our taxes are so high; we have to pay goof-offs like you."

Lorraine took a deep breath as she watched the out-of-state car whisk away.

"Thank you, sir," Lorraine addressed the next traveler. "I hope you enjoyed your trip."

"I surely did! What a beautiful highway, and the scenery is just exquisite through this valley!"

Lorraine smiled as he pulled away.

Finally, she thought to herself, *someone appreciating the choice colors of the beguiling autumn.* She looked out of her workplace to the rolling hills; her head tilted slightly to the side as it always did when she saw something lovely.

"Mmm," she heard herself softly utter as she saw the blending of mauve, crimson, and maize. She knew if she turned around and looked out of Karli's window she'd see a different blending. *That's just how nature is in this great country,* she thought to herself as she smiled.

Lorraine's scenic wonderment ended as the roar of a truck startled her.

"Sorry about the noise, miss," a man shouted hoarsely above the din. "I'm taking her now to get it fixed."

"That's good," Lorraine shouted back.

The roar could be heard as the truck wound around the curve of the exit. Lorraine knew the embarrassment of driving with a hole in the muffler; she snickered to herself, however, knowing that the young man in the truck hadn't been embarrassed.

What on earth? Lorraine thought as she looked into the next car. She extended her hand for the card and the money but her eyes were on the bundles, boxes, and bags in the back seat. Actually not on the bundles, boxes, and bags but on what looked to be a person buried in the debris.

"Is that a person in the back seat?" she asked.

"Oh, yeah, that's grandpa. He's taking a nap."

"Is he all right?"

"Well, I know it's a little crowded back there, but he's fine."

When Lorraine heard grandpa snore and saw a few boxes move on top of his chest, she realized he wasn't dead. "I hope you don't have too much farther to go," she said quickly. "Have a nice day."

Lorraine giggled as she put the seven dimes and eight quarters into the box.

"What's so funny?" Karli asked.

"Oh, you had to see it to believe it!" Lorraine replied still laughing.

"I don't know how you can laugh about anything on this job—this has to be the worst job I've ever had."

"Really? How many jobs have you had?"

The chitchat ended as they both turned their attention to their travelers at the windows. There was a heavy flow of traffic for a weekday. Lorraine attributed it to the sightseers.

The comforting softness of the autumn air was suddenly pierced when Karli screamed, "Don't you dare talk to me like that, you bastard."

Lorraine swung around even though her customer's hand was midway to her. "Karli, stop, stop. Switch sides. I'll handle this."

"What's the problem here, sir?"

"Oh, damn, where'd the pretty one go?" The inebriated man slurred his words. "I want to get my hands on her."

Lorraine pushed the black button as she asked, "So where are you headed?"

"To hell and back if I'm lucky," he laughed.

"Well, I don't know if you'll find that on this road," Lorraine said, keeping the conversation going.

"Say, I guess you're not so bad, I know of a little place down the road. What time do you get off work?"

Lorraine looked up to see a trooper car sail past and then swing in front of the man's car. Two officers took over as Lorraine went to the next station to open up for traffic. She looked over at Karli, alone in the booth.

"What's going on over there?" a woman asked as all five people in her car gaped at the highway excitement.

"Just routine. Enjoy the rest of your trip."

The following car of people brought more questions. "Was he speeding? Is this a drug raid? Are we all going to get searched?"

After the incident, Lorraine returned to her station.

"Boy, am I glad you're here! It's spooky doing this by myself," Karli uttered as she deposited a fee in her box.

Lorraine knew what she meant—she remembered her first few weeks of work.

"Is that a kid driving that car?" Karli gasped.

Lorraine watched a car slowly creeping into her lane. "No, I think it's a tiny, little lady," Lorraine replied. Sure enough, as the window slowly went down, a woman sitting very low in her seat stretched out her hand with the card and said, "Excuse me, could you tell me how much I owe you. I think my glasses must have fallen under the seat and I can't seem to reach them."

Lorraine looked at the card and told her, "Ninety cents."

"Oh, that's not so bad." The little lady smiled as she reached for her pocketbook. "I thought it was going to be a lot more than that."

Lorraine noticed she was feeling her way through the process of obtaining the change. "Oops," she heard the tiny voice say, "that must be a nickel. Here is another quarter. There you are, Miss, four quarters and you may keep the change."

Lorraine smiled as she handed her a dime, "Thank you ma'am, but we're not allowed to accept tips."

"You're not? Oh, that's terrible."

"Do you need your glasses for driving, ma'am?"

"Oh, no, I can see perfectly well at a distance; it's just the close things that become blurry."

"Okay, do you have much further to drive?"

"No, only two more miles—I'm almost home." The little lady tipped her head toward Lorraine and giggled, "Don't tell anybody, but this is my first time on this big road. I vowed I would try it before I died."

"Well," Lorraine paused, not knowing quite what to say, "You did it!"

"I sure did, honey, I sure did!"

Lorraine watched as the light blue car crept off the exit.

Five cars had passed through Karli's station while Lorraine tended to the little lady. "Why do they let those old people drive?" Karli said out of the side of her mouth.

"Karli!" Lorraine retorted. "You'll be there some day."

"Oh, no, help me and save me," the young girl moaned as she turned to her next car.

Lorraine pulled into her own driveway only to stop short to avoid hitting an abandoned bicycle. A wide-eyed sweep of her lawn displayed more bikes, a tricycle, toys, toys and more toys. Lorraine sighed as she got out of the car. She set the bike up and pushed it into the garage, grabbed hold of a few more handlebars and rustled the toys together into some semblance of order in one area. Stepping into her house brought more of the same. The older children were sprawled amidst the chaos watching TV while the little one sat tearing pages very meticulously from Lorraine's new magazine. She could hear her daughter talking on the phone in the kitchen.

"Grandma's home!" Lorraine sang out to a deaf audience. Only the baby looked up to show Grandma her tearing accomplishment of the day. Lorraine knew she couldn't let the baby think that destroying was acceptable so she walked over to remove the nearly obliterated tatter. Immediately little Jessica started to cry as Lorraine spoke in elementary sentences of, "No, Jessica, no. No magazines. No ripping."

Linda yelled from the kitchen, "You kids stop it—don't make the baby cry!"

Billy Joe yelled back not missing one pulse of the show, "It's not us, it's Grandma!"

Linda came to the doorway. "For God's sake, Ma, let her have the stupid magazine. It's all torn anyway."

"How is she going to learn if we allow this?"

"Learn, learn. Is that all you can think about?"

Lorraine knew she wouldn't get anywhere in trying to explain herself with the TV blaring, the baby crying, and Linda, still talking to someone on the phone. She went upstairs to shower and change while pausing several times to pick up clothes and toys. Lorraine looked at the jobs chart that she had laboriously worked on and hung in the hallway. She stared at the gold stars the children had earned the first few days. Now, the chart had become someone's scribble picture and hung loosely with the bottom corners torn off.

Lorraine scanned her bathroom with the wet towels and the clothes on the floor. The toothpaste drooled into the dirty sink. She let the water flood her head as she positioned her face directly into the deluge of the shower. How much longer are they going to be here, she moaned to herself? "Just a couple of weeks, Mom, while Sam gets us relocated," Linda had told her mother. That was a month ago.

Dear God, help me, Lorraine prayed.

"Good morning, Lorraine."

"Good morning, Karli. How are you today?"

"Great, but I need to ask you a big favor."

"What's that?"

Karli took a deep breath and quickly asked, "Can you work for me tomorrow? I know it's Saturday and it'll be a busy highway day and it's your day off, but my boyfriend really wants me to go to the lake with him."

"Sure."

"You will?"

"Yes." Lorraine laughed. "I will!"

"Oh, super! Thanks!"

Lorraine had come to realize that working was better than being home these days.

"Good morning, ma'am, how was your trip?"

"Excellent!" the woman exclaimed as she handed Lorraine the fee. "Watching the first rays of sunlight dance across the tops of the trees was like watching a black and white movie turn into color!"

"Great stuff, isn't it?" Lorraine remembered last Saturday when she tried to excite her daughter and grandchildren about the foliage. The little expedition they had gone on turned out to be a total bomb—none of them had a good time.

"Good morning!"

"Good morning," yawned the man. "I should say good night," he laughed. "I've just about had it for one day. I'm glad I'm almost home—I drove all night. But I'll tell you when that sun started coming up and I saw the colors of the trees, I couldn't believe it!"

"They are stunning, aren't they."

"We sure are lucky to live in this neck of the woods! Take care."

Gosh, thought Lorraine, *I love these little conversations even though they are so short. At least it's more than what I get at home.*

"Good morning, sir."

"Good, beautiful morning to you! You don't mind if I preach on the beauty of this valley this coming Sunday, do you?" he asked with a twinkle in his eye.

"Why, heavens, no. It certainly would be the truth," Lorraine replied with a laugh.

"Very well then. Have a nice day!"

I wonder if I can convince Linda and the kids to go to church with me Sunday? My asking hasn't worked yet, but you never know. Her thoughts went back to last Tuesday evening when her daughter reprimanded her for saying something about God to her children. "That's my and my husband's business to teach them about that stuff, not yours—we'll tell them what we think is appropriate for them to know."

"Eeeek!" Karli screamed.

"What's the matter?" Lorraine questioned in horror.

"Look!" Karli gasped as she pointed to the back of the car that was pulling away.

"I think it's one of those fake hands; I've seen them before." Lorraine said calmly. "But I'll call it in anyway," she mumbled as she jotted down the license number.

"And people think this is such a dull job," Lorraine heard Karli say to herself.

"Good morning, sir, I hope you had a nice..." Lorraine stopped, not wanting to continue with any pleasantries after she saw the messages that were plastered all over his car.

"Those signs are disgusting!" she said to the man.

"Good! I'm glad you think so, because I think you're disgusting!" he retorted as he stepped on the gas pedal. Lorraine grabbed her notepad again. Well, she thought, I'm giving the troops plenty of business this morning. She was sure there must be some sort of law against displaying signs like that.

When there was a lull, Lorraine said to her coworker, "Karli, when your sister and her kids moved in with you and your folks, what was it like?"

"What was it like? It was like all hell had broken loose! Why?"

"Well, maybe I'm selfish or maybe I'm too set in my ways, but I am losing it. I can't handle anything in that house anymore. If my daughter wasn't there, I'd run that ship with all confidence, but she lets me know in no uncertain terms that she is in charge of those kids and for me to butt out. Was that the way at your house?"

"Gee, I guess I didn't pay that much attention to what my mother and father were thinking, I just knew I had to get out of there as much as possible. I don't remember either one of them saying too much, however. Yeah, I guess they just kept quiet about a lot of things. I know Dad never let us get away with things that my nieces and nephews did."

"Maybe that's the answer. Maybe I should just shut up," Lorraine said sadly. "Trouble is, now I know more and could help train the children so much better than I did my own. When I was a young mother—what did I know?"

"Maybe that's what your daughter thinks."

"No, she thinks she knows it all."

"Oh."

The next hour left no time for the coworkers to chat, but still Lorraine tried to think of ways to successfully get through to her daughter and the kids. *If I don't do something or say something*, she thought, *those kids are going to grow up with no manners, no respect, no work ethics, no spiritual training...*

"Ouch," Lorraine said as she felt her forehead, "something just hit me, I think."

Her eyes spotted six or seven kids duck down into the back seat.

"That's it, you kids," the woman behind the steering wheel screamed as she turned around. "Give me that pea shooter right now! I mean it! Right now! Give it! Do I have to count to ten? Give it to me!"

Lorraine watched as none of the kids moved.

"That's it, you're all grounded!"

As the car sped away, Lorraine watched all the heads pop up as they looked from the back window to stick their tongues out at her.

Oh, dear God, Lorraine thought, *I don't ever want my grandchildren to be like that.*

Lorraine took the long way home, hoping she would have more time to come up with a plan of action. "Maybe it'll have to be bribery," she moaned.

Well, this is a switch, she thought, as she drove her car clear into the garage. *No bikes in the way, no toys?*

She slowly turned the door handle wishing she were leaving the house, not returning. She stopped in surprise when her neighbor, Mary, met her in the foyer.

"Mary! What are doing here?"

"Don't be alarmed, dear. Linda asked us if we'd sit with the kids until you got home. She had to meet her husband to look at a house."

"Oh! This was very nice of you. I appreciate it."

"It was quite all right; we've really enjoyed it."

"You have?"

"Yes, certainly!" Mary proclaimed as the two women walked into the living room. Lorraine's eyes scanned the room so quickly looking for the mess that she felt dizzy. The TV was off, everything was orderly, Mary's husband, Dom, was reading to the older children and the toddler was in a...playpen?

Dom stood as Lorraine entered the room and said, "Hello," the children said, "Hi, Grandma."

"Keep reading, Dom," Eric begged.

"Oh, I will, but it's always polite to ask your grandmother how her day was first."

"It is?" Eric and Sonya both asked at once.

"Yes."

After Lorraine told them about some of her highway adventures, Billy Joe said, "Gee, Grandma. I didn't know you worked at the tollbooth. That's cool!"

While Dom recaptivated the children with the story, Lorraine quietly asked Mary where the playpen came from.

"Oh, we brought it over from our house. After ten minutes of trying to keep up with Jessica, I cried *uncle*! and sent Dom to the attic to get it.

"You are exactly right, Mary. But you must have spent all day picking up from the cyclone..."

"Oh, no. As soon as the children came home from school, we sat them down for snack time and explained how they had to pitch in. I'll admit, we did use a little bribery and a lot of just plain honesty, such as: we are too old to do it; it's their stuff; all their heroes had to work at home when they were young...you know things like that."

"Well," Lorraine said thoughtfully, "I wouldn't mind coming home to something like this."

"You know, Dom and I wouldn't mind helping out anytime you need us. It seems that Linda is about ready to pull her hair out, the poor girl. It isn't easy to live temporarily with someone else—not knowing what your situation is and not having the support of your husband."

"I guess you're right, Mary. I've been so confused and frustrated by this situation; I've just about been beside myself. I've been praying that God would help me, and look—He sent me my own dear neighbors. I can't believe it!" Lorraine hugged Mary while the neighbor uttered that they hadn't done anything special, just helped out like good neighbors do.

"Mary? Can you and Dominic stay for dinner? That seems to be the wildest time of the evening. I'll really need your help."

"Sure, we'd love to. It'll be fun."

"I hope so," Lorraine answered timidly.

Mary turned to Dom and told him of the plans. "So now I'll trade with you, dear."

"Okay, kids, we'll finish this story after dinner. You are needed in the kitchen and it's my turn to entertain your baby sister."

"Aww," they groaned.

"No complaining now. I expect you guys to cook me up something good. I'm as hungry as a bear."

"All right!" they exclaimed in chorus.

"What are we going to make, Mary?"

"How about some lizard's breath, jungle grass, and the giant's bellybuttons?" she said seriously.

"What?"

"Sure. That's why I need lots of help out here."

Lorraine watched as Mary conducted the young troupe of chefs as smoothly and refreshingly as the "orange froth lizard's-breath milkshakes" Eric was blending. Billy Joe and Sonya washed all sorts of vegetables for the "jungle-grass salad" while Mary put the burgers on the grill. The children set the table, wondering which utensil, plate, or napkin Mary was going to put the "free pass" under. The pass was for an ice cream cone at Dilly-Deli's. Lorraine was mystified with their newfound enthusiasm and helpfulness.

Dom put Jessica in the highchair, while everyone took their places. "Who would like to say the grace?" he asked.

"Not me!" the three older children chorused as their hands started grabbing at the food.

"Whoa, whoa, whoa," Dom ordered. "We don't eat until we thank God for this food."

Three hands retracted, and Dom did the honors.

Sonya found the free pass under her napkin, and they all got a chance to tell two things about their day at school.

Mary giggled as she said to Lorraine, "You can't tell Dom was a school teacher for thirty-five years, can you?"

Clean up started just as the phone rang.

"Oh dear," reported Lorraine when she came back into the kitchen. "Linda and Sam want to look at two more houses tomorrow, and I promised my coworker I'd work for her."

"Not a problem," said Dom quickly. "We're available tomorrow. How about we pack a picnic lunch, kids, and go to the lake? The trees are gorgeous this time of year."

"Yeah!" they echoed and clapped.

"Mary?"

"I wouldn't miss it for the world."

"Thank you so much," Lorraine added as she hugged Mary. Now she wished she didn't have to work and could go with them— she needed to learn so much.

Lorraine worked through the busy Saturday with car after car passing through her domain. Situations transpired, but none seemed to have much effect upon her. She looked at the people but didn't see them; she listened to the people, but didn't really hear them. Lorraine's thoughts were on learning how to deal with her role as a grandparent; it should be one of the simplest transitions in nature—but for her it wasn't. *There must be others in the same boat*, she thought. Maybe it was the times; maybe it went back to not raising the last generation properly or the generation before? Why were Mary and Dom such naturals with the children? She could learn those skills; she could develop that positive attitude. Linda could learn, too. Lorraine knew that her daughter would need to be involved with this learning process, or it would never work.

"Grandma, Grandma!" Lorraine heard the children calling her.

"What are you doing here?" She laughed with delight to see them in front of her.

"We wanted to surprise you and see where you worked!" Billy Joe exclaimed excitedly.

"Well, you surely surprised me. Are you all having fun today?"

"Yeah!" they all said in unison.

"Well, I can't wait to see you at home. It'll be about an hour from now. Thanks, Dom. And Dom? I have an idea for an adult education class that I think you and Mary could teach. I'll talk to you about it later."

"Bye, Grandma, bye, bye, bye."

Lorraine watched the white car with the happy children exit the highway.

Chapter Eighteen

The Connection

"Grandma, look! I got a birthday card from Sister Agatha!"

"She never forgets you, does she? I remember her coming here after school when you were a little tyke. I felt kind of sorry for her, growing up in a foster home and all."

"Grandma, did her mother and father go away like mine did?"

She allowed the creases to glide between her fingers. The three pleats on her right-sided lap were in order. The three pleats that she knew so well on the left were also in good order. The same six folds that stemmed from her waist and journeyed to the floor were as familiar as roads to someone's home.

The thought of home fluttered through her mind. How many years had it been since she last turned to wave to her mother? Were the lilac bushes still crowding the front porch? What became of her mother's slightly faded apron with the little geraniums that crept inside the pockets?

Again the folds were examined with her fingers. How familiar they were. How comforting were the trillions of smooth threads that she imagined had been counted by someone at the cloth factory.

Black, she knew they were black, she could see black, she remembered black. Everyone knows black, she conjectured.

She laughed to herself with the idea of having a new garment with five pleats, or four, or none. "What would we do with such a change in our lifestyle?" she murmured to her pleats. She pressed them down as if they were going somewhere.

Her toes pointed upwards inside of her small heeled, laced shoes. Black, she knew they were black. She lifted her heels, not high enough to lift them off of the concrete, but enough to make movement possible between toe and heel. Grit—she felt the smallest pieces of grit beneath the soles of her shoes. Her feet responded with tiny sideways movements in order to shush away the unevenness it was creating in her symmetrical body. More little movements on the ball of her foot made her remember her father's huge shoe putting out his cigarette in the dirt. Her foot stopped as she thought of her little childish eyes checking each cigarette after her father had walked away. She would never want her father to set a fire to the world.

The grit seemed to have dissipated or vanished or blown away. She wasn't sure by which means it disappeared, but it had, as far as she could feel.

Her white collar fluttered a bit, not an ordinary flutter as with the soft material around her ankles, but a controlled flutter of material heavily starched. Her hand ascended to the collar and all five fingers lay upon it as if another gust of wind might enter from underneath to lift her off the chair and sail her out onto the lawn.

She sat as if giving the Pledge of Allegiance to the flag. White, she knew the collar was white. She remembered white.

Would it crack, she mused, this stiff cloth? How many gallons of starch had they used over the years just on her collar?

Her fingers lowered to touch the rim of the stiffened orb. She followed it up and around to her left shoulder. She started the trek back down the circumference and after reaching its lowest point started the upward journey to her right shoulder. The motion became a steady pendulum making her unaware that she was engaged in the exercise—only letting her think of the wringer washing machine with the agitator that turned only so far to the right and then symmetrically to the left.

"Are you going to stand there all day, staring into the washing machine?" she could hear her mother ask.

Her hand stopped its hypnotic journey along the ridge between white and black to adjust her crucifix.

"Ah," she uttered as she did each and every time her two first fingers rested on the corpus with the thumb giving strength to the back to balance the push coming from the front. "*Ah*" like the feeling of being at home base; finishing the exam paper; the end of war; the last stitch of the afghan; to the words: not guilty. *Whatever people needed, the "ah" was there*, she often meditated.

She clutched the metal on the wooden cross until her hand gave it warmth from her own body—it made her feel that it was the least she could do. She brought it up to her cheek. It was warm.

With great ceremony she lowered her love back to its place of her center body. *This is what holds me together*, she thought. It centers me and disallows my wild thoughts to veer to the right or to the left. The old nun giggled as she thought of herself being dragged off in one direction and then in the other not knowing what to do…being confused.

"C-o-n-f-u-s-e-d," she spelled aloud. She could see herself boldly writing it across the chalkboard and dramatically turning toward her class with her black skirt sailing around her ankles. "Who can explain what this word means?"

"Oh," she reminisced as she cradled her chin in her hand, "the answers, the answers!" From the young ones came absolute truth and simplicity. From the junior high—reservations about giving the "right answer" hence, confusion over "confused." The senior high—a sense of fear creeping in; a sense of "maybe that's me, maybe I have *it*."

She clasped her crucifix again, wondering how it could be off-center so soon. "Help them, Lord," she prayed silently as she prayed every day for her former students.

Her left hand went to her beads. Black. She knew they were black. She remembered black.

"Ah," she uttered as she felt the smooth prayer-worn beads. The feeling of the softness, the familiar shape, the chain that was her lifeline gave her peace before any words were uttered.

"What might we have as a lifeline, class?"

"A house key attached to a piece of yarn and worn around our neck...A telephone directory with emergency numbers...A cell phone...An oxygen supply...A family support system...Friends..."

"Good answers, class, very good answers. Now," she proceeded as she stared at her piece of chalk and picked off the tiniest of specks that she imagined had been making an irregularity in the formation of the words, "what might be a lifeline to God?"

How many times have I said "the rosary"? she silently pondered as she held the large beads in both hands. As she let them slip slowly back and forth between her hands, listening to the little clinking sounds that she cherished, she reckoned in huge numbers of a trillion or a "double kadrillion" as she often heard the children in the early elementary classes say.

"I'm sure I don't know," she answered herself as she laughed at her own question.

"S-O-S, God, S-O-S. We're sending up an emergency signal via your mother, Mary!" Billy animated his answer.

If anyone could bring humor to the class it was Billy, she thought as she used one hand to toss the bulk of her beads up and down like a tennis ball. What a character he was; always right, but with an uncanny, whimsical way of answering that was never excelled, as far as she was concerned.

"Watch over, Billy, Lord," her thoughts suddenly became serious as she stopped playing with the beads and started praying. "This really is an S-O-S to you via Mary."

"William" was now all over the news with a fraud scandal going on in the city's biggest financial company.

Sister leaned her head back on the wood of the porch chair that tilted her head upwards. She knew the sky—it was white. She knew white.

If I could fit all the faces of my students onto the sky, would they fit? she wondered. She had taught every grade, every aged child, sometime or another in her lifetime.

I would like to see their faces again, she thought. *Altogether, right there before me painted onto the sky!*

She smiled as if she was looking at a portrait of "her children."

She could hear Sister Cecilia's footsteps coming through the inner room. *A kind soul, Sister Cecilia,* she thought, as she listened to the quick little steps crossing the threshold to the porch.

"Sister Agatha, aren't you chilly out here?" Sister Cecilia chirped in the happiest little way of hers.

"It is somewhat chilly this morning, but so refreshing, Sister Cecilia."

"How did you know it was me Sister, with so many novices buzzing around all the time?" she asked with surprise in her voice.

"I heard those quick, little footsteps, of yours, my dear. Who else could it be?"

"I don't know how you do it, Sister Agatha."

"That's not so amazing, but what might be especially amazing is the nest that the robins are constructing in the tree to our right."

Sister Cecilia put her tray of medications on the little wooden table and stretched her body over and upward to look into the tree.

"I don't see anything, Sister Agatha," she uttered.

"No, I didn't either, dear."

The old nun could just picture Cecilia in her Postulate's habit with the black stockings and the black shoes. The shorter length black dress with the white veil that would be accentuated by her youthfulness. Cecilia's hair around her forehead would still be allowed to show.

Sister Agatha could tell that her young friend was still stretching and straining to see the bird family by the way her voice sounded tighter when she announced again that she couldn't see a thing.

"I'll keep you updated on the progress, dear. Now, would I be mistaken if I thought you came out here with something for me?"

"Oh, my, gosh," she giggled. "I forgot for a minute. Here are you medications, Sister."

After each swallow, Sister Agatha grimaced.

"Sister Cecilia, tell me, why doesn't God just heal me so I don't have to take all these pills?"

Sister Cecilia stopped her customary chattering; she knew she had been "caught" by the teacher. Sister Agatha's face was turned directly to hers and she was waiting.

Maybe she's joking around, hoped Cecilia. *I don't think she really wants me to answer that.*

"Cecilia, my dear, what is your answer?"

"Um, maybe God wants you to suffer, Sister Agatha. No, I don't mean He wants you to suffer; He doesn't want you to suffer, He is letting you use your suffering to get closer to Him," the young Postulate answered with hurried little puffs of air being released in between words.

"Very good, Sister Cecilia; that's a good answer and you're going to do very well in your classes this afternoon. I can just tell!"

The old nun could "see" the beam of pleasure that went across the young, pretty face. There was always of beam of pleasure when students were successful, she knew.

"Would you like this afghan to put across you, Sister?"

"Maybe I will take it; I plan on being out here for a while."

Cecilia gave a quick look up into the tree before she darted back into the building. Sister Agatha could hear the young Postulate's beads clicking with excitement to accompany the spry, youthful steps of the novice.

$$\sim$$

"Ah, Mother Veronica, I thought it must be about ten-thirty. Come, sit with me," Sister Agatha said as she gestured to the chair next to hers.

"How are you this morning, Sister?" Mother Veronica asked with the same deep concern that she uttered each and every morning.

Agatha extended her hand to grasp that of her Mother Superior's. She leaned over to her confidant and friend and whispered, "Jesus and I had a time of it last night."

"You had another bad night, Sister?"

"We suffered together, Mother Veronica. I am so grateful that He allows me to share that precious time with him. Talk about buddies in the same foxhole; you get to know each other pretty darn well," Sister said with a laugh.

"Well, that's a different way of saying it," replied Veronica with a pleasure that always emanated from their conversations.

"So, what's on the docket today, Mother?"

Mother Superior took in a deep breath of the spring air and stretched her feet outwards toward the porch rail. She crossed her feet and folded her hands in her lap at the same time.

"Oh, you know, budget meetings, faculty meetings, construction meetings, diocesan meetings, on and on and on."

With the long pause, Sister Agatha used the time to pray. One hand went to her crucifix and the other hand went to her rosary. She remembered Billy once saying, "And sometimes you've got to use the double-barreled shotgun!"

"Oh, Lord have mercy," Sister prayed as she stifled a laugh. She wanted this to be a serious moment of prayer for God to give some relief to Mother Veronica.

The director of so much responsibility broke the silence. "Are you praying for me, Sister?"

The old nun looked up after being startled by the remark. She didn't know why she should be startled until she remembered the feeling of being caught by her father when he said, "I know exactly what you're thinking, young lady. Don't ever think you can get away with me not knowing what's on your mind."

"How did you know I was praying for you?" she asked sheepishly feeling ashamed that she had slipped back into her past.

"Because, Agatha, I feel better. It might be a combination of resting my feet for a few minutes, and the fresh air, and being with my friend, but I have a funny feeling," she leaned over to whisper to Agatha, "that someone is pumping strength into my being."

"It's that high octane that'll get you every time," laughed Sister.

Mother Veronica broke into her famous "big as the outdoors" laugh as she squeezed her friend's hand.

"How are the Postulates doing, Mother?

"They're praying, and searching, and studying hard."

Both women silenced their chatter, looked outward over the porch rail, breathed a deep breath of air and exhaled it slowly back to the universe to be recycled. Their own days of praying and searching and studying hard seemed like yesterday. The memories of being young women and contemplating the giving of their lives to God were instilled in every pore of their souls. They knew the joys and the reflecting, and sometimes the sorrows that Postulates went through. It was a very personal choice. No human could lead another into the convent, or out of the convent. Mother Veronica and Sister Agatha knew they could only be of assistance to the young women if they asked for counsel.

"Well, my dear, I have a meeting coming up, so I must bid you adieu. I'll see you at evening prayers."

"Lord willing and the creek don't rise," exclaimed Sister Agatha as she waved goodbye. Creek...ahh, her Lone Moon Creek! She wondered about the people in the place where she grew up. She owed Agnes and Marjory a letter. She thought about the times of going to their house after school to help with Marjory.

She sat listening to Mother Veronica's slower than Sister Cecilia's footsteps decrescendo through the inner room. *A strong woman, a good woman, a fair woman*, thought Agatha. *God help her.*

"Hey," she shouted louder than she intended, "all you saints and angels up there, put in a good word for Mother Veronica with the main man! My Lone Moon Creek friends, too."

Birds fluttered out of the tree. She could hear wings against leaves.

"Oops, sorry birds, I didn't mean to scare you." And this she said with all honesty.

Two years ago Sister Agatha would not have had to retire to her room after lunch to rest. Now she did.

There on her bed, the same bed that she had occupied for fifty-three years, rested the slight frame of a woman. Without her eyesight now, she still turned her head to look up at her cross on the wall. As she prayed, she touched her gold band on her right hand, her wedding ring. She married her beautiful bridegroom, Jesus, forty-six years ago.

"Well, Jesus, what do you think? Here I am, all these years later and we're still together. I'm not that cute, young girl that I once was but you're still the most handsome man in the world to me. I still can see your face, your beautiful face. We've shared a lot of memories, haven't we? And not one day did I want anyone else but you. You could never be replaced. No one holds a candle to you, my sweet heart of Jesus. You are always here for me. I can talk to you day or night. You have guided me well, Lord. How many, many times you saw me stumble and led me to the right decision or the right path. You never wanted me to stray from you, did you? You saw me when I cried; you saw me joyful in the classroom. You were always there waiting for me to say, 'Jesus, I need you. Jesus, help me.' And you did!

"Remember when I would ask for things and have a fit when I didn't get them? What a fresh little wife you had at times! Forgive me for being so self-centered and arrogant. Now I know why I didn't get all the things I asked for. You knew the consequences of it all, didn't you? I love you, Jesus."

∿

Sister Agatha stopped her praying to kiss her hand and blow the kiss to her bridegroom. She remembered her Mama always doing that when Papa took her away in the car. Agatha swallowed hard and returned to her prayers.

"And to think how you suffered for me and for all the people. I finally know, dear one, what suffering is. I had no idea before. Thank you for sharing that feeling with me, it has brought us closer. I am now able to better understand what you went through, I would not have really known without it.

"I'm getting closer to being with you in eternity...I can't wait! I need to be with you, Jesus. You have been my wonderful companion and suffered so much so that I could be with you in the next life. Thank you.

"I must sleep now, my dear Jesus. I'll visit with you more when I awake or maybe, just maybe...it's up to you."

∿

"Good afternoon, Sister Agatha."

"Hello, Sister Ann. Isn't it beautiful out here this afternoon?"

"How can you tell us all apart, Sister?"

"You're the only one who props the door open first and then comes through with my medications."

"Well, yes, I always do that since the time I spilled the tray. You wouldn't think I was once a waitress, would you?"

"I remember Mother Superior telling me that waitressing had been your summer job through college. A noble job, I'm sure."

"I don't know how noble it was, but it was a job and yes, it is beautiful out here today."

"See, you remember what your customers have said to you!"

"One more little pill, Sister, and I won't have to bother you any longer."

"Bother? Dear child, you are no bother. You young women bring some pizzazz into my day!"

"Pizzazz? I didn't know a Sister would use a word like that."

"Good grief, child. What do you think we are, old fence posts?"

Sister Ann couldn't keep from laughing and Sister Agatha couldn't keep from making her laugh. The robins must have ceased their work just to regale in the sounds coming from the porch.

"Oh, Sister, you're too much," the young Postulate added with a deep breath. "But seriously now, if you could just help me a little bit, I have a paper due tomorrow on the virtue of Obedience. I'm kind of stuck on that one."

"Tomorrow?" Sister Agatha gasped with the dismay that only a teacher can gasp. "Tomorrow?"

"Well, I've been trying for a week to get my thoughts down on paper, but everything I write sounds ridiculous."

"Oh, oh, oh." The younger Sister heard Sister Agatha moaning into her clasped hands.

"Sit down, Sister Ann," the moaning nun said assertively, seemingly able to pull herself together very quickly. "Have you ever thought of a career in the military?"

"The military?" exclaimed Ann in great surprise.

After affirming the negative, Sister Agatha then inquired about business fields and civil servant positions and concert pianists and motherhood.

"Would any of those fields be without obedience to someone or something?" she asked, looking her student squarely in the eye.

The young girl tilted her head and thought.

"I don't see what the concert pianist would have to be obedient to."

"How does he or she get to the highly sought after position of being the best?"

"Well," the young girl exclaimed flippantly, "just practice, practice, practice."

"What if he or she refuses to practice?"

"Well, that's obvious; he'll never reach the higher standards that he dreams about."

"And, he has that choice, right?"

"Yes, we all have free will."

"So, the pianist can follow his teacher's advice, his own advice, or even listen to the advice of the piano..."

"The voice of the piano? That's a silly thought!"

"It is silly in a way," agreed Sister Agatha, "but think of the pianist trying to play a beautiful piece of music and, because of lack of practice or of being uncaring to the beauty of the sound, he misses several notes."

"What does this have to do with obedience, Sister?"

"We all have to be obedient to something, even if it is as abstract or intangible as sound."

"Hmm," was Ann's only comment, as she seemed to look past the crevices of her mentor's face and delve into her brain.

The old woman continued, "If obedience is constructive, and believe me there can be obedience that will lead you astray and ruin your soul, it will only enhance your life on this earth and prepare you for the next."

"So taking the vow of Obedience is not meant to punish me?"

"No, my good child, no. Being obedient to God puts you on the 'super highway of the world,' as my former student Billy would say."

"Well, I'll be," replied Sister Ann.

All that food for thought and all she can say is, "Well, I'll be"?

"Obedience isn't something I have to fight against, is it Sister."

Now the teacher could sense the young Postulate's reasoning powers starting to work.

"Not at all, child, not at all."

"Oh, my goodness, look at what time it is," Sister Ann suddenly exclaimed jumping up to gather her supplies. "I'll see you at evening prayers," she called out.

Agatha was sure the young girl's skirts were flying.

⁂

"Sister, let me help you."

"Thank you, dear, but I could walk to the chapel in my sleep if I had to."

"I know, Sister Agatha, but I would feel better if I walked with you."

"Very well, Sister. Shall I take your arm—or do you want to take my arm?" she asked with a laugh.

From there they walked in silence, quieting their hearts, minds, and souls in preparedness for the evening's audience with God. It was a time to pray for the whole world. Sister Agatha wondered how many people out there knew that they would be prayed for this evening, and every evening for the rest of their lives. In fact, all over the world—now her math-teacher mind was kicking in—in every time zone, her sisters in Christ would be on their knees praying. Praying for children; praying for new mothers and fathers; praying for world leaders; for the unemployed and the employed; for addicts; for abortionists; for class bullies; for the handicapped; for school bus drivers; astronauts; prostitutes; the homeless. Now, if there are twenty-four time zones and maybe a million nuns who would say

329

their evening prayers, how many prayers would that be? She wished that she had asked that question in Billy's class. *Well anyway,* she thought as they neared the door to the chapel, *God certainly is on alert to help a lot of people.* She wished the people knew He was right there waiting for them to call on Him.

"Just ask," she said aloud.

"Excuse me, Sister?"

"Oh, sorry, I was thinking out loud."

They entered the chapel with Agatha "seeing" every aspect of the sanctuary. This was one of the spiritual centers where she could feel so very close to her savior. She could "see" the candles glowing in the darkness, twinkling out their little lights of hope. She could "see" her Blessed Mother waiting for special requests from the Sisters who would then present them to her son. Oh, if there ever was a son who loved his mother, it was Jesus. If she asked a special favor of Him, He would grant it. Even through God is divine and we are human, we are able to understand this.

And, if there was ever a mother who loved her son...Sister Agatha groaned as she knelt.

"Are you all right, Sister? Are you in pain?"

"No, no, a thought of my baby brother and my mother just came to my mind."

"I'll say a prayer for them, Sister."

"Thank you."

During their silent prayers they could hear the soft crying of someone seated toward the rear of the chapel. They knew who it was. Every evening for two years, their little Postulate Marian prayed with tears. Oh, the sadness of that child. What is on her soul that burdens her so? Dear God, bring her to your peace. Give her relief for her soul.

"Good night, Sister Agatha. May God be with you through the night."

"He will, Sister, he will. And with you."

"Thank you. And Sister? I'm sure it would be permissible for you to sit in the chapel and not to kneel."

"Why, thank you for your concern, but I'll kneel as long as I'm able."

"I know you will, Sister. Goodnight."

Agatha entered her little room and used her sense of touch to ready herself for bed. She knew how to find everything and fold everything and place everything in its proper space.

Whoever would have thought, she contemplated to herself, *that one day I would have to give up kneeling. Kneeling—the simplest act of humility, an outward sign that you understand the relationship between you and God. That God is divine and you are human. That He can do everything and you can do nothing without Him.*

"Let me kneel before you for a long while yet, dear God," Sister Agatha prayed. She wiped away a deluge of tears.

In complete blackness, the old nun retired for the night, still praying for people around the world in every situation of life.

"Now who do you think possibly receives the least number of prayers?" came a question she would sometimes pose to her students. She remembered answers of: cafeteria workers, psychiatrists, car mechanics...

"That's exactly who we will offer up our prayers for today!" she would tell her class. She did this on a daily basis; it really made the students think.

She navigated her gold band around and around her finger while sending loving thoughts to the one she adored. She thanked Him for the day and the opportunity to share His wisdom. She thanked Him for sharing His life with her and letting her share her life with Him. She promised to visit with Him later in the night when they could share their sufferings together.

"Sister—Sister. Here, take these. I heard you crying out in pain."

"Oh, I'm sorry, I didn't realize I was making noise."

"Please, Sister, you are way past due on your medications."

"I'm offering up my pain for the souls in Purgatory, Sister."

"I know you are, Sister Agatha, but I think you've gotten your quota of souls released for this night."

"Do you think so?"

"I really do think so. Even Jesus needed some relief when he called out to his father, 'Why have you forsaken me?' Come now, take these, Sister."

"I know I will be asleep soon, my angel girl. Can you imagine going through the suffering of being crucified on the cross to save your people? Crucified so we could rid ourselves of our sins; crucified so we could spend eternity with God? Is it any wonder I love God so much?"

"It's no wonder, Sister Agatha. That's why I'm in love with him, too."

"I'm glad," the old nun said weakly as she smiled at the young girl.

"Good morning, Sister, are you ready for Mass?"

"Yes, yes. Come in."

"I'll walk with you if you'd like."

"I'd love that. Thank you, Sister Ann. Did you complete your paper on Obedience?"

"I surely did," she said excitedly. I've been up all night writing it, and it's finished!"

"Well, that's good. I'll be anxious to read—I mean—have you read it to me."

"I will, Sister Agatha. Especially when I get an A on it!"

"Sister Ann! I think you need to write a paper on Humility."

"Sorry, Sister."

"Come along. Let's not dawdle."

"Ah, the grandest part of the day," Sister Agatha whispered to her young friend as they entered the church for Mass.

The elderly nun knelt.

Soon the church was full of nuns ready to start their day with the Holy Sacrifice of the Mass, the place where they received their sustenance, their strength, their love. Here they were reminded of Jesus' supreme sacrifice for them and for those of the whole world. Here they were given the opportunity of taking Jesus' body and blood into themselves—to be nourished, to have Jesus dwell in themselves, to be given the courage to follow His ways, to take any adversity and face it in His name. The nuns came readily for this sustenance.

It was when they were reciting the "Lamb of God" prayer that Sister Agatha felt something quite heavy lean against her arm. It only took a second to realize that the heavy breather was Sister Ann— sound asleep. As a shepherd takes care of his flock, it was Mother Veronica who leaned forward with her shawl rolled up like a pillow to put under the little lamb's head.

I can't imagine living in a country where the people are not allowed to celebrate the Mass, to be denied receiving the body and blood of Jesus Christ, Sister Agatha thought to herself as she sat on the porch basking in the morning sunshine after breakfast.

Her fingers went from bead to bead, as occasionally her head would lift to "watch" the birds.

"Good morning again, Sister. What are you praying for today?"

"Hello, Mother Veronica. Thank you for bolstering up our little friend. I don't think I would have had the strength to hold her up for too long."

"She and I had a little chat after Mass about getting assignments done in good fashion and being 'Obedient' to curfews and lights-out."

"Aha, curfews. Such excitement to break them!"

Mother Veronica gave Sister a look (Sister Agatha could just feel it) before she asked again, "So, what's the prayer today?"

"The prayer is for Michael and for my mother."

"I see. Don't you think Michael and your mother are in heaven?"

"Yes, I do."

"When are you going to include your father into your prayers, Sister?"

"I try, Mother Veronica. I really try."

There was a silence before Mother Superior went on.

"To be very blunt Agatha, you're not getting any younger. I think you had better get this thing squared away with God before you get up there and have to sort it out then."

"I know you're right, Mother. I know you're right."

"Why don't you talk to Father Ben about this?"

"I will. I will try again."

Another silence gave the mama robin a chance to call out for her mate.

"Well here I go. Up and at 'em," commented Mother Veronica as she rose from the chair. "Do you want me to say a prayer for you, Sister?"

"Yes, please. I need it very much."

Sister Agatha straightened her pleats, straightened her crucifix, squared off her feet, felt for the edges of her veil to discern their symmetry, and lifted her face to the heavens.

"Baby brother, Michael, you who didn't get a chance to be born, and Mama, you who couldn't face life after the abortion, help me. Please intercede for me. Ask Him please to send me the grace I need to forgive Papa. I need to forgive him; I have to. I am no better than the common sinner. I have to cleanse my soul. Please let me come to grips with this.

"I know if Papa came to me right now and said he was sorry, I would forgive him. But who knows where he disappeared to? I never saw him after Mama died. I'm sure he has passed away by now; he'll never have a conversation with me now."

"Hi, Sister Agatha," bubbled Sister Cecilia as she flitted out onto the porch. "What's happening with the birds today?"

"Oh, hello, Sister Cecilia," the older nun greeted her in an apparent daze. "Um, to tell you the truth, I haven't been paying much attention to the birds."

"Have you been in a lot of pain?" the young girl asked compassionately.

"No, dear, I've just been busy with my thoughts. Say, what are doing out of class already?"

What student isn't excited about getting out of class early? thought Sister Agatha as she waited for the answer.

"Father Ben had some sort of emergency. Rose, I mean Sister Rose, said he had to go and be with Sister Marian. I'm not sure what's going on.

"It was too bad he had to leave, we were having a really great discussion on the vow of Chastity."

"Oh, my. That would be a difficult lesson to be interrupted. Isn't that always the way though?"

Sister Cecilia couldn't tell if Sister Agatha was being facetious or not.

"Sister Cecilia, could you pray with me?" the old nun asked in all seriousness.

"Me? You want me to pray with you?" asked the young one in the same tone of voice as had Agatha fifty-four years ago when the bishop chose her to assist him at the graduation. Of all the boys in the senior class, he chose Agatha to pray with him in front of the entire auditorium. Agatha had felt very unworthy to stand side by side with such an important man of God, but on the other hand, she felt honored. That afternoon, Agatha felt her soul soar through the sky, through the heavens and through all of eternity. It was beyond being physically close to the bishop even though his nearness almost took her breath away. It was as if her words, when entwined with his, could not be corralled. They were free...free to leave the auditorium and search through the universe for their God. The timid high school girl felt power as she had never felt; power because she had attached herself to his coattails.

All those years ago, and she still felt that it should have been her own father who made her feel such ecstasy. That's what fathers do for their daughters, she discerned. Young girls should not have to wait for the bishop to come along to do the parent's role.

"Dear Cecilia," Agatha whispered as she reached over for the young girl's hand, "I am a sinner, I need for you to give me strength."

"Me?"

"You."

The young Postulate knelt at the knees of Sister Agatha and prayed with all her heart. She didn't know the exact reason she was praying, but because her revered Sister had asked her, she prayed with such voracity that the old nun wept into her hands.

After Sister Agatha wiped away her tears, she held the young girl's face in her hands and whispered, "Thank you Sister Cecilia. You did me a world of good today."

"I did?"

"You did."

The chapel was heavy with quietness that evening. Even the life of the candlelight stiffened, to say nothing of the alabaster statues. Nuns in rows were as unmoving as the iron fence around the convent. The only thing moving were the prayers being offered up for Sister Marian. Thousands and thousands of prayers just for her. Sister Marian's cry was not heard in the back of the chapel that evening; Sister Marian's cry would not be heard again in the chapel. Sister Marian had gone home.

Sister Agatha remembered when her best friend had left the convent. Oh, how she missed her. They had met on the first day of orientation and became the greatest of companions. They had such plans and aspirations for serving God forever and ever and ever.

But Janelle was called to a different direction. How they prayed and prayed that it wasn't so, but it was, and Janelle knew she had to leave. Agatha remembered being in mourning for almost a year. She cried and prayed and prayed and cried. Finally one day, Agatha understood and she thanked God for that understanding.

"Good morning, Sister, I understand you want to see me?"

"Father Ben. Yes, yes. Come. Sit down, please. Isn't it beautiful out here today?"

"That it is, Sister Agatha. That it is," he spoke looking all around the landscape as if he would later go inside to paint it.

"What can I do for you, Sister?"

"I need to go to confession, Father,"

"Well, mercy sakes, Agatha, is that all? I thought it was something serious," he laughed.

She drew closer to him, as she would have done to a student who was just on the verge of being expelled from her class.

"Benjamin," she said directly and slowly, "I would not have called you here on a whim; this is something of the utmost importance."

It wasn't until he apologized that she released her stare from him and let her body rest back onto the chair.

Sister Agatha sighed; she felt exhausted and knew she had yet to climb the mountain. Her words were not formulating in her head. She started to panic. "Lord, help me," she prayed silently, "I'm not a teenager; what's the matter with me?"

Father Ben took his holy scapular out of his pocket, kissed it, and then put it around his neck.

"What is troubling you, Sister?" he asked.

"Father," she began very, very slowly, "in all my years of confessing my sins week after week, I purposefully never mentioned my scorn and my unforgiveness towards my own father."

"Oh, my dear child," the priest said recognizing the gravity of her statement.

"I know, I know Father. My heart has been closed on this matter. I want God to release me of this burden. I need God to forgive me; I have no right to take on God's responsibilities. He will settle things with my father; I can't do it."

"That's right, Sister. Hatred will only destroy yourself; it won't do a thing to your father."

"After he made my mother abort the child, she went out of her mind and died soon after. I think I held onto the hatred because it made me feel as if I had some power over him, that he wasn't able to destroy me, too."

"You're probably right, Sister," he said softly as he cradled his chin in his hand. "Many people think that in order to survive, they need to hold the crow bar under the rock in order to feel some sense of power. Unfortunately, all they do is wear themselves out; the rock most generally isn't going anywhere."

Agatha sat in silence soaking in Father Ben's words just as she remembered her students doing to hers.

He let her reflect without saying more.

Finally Sister Agatha asked as would a child, "What does God think of me for not wanting to confess this before?"

Father Ben was no longer "the young kid on the block" as Sister Agatha and some of the older Nuns had jokingly referred to him.

"Sister Agatha," he said gently, "God has been waiting a long time for this day. God is now joyful, probably jubilant! He never wanted you to carry this for so long by yourself."

"I didn't do anything but hurt myself, and hurt God, did I Father?"

"You're right, Sister. But just think, you came out of that dark tunnel. You came out into the sunshine."

"I'm sorry I hurt God, Father."

"I know you are, Sister."

"Father? I wish I could say I had a Papa whom I loved."

"I know. God doesn't expect you to love the wrongs that he did, but try to look at your father as a child of God, too."

Sister Agatha looked up suddenly. "A child of God? I never thought of him as a child of God. A child of God?" she repeated.

All remained silent for quite some time until Sister Agatha finally said, "I guess he was." She sounded as surprised as would an elementary student conducting a science experiment.

Father Ben took her small, thin hand in his and said, "Sister Agatha, from whom did you inherit all of your nice ways, and intelligence and beauty?"

She wasn't exactly sure where he was going with this question but she answered as a dutiful student, "From my mother."

"And?" he asked as he waited for her answer.

Quite reluctantly she replied, "and from my father."

"And from you father," he reiterated.

"Is there anything else, Sister?"

"No, Father."

Then came the words, the words that take away the sins of the world. The words that restore the soul to God's likeness, the way He created it to be. God took away Sister Agatha's sin. She felt the weight of the world being lifted from her shoulders as she cried and wept into the blessed hands of the "young kid on the block."

❧

Sister Agatha opted to have her lunch on the porch that day; she needed the solitude that only nature could provide. Through her blind eyes, she looked out into the realms of the universe, sometimes pausing at her childhood, sometimes pausing at her foster home, sometimes navigating far beyond anything she had ever known.

She pictured herself without sin. She lamented her years of carrying burdens that God would not sanction.

Why did I think I was such a good person? How could I counsel everyone else on the state of his or her soul and neglect my own?

As she ate from her dish at positions of 3:00 and 6:00 and 9:00 and 12:00, she meditated on all of those things. When she finished her meal, she thought of the food that had been removed to reveal the solitary plate. *When everything has been said and done in this lifetime, all that is left is our solitary God,* she thought. *It's good to clear your plate before you go to eternity.*

As she sipped her tea, she heard the porch door open and close. Someone was coming for the dishes.

She suddenly swung to the direction of the person and shouted, "Janelle?"

"Sister Agatha?" the person inquired.

"Yes, I'm Sister Agatha. May I help you?"

"It's Jillian, Sister. Why did you say Janelle?"

"Oh, I'm sorry. I once had a very good friend who wore the same perfume that you are wearing. It floated across the air when you walked out, and I immediately thought of Janelle. I'm sorry. How may I help you?"

"My grandmother was your good friend, Sister. My grandmother was Janelle."

"Oh my heavenly soul. Come, Jillian, come, sit by me."

"How are you, Sister Agatha? I haven't seen you since I was a little girl!"

"I know, I know," exclaimed Agatha as she hung dearly to Jillian's arm. "When your grandmother brought you here to visit you were the cutest little girl we had ever seen. And what a performer; you had everyone in stitches!"

"I know," Jillian groaned as she put her hand in front of her face, "my grandmother would tell the stories about our visit to the convent to everyone."

"Oh, Lord help us and save us," the old nun laughed. "Those were the days. Well, anyway, what brings you here today, sweetie?"

"Well, Sister, my grandmother always told me, before she passed away, that if I ever needed someone to talk to, I should go to you."

"God rest her soul and give her peace," said Sister Agatha in respect for the dead. "She did, did she? Well, I don't know what help I can be to you, Jillian. You see, just this morning I made my first confession. I'm pretty much a novice around here. If you need any counseling, you ought to talk to Mother Superior or one of the older nuns."

The young girl looked at her grandmother's best friend like a child would look at a gumball machine after nothing rolled down the shoot. She knew she had put the coin in and turned the crank.

"Sister?" she finally said.

"I'm sorry, Jillian, but it's difficult to face up to your character defects and sins when you're an old lady."

It was obvious that the twenty-year-old was unsettled and confused by Sister Agatha's responses, and it was obvious that the little nun in black was very unsettled, too."

"Maybe I should come back another time," Jillian said sadly.

With those words laced with disappointment, Agatha resumed her composure of dignity, teacher, and service.

"Forgive me child, today has left me a little out of myself. Now, you go ahead and tell Auntie Agatha what's troubling you."

"Well, Sister, I'm in love."

"And you're sad?"

"Why do you think I'm sad?"

"I can't see your face but your voice sounds sad."

"Oh," she said quickly, "I didn't realize that."

"So, what's this boy like? Is he nice?"

"Yes, Sister, he's very nice," Jillian continued with words that were starting to quiver.

"Sweetheart, what's the matter?"

"I'm pregnant," she sobbed.

"Oh, my," Auntie Agatha voiced softly. "Well, that's not the worst thing in the world, you know. It happens in the best of families," she spoke more cheerfully to compensate for the degree of crying from Jillian.

"What am I going to do?" Jillian wailed as she went down on her knees and hugged Sister Agatha's legs.

"Child, child, it's okay, you'll have the baby and make a life for yourself. I'll get you the help you'll need."

"No, Sister Agatha, no! This child will ruin my life!"

The old nun bent forward and hugged the sobbing girl's head. "That is not true, Jillian. The child will not ruin your life."

Jillian jumped up. "I don't want it," she screamed, "and I never should have come here."

"Jillian, Jillian, stop," Sister Agatha called after her.

Jillian did not stop. The birds stopped building their nest; the spring air stopped emitting its sweet scent; the tulips stopped standing at attention; Sister Agatha felt that her heart had stopped, but Jillian did not stop.

Agatha got up from the chair and knelt immediately on the porch floor. She grasped her hands together and called out, "Oh, Mother Mary, Mother of God, Jillian needs you. Dear friend, Janelle, I couldn't stop her. Send the angels, Janelle, send them quickly. God, in your mercy, send your grace and wisdom to Jillian."

A tremendous flurry came out of the door with Mother Superior leading the troupe.

"Sister Agatha, Sister Agatha, are you all right?"

"No! I'm not all right at all! Here, everyone, get on your knees immediately. We've got to pray right now!"

There, on the porch knelt the nuns praying their hearts out for Jillian and her baby.

The birds didn't know what to make of it, the sunshine stared with curiosity, the hyacinths bobbed their heads in wonder, and God listened.

Sister Agatha lay on her little bed, not able to move. Her entire body had been seized—seized by pain, paralysis, sorrow, helplessness, and desperation. She didn't know what all the iron grips consisted of, she only knew they were many. Her heart cried out, her soul cried out, tears dampened her pillow. She prayed, she agonized, she thought of Janelle, of eternity, of sin, of human nature, of compassion, of understanding. *Why*, she asked herself, *why were God's humans relegated to this life of hell?*

"I need to see the priest again," she whispered to the crucifix on the wall.

Father Ben knew better than to take this visit lightly. He entered with all solemnity and respect.

He pulled a chair over to the bedside and remained very close to the ear of Sister Agatha.

"I need your counsel, Father. I am deep into the sin of humanity," she whispered. "I am trying to take over God's responsibilities again; I must think I am God. I think I can handle everything that comes along, that I'm strong. Father, I can't handle anything."

"Oh, Sister," he leaned to her cheek to kiss it, "you are so blessed. You have no idea how the rest of us gather strength from you. We learn from you each and every day. Do not be despondent. God loves your humble heart, your good spirit. You're right about not having to take on the trials of this world, however. He will tend to that. Relax, Agatha, regain your composure. Just pray and speak to Him; love Him—that's all he wants from you. Relax."

Sister began moving her arm, and then her other arm. She turned her head side to side as if to loosen the neck muscles, then her knees moved upward under the blankets and then downward.

"Father," she reached out her hand to him, "thank you. I know Jesus was speaking through you. I could feel His presence."

Father didn't respond, except for his tear that Agatha felt drip upon her hand.

"It's so good to see you up and around again, Sister," Mother Veronica boomed her voice out onto the porch.

"It's wonderful to be outdoors, Mother," Agatha responded as she took in all of nature and then some.

"Ah, I wish I could sit here all day," Mother Veronica voiced. She comforted herself by getting into her favorite position of feet and legs extended, with ankles crossed and hands folded in her lap.

"Someday you will. When you're old like me," Agatha said rather sadly.

"Oh, I'm sorry, Sister Agatha. It's just one of those days. By the way, Sister, I've been waiting for you to regain your strength before I brought this up."

"What is it, Mother?" Agatha questioned with a trace of delight of being possibly presented with a problem to solve.

"It's your Billy. He has been calling, wanting to speak with you."

"My Billy, from school?" she asked excitedly.

"Yes, one in the same."

"I would love to speak with him. When is he coming?"

"That will have to be arranged, Agatha. I don't think it will be much longer before he's convicted for that mess he has gotten himself into. It's rather evident that he's going to go to jail, Sister."

"Oh, no," sighed Sister Agatha. "What happened to that boy? He knew better."

"We all know better. Especially after the fact," reminded Mother Veronica.

"That's certainly true," the reflective nun uttered remembering her own recent declaration of sin.

"Could you call him for me, Mother Veronica? Late morning or late afternoon of any day would be a good time to meet with him."

"I will, Agatha," she replied and as she uncurled from her position of comfort. "Do you want me to say a special prayer for you, Sister?"

"You must be kidding?" hastened Sister Agatha's answer.

"Yes, I was," Mother Veronica interjected as she sailed across the porch to meet the world.

Without knowing it, Sister Agatha began proceeding through her regimen of straightening. The only thing she was aware of, were her thoughts of Billy. *"I loved that kid."*

Sister Agatha went to the dining room at noontime with a mission in mind. She always worked that way, back in her teaching days that is. It invigorated her to set out with a goal; it brought back the excitement of planning and research that she had excelled in. She listened for Sister Ann's voice, and then proceeded over to her.

"Sister Ann, hello. May I join you for lunch?"

"Oh, my, yes Sister. Please sit down. You know Sister Lena and Sister Claire?"

"Yes of course. How are your studies progressing Sisters?"

And so, lunch flowed with chatter and laughter and stories, both from the present and from the past. The young entertained the old and the old entertained the young; a much-needed mixture, Sister Agatha discerned to herself.

Later that afternoon, when Sister Ann delivered the medications to the porch, she called out excitedly, "I have them, Sister—the old yearbooks from the library!"

"Good girl," Agatha said excitedly. "Would you mind looking up a few things for me?"

"Not at all, Sister. What are you looking for?"

"Not a 'what' but a 'who.' Billy Bransen, William Bransen. I remember him from his tenth, eleventh, and twelfth grades."

"Okay, let's see. Gosh, this was quite a few years ago," she said as she started with the index of names.

"Indeed it was," Sister Agatha agreed.

"Sure," the young one voiced, "there is information about him on pages twelve, twenty-nine, thirty-three, thirty-seven, fifty-two, and sixty-eight."

"Is that his sophomore year?"

"Let me check. Yes."

"Okay, could you read everything about him during that year? And then we'll go to the next and onto his senior year."

"Sure."

Sister Agatha rested her head against the back of the chair as the life and times of William Bransen came to life.

"My word, he was busy in school," Sister Ann announced a few times as she went on and on about clubs, sports, drama, and service groups.

"He had unbelievable energy for sure," Agatha remarked looking way beyond the horizon.

"And that's it!" Sister Ann proclaimed as she closed the last book. "What did he do after high school?"

"Oh, he went on to college and got himself a good job. He has a wife and children."

"Where is he now?"

"Ready to go off to jail," Sister said unemotionally.

"Jail?"

"I think he tried to get a little too smart for his own britches."

"Oh," sounded Ann. "Do you want me to take these back to the library for you?"

"No, dear, I'll need them for a few days. I'll let you know when I'm finished with them."

"Okay, Sister. Have a nice rest of the day. I'll see you at evening prayers."

"Thank you for doing this for me, Sister Ann."

Her, "You're welcome" drifted across the porch and in through the door while Billy Bransen remained on detention right next to Sister Agatha.

A man's voice torpedoed through the still air and exploded in Sister Agatha's ear, "Sister, thank you for seeing me. It's so good to see you."

"Billy?"

"Yes, Sister Agatha, it's me."

She listened to his assertive footsteps approaching and tried to calculate his presence. She had a sense of hugeness, of power, of after-shave, of a briefcase, a suit, of having a styled haircut. He bent to kiss her cheek—smooth-shaven, probably debonair, she imagined from images of the past.

"Sit down, William," she said almost shyly. Her sense of him loomed with such command she couldn't conjure the old teacher-student relationship.

It wasn't until he noticed the yearbooks and started to laugh that she regained the atmosphere she wanted.

"Oh my Lord. Don't tell me you still have these?" he asked paging through the top book.

"Well certainly. Don't you?"

"Oh, I suppose I do someplace. I couldn't tell you where they are right off hand."

He came across his team picture. "Ah, those were the days, Sister. I never thought that the world would change; I thought I would stay young and invincible forever."

"You certainly were full of life back in those days, Billy. Risk-taking, and yet right on target as far as standards and morals were concerned. You were such a natural leader; the other kids looked up to you and trusted your decisions. Didn't they?"

"Yeah, I guess they did," William said slowly.

Sister Agatha could feel his exuberance being deflated not only from his self, but also from his suit and his briefcase and even from his after-shave. He no longer was the CEO; he was the boy from school.

"Why did you want to see me, Billy?"

"I need your forgiveness, Sister."

"Oh, Bill, you don't need my forgiveness; you need God's forgiveness."

He lifted his head up out of his hands and said, "I can't speak to Him, Sister Agatha. I'm too ashamed."

"What do you think I am, chop suey?"

"Sister, no!" he laughed. "This is why I can come to you, I know you can laugh; I know you're fair; I know you are forgiving. Do you remember the time you handed back our essays on 'What It Means to Live in America' and you were so angry at us for doing a mediocre job?"

"Yes! And you, Billy, yelled out: 'Get out of the boat and walk on the water'!"

"Exactly, and you laughed for the next five minutes! Then you handed back our papers and told us to 'walk on the water.'"

"But I wasn't a very good teacher."

"What are you saying? You were the best!"

"Apparently not, I didn't teach you that you could go to God with anything at anytime."

"You did teach us that, Sister. I remember you saying it." He paused and then added, "I guess I opted not to do it."

"Billy? What went wrong? It's so out of character for you to be fraudulent in anything you do. You were always so honest. I loved you for that."

"Oh, sister," he groaned as he took her hand. "I wish I could go back to those days." She could feel his wedding ring press against hers. This, she realized was a symbol of their adult life; he was no longer her teenager Billy. "I became successful, Sister, and then more successful with more and more of an income. I finally could give my wife and my children everything. I was on the ride of my lifetime, Sister. I was on top of the world."

"I don't hear anything sinful yet, William," she interjected.

"No, that part wasn't sinful. It began when I wanted more—more to the tune of getting it dishonestly."

And that's when Sister Agatha's prayers that she so generously offered up over all those years for her students came back a hundred-fold and pierced Billy's soul as would a torpedo ripping through the ocean.

William wept to the very core of his being. His tears totally immersed their golden wedding bands and squeezed through their fingers until they dripped down to the porch floor to be devoured by the hot sunshine. They would, Sister Agatha knew, return back into the heavens.

"I am so sorry, Sister," he cried.

"I know you are Billy. I know you are," she cried. "Tell God."

"I will, Sister Agatha, I will."

As she held his huge body in her little arms she could hear the pages of the yearbook being turned by the breeze.

❧

Sister Agatha lifted her head towards the Holy Eucharist just as she had done every morning during the Mass. She needed no eyesight to see it. She could see her bridegroom, Jesus. He was there, always there to counsel, to give her courage, and to tell her he loved her.

"I love you, too," she whispered, just as she had done every morning. And that was all Sister Agatha remembered of that day. She slowly crumbled downward onto the kneeling bench, not making a sound, not making as much as a sigh. The nun to her left, the nun to her right, and those in the pew behind her were the only ones who witnessed the crumbling of Sister Agatha.

The little nun lay on her bed totally unaware of the world around her. She was attended each day by her sisters, every hour upon the hour, day and night. The Christ from her crucifix looked down upon her. The statue of Mary gazed relentlessly upon her daughter. The priest came to give her the sacrament of Last Rites. It was very unlike Sister Agatha to be unresponsive to a sacrament.

Her sisters prayed for her, prayed for her happy union with God, if that was to be His Will. They prayed for her speedy recovery, if that was to be His Will.

They didn't know that Sister Agatha was only unaware to the things of the world. In her time of stillness, Agatha saw many things and heard many things. And smelled and touched and tasted many things.

She shared raspberries with her mother. Oh, her dear mother, what a joy!

She held little Michael on her lap and bounced him up and down. He laughed and laughed and laughed.

She watched her father as he carved out her cradle. She had never known how lovingly he waited for her to be born.

She and Janelle went arm-and-arm through the apple orchard, talking and laughing and crying. Agatha told Janelle they had to find Jillian's baby but Janelle kept telling her not to be silly, "I have no great grandchild here, Agatha. Stop saying that."

Sister Agatha begged Janelle to find the baby; she could hear him crying. Janelle always said the same thing, "I have no great grandchild here."

She knew she heard the baby crying. She twisted and turned trying to look behind each apple tree.

"Sister? Sister Agatha, wake up! Sister, you're awake!"

Indeed Sister Agatha had returned to her consciousness.

"Who is it?" she said weakly.

"It's Jillian, Sister. It's me. I've been coming here every day to tell you I'm going to keep my baby!"

"Ah, Janelle, congratulations," she murmured.

Sister Agatha did some of her recuperation on the porch. There she mentored to the young ones and conversed with the older ones. There she soaked in her God and smiled to know that the baby birds had grown up and flown off into the world.

Chapter Nineteen

THE JOURNEY

"**N**o Marjory. No one has ever heard what became of Miss April.
I'm sure one of these days she'll show up."

April laughed to herself as she started over the mountain. Three months ago she had strategically angled the map on the console to check it after every turn onto the next road, and to the next road, and the next. That's how it was on her weekly trek, one little road after another.

Now there was no map, just that which was in her head. She knew how many miles each segment was and it all added up—each time the same. There had been landmarks, which April had used over and over with a feeling of relief when each was spotted. The landmarks had then been replaced by others, or encountered with no great exhilaration.

April felt relaxed; a feeling quite contrary to three months ago when it was a toss-up as to which was more rigid: April's neck or the axles on the car.

She looked to the left to see a long row of sunflowers by the red barn with the cupola, and wondered why they had escaped her notice. She quickly looked to the other side of the road. That's why— she always looked at the pond with the ducks. *I've got to branch out more*, April amused herself with the thought as she realized there was another whole world on the other side of the road. For the rest of the trip she vowed to concentrate on the unfamiliar. Sometimes it worked, but most times it didn't. The familiar was comforting, but finding something just a little out of place became a game to April.

Oh, look at the young woman carrying a baby in the flower garden. I wonder if they live there... Probably the baby had been fussing and the new mother needed a change of scenery. What a wonderful idea. Now the mother would know what to do next time. *I'm glad I got to see them; they looked so sweet among the blossoms— happy times that the baby will never remember. And when the child grows up and tells her mother that she never did anything for her, the mother can tell her about the 'garden tours'. I hope the mother doesn't forget; it would be a nice story. It might soften her daughter's heart.*

April drove on. *Hmm, when did they get chickens? I'm sure I would have noticed chickens in the front yard! I hope they stay put and don't go wondering out into the road. The kids will have a good time finding the eggs, if those are the kind of chickens that lay eggs. I think they are.*

Woah! Sorry mister. I better pay attention to what I'm doing, April reprimanded herself as she jolted the wheel.

I can't believe that the leaves are starting to turn color, April thought as she looked onto the puffy treetops. *There must be a billion trees on this mountain, a trillion, a...what on earth? Oh, no, what has burned to the ground? What was there?* April slowed the car as she went by the black charred remains. What had been there, a house? Yes! But why couldn't she picture it? *How terrible to lose your home, I wonder where the people are now? I can't imagine losing everything. I guess that's why you don't store up treasures on earth.* April tried to think of "treasures" that she had. She didn't really have any. *Good,* she thought. *Good,* as she drove on.

Hmm, that's odd; I wonder why that front door is wide open? Oh well, must be some reason. There are so many side roads up here, April thought as she read each and every name as she went by. *How do they come up with these names?* She laughed as she sailed by Beaver Tail Road. *There must be a huge beaver pond down there,* she thought as she stretched her neck only to see trees. *Maybe someday I'll go early and take a tour of some of these side roads.*

Ah, the horses, five horses always grazing in that field. *So you two are buddies today, are you?* She noticed that the Palomino was closest to the black horse today. Usually the Palomino was off by himself. She wondered where they would be kept in the wintertime.

Well! What's going on here? There were cars and trucks lined on both sides of the road and up into the driveway. *Must be a party or a reunion, but in the middle of the week like this and at this time of day? Oh, maybe it's a gathering after a funeral.* She wondered who died. She wondered if anyone would be at her funeral; it didn't matter to her. She grinned. She wasn't going to be there.

How can they have that place landscaped so beautifully all the time? She looked at the chalet on the hillside. Now both sides of the long driveway were lined with mum plants. "That is gorgeous," she sighed. She wondered when they did all the work; never had she seen a person outside. She recalled the rows of red and pink geraniums that had processed up the hill before the mums appeared. *That is a large piece of land to keep mowed, too.* She thought of her own tiny plot.

Oh, oh, oh. Why are the cows in the road?

A man in blue denims sauntered over after she had come to a stop, "Sorry, ma'am. Just taking these critters from one pasture to another."

April watched the big bellies of the cows sway from side to side as they walked past her car. One stopped and looked squarely at April. "Okay, you just go along now you old bossy cow," she said as she envisioned the entire herd coming to a standstill.

She and the cows parted company, with April traveling south trying to avoid the remains left upon the road—as the bovines headed north with no worries of leaving remains.

Isn't it odd that the milk we drink comes from those animals? She pondered the thought while she returned the car to its normal speed for going over the mountain. With the constant need to diminish speed for curves and unexpected circumstances, she learned it was futile to apply the cruise control.

Wow! Look at all the sheets hanging on that line! From a distance it looked like a huge sea of sailboats blowing across the ocean. The whiteness was startling as the waves rose and fell with the wind. *White? They were all white? That was a rarity these days.* She wondered if someone in that house was ill. She checked the sailboats in her rear view mirror. They were still sailing.

She looked at the huge stone house that was partially dug into the side hill, and then quickly glanced to the right hoping there wasn't anything of significance there. *Good, just trees.* April took her foot off the gas pedal as she always did in that stretch; there was so much to see, so much to wonder about. *What had it been? Who lived there at one time? Why were there barns and carriage houses and sheds and...a gazebo!* She had never noticed that before; it was partially secluded behind the apple orchard. The grape arbors were heavy with clusters of dark blue grapes that she could see from the road. There were still perennials that would not give up the ghost, even though they were tight in between the weeds. April could see stonewalls and stone walkways. Someday she would go early just to stop at the edge of the road and look at the estate.

Beep!

"Judas Priest!" April emitted with a start. A pickup truck raced past with a stern looking passenger glaring at "the stupid woman driver." She quickly closed the window to keep the dust out.

April didn't accelerate very much after going past the stone building, because just around the bend was the beer-can house, as she called it. She always got a kick out of seeing how many cases of beer cans were stacked around the garage. She assumed they were the empties. All summer she had observed the stacks grow and multiply. They were now rising on the south side of the building as well. *Why was someone doing that? Where were those cans coming from? You would think they would be turned in for the refund. Oh, maybe it's an organization collecting for a charity.*

356

April drove through a little hamlet of six houses. It almost seemed that it was a small community with the neighbors outside talking to each other and the children playing together. It seemed like they had each other for protection, but who would those people living out in the country have for protection? April felt her forehead break into a sweat. She turned on the air.

Ah, the vegetable stand. April slowed to look at the huge pile of pumpkins. That was new from last week. She quickly opened the window, hoping the apple aroma would drift into the car. She had stopped there a few times. She thought of the blackberries and their dark color, which glistened out from the surrounding white milk and sugar in her bowl. The thought made her swallow.

She exhaled loudly as she came up behind the back end of a tractor. Oh, well, she knew the farmer would pull over as soon as he realized she was there. It took a few minutes but over he went. She waved. He waved. What was it about farmers? Why were they so kind? Did they get it from working in the soil?

There's the little church. Tonight, when she returned in darkness, she knew there would be cars parked under the huge maples and the lights would be on inside the building. This was their meeting night of some sort. Even though there never were more than five cars, they were always there; they must be a good and faithful group.

Stop ahead. Another landmark. She entered the tiny town with the one store—a very busy store nevertheless. She always saw cars out in front. Probably a lot of chatter inside with, *What's going on?* She imagined if she stopped and went in, everyone would cease their conversation and look at her. She didn't envision having to go in for any reason, but she might have to someday. Just as she turned onto the next road it came to her that there must be more of the town to the right. Someday she would drive that way and see.

There was the bar with the never-changed sign for "Karaoke on Sat. Nites." There were always vehicles at Big Ideas. April wondered if the people who drank there during the week came back on Saturday nights to sing. She wondered if the beer-can house contributors ever met at Big Ideas.

April liked the next road to the right because in a few minutes she would pass by a restaurant fashioned out of an old Victorian house. Someday she would stop there. She especially liked to look at it on her return trip; the five-globe lampposts would be lit and, if she went slow enough, which she always did, she could peer in to see the patrons sitting under the sparkling chandeliers. There were two dining rooms on the roadside. She wondered if there were more on the other side of the house. April thought about the excitement of going there someday. Someday soon. Just past the restaurant was the lake. *Oh, my...*April gushed as she nearly stopped the car to see the colored foliage reflected upon the water. The bluest of blue skies was also painted across the lake as the colors spread themselves calmly over the top. Two rowboats dotted the center, as the navigators seemed to be having a conversation. *How interesting*, April thought. *What a lovely place to meet and visit.* The thought carried with her for the next few miles when she suddenly realized she hadn't been looking for landmarks. She panicked when she didn't recognize anything. Then she saw the road sign: "Shoe Fly Road." *Whew!* Now she knew where she was.

Well, that's pretty, she thought as she saw an arrangement of cornstalks, pumpkins, and mums in a wheelbarrow. *They ought to have a black cat in there.* She smiled with the thought—just as she slammed on the brakes for a real black cat to dart across the road. April watched the black paws scurry across the lawn to the wheelbarrow. "I can't believe it!" she laughed. The cat ran underneath the old boards of the antique and looked out with great superiority.

Bang! April flung forwards as the seat belt dug into her neck. Her head bobbed up to see a car in the rearview mirror. Before she could think, a man was at her window banging on it and motioning her to roll it down. "What the hell is the matter with you? Why did you stop in the middle of the road? Don't you know anything?"

"The cat," April said weakly.

"You stopped for a cat?" continued the gruff voice.

"I-I..."

"Never mind, let me see your insurance card and your license."

April didn't know if she was supposed to show him but she did. She watched as he scribbled down his name and insurance information and flung it through the window. The dust flew as he squealed his tires past her; April looked over at the cat that had turned its back to her. She drove off wondering if she was supposed to call the police.

April thought about the police. She rubbed the back of her neck. She knew there were a few more interesting spots she always looked at but now she didn't move her head left or right. She stared at the road wondering how it could sail underneath the car as she sat basically motionless. The reality of...*when you're walking, you do the moving and the road remains still*...meandered through her mind.

She arrived.

"Late again?" Mr. Farley grunted as he looked from her to the clock.

"I'm sorry, Mr. Farley," April almost whispered.

"You criminal broads sure know how to take advantage of the system, don't you?"

"Yes, sir. I mean, no sir," she stuttered as she felt her face reddening.

"Sit down and give me your weekly report."

April fumbled through her folder. As she handed him the report, she gasped as she watched her pencil drawing drift to the floor; she swooped for it like a bird for a worm.

"What is that?" he demanded as he arose like a geyser.

"It's nothing," she murmured.

"Let me see it!"

April slowly handed him the drawing.

He lowered himself to the chair as he looked at the landscape.

"I suppose you did this?"

"Yes."

"You don't think you have talent now, do you?"

"No, sir."

"That's right, because you don't. You jailhouse sluts have no talent except for killing and getting your men into trouble. That's the only talent you have."

April looked at her probation officer with her hollow, bottomless eyes. She thought of the lake, the sunflowers, the clothesline—they all had substance. He had none.

"So this is what you do in your spare time?"

"Sometimes," she muttered.

"Why didn't you ever mention it in your weekly reports?" he questioned as she watched his nostrils pulsating.

"I didn't think it was important," she answered as she looked at the bottom of his desk; a ridge of dirt had formed on the edge probably from a dirty mop.

"That's true, it certainly isn't anything of importance. But you know the rules: you write down everything that you do during the week. Right?"

"Right," she managed to squeak out.

"So," he continued as he leaned back in his swivel chair and spread a hauntingly sly grin across his face, "you sit around and draw instead of taking your drugs?"

April's stiff, aching neck pulled upwards. "I don't take drugs. My husband did."

"Oh sure, yeah, all you women sing the same tune; you are as innocent as hell when the law comes knocking at your door. It's always the man who's guilty, right?"

"I don't take drugs," she reiterated.

"You women are all the same, don't try to kid me," Farley said as he suddenly lurched forward with his nostrils moving similarly to the pulsation of milking machines. "Just because you're out of the pen, don't think we're not watching your every move. Now, here is another example of your lying and deceiving," he growled as he waved the drawing in the air. This," he said dramatically, "will go into your file as evidence."

"Evidence of what?" April exploded negating the vow she had made to herself last week that she would never lose her temper with Farley again.

"Evidence that you're a liar and you have a history of hiding evidence; that the self-defense plea you gave at your trial was a lie; your husband didn't attack you, you killed him because you were sick of him, you wanted another man!"

April dug her fingernails into the palms of her hand and when Farley heard nothing but silence, he obviously took it to mean he had scored the point and went on. "All week and this is all you did?" He asked as he looked up from the report. "What are you not telling?"

"I told everything," she replied, hating every minute of the meeting.

"Yeah right: Thursday—grocery shopped; Friday—did laundry; Saturday—went to the park; Sunday—went to Church; Monday—cleaned house; Tuesday—went through photo albums. Why can't you be truthful enough to put everything down? What are you ashamed of? What are you hiding?"

April felt her neck pain traveling and tightening throughout her body, as a piano tuner twisting each string until it was ready to snap.

When there was no reply, Farley continued, "You know, you are just getting yourself deeper and deeper into trouble. I can see where it won't be long before you are right back in the slammer."

"I haven't done anything wrong!" she screamed as she jumped out of the chair.

"Well, well, well. What do we have here? A belligerent, hostile, uncooperative ex-con?" he cooed sweeter than a morning dove.

April slumped down into her chair and unconsciously began rocking forward and backward.

"That's better," Farley grinned. "You need a little taming, don't you, honey? Now, I'm sorry I have to write you up for this unfortunate meeting we had today, but maybe next time things will run a little smoother. Don't you agree?"

April left without saying a word and ran to her car. The tears flowed as soon as she closed the door.

"God, help me, help me," she sobbed into the steering wheel. April didn't know how long she had sat in the parking lot, but when she raised her head, the two streetlights seemed to signal her to go home.

She drove slowly with heaviness bearing down upon her shoulders; everything felt heavy, even the blackness of the night seemed to weigh down upon her. She realized that she was so slumped in the seat, her eye level was only one centimeter above the steering wheel. She pulled her body up, feeling pain in each movement. Words from her counselors began filtering into her thoughts. She remembered her discussions of focusing, inner strength, faith, courage, determination, and—she straightened her posture because, as they used to say—"You are worth something, you are." By the time she got to the Victorian restaurant she was able to look at the twinkling chandeliers and the couples inside. "Thank you, God, for helping me with my thoughts," she humbly said.

The way home looked so different in the dark. She liked seeing light in the houses, but it was hard for her to know which house she was actually looking at. Yet some she always knew. Those that were strategically located, or those that were well lit.

The bar always stuck out like a sore thumb, with its neon beer signs, but a cold chill crept over her as she noticed some sort of ruckus going on in the parking lot. It looked like a woman was being pushed into a parked car. A screaming siren and flashing lights suddenly came up behind April. The police car pulled into Big Ideas. April kept going.

There were still customers at the little country store. Soon they'd have a new story to talk about. April envisioned the gossip that must have run rampant when she killed her husband. She felt her stomach churn like a slow-kneading bread maker. April quickly rolled down the window for air.

She drove somewhat in a trance until she saw the church, and sure enough, the lights were on with four cars outside. April thought that some evening she would stop and ask if she could be included.

Shining animal eyes were occasionally caught in the beams of her headlights and she thanked the deer for waiting as she went by. She wondered what the black cat was doing and wondered if there had been a funeral, and wondered if the baby from the flower garden was safely tucked into bed. She couldn't recall where she had seen the white sheets or where the large stone estate was—it had no caretaker to turn on the lights. Well, next week she would try to notice everything.

April started her trip thirty minutes earlier than last week, to take in more of the mountain's life. Well, in actuality, she didn't want to be late. She began having thoughts of the Farley "demon," but tried to dismiss them as she had been taught. "Change your train of thought when it starts to engulf you," she could still hear Betty say. She liked Betty; Betty was compassionate and kind.

Oh, look! April rejoiced to herself as her eyes absorbed every mauve, gold, and yellow ocher. Every tree was showing its originality. They weren't just a mass of green anymore; they were unique individuals. April laughed at her thoughts, which resembled the sessions with Betty: "We are unique individuals; we're all special to God."

Maybe I'll add some color to my pencil drawings, April thought. *Maybe it's color that I need.*

Hello, sunflowers; hello, ducks; oh, the baby! April waved to the young mother with the baby. The mother waved back! "I love you, sweet child," April whispered as tears came to her eyes.

She dove into the cache of clichés that had been passed on to her from her group-mates and counselors. She came up with, "Live in the present; it's your gift from God." She took a deep breath and journeyed on.

Well, there it is—a chicken in the road. April laughed as she slowed and watched it waddle across. *What do you get when a chicken crosses the road?* she quizzed herself. She didn't know why she couldn't remember the answer.

Oh, dear, the fire, April recalled as she drove past. That definitely didn't show up in the darkness last week. She pictured it in full blaze during the nighttime; the night must have been in startled horror as it was exposed to the phenomenon of fire.

Well, look at that. April's attention was drawn to three backhoes carving out the sod of the mountain. Someone must be building a new home. *How exciting.* She had once had a dream of having her own house to share with her husband and their little girl. She hoped those people would have better luck than she did. April sighed as she rubbed the back of her neck.

"Oh, nuts!" she groaned after she realized she had gone past the horses.

There was no big crowd at the funeral house like last Wednesday; all had gone back to their regular business. She thought of her husband's funeral—she hadn't been there.

She flipped on the air conditioner to jolt herself out of the past. "Do not dwell in the past," her mentor's words resounded in her ears. *You're right, you're right,* she inaudibly responded. Her past dissipated just as she approached the remains of the once glorious stone house. *Oh, my goodness, there is a car.* April slowly drove by with her imagination running wild as she conjured up scenarios as to what was happening. Her greatest hope was that someone would restore it to its glory.

How did I get to the little church already? April wondered in disbelief. What am I doing? She held tighter to the steering wheel as she counseled herself to pay attention. Okay, there's the Stop sign and the store and Big Ideas. That damn name, I hate it. She unconsciously fell back into her muck and mired past.

It wasn't until she saw the wheelbarrow that she came back to the present. By then, her disappointment of missing the restaurant and the lake—combined with the fender bender incident—gave her an immediate headache. "Oh," she groaned as she massaged the back of her head. She remembered the paper the man had flung at her; it still lay on the counter by the telephone. She couldn't bring herself to call. Maybe she didn't need to; the dent wasn't that bad.

❧

"Well, well, well, don't tell me you're on time?" Farley looked up from his paperwork.

"Am I?" April appeared surprised, then chastised herself for giving him an opening to disparage her from the very start.

He didn't take that opportunity however. Instead, he slunk into his cunning mode with, "I have been waiting all afternoon to see you Ms. Randall; we have a little situation to talk about."

April sunk into the chair knowing she was headed for the hot seat. She immediately hung her head but snapped it back to eye level when she remembered how important her comportment was going to be.

"It has come to my attention, Ms. Randall, that you had a vehicular accident last week, and you never reported it."

"It was nothing, only a little dent."

"Well, the other party reported it saying you were stopped in the middle of the road. Is that correct?"

"I had to stop for the cat."

"You had to stop for the cat," he said slowly, trying to mimic her voice. "Now isn't that interesting; you wouldn't kill a cat but you would kill another human being?"

"I've told you a million times," April screamed as she jumped out of the chair, "my husband was going to kill me; I had to defend myself. I didn't try to kill him. I didn't know he was going to die!"

"You are totally irresponsible," he erupted. "This business of causing an accident is more proof of that. My folder on you is getting fatter and fatter, you better believe that!"

"What's going on in there?" a voice came to the door.

"Nothing, nothing," Farley bellowed.

"You see," the probation officer said in a quiet voice, "everyone is aware of your transgressions."

"I can't take this any longer," April cried as she swung open the door.

"Where is your report? I have to see your report!" he screamed down the hallway after her. April knew he would use that against her, too. He might even send the police after her tonight. "Oh, God, oh God, help me," she cried as she ran to her car.

∽

No one ever saw April Randall after that night. The woman with the baby remembered her waving, the farmer with the cows recalled seeing her the previous Wednesday, and the people at the store wished they had seen her. There was no one left in April's life who cared; everyone had abandoned her. Now she was just a piece of information waiting to be a statistic. Her case didn't have to be solved. No one made it a priority.

But, interestingly enough, ten years later the owner of the Victorian restaurant claims he has seen a woman on several occasions walk across his dock to a rowboat and then disappear.

366

ꙮChapter Twentyꙮ

JUST WORDS

"**I**t's a new business in town, Marjory. Isn't it nice to have some of the empty storefronts occupied again?

I can't believe you remember that. Yes, years ago it was a toy store.

Sometimes you absolutely amaze me, Margie."

"Lily, what can I say about this thing?"

Lily looked up from her keyboard and asked, "What is it?"

"I don't know. What do you call those things that tie in the back and keep your clothes clean while you're cooking?"

"Good grief, Maddy. It's an apron," Lily laughed.

"Yeah, that's right. My Tanta Lena used to wear one all the time."

"Maddy, you have to be creative. Look at the material, look at the pattern, notice the details, and think why a prospective customer would buy an apron. Make it appealing through your words. Make it irresistible." Lily spoke with such a flair of excitement, it motivated the young novice to delve into her mind's pool of adjectives.

Lily went back to her work of describing a silk scarf for the new fall catalog.

Wrap your shoulders in a cloud of silk with the illusion of a fall garden. Golden splashes will intermingle with an azure sky. This scarf is a must for your autumn wardrobe in a generous 36" x 36" landscape of tranquility and surprise.

The young woman interrupted the silence of creativity, "How does this sound, Lily?"

Keep clean the bright way. Order this apron for a fun way of fixing dinner. The sunflowers will brighten any kitchen.

Oh, my, thought Lily. *Four years of college for this?* "Actually Maddy, you are on the right track. Try to add more of an allure—a feeling that the customer will want to achieve when she adorns herself with the apron."

Maddy went back into her discerning mode. She stood and swirled the apron around. She put it on...she fluttered it. *That's good,* thought Lily, *a necessary procedure for bringing it to life.*

"I've got it!" squealed the newest writer as she sailed into her desk chair causing it to wheel past the keyboard. "Aha, aha, this is it! Listen to this Lily:

"Dance into dinnertime with your significant other and these cheery sunflowers. You won't miss a step or an ingredient in this romantic apron.

"How's that?"

Lily looked into the anxious, excited eyes of the beginner and smiled. "You're getting into it now. Work on it a little more; polish it up a bit, and I think you'll have a winner," came the answer laced with delicacy.

Lily printed out her description and laid it in the box with the scarf, which would be picked up by Leslie for the secondary approval. She then walked to the table to select another box. *How exciting,* she thought. What would it be? Which one should she choose? *Ah, look at the tiny one. I wonder what this is?*

Lily sat at her desk and very carefully opened the lid. "Oh, my goodness!" she uttered softly.

"What did you get?" Maddy called out from the adjacent desk.

"It's a tiny glass turtle with its back painted with pink roses."

"What would anyone do with that?"

"It's just for decoration," Lily said gently as she held the little turtle up to the light.

"Well, good luck with that thing, and can you listen for a second?"

"Sure."

"Dance into dinnertime with these cheerful sunflowers. You won't miss a step or an ingredient in this lovely apron."

"I like it! Put it in for submission and we'll see if it makes the grade."

Maddy almost skipped to the "finished" table, and then over to the "select" table. Lily hoped that Maddy was feeling the fun and excitement of the job; she hoped that the young woman would feel fulfilled and stay longer than the last three had. "Which one shall I choose? Which one shall I choose?" she heard Maddy singing to herself.

Lily looked at her new little turtle friend and placed it on her highest shelf, followed by the middle shelf and the lowest. Each time she noticed how the light played with it and noticed too, its shadow. She experimented with different positions, even putting it upside down.

"Oh, nuts," Maddy exclaimed in a disappointed tone.

Lily looked up from her turtle. "What did you get?"

"A stupid umbrella," Maddy whined as she slumped in her chair resting her chin in her hands.

"Maddy! Rain is a terrific subject to work with!"

"Rain? Oh, yeah! I didn't think of that angle."

Lily smiled and shook her head as she went back to her wee, glistening creature.

Can you imagine this little turtle on your shelf or on your desk, always there to greet you with pink roses? A faithful friend to comfort you when the day is tedious. With its glistening glass, it will gather every bit of light for you and save it for that rainy day.

Thanks for the rainy day theme, Lily thought as she looked over at her coworker. Lily burst into laughter when she saw Maddy sitting under the umbrella with her feet up on the desk.

"What on earth are you doing?"

"Just trying to get in the mood of this thing." Maddy explained as she extended her hand as if feeling for raindrops. "What did you write about the turtle?

"Cool," Maddy sighed after she heard it.

Leslie came in to gather the objects from the "done" table. "Boy, I wish I had your job," she said looking directly at the relaxed umbrella girl. Lily couldn't help but think of what Leslie's "real" job was.

"This isn't easy, you know," Maddy said defensively as she swung her legs down to reality. "It takes a long time to come up with just the right description."

"Seems to me that it's Lily who is coming up with most of the descriptions," Leslie said arrogantly to the newcomer as she swooped boxes into her arms.

Don't patronize me, thought Lily as she turned her seething face away from Leslie. *Just because I know what really goes on in Mr. Morrison's office, don't do me any favors.*

Lily let her leave without adding the turtle to her menagerie; the turtle could go with the next swoop.

"Never mind her, Maddy. No one expects you to write as quickly as someone who has done this for twelve years."

ᙅᔕ✧Chapter Nineteen✧ᔕᙁ

THE JOURNEY

"No Marjory. No one has ever heard what became of Miss April.

I'm sure one of these days she'll show up."

April laughed to herself as she started over the mountain. Three months ago she had strategically angled the map on the console to check it after every turn onto the next road, and to the next road, and the next. That's how it was on her weekly trek, one little road after another.

Now there was no map, just that which was in her head. She knew how many miles each segment was and it all added up—each time the same. There had been landmarks, which April had used over and over with a feeling of relief when each was spotted. The landmarks had then been replaced by others, or encountered with no great exhilaration.

April felt relaxed; a feeling quite contrary to three months ago when it was a toss-up as to which was more rigid: April's neck or the axles on the car.

She looked to the left to see a long row of sunflowers by the red barn with the cupola, and wondered why they had escaped her notice. She quickly looked to the other side of the road. That's why— she always looked at the pond with the ducks. *I've got to branch out more*, April amused herself with the thought as she realized there was another whole world on the other side of the road. For the rest of the trip she vowed to concentrate on the unfamiliar. Sometimes it worked, but most times it didn't. The familiar was comforting, but finding something just a little out of place became a game to April.

Oh, look at the young woman carrying a baby in the flower garden. I wonder if they live there… Probably the baby had been fussing and the new mother needed a change of scenery. What a wonderful idea. Now the mother would know what to do next time. *I'm glad I got to see them; they looked so sweet among the blossoms— happy times that the baby will never remember. And when the child grows up and tells her mother that she never did anything for her, the mother can tell her about the 'garden tours'. I hope the mother doesn't forget; it would be a nice story. It might soften her daughter's heart.*

April drove on. *Hmm, when did they get chickens? I'm sure I would have noticed chickens in the front yard! I hope they stay put and don't go wondering out into the road. The kids will have a good time finding the eggs, if those are the kind of chickens that lay eggs. I think they are.*

Woah! Sorry mister. I better pay attention to what I'm doing, April reprimanded herself as she jolted the wheel.

I can't believe that the leaves are starting to turn color, April thought as she looked onto the puffy treetops. *There must be a billion trees on this mountain, a trillion, a…what on earth? Oh, no, what has burned to the ground? What was there?* April slowed the car as she went by the black charred remains. What had been there, a house? Yes! But why couldn't she picture it? *How terrible to lose your home, I wonder where the people are now? I can't imagine losing everything. I guess that's why you don't store up treasures on earth.* April tried to think of "treasures" that she had. She didn't really have any. *Good,* she thought. *Good,* as she drove on.

Hmm, that's odd; I wonder why that front door is wide open? Oh well, must be some reason. There are so many side roads up here, April thought as she read each and every name as she went by. *How do they come up with these names?* She laughed as she sailed by Beaver Tail Road. *There must be a huge beaver pond down there,* she

"Sounds good to me. Let's walk down to the park, shall we?"

As the two women gathered their things, Leslie drove off in her car. She never ate lunch with them.

Both women studied the trees and the flowers and the breeze. They looked at the shadows and the knotholes and the depth of the woods. Before either one had eaten even half a sandwich, Lily brought out her notepad and Maddy had secured her pencil and sketchpad. Both worked in silence, one in words, and the other in pictures. Lily wiped a drop of peach juice from her prose and Maddy could be seen occasionally brushing cookie crumbs from her illustration. The entire hour was a quiet, creative experience, which both women languished in.

Suddenly, Lily looked at her watch. "Oh! Come on Maddy, we're going to be late!"

"Already?"

"Yes! Come on!"

The two women were panting when they came face to face with Leslie. "Late again?"

"Sorry, Leslie. The time got away from us. We'll make it up on the other end."

"I know you will," Leslie replied curtly as she walked away.

As the women settled at their computers, Lily quietly said to Maddy, "Let me see what you drew today."

Maddy reached into her satchel and brought out her sketchpad, holding it up for Lily to see.

"Oh, Maddy! It's exquisite! How are you able to put in so much detail?"

"I love detail in my drawings; the more the better," she laughed.

"And what did you write?"

Lily brought out her tablet and handed it to her young comrade. Maddy read in silence as she occasionally looked up to her own drawing. Of course the piece was filled with Lily's forte, her descriptive way of painting a picture with words. "I can't believe it," Maddy sighed.

"What's that?"

"The way you can write like an artist!"

"But look how you can illustrate like a writer!"

"Well, we better get cracking here, before Miss Beetle Bomb comes in," Maddy laughed.

"Maddy, don't call her that," Lily whispered to her.

Lily could hear the charm bracelet tinkling as Maddy turned it around and around. "I don't know what to say about this thing other than what I've already said," Maddy whined.

"Why don't you try looking at it like you were going to sketch it. I think you'd see lots of details if you thought of it in that light."

"Now that's a unique thought," the artist said quietly as she looked at the bracelet with new interest.

It wasn't long before Maddy called out, "How does this look?"

"Look?" repeated her mentor. Lily glanced over to see that Maddy had sketched the charm bracelet. "Well, it looks great but we're getting paid for the words, not the pictures."

"Yeah, I know," Maddy said, disappointed. "Too bad. Hey!" She suddenly bolted upright, "Why don't you write the words and I'll draw the illustrations. Wouldn't that make a neat catalog?"

Lily became very pensive and finally answered, "You know, you're right. But all of that would have to be presented to Mr. Morrison. For now, we'll have to continue with the same format, using the photographs. But why don't you work up your idea and present it to him? It can't hurt to ask. Maybe we could do it for the Christmas catalog or the spring catalog!"

"Ooo, I'm so excited," chirped Maddy as she settled into trying to write about the charm bracelet. She knew she'd have to work on the proposal at home.

Two mornings later Maddy radiated into the room waving her neatly typed proposition. "I've done it! Lily, read this and see what you think."

Lily read through Maddy's proposal and looked over the accompanying pages of illustrations. She was amazed at how direct and precise Maddy explained her idea. There was no fluff or endless adjectives that Lily was so good at in describing the products. Now she realized that Maddy was a different type of writer, and a good writer at that.

"This is wonderful, Maddy!" Lily said in all honesty. "Do you want to take it into Mr. Morrison now?"

"Sure! He might be in a good mood this early in the morning." The young entrepreneur giggled.

Lily walked to the table for her first mystery package of the day hoping that Mr. Morrison would at least listen to her coworker's idea.

"Lily!" Maddy whispered as she swept back into the room and braced her body against the door.

Lily looked at the horrified face of her friend and watched the papers in her hand shake.

"My gosh, what's the matter?"

Maddy's eyes were huge, her mouth was open, but no words emerged.

"What on earth is the matter with you? Here, sit down."

Lily removed the jittering papers from the girl's hand and wheeled her desk chair close to hers.

"What is it, dear?"

"Leslie...I walked in...Mr. Morrison...Leslie...I forgot to knock...they..."

"Oh, no."

Maddy clasped her hands over her mouth and became a statue. Lily became half a statue, as well. The two women sat in silence each wondering what was going to transpire in the next few minutes. Maddy was sure she was going to lose her job and Lily thought she would just as soon work somewhere else. The silence dragged on.

"What should we do?" Maddy whispered to her mentor.

Lily lifted her eyebrows and her shoulders. She herself had been through this embarrassing scenario before. The door didn't open nor did the intercom sound. Finally Lily whispered, "I guess we should just go back to work."

"I can't work after what I saw!"

"I'm sorry you had to experience that, dear," Lily said sympathetically. "Maybe…"

Three loud raps came upon the door. The two women jumped.

"Oh, God," Maddy groaned.

"Just remember, you didn't do anything wrong."

"Are you girls working?" Mr. Morrison questioned much like the Gestapo.

Lily stood up tall, and as Maddy peeked over at her, she never recalled Lily ever standing so tall and erect.

"Actually, no, Mr. Morrison," Lily spoke calmly, "we're not working."

"Well that's why I'm here," he paused to glare at Maddy. "It has come to my attention that Miss Jorgeson's work is not up to the standards of this company and I need to let her go."

"That's okay, I want to go," Maddy muttered, seemingly very much intimidated.

"And me?" Lily asked without flinching a muscle.

"Oh, no, no, your work is superior," he uttered as he flashed a fake smile and began showing signs of nervousness.

"I'll be leaving, too, Mr. Morrison."

"What? After twelve years? Who's going to hire you at your age?"

"Well, this talented lady," Lily paused to look at Maddy, "has a brilliant plan for a new business, and I'd be honored if she would hire me!"

Chapter Twenty-One

VISIONS

"*D*on't ask me what's going on in that school. *All I know is that rich woman left them some money.* Yes, the school you used to go to.*"

"You've got to be kidding me! Ceasar the Snake did this?" Ms. Wilson exclaimed as she stared at the oil painting of delicate lavenders and pinks cascading across the field of blowing grass.

"Shh," her colleague whispered. She peered in either direction of the hallway to see if a student had been close enough to hear the "snake" title.

"I can't believe that idiot has this kind of talent and…and…sensitivities," she continued, deriding Ceasar Bellimore, alias Ceasar the Snake.

"Well," the English teacher interjected weakly, "I suppose all of these kids have some sort of hidden talents."

"Hidden talents, I guess!" Lori Wilson proceeded with her bulldozing affect upon the troublemakers of the school. Her notorious gift, her hidden talent, of which she was proud.

"Take a look at this one." Sonja Frank directed her friend's attention to the next painting in the mid-year art show. She liked fueling Lori's math-teacher mind into hysteria.

"You've got to be kidding me!" Lori erupted.

"Shh," Sonja cautioned again, feeling adrenaline surge with nervousness and strange excitement which Lori always brought to their conversations. *A math teacher's bravado*, she thought.

"Goose Neck Schwan did this?"

"I guess so, but, shh," Sonja uttered. "There's his signature."

"That blithering moron hasn't handed in an assignment in two weeks, and yesterday he pretended he was sleeping at his desk."

The two teachers stared at the old, black woman in the painting. Her bowed legs rested against the steps of a porch at the back of a house. She was reading a letter, tears running down the wrinkles of her face. The letter had tear spots on it. Goose Neck had even painted in the effects of water on paper. "I don't believe it," Lori muttered.

Ms. Wilson and Mrs. Frank walked on, the latter hoping that her colleague of the left-brain department would expound and erupt one more time before they parted to opposite hallways. Mrs. Frank, from the right-brain English department lacked the gift of belligerent, razor-sharp descriptions and received quite a thrill in hearing them, especially from Lori—one of the masters.

"What the hell is that?" Lori stopped short to stare at a sculpture of metal, corn silk, and dried peach pits, which was labeled "The Battered Child." "First prize! This thing won first prize?" she snarled as she lifted the blue ribbon. "Who the hell did they have for a judge, Elmer Fudd?"

"I think a group from the Butternut Art Association came in to do the judging," Sonja answered with the slightest of giggles exuding from the corners of her well-groomed lip liner.

"Butternut Nuts," the relentless critique continued from Lori. "Don't they know anything about art?"

"You mean you don't like this?" Sonja asked deviously.

"Oh, please. It's no wonder the kids are so messed up and can't do their schoolwork; look at what they're allowed to do in art class." Lori looked at the artist's name card.

"Aha! Case in point!" she raged as Sonja wriggled with anticipation to hear the pronouncement.

"Regina Alexly. Regina Alexly. I might have known that weirdo girl would create something like this," she delivered on cue.

"Shh," warned the elated Sonja as a group of students walked by.

"I don't care if they hear me," Lori snapped. "Everybody thinks she's weird. Have you ever seen anyone look the way she does? She reminds me of a walking corpse; she gives me the creeps. What's with her anyway?"

Mrs. Frank had no chance to answer; the fifth period bell rang and both teachers hurried along their prospective hallways with Ms. Wilson looking back to give "The Battered Child" one more disgusted look.

"Congratulations, Regina," Lori could hear some of the students utter to the artist, as she entered her classroom.

My God, you'd think she'd at least be pleasant to them, Lori thought when she heard only a soft reply of, "Uh." The "corpse" sat at her desk like a statue, wearing her brown Oxfords and white ankle socks, a long dress, and black lipstick. She walked up and down the aisles collecting papers. *At least she'll have her homework done,* Lori appeased herself, *even though it will be full of bizarre sketches. Why didn't they tell us in college that we'd have to put up with so many weird students?*

Lori stopped at the Snake's desk. "Where's your homework?"

"Homework?" he asked. "What homework?"

Lori could hear the class chuckling. "That's it. Go to the office. This was your last chance."

"Last chance for what?" Ceasar asked innocently. The volume of the chortling rose.

"Don't even talk to me. Go!"

Ceasar slowly stood, refusing to take his icy stare from the teacher. His large frame, donned with the latest fashions for men, posed like an Adonis, as he slowly clipped his expensive pen onto the top fold of his meticulously ironed shirt pocket. Lori noticed the startling silence lying thick upon the room while Ceasar the Snake lifted his book bag, never breaking his stare from her.

Finally, as he turned she took a breath. Everyone watched in silence. Before he got to the end of the row he stopped alongside Regina and said, "Congratulations. It's a fine sculpture."

"Thank you," she said softly.

The statuesque student left the room as fidgety Goose Neck Schwan entered like a whirlwind, with papers fluttering out of every book and pocket. Pencils were sticking out of his hair.

"Schwan, you're late!" Ms. Wilson stated with the authority that she knew she had to re-establish.

"Sorry, Ms. Wilson. I had to find some stuff in my locker."

The class started laughing.

"Where's your homework, Schwan?"

"I've got it, I've got it. It's here someplace," he said as he started the mad search through his papers.

"That's it, I can't wait any longer," Lori retorted as she marched to the phone. "Get yourself down to the office and explain this to Mr. Winthrop."

"But I did it, it's here somewhere." Curtis Schwan tried desperately to find it as papers, gum wrappers, and pencils fell to the floor.

"I've had it with your excuses. Go."

She picked up the phone. "This is Lori Wilson. I'm sending two students, Ceasar Bellimore and Curtis Schwan.

And where do you think you're going?" the irritated teacher directed her question to the "walking corpse."

The walking corpse didn't answer; she only floated silently out of the math room.

"Get ready for Regina Alexly, too," she said into the phone as she rolled her eyes. Ms. Wilson slammed the receiver to the cradle.

"Hello, George, come in, have a seat," Mr. Winthrop said as he simulated a smile at the art teacher. He tried to button his suit jacket over the bulging stomach he'd told his wife was brought on by his frustrating job. Mr. Winthrop wasn't expecting five minutes of small talk from George, so he wasn't disappointed when he didn't get it. George was a man of few words, and in the twenty some years that the two men had worked together, Jim Winthrop knew and respected George's quietness.

"George," Mr. Winthrop began, aborting the idea of forcing the button through the hole, "I need a huge favor from you."

For some reason, the superintendent did wait for a reaction, but when there was none he continued. "George, we've run up against a situation here and we're about ready to pull out our hair." Mr. Winthrop probably didn't realize that as soon as he said 'hair', he reached up to his bald scalp, but George noticed. "We've got a handful of students who are ready to get axed from the system. If it wasn't for the guidance counselor they'd be gone by now, but Charles insists we have to keep them. We have to do something with them." The superintendent hoped for...a question?...a comment?...a facial expression?

"Anyway, according to Charles those damn kids are on the genius level and just need to be challenged. I said, 'What the hell is Math and Science and History? Isn't that a challenge? I know it was when I was in school." Mr. Winthrop went back to his button as he drew in a stomach-rising breath. "So, I said, 'Genius level? Have you seen their report cards? Have you any idea how the teachers are complaining about them?' He told me he had the 'real' records."

"Do you want some?" Mr. Winthrop asked George as he pulled a bag of caramels out of his desk drawer.

"Oh, no thank you," George replied in his notoriously soft, soothing voice. At least that was what the women teachers always said about George's voice. Mr. Winthrop thought about George's voice as he exuberantly moved his jaw to accommodate the stickiness of the caramel.

After a big swallow and the crinkling sound of another caramel being unwrapped, Jim continued, "Well anyway, and this was my wife's idea, so if it's no good, don't be afraid to tell me. She told me about the mayor looking for an artist to paint a mural for the new park. Candice thought it would be a good project for one of your art classes." In went the caramel as George watched the voluptuous movements that accompanied it. "So what do you think?" Jim spoke before he swallowed making the words stick to the goo.

"Which students are you referring to?"

"Well, there's that Ceasar Bellimore, Curtis Schwan, Regina Alexly, Virginia Lamont, and Guy a-a...

"Mixtore," George added quietly.

"Yeah, that's right. Mixtore," Jim uttered as he swung his chair around to his filing cabinet. George watched as he moved bags of chips to retrieve a folder.

"Here's some of the info on that bunch," he exclaimed as he slung the folder towards George. He swung back and held up a bag of potato chips. "Want some?"

"No, thanks," George uttered as he picked up the folder and opened it.

The office was quiet while George read through the reports; only the occasional squeak of Mr. Winthrop's chair was heard as he rolled back and forth deliberating the concept of opening the bag.

"Well," George finally said, "they all are my students." He paused as he looked pensively at Jim. "That's rather interesting isn't it?"

"It is?" George asked in bewilderment wondering what the art teacher meant by that.

"These kids are so talented and become totally involved when they are in with me, I'm shocked that they are causing all these disturbances in other classes."

"Well, we've got to do something with them. What do you think about the mural project? Maybe we could bribe them to be cooperative in school if they had the privilege of working on it. What do you think?"

George thought about that comment as Jim looked at his colleague's wardrobe. The same style—the corduroy pants with the suede shoes; the shirt collar turned neatly over the soft sweater—that had been George for as long as he had known him.

"I don't quite understand the bribery part of this, but I do understand their need to be creative. And yes, maybe they'll grow up a little bit through all of this."

"Well," Jim said jubilantly—jubilantly enough to give himself permission to open the bag of chips, "you write up the plans and I'll present them to the board and to the town supervisor. This is great, yes, this proves that we have the best interest of the students in the foreground. Thanks, George," Mr. Winthrop said, wiping the salt on his pants then extending his hand. "And George, maybe you could talk to them about their behavior."

He didn't expect an answer.

"Would you like to work on the project?"

Ceasar looked from Guy to Virginia to Regina to Curtis. It was always harder to answer Mr. Vondon's questions, because he gave options and choices, very unlike the other teachers.

"This will be for the new park, downtown," Guy filled in.

"Yes."

"We can design it ourselves and choose our own theme?" Virginia asked. She fluttered her long eyelashes and scooped dollops of long silky hair through her fingers.

"The theme will have to be submitted for approval."

"And we can get out of study halls if our homework is done?" Curtis asked as he rummaged through his pockets for his notepad, spilling bits of papers and wrappers to the floor.

"Yes."

Regina and Ceasar were making notations in their notebooks; Regina's of handmade paper tied with a mauve ribbon, and Ceasar's much like a businessman's portfolio with a zippered leather case.

"Oh, I have to tell you," Mr. Vondon said softly...

"Here comes the catch," Guy piped up sensing a scenario.

"...if I hear of you causing trouble in any of your classes, this project will be off limits to you."

"Why? What's the scuttlebutt about us?" Goose Neck Schwan asked.

"Let's just say I don't want to hear any more of it," Mr. Vondon answered in his effective style. "Let me know when you have your theme," he added as he walked to the other side of the room to mix paint for his next class.

"Do you have ideas already?" Virginia asked Ceasar and Regina, as she had noticed them jotting something in their notebooks.

"Ladies first," Ceasar nodded to Regina.

"I was thinking of a beautiful landscape, maybe something depicting the four seasons but using a modernistic approach."

"Yeah, because the park already has its own landscape, we could bring in something a little different, something that everyone doesn't see when they open their back door."

"I like that. How about adding depictions of the world today—how young people see the world."

"Yeah, let's not make it just our little niche. Let's open it up to all peoples and all concerns."

"Great, let's start formulating our ideas on paper."

Within three days the team presented Mr. Vondon with their proposal of "Today's World." They listed the inclusions of the family, business, entertainment, technology, God, recreation, war, and the environment. He in turn presented it to Mr. Winthrop, who passed it on to the Board of Education and to the supervisor.

Within two weeks all systems were go. A massive plywood display board was constructed by the town crew and moved into the back of the art room, section by section. Later it would be hinged together and mounted on four-by-fours in the park. After the PTA heard about the project, a group of elementary students were selected to paint the other side. Mr. Vondon thought it was a wonderful idea and spent three Saturday afternoons with the kids and the parents in the art room until it was finished. Their finished project was exposed to the classroom and everyone who entered thought it was "pretty neat" for little kids. *It does add color and vitality that only little ones can portray*, George thought. They had a way of making flowers and trees and kids and sunshine unique and joyful.

The five high school students began their project on the backside of "Happiness." They sketched their plans onto the base coat and were anxious to start. Hour upon hour, whenever they had a study hall, they converged to the mural to paint. They also got permission to eat lunch in the art room while they worked.

"How's your grandmother today Goose?" Regina asked as she painted.

"She's suffering real bad now; she can barely walk."

"I'm sorry," she softly responded. "That was your grandmother in the painting you did for the art show, wasn't it?"

"Yeah."

"What was in the letter that made her cry?" Regina asked as she lifted her brush to look at Curtis.

"It was the letter from my father. The last letter she got before he was killed in the war."

"Oh, my gosh. Did you paint that from memory?"

"Yeah, it was an image I'll never forget," he half whispered as he turned his head away from her. When he turned back, the tear he hadn't wanted her to see on his cheek was replaced with a blue streak of paint.

"Did she and your mother bring you guys up?"

"Well kind of. My mother wasn't around much of the time but Grandma was always there."

Goose Neck quickly turned the conversation. "How about you? Where'd you get the idea for 'The Battered Child'? And by the way, I think it is a sculpture of genius."

Regina blushed, giving color to her face that Curtis had never seen before. He looked, trying not to stare. "I—I don't know, I just dreamed it up, I guess." Her blushing continued.

Curtis had an idea of what was going on so he quickly said, "The materials you used were totally rad! How did you ever think to use metal, corn silk, and peach pits?"

Regina's tall, thin body turned to Curtis and with the sincerity of an angel, she said, "I don't know. I searched the tool shed and the barn for materials and the only thing of interest was the old scrap metal that my father said I could have. There was a wagonload of corn ready to be chopped for silage and the silk that was sticking out of some of the cobs looked so desperate, I immediately wanted to save it, I guess. When I went into the kitchen my mother and the other women had started blanching the peaches to can for the winter and it was my job to pit them. So, of course I wanted the pits," she said with a little grin.

"Do you live on some kind of a farm or something?" Goose Neck asked in such a way that Regina blushed again.

"Well, yes, it's a communal kind of farm with everyone doing the work. The old fashioned kind of work."

"Oh."

He wondered more about "The Battered Child" but thought he had asked enough for a while. He glanced sideways at her long skirt and the brown, tied oxfords with the white socks. At least her get-up can pass for fashionable in this day and age, but she probably hates that she has to wear it every day. He wondered where she got the black lipstick. He sighed as he dipped his brush into two primary colors to create a new hue. Curtis thought about mixing two people in order to make something brand new. *I guess that's what a child is*, he thought.

The five-minute bell rang. Regina and Goose Neck dipped their brushes into turpentine.

❧

"Come in for a minute, George. How's the mural progressing?" Mr. Winthrop asked as he pointed to a chair.

"Very well."

"I'm glad. I'm glad," Jim reiterated as he swept crumbs off his desk. You know, I haven't had one bad report on that bunch. You sure did the trick."

"I didn't do anything. This is apparently something they are interested in and want to continue."

"Well, whatever. A little bribery goes a long way, I always say."

George didn't respond and Mr. Winthrop wasn't surprised.

❧

"I want to work on the sky. I want to work on the sky," Virginia whined as she bounced up and down in front of Ceasar. He took a second to watch the voluptuous activity exhibited under Virginia's tight blouse.

"That's fine with me," he stated. "I want to work on the forest."

After a long stretch of quietness with a sound from neither the brushes nor the artists, Virginia broke the silence. "Ceasar, why are you so meticulous?"

"What?" he asked as if someone had drawn him out of a trance.

"Meticulous. Why are you so meticulous?" Virginia asked again as she peered down from the clouds she was billowing. Ceasar looked at her long, black-stockinged legs as she stood on the chair.

"What are you talking about?"

"I mean the way you dress and stuff. When you come to school you look like you're going to a business meeting or something. And your leather-cased notepad and fine pens... How did you get that way?"

"My mother brought me up that way, I guess. She has always spent a fortune on me. She just can't stop."

"Huh," Virginia uttered pensively. "I have to beg and plead my mother for every damn thing I want, even a stupid new lipstick or a bracelet. I can't imagine someone wanting to give me everything."

"Well, it's just the way she is, I guess. My dad makes tons of money, and since he's away on business all the time she has nothing to do except shop."

"But why don't you tell her you want teen clothes—not those preppy things you wear all the time?"

The Adonis stopped painting and sternly said to Virginia, "I would never upset my mother."

"Oh," she said meekly.

After a thick-aired, linseed oil-scented second or two, Ceasar quickly said, "I'm sorry. I didn't mean to snap at you."

"That's okay," she mumbled humbly, not accustomed to anyone ever apologizing to her, especially over such a little matter as this.

"It's just that my mother is very vulnerable to stress and since I'm the only one left. I try very hard to keep her calm."

"What do you mean, 'the only one left'?"

Ceasar looked up to the lady in the sky, letting his eyes pause when they reached her tiny bare waist. "Well," he began when the journey was complete to her eyes, "she says there were three other children—or supposed to be three other children besides myself."

"Huh?"

"My dad made her get them aborted."

"Oh," the longhaired beauty exhaled as if she knew exactly what Mrs. Bellimore had gone through. "I'm so sorry, Ceas." She crinkled her nose as tears dripped from her elevation to the seat of the chair.

Ceasar immediately handed her his perfectly folded white handkerchief. "Virginia, I didn't mean to make you cry—I'm sorry."

Virginia kept the handkerchief and used it to dab her eyes with one hand while she painted with the other. Both were silent as they added more and more to "Today's World."

"Virginia!" Ceasar said abruptly making the teenage girl jump. "Oh, sorry, I didn't mean to scare you. I just wanted to ask you something."

"Fire away," she replied, not stopping work on her cloud to look down.

"Why do you, I mean, well I know it's none of my business, but why do you dress the way you do?"

The cloud work stopped.

"What do you mean?"

"I mean, well, so revealing?"

"You mean sexy?"

"Yeah."

"Because I am sexy, right?"

"Well, yeah, but…"

"But what?"

"But you're showing to everybody. Don't you want to show to just one person?"

"Oh," she cooed lasciviously, "do you want to be that person?"

"No, no I don't mean that!" Ceasar stuttered in a totally uncharacteristic manner. Virginia laughed aloud to see the Greek Adonis fall out of composure. "I'm just asking why you want to please so many men day after day?"

"But I don't," she said defensively. "I'm lucky if I can please even one."

"Now I don't understand that," her painting partner stated.

"I wish I could get just one man to really like me, or love me, or something nice like that," she said forcefully as she leaned forward to wag her paintbrush in her partner's face.

Ceasar suddenly exuded the compassion that he undoubtedly used when he dealt with his mother, "Virginia, dear Virginia. You need to show nothing to no one. When they discover your beauty from within, they will be magnetized by its allure."

The handkerchief again was manifested for sorrow and…an awakening? The last tear, of which there had been many, was finally dried when they heard running footsteps.

"Sorry I'm late," Guy panted.

"What happened?" Ceasar asked.

"I had to finish my physics homework before I came down."

"Couldn't you have done that last night at home?" Virginia asked as she looked down and over.

"I didn't get home from work until quarter past nine, and all hell had broken out at my house."

"What do you mean?"

"The cops were there hauling my father away again. Ma was crying, and the neighbor was trying to patch her up. She finally said she would go to the emergency room. The kids were hysterical, and I spent hours trying to settle them down. Two of them finally fell asleep on the couch, but shit, man, I fell asleep, too."

"Geez, that's too bad," Virginia said compassionately.

"I don't know," Guy mumbled as he started painting on his section—the city. "I'm thinking of quitting school anyhow."

"What!" his partners resounded together.

"Yeah, this is getting too much for me. What's the sense of me spending hours learning stupid stuff when I could be out working full time? My father can't keep a job; he's drunk all the time. Ma is getting desperate. I don't want her to kill herself or something."

"Today's World" received more paint as the artists worked in silence.

On Tuesdays they all had the same study hall. Mr. Vondon had no class at that time either, so he always made it a point to converse with them about their ideas in relation to the theme. Sometimes he questioned their motives, and sometimes he nixed an idea, but in general he was receptive and understanding of what they were trying to convey. After the inventory, George would either work at his desk or scurry around the art room getting projects and materials ready for the next class.

He always smiled when he heard Curtis break into song. He knew what was to follow—it wasn't long before all five of his protégés behind the huge plywood wall would be sending forth music that brought delight to the roomful who loved creativity. *Those five are talented in so many ways,* George thought as he quietly hummed along with them. Mr. Vondon also heard about the strict communal farm, the meticulous abortions, the chastity lessons, and the false need to be sexy, the absentee fathers, the alcoholics, and the desperate families. He heard much discussion about the wrongs of society and of the school. He listened to their discussions about God and how the world was keeping Him out of their lives; they claimed they knew of no one who spoke about God—except Curtis' grandmother. Mr. Vondon realized that the songs they loved best were the spirituals that Curtis taught them, the spirituals that his Grandmother had taught to him.

George listened with admiration to the reasoning and logic they gave Guy about the notion of quitting school. Guy would listen to them more readily than to any adult, the teacher knew.

In eight weeks to the day the mural was finished. Mr. Winthrop worked on scheduling an unveiling for the school board members, the supervisor, the councilmen, and the park organizers.

Tuesday's study hall time period was finally settled upon, because Regina was not allowed to leave the farm at night, and Guy had to work.

The custodians had moved the mural further away from the wall and had placed casters on the bottom so the sections could be turned.

When the artists entered the room the invited guests were chatting and eating packaged cookies from the cafeteria and sipping fruit punch from paper cups.

Mr. Winthrop welcomed the guests and introduced everyone. The program began with the front side of the mural being unveiled first. The playfulness of the colors and the primitive representations from the elementary students brought a joyful response with applause and exclamations of approval. Those artists would be acknowledged next month during a separate program for the elementary grades.

Mr. Vondon then turned the sections and scooted them around to the proper 1-2-3 order. He unveiled the work.

Silence.

There was no applause. No cheering. No smiles. No words...

The five artists looked at each other; the adults looked at each other; Mr. Winthrop had beads of sweat festering from his forehead. All eyes went back to the mural to study the cornfield with battered children tied to the cornstalks and a city of drug dealers on every street corner. It looked like thousands of fetuses stacked meticulously in a box and men strewn on the battlefield. Men and women were trapped in a liquor bottle and a large grandmother with wings sheltered chicks under her feathers. God was sitting on a cloud, crying and there was a sign in front of a school reading: All Sex Allowed.

At last the president of the Board of Education cleared his throat and asked that the artists be dismissed—he wanted to speak with the adults.

The mural was placed in the Park with "Today's World" painted totally black.

Mr. Vondon was put on probation.

Chapter Twenty-Two

THE INTERVIEW

"**Y**es Marjory. Saratoga went to the big city, too.

Oh, I see, you're looking in that old photograph album again."

Yes...that's Auntie Anna and Saratoga and me. What good times we had; every summer we'd take you to the county fair. Aren't you cute riding on the merry-go-round with Saratoga holding on to you?

Don't cry, my little Margie, I miss them, too."

"Excuse me ma'am," this is W-W-O-W. Can you tell our viewing audience what you are most thankful for this year? Here, speak right into this."

"Um, I guess I'm thankful for my family, except none of us gets along—but I suppose I have to be thankful for them."

"Thank you, ma'am. Excuse me, sir, can you share with the nation what you're thankful for?"

"Well, let me think. Hmm. Maybe it would be for my house. No, not the house—my wife got that. My business, no—that's gone. My...my nothing...get away from me!"

"Sorry. Excuse me ma'am, can you tell W-W-O-W what you're thankful for?"

"Oooh! I'm thankful that my boyfriend can see me on television!"

"Okay! That's it ladies and gentlemen, our weekly on the street interview...wait a minute, I see Saratoga. Let's ask her.

"Saratoga! Saratoga, can you tell us what you're most thankful for?"

Saratoga pulled herself up from the bench and yanked the opening of her coat closed. The cameraman zoomed in on three of her fingers that had pushed through the yarn of her brown gloves. "Thankful for?" she asked as she pulled the orange hat over her left ear.

"Yes," Jeffrey answered as he let his perfectly white teeth gleam for the camera, while posing his best side for viewing.

"Well," said Saratoga pensively, "what have the other people answered?"

Jeffrey chuckled for the camera and answered, "Food; cars; jobs; health; family; houses; being on TV."

"Hmm," the woman uttered as she nodded her head, "good answers I suppose; quite typical. Here, you want some popcorn?"

"No thanks, Saratoga," the TV interviewer smiled and winked for the amusement (he thought) of his audience. He watched the homeless woman take kernel after kernel out of the greasy bag, five pieces went to the sidewalk for the pigeons and one piece went into her mouth.

It was with the next set of five that Saratoga answered, "Abortion."

"Excuse me?" Jeffrey laughed as he quickly sat on the bench with the tattered woman, hoping to gain her confidence by nuzzling close to her. "Are you saying you are thankful you had an abortion?" His voice mellowed like a sleazy soap opera character.

"No! You damned fool—I'm thankful I never had an abortion!" Saratoga snapped as she tucked the popcorn bag under her arm and pulled the plaid scarf tighter around her neck.

"Well folks, you heard it live on W-W-O-W. See you next time."

"What the hell are you sitting so close to me for? Move on down, Mr. Big Shot."

"Gary! Why didn't you stop the camera?"

"Sorry, boss."

"Oh, please, Christina, no more of Saratoga."

"Are you kidding me, Jeffrey? She's the hot spot of the live interview. We've gotten tons of mail and email about her. Everybody loves Saratoga."

"But she always makes me look like a fool!"

"Yeah, she does, doesn't she?" Christina laughed. "I guess that's what's so appealing."

"Thanks a lot, Christina."

"Oh, come on, you've got broad shoulders; you can take it. Just think, everyone is tuning in to your segment."

"Yeah, that's right."

"So search her out; interview whomever is around, and then get her on last. I hear there's going to be a bonus for you."

"Really? All right. I'm out of here."

"Excuse me sir. It's W-W-O-W. Can you tell our viewing audience what you enjoyed most at the Thanksgiving table?"

"Oh, man. My mother made some sort of dressing that was out of sight!"

"What kind was it?"

"I have no idea but it was, like rad, man."

"Thank you sir.

Ma'am? What did you enjoy most about your Thanksgiving dinner?"

"Oh, hi everybody! Hi everybody! I loved the turkey, of course. What would Thanksgiving be without turkey? That's why we call it 'Turkey Day.' Doesn't that make more sense than calling it Thanksgiving? What's Thanksgiving got to do with it anyhow?"

"Thank you.

"Excuse me, you're on W-W-O-W. What was your favorite part of the Thanksgiving dinner?"

"Oh, it had to be the football game."

"No, the dinner—what did you like best?"

"To tell you the truth I don't know what was on the plate. I just shoveled it in as I watched the game."

"Okay. Let's go on to our next woman on the street. Hello ma'am."

"Get out of my way, you jerk!"

"Jeffrey, you better get over to Saratoga; she's packing up her stuff," Gary whispered. "Looks like she's going to be heading out soon."

Damn, Jeffrey thought to himself as he looked over at the vagabond. Gary was right. She stood up to push her cart along.

"Morning, Saratoga! Got a question for you."

Saratoga didn't stop.

Oh great, Jeffrey thought, a walking interview. He knew it would be especially tedious for Gary who would have to walk backwards while he filmed.

"So, Saratoga, what did you enjoy most about your Thanksgiving dinner? Oh, wait a minute! Did you even have a dinner?" Jeffery asked wishing he had a manhole to fall into.

Saratoga stopped to stare at Jeffrey. "Of course I had dinner, you fool. Don't you know there are good people in this city who see to it that we're fed?"

"Yes, yes of course, I know that," Jeffrey uttered, relieved to know that he was telling the truth. "And what did you like best, Saratoga?"

Saratoga looked up at a broken window and stood as still as a statue. It wasn't long before Jeffrey, too, looked at the window that she was transfixed upon and Gary zoomed his lens to the area.

"Saratoga?"

"Oh! Yes, my favorite food for Thanksgiving."

"Yes."

"I would have to say it was the Holy Eucharist."

"Holy Eucharist? What on earth is that? Is it tasty?"

Saratoga bolted her cart forward. Gary swung to the side as the woman walked past wiping away a tear with the ratty, brown glove.

"Jeffrey, you are just superseding yourself all the time!" Christina commented as soon as the live crew returned to headquarters.

"I am?"

"You sure are! The emails are non-stop."

"Great...Right?"

"Right," Christina drawled the word to quite a noticeable length.

"Is there a problem?" Jeffrey asked nervously.

"No...keep doing just what you're doing."

"Ok! Great!"

"What's the question this week, boss?" Gary asked excitedly as he grabbed his satchel.

"I don't know yet, Gary. I wait for the last minute; I do my best thinking that way."

"Wow! Cool!"

"Where the hell is she?" Jeffrey muttered as he stared out of the car windows.

"I don't know, but I've used up a quarter tank of gas going up and down these damn crowded streets."

"Wait! There's Burke. He might know where she is."

"Hey, Burke! Where's Saratoga?"

"What's in it for me?" the whiskered man growled at Jeffrey as he held out his hand.

Jeffrey placed a five-dollar bill on the palm of the man who looked like an Aleutian with a fur-trimmed parka.

"She's over at St. Anna's. She found a baby in a trash can last night. Can you believe it?"

"Yeah, I can believe it. Thanks Burke."

"Gary? Were you filming that?"

"Yeah. You were interviewing weren't you?"

"Never mind, come on."

"Excuse me, ma'am. What do you think of all the Christmas lights around the city?"

"Oh, you're from W-W-O-W aren't you?"

"Yes ma'am."

"Oh, they're pretty I guess. They do add a little cheerfulness to this dreary city."

"Thanks.

"Excuse me, sir. How do you like the Christmas lights around the city?"

"What a stupid waste of money."

"Say, little fellow, do you like Christmas lights?"

"I love them! Now Santa can see where he's going."

"Maybe so..." Jeffrey grinned just as he spotted Saratoga coming out of St. Anna's.

"Saratoga! Over here! What do you think of all the Christmas lights?"

"Lights?" she asked.

"Yeah! The whole city was lit up last night. You must have noticed."

"Hmm," she uttered as she furrowed her brow. Gary zoomed in to catch her expression. "Isn't that something," she said slowly as she pushed a lock of hair up under her crocheted hat. "I never noticed the lights last night."

"You were probably too busy rushing that baby to St. Anna's. Right?"

"I guess I was," Saratoga said quietly. Gary kept the close-up on her as she put her index finger on her tooth and wiggled it back and forth.

"So," Jeffrey interrupted the silence, "do you think there should be lights for Christmas?"

"Mary's baby deserves lots of lights," Saratoga replied as she pulled the scarf over her mouth to keep out the cold air.

"You know the baby's mother?" Jeffrey asked breathlessly, hoping to get a scoop on a real story.

When Saratoga walked away, he called out, "Mary? Did you say the mother's name was Mary? Don't forget that Gary, we might have a lead! Turn that thing off!"

"You never cease to amaze me, Jeffrey."

"Thank you, Christina. How about letting me go out to investigate the kid who was in that trash can? I've got a lead on the mother, you know."

"Oh, I know. I watched your segment."

"Well?"

"I don't think so, Jeffrey. But I'll tell you what you can do. You can help Lori with all the packages that people have sent to the station."

"Packages?"

"Yes, for some odd reason our address is being used for Saratoga's mail."

"Is that bad or good?"

"We shall see. We shall see," Christina exclaimed as she walked to her office.

"My God!" Jeffrey gasped. "These are all for Saratoga?"

"Yeah," Lori said, grinning. "Can you believe it?"

"Why is she getting all this mail?"

"I think people like Saratoga."

"What people?"

Lori stopped to stare at Jeffrey. "The people who watch your 'Street Talk.'"

"Oh…Oh! I'm going to be famous, aren't I Lori?"

Lori turned to another stack of presents.

Jeffrey and Gary scoured the streets looking for Saratoga; looking for any of the street people.

"I guess it has gotten too cold for them," Gary uttered as he made a sharp turn and felt the car slide. "Damn, it's getting miserable out here."

"Yeah, maybe we should check out the shelters. There's one a block and a half from here. Wait! Let's get these people before we go in."

"Excuse me ma'am, it's W-W-O-W. Is there something special you'd like for Christmas?"

"Oh yes! I'm hoping for a new range; I want one with a barbecue grill on the side, even though my other one is only two years old. My husband is having a fit, but I'll get it!"

"Thank you.

"Ma'am? Can you tell us what you'd like for Christmas?"

"I hope I get a new diamond; this little thing is ridiculous," she exclaimed as she pulled off her glove to expose the ring.

"Well, good luck. Come on Gary, we're going inside."

The two men walked into the bleak, dim building. They saw rows and rows of cots.

"Can I help you?" a woman asked as she halted her mopping.

"Is Saratoga here?"

"Nope."

"Has she been here?"

"Nope."

"By the way, what would you like for Christmas?"

"Christmas?" After a long pause she looked at the floor and uttered, "I'm too old for Christmas."

"Come on," Jeffrey cajoled as he winked into the camera, "what would you like?"

"Well, a nice pair of warm socks would be nice," the woman blushed.

"Socks? That's pretty funny," the host smirked as he looked into the camera. "Let's go, Gary."

"Here! Pull over."

"Hi, kids! Do you know what you want for Christmas?"

"Oh please," the mother whined, "we'll be here all day; they want everything under the sun."

"Excuse me Sir, what do you hope you'll get for Christmas?"

"Ha!" laughed the man. "I don't think I can say that on TV!"

"Let's go in, Gary."

Again, another dreary headquarters stared back at the two men.

"Saratoga!" Gary nearly shouted.

Saratoga looked up from her mending.

"We've been looking for you," Jeffrey explained as he felt his gelled hair.

The woman lowered her eyes to her work.

"Tell us, are you hoping for something special this Christmas?"

The needle didn't go through to the other side of the button, the needle stopped. The rough, cracked hand, poised with the smooth shining needle, might have won Gary an award if he had had a propensity for creativity. Needless to say, the captivated nation watched the homeless woman and waited for her answer.

"I would like," she began, "I would like to see my Lord."

Jeffrey squirmed and rolled his head trying to get more space between his neck and the tight collar. He put his finger in the constriction seemingly trying to stretch the material. "Your Lord? How on earth would you do that?"

"I don't know," she simply replied as she stood and walked out of the room.

※

"Christina, she's getting too weird for me, you've got to give me my release from her," Jeffrey implored as a kid begging for a cookie.

"You must be kidding me. Don't you realize what's happening?"

"What *is* happening?"

"I guess if you don't know—that's it! Because you don't know! That's where the magic is!"

"Magic?"

"I've got to dash to a meeting. See if you can come up with a plan for delivering the mail and packages to Saratoga. We can make a big production of it, and maybe give you a half-hour spot."

"Really?"

※

"Lori, I might get my own show! I'll have Saratoga opening all her presents on TV! Maybe we can do it downtown in front of the huge Christmas tree! Wow, this is exciting!"

"Okay, Mr. Exciting, help me with these boxes."

※

"Gary, I can't wait! And you're going to be my 'main man' at the camera. Come on, I can't wait to tell Saratoga."

※

"Excuse me, sir. Can you tell our viewing audience where you're going to be on Christmas?"

"Oh, we'll be right to home with all the children and the grandchildren around us. When it comes to Christmas, I don't think of anyone except *my* family. That's what Christmas is—your *own* family."

"Thank you sir.

"Ma'am? Ma'am, would you like to tell us where you'll be on Christmas?"

"That's a sore subject with me, I'll have you know! I have to work. Can you believe it? Do you think I want to be at the nursing home with them? I want to be home with my family. Don't they know what Christmas is? I am so mad!"

"Well, thank you, and sorry. Hey Burke, old buddy, have you seen Saratoga?"

"Why the hell are you always looking for her? You got something going on that we don't know about?" he snickered.

"Nothing like that Burke, my boss just likes to see her on TV."

"I don't know where the hell she is; she must help out at fifteen different places."

"Really?"

"Yeah, try the waif's house, over there."

"What's that?"

"Some dump where the runaways go. How do I know? I got my own problems."

Gary kept the camera on Burke as he sauntered away in his fur-trimmed parka and tall hunting boots.

"Were you taping all that?" Jeffrey suddenly asked Gary.

"Yeah. Why?"

"*Why* is what I wonder. Why waste all that footage on junk?"

"I don't know. It's kind of interesting to me."

"Good morning! We're from W-W-O-W. You've probably seen me on television. We're looking for Saratoga."

"You can't come in here; we protect the confidentiality of our clients."

"Okay, okay. We'll wait out in the van."

"Can't the heater put out any more heat than this?" Jeffrey whined.

"I'll go and get us some hot coffee. Wait. Here she comes."

"Saratoga! Can you tell us where you'll be on Christmas?"

She kept walking and didn't answer.

"Well," said Jeffrey after he knew she wasn't going to respond, "let me tell you. You are going to be three blocks from here sitting in front of the city's huge tree opening all the presents people have sent to you!"

Saratoga stopped. Saratoga looked at Jeffrey.

"And what's more, all of America will be tuned in to watch you enjoy your presents!"

Saratoga walked away.

"You're going to have a real Christmas this year!" Jeffrey called to her as Gary faded the image.

"I've got it all set up, Christina. Saratoga will be by the tree for her presents."

"Are you sure?"

"Oh, yeah! This is going to be a hit. I bet the network will run this clip every year."

"Okay. I hope you've got it all under control. We'll have a truck take everything downtown on Christmas morning."

"Great."

Jeffrey looked dapper in his red beret and matching scarf over top of his new woolen coat. He spoke to the hundreds of people who had gathered to watch Saratoga. People in their homes turned in to W-W-O-W to see their beloved Saratoga. This was to be a Christmas story for sure. The host was at his pinnacle of personality and charm. He never looked better and worked the crowd like a well-oiled machine. The diner from up the street delivered hot chocolate, and Steiner's bakery brought over pastries. The city was warmed with Christmas love for their Saratoga.

Jeffrey did everything from leading the crowd in singing carols to guessing what was in the packages. He nervously realized they had been waiting for over two hours.

"Christina! What are you doing here?"

"I need your mic, Jeffrey."

"Ladies and Gentlemen, boys and girls, let me update you on Saratoga; she's had a busy morning. She left her own shelter at five a.m. to go directly to the orphanage. There she played Santa Claus for the third year in a row. After that she made visits to her regular stops including the maternity home; Youngsters, Inc.; St. Luke's; St. Bridgett's; our two infirmaries; and the shelters around the city. And today," Christina paused and smiled, "she traveled first class through the generosity of Clark's Cab Co."

The crowd clapped and cheered.

"Saratoga has sent you a message," Christina continued. "She thanks you and all the people from around the country who have remembered her. She has designated the Halo Organization to be the distributors of the presents; she wants everything to go to needy organizations. She told me she couldn't be here today because she's with the Lord."

"What?" Jeffrey shouted. "She died?"

"Oh no, Jeffrey. The two are working as a team."

The crowd cheered wildly as Jeffrey said, "Team?"

Chapter Twenty-Three

The Wind

"**M**arjory, the girl has gone off the deep end; of course she had to go to the big hospital in the city.

Wouldn't you think the girl would like living in a place called Lone Moon Creek?"

❧

"Why do you want to die, Cheyenne?" Andrea whispered as she gently swept a wisp of black hair from her patient's eyes.

Cheyenne didn't move; Cheyenne didn't answer; Cheyenne saw only the lone eagle circling the mountaintop waiting for her.

Andrea remained by the bedside of Cheyenne, looking at her face, wishing to see through to her thoughts to her anguish. The long black hair streaked over the young woman's shoulders like the spears of her ancestors.

Andrea's eyes crept slowly to Cheyenne's wrists, bandaged tightly to keep life in—exactly the area where life was to escape. As a black bear charging out of her den, Cheyenne had planned the wrists to be the opening to where her life would emerge. But now the opening of the cave had been barricaded closed. "Let me out," her head screamed. "I need to be set free."

Andrea placed her warm hand on Cheyenne's arm. The skin felt cold. "Why are you cold, Cheyenne?" Andrea whispered, again knowing there would be no response. She needs the sunshine, Andrea thought. She knows she is without the sun; her bronze skin is paling as each day goes by. The doctor knew fluorescent lights and white walls were not the nature of Cheyenne; she needed the sunshine.

Andrea closed her eyes and lifted her face. She let her neck loll back and forth as a stem of grass on the prairie, trying to capture the thoughts of Cheyenne. Somehow she had to reach this girl. *What was she thinking? Dear God, let me somehow reach this girl.*

Andrea periodically lifted her warm hand and placed it gently a few inches higher or lower on Cheyenne's arm. Her fingers radiated heat into the cold body. With the heat, Andrea wanted it also to carry in her presence, her concern, her love—three gifts of which people in terrible despair are barren.

In the total blackness of her frigid cave, Cheyenne knew something was trying to move the boulders from the entrance. Cheyenne envisioned it to be the beautiful, graceful doe. "What help can you be?" she called out, without a sound.

Andrea removed her hand and straightened her shoulders, which had stiffened with the pose of heat giving.

Cheyenne knew the doe had given up and walked away. The young girl knew she could do nothing except close her eyes and sleep in despair.

The doctor walked to the foot of the bed and her eyes started their slow journey. Andrea saw a beautiful gift from God—what was it that made you want to leave this earth, Cheyenne?

Andrea gently clasped Cheyenne's left foot in her hands. The clasp turned into folded, warm hands that Andrea used as her prayer center. *What happened, Cheyenne? What happened, God? You both know. Help me to reach this special child of yours, dear God. She is broken in every nature of her being; let her be mended before she goes home to you.*

Andrea's prayer center felt the left foot twitch. "Life! Dear girl, that's life!" Andrea let her words drift up to the sleeping girl's ears.

"Doctor, excuse me, here is more of the police report."

"Thank you, Louise."

Andrea sat by Cheyenne and read that the now immobile girl was twenty-two years old and living in a rural area called Lone Moon Creek, but was found by her friends at a campsite in Oklahoma, where there was an environmental-saving rally. In parenthesis, it said: (The friends were not overly surprised by the attempted suicide.) More interrogation is in progress.

"Not overly surprised," Andrea read again.

Oh, majestic eagle, wait for me, Cheyenne called out in silence, do not abandon me, I beg of you. She felt herself crawling to the barricade at the entrance of the cave. In blackness her hands touched the huge boulders. On her knees, she stretched wide her arms and felt her fingertips cleave to the curve of the stones. She walked on her knees to the right. Again her touch indicated a stone of massive proportions. On to more boulders. But in the cracks? There must be cracks? What has been put in to block the light? She touched, she pulled her hand back, she touched again. What was it? She smelled her fingertips. Oh, no! Cheyenne lurched back onto her heels and rubbed her hands against her pants to remove the sins against the earth. They had used the sins of apathy, neglect, and destruction to seal her into this cave! Forward again she crept to the wall and began scratching at the hard mortar.

Andrea stretched her arm to reach her tape deck and pushed the button. The tones of a lone flute could be heard intermingling its pure sounds with those of the wind. Andrea pictured a person high on a mountain with his flute and the winds.

What was going through Cheyenne's mind? The clawing stopped; her hands relaxed.

This is good, thought Andrea, *she can still permit peace to enter her body through music; this is good.*

Andrea touched Cheyenne's forehead using a circular motion, which matched the flow of the flute, which mimicked the flow of the wind.

"Why Cheyenne? Why do you want to leave?" Andrea whispered like the wind.

Cheyenne's eyes opened quickly—quickly as a wild morning glory blossom that had twisted itself around an iron-gate. Her dark, dark eyes seemed to pierce the ceiling, never swaying to the left or to the right. *What is she looking at,* wondered the doctor?

Cheyenne remained in that stare while Andrea read a note stating that the girl's mother and father were waiting in her office. *Here,* she thought, *would be a major piece to the puzzle.* Now, I'll find out what terrible things this girl has had to face. She paused to subdue her sudden anger.

Andrea felt like throwing open the door and screaming, "What dastardly things have you done to your daughter? Why did you neglect her as a child? Why didn't you listen to her?"

"Hello, Mr. and Mrs. Blackstone, I'm Dr. Linqua," Andrea said in a controlled manner.

Huddled together were a man and a woman with grief-painted faces, swollen eyes, and outdated pieces of luggage at their feet. The man stood and shook Andrea's hand; the woman remained seated with weights of sorrow resting upon her shoulders.

"How is she doctor?" the man asked with furrows in his face deep enough to hold the sadness of Job.

"She's alive. I've been working with her—trying to bring her back to reality."

"Can we see her?" the woman with the tears asked.

"I'll need to ask you some questions first: Does Cheyenne live with you?"

"Yes, except when she's traveling."

"Traveling?"

"She works long enough to save some money, then off she goes on another crusade to save the earth. She has been all over the country, up into Canada, and even into Central and South America."

"What does she do on those crusades?"

"She speaks, demonstrates, carries signs, goes to jail...anything she can do to get the peoples' attention about protecting the wildlife, air, water, land."

"Was she a happy child?"

The mother and father looked at each other. "Yes, she was happy," the mother spoke for the first time. All seven of our children were happy. We loved them all. Cheyenne was just—serious. Always so serious about everything. When she was still little, it would break her heart to see trapped animals or construction crews digging up the landscape. Or litter! If she saw litter on the ground she almost went hysterical. She...she cares for this earth beyond anyone I've ever seen. Maybe it comes from my mother who would tell her stories about the land, the way it use to be, so sacred, so pristine."

"Little Flower, shh," her husband tried to console his weeping wife.

Oh, dear God, Andrea thought to herself, *what have we done to your people?* Andrea suddenly wanted to hug Mrs. Blackstone, too, but she stood stiffly and announced that they could see their child, now.

The Blackstones looked down upon their girl, like Andrea imagined survivors of a raid would look down upon their devastated village. Their silent tears dropped onto the edge of the bed. Tears fell upon Cheyenne's hand.

∞

Cheyenne felt water! Somewhere there was a crack in the barricade! A weak spot! A spot that Cheyenne could dig through with her fingers. A place for her sunshine to spear through! Where? Where was the crack?

∞

"Doctor, help her!" Mrs. Blackstone said sharply. The mother knew her child was in distress. Cheyenne's fingers were frantic. Andrea quickly pushed the "play" button to bring the flutist and the wind into the hospital room.

Little Flower cried from the combination of Cheyenne's desperation and the eerie music. The parents saw the demons being released from Cheyenne's hands. Very softly, Little Flower began singing in native syllables as the flute and the wind wound in and around her hauntingly beautiful tones. The father used his thick, stiff hands to create the sound of a deer-hide drum.

Cheyenne turned her head toward her lifeline and Little Flower cried into her daughter's hand.

"Mama," Cheyenne whispered.

"Baby, you can't change the world by leaving it. You have to stay and do what you can."

"There is nothing more that I can do, Mama. I want to leave and soar with the eagle."

"Cheyenne, no. It's not your time."

"Your mother is right," the man said. "You must stay to bring about change."

Cheyenne's fingers started their frantic movements again as she drifted out of consciousness.

Andrea and the Blackstones left the room as a team of nurses and Cheyenne's internist began their procedures.

"Have you made arrangements for lodging?" Andrea asked.

"No, not yet."

"Here. Take my card and register at the hotel across the street. They'll accommodate you at a very reasonable rate. Maybe we can rejoin in a few hours."

"Thank you, doctor. Please save her," Little Flower whispered pleadingly.

Dr. Linqua found a new folder on her desk labeled "Blackstone, Cheyenne." School records and information from previous employers were included, but the statements from her friends at camp caused Andrea to look at them first:

"I have been so worried about her."

"She has been very depressed."

"I never saw anyone so saturated with the cause as Cheyenne."

"She wants to do it all—she doesn't seem to realize it takes time to bring about changes."

"She can act really weird sometimes. She acts like she can get into the heartbeat of the animals and the birds and nature. It's like she becomes one with nature. I really can't explain it."

"She told me she wants to leave her body and be with the eagles. She really had me worried."

"She said to me that she's a failure—she can't get people to clean the land and stuff. I tried to tell her she's not responsible for the whole world or even the country. We just go out and do what we can. A lot of changes have been made, I told her. I told her, too, to focus on all the good things that people and governments are doing to return the environment to the way it was."

"Hmm," Andrea uttered and then picked up the school records: Quiet, kind, caring, a definite environmentalist, artistic, creative, excellent stories, beautiful paintings of nature and animals in nature, musically inclined.

"Hmm," she uttered again as she digested the information.

Employee records: Hard worker but no reason given for abrupt departure. Took job seriously, no idea why she left. Was a fanatic about other people's litter. Left to be in a rally against oil killing the fish.

"Hmm."

Andrea returned to Cheyenne's room. The face of the past, the present, and the future was turned toward the wall. Andrea gently put her hand on Cheyenne's arm.

"Cheyenne," Andrea whispered.

The face did not turn toward her.

"Where are you, Cheyenne?"

Cheyenne's fingers started to claw at the mortar of man's sin against the wholesomeness of the world. She knew there was a weak spot because she had felt drops of water before.

"Are you trying to get out?" Andrea guessed by the movements of the hands.

Suddenly Cheyenne stopped her feverish digging and tenderly used her index finger to feel a soft spot in the mortar—a spot man had forgotten. Now Cheyenne worked only in that one area.

"What are you digging out, Cheyenne?"

With one last movement, the young woman put her hand down and smiled a smile that spread across her bronzed face as the sunshine spreads across a field of bluebells in Texas.

"What is it, Cheyenne?" Andrea whispered excitedly.

Cheyenne let the light glow upon her face, turning her head slightly from side to side as if to get the affects evenly distributed.

As Andrea made notations in her book, she abruptly lifted her head when she heard high, shrill tones coming from Cheyenne. Her notebook fell to the floor as she bounded towards Cheyenne. The girl had her hands cupped around her mouth and was repeatedly calling out a strange tonal pattern.

"On, no," Little Flower gasped as she and her husband came into the room.

"What is it? What is she doing?" Andrea asked fearfully.

"She's calling the wolves!"

"What?"

"Yes, her grandmother taught her how to do that."

"Why is she calling them?"

"Somewhere, in her mind, she's trapped."

"And the wolves will get her out?"

"Yes," Little Flower answered as simply and poignantly as wouldn't be written in a thousand pages of a psychiatry text.

Little Flower suddenly swung to Andrea and tightly grabbed her arm. "Don't let her out, doctor. Don't let her get out!"

"Why, Little Flower, why?"

"She'll try to fly with the eagle again," sobbed Cheyenne's mother. She fell to her knees, weeping desperately into her hands.

Andrea quickly looked to Mr. Blackstone for help in explaining all of this.

"Cheyenne will try to kill her body again so that her soul will be free to fly with the eagle," he answered desperately as he wiped the tears from the furrows of his face.

Cheyenne stopped calling the wolves and began digging again.

"We have to get her out, Little Flower! We can't leave her in that entrapment."

"I know, but I'm scared," she answered as she let her husband lift her to her feet. "I know we do."

"We have to think of ways to convince her to stay on this earth. We can't let her go with the eagle," Andrea stated emphatically.

More of the mother's tears fell upon Cheyenne's arm.

"Hi, Jane, it's Andrea. What do you have in the gallery related to Native American culture?...Ooo, that sounds interesting! I'll stop by later this afternoon. See you then, bye."

"Looks like you've already been shopping," Jane remarked when Andrea entered the gallery with her shopping bags.

"Yes, I've found all sorts of interesting things. Look at these tapes. I didn't know so much was available."

"Tapes about the wind, the water, birds, rain, the sun?" Jane questioned.

"It piqued my curiosity," Andrea said exuberantly.

"Are these for you?"

"Well yes, but I want to share them with a patient. I luckily had one tape already, featuring a flutist and the wind. It calmed her immediately."

"I always admire your approaches—they surely beat medications."

"I think so, too." Andrea smiled.

"Listen to these intricate wind chimes I bought."

"Oh, what a sound! It's so clear and clean."

"Isn't it though? Here, you must listen to this. Where can I plug it in?"

Jane sighed with delight. "Oh, listen to the water bubbling...I need to get one of those in here. What a perfectly lovely, soothing sound."

"So, Jane, I'm here to add to my nature collection. What do you have?"

"This patient of yours must be pretty special."

"Oh, yes," Andrea said softly, "she's as special as all of creation."

"Well, my goodness. I didn't know anyone was that special."

"Jane!" Andrea stopped suddenly and looked directly into her friend's eyes, "Everyone is that special in the eyes of God."

"I suppose you're right. Well, anyway, let's go into this section of the gallery."

Andrea spent nearly two hours going from painting to painting, print to print, sculpture to sculpture, and back around again.

"Have you decided?" Jane asked excitedly as she reentered the room.

"I think I have, Jane. I'm going to take the painting of the young Native American girl standing on top of the mountain looking out at the world. I like the way her arms are outstretched."

"Mmm, that is a beauty, isn't it? What do you think that girl on the mountain is thinking about?"

"I don't really know, but I'm going to find out," Andrea responded confidently. "I am also intrigued with this print where the wolves are circling around the eagle with the broken wing."

"Oh, I don't like that one," Jane said, shuddering her shoulders. "That one scares me."

"Me, too," Andrea murmured.

"Anything else?"

"Yes, this statue of the mother and child. I think the child represents hope."

"You might be right," Jane said as she stood by her friend, both looking at the gift of hope.

⁂

"Good morning, Mrs. Blackstone. Where is your husband this morning?"

"He had to fly back. He couldn't take anymore time off from work and we still have three children at home."

The doctor looked intently at her and asked, "How were you able to decide, as a mother, what to do? To stay here with Cheyenne or to be home with three of your other children?"

"I think a mother goes to the child who needs the most help."

"I think you're right, Mrs. Blackstone."

"Like God, too," Little Flower interjected quickly. "I know God is right here with Cheyenne."

Andrea put her arm across the mother's quivering back, "He surely is, Little Flower. He surely is."

The mother's dark eyes looked up from her daughter's face to the new painting on the wall. Little Flower gasped as she put her hand over her mouth.

"Do you like it, Mrs. Blackstone?"

"It's beautiful. Cheyenne will love it."

"I brought in some other things, too; I thought it would make it a little more homey in here."

"Cheyenne loves things like this," her mother commented, looking from the painting to the wind chimes to the statue.

"Little Flower, listen."

Andrea plugged in the bubbling water tape.

"Oh, my! You know?" Little Flower hesitated as her brow wrinkled, "sometimes I think Cheyenne wants to go back to her grandmother's era, which of course is really her great-great grandmother's era."

"What do you mean?" Andrea asked intently.

"The two of them would go way back into history, through stories of course, and then they would play-act those times constantly. Cheyenne and my mother would dress up in native costumes and live the whole day in fantasy. I'm not saying my mother didn't teach her some wonderful customs and ways of our people, but Cheyenne just became immersed in it. I think she got to the point where she couldn't accept today's world very well. Not that I'm condoning pollution, land devastation, or animal cruelty, but even I know that by going about it the right way, we can bring changes for the better. Many laws have been passed because people were concerned. I'm afraid Cheyenne isn't able to see the long-range picture. I don't know, maybe she just sees today. Or," Little Flower went on trying to piece the whole thing together, "maybe she doesn't see the positive things that are happening. My mother was very negative in that way, too." She ended, looking up at the picture of the girl seemingly accepting the world.

"Thank you for sharing that, Little Flower. It will be a tremendous help to me. Are you going to stay for awhile? I really need to see another patient of mine. There are new music tapes on the stand, help yourself."

Little Flower sat by the bedside holding the statue of the mother and child. *Where did I go wrong?* she thought, as she traced the folds of the mother's dress. She ran her finger over the tiny face of the child thinking of Cheyenne's baby features.

Cheyenne's eyes fluttered open. "What do you have, mother?"

"A beautiful statue. Look," Little Flower said nonchalantly as if it had been the day before the tragedy.

Then she realized what was happening as her daughter replied, "Oh, how nice."

The mother handed the statue to her daughter thinking, *Isn't it strange how I never delve into the past, and Cheyenne can't look into the future?*

"Well, hello!" Andrea entered with surprise and delight to hear the two women conversing. "Hello, Cheyenne, I'm Dr. Lingua. Andrea Lingua."

"Hello, doctor, this is my mother."

"Yes, we've met. I see you're examining the statue."

"It's beautiful—there's nothing like a mother and child, is there?"

"You're right, Cheyenne. There is nothing like it. Are you going to have children someday?" Andrea asked, knowing she was getting into this kind of analysis way too quickly, but she feared she might not have this opportunity later.

"Me?" Cheyenne laughed. "What would I do with a child?"

"You could teach him or her all about the beauties of the earth and how to protect those beautiful things. Like this girl in the picture," Andrea pointed. "She is ready to show someone the entire world, in all its splendor. Maybe she has a little girl or boy to show it to."

"Yeah, maybe," Cheyenne said sullenly as she turned her back to the doctor and faced the wall.

Andrea motioned for Little Flower to exit with her to the hallway.

"I'm sorry, Little Flower. Maybe I should not have said that."

"Don't be sorry. You sounded like a caring mother. Do you have children?"

"Yes, two. There used to be three."

"Oh, I'm sorry."

"Yeah, me, too. She took her own life one day."

Little Flower gasped, then she put her arms around the other mother.

"How are you today, Cheyenne?" Dr. Lingua asked as she went in for a chat. She placed a rolled print on the floor by her chair.

It was a month to the day of Cheyenne's entry into the hospital.

"Oh, I'm okay," Cheyenne replied as she sat at her little table finishing her lunch.

"Is that the 'Wind' tape you're listening to?"

"Yes. There's something about the wind that draws me to it, I guess," she said pensively as she focused her eyes on the painting.

"Who made the wind?" Andrea asked.

"Who made the wind?" Cheyenne reiterated.

"Yes."

"Well, I suppose God did."

"Yes, I suppose He did. And who made all of nature?"

"God."

"And who made you?"

"Well, this is getting a little annoying," Cheyenne said arrogantly as she threw her spoon into the soup bowl.

"I'm sorry. I didn't mean to annoy you."

There was a long silence until Cheyenne looked up sheepishly and said, "I'm sorry, too. God made me."

"Thank you. So, we pretty much have established the fact that God made everything in nature and that He made the people."

"Yeah."

"So when you demonstrate and rally for the good of the environment, you're doing it to preserve God's creation, right?"

"Yes, I guess I am." Cheyenne looked surprised at this revelation.

"Do you think it pleases God to see people like you making an all-out effort to save his property?"

"Why, yes. Yes! He must be very pleased with us," Cheyenne smiled.

Andrea wanted to stop and comment on the young woman's beautiful first smile, but she continued, "You're right, Cheyenne. God is pleased that people care about His creations. Now let me ask you this, do you think you have the right to destroy your own life?"

Cheyenne's smile dropped as she glared at the doctor. Andrea thought lightning bolts were going to come out of the girl's eyes and pierce her body.

"How dare you talk to me like that?" Cheyenne screamed. "Get out, get out of here!" The tray flew off the table and the hard plastic dishes clattered to the floor. Cheyenne ran to the "Wind" player and turned the knob to full volume. It was like a cyclone in the room, with Cheyenne whirling around and Andrea keeping out of her way. Two attendants ran in but Andrea motioned them to leave the room.

"Who do you think is going to save you from me?" Andrea shouted above the wind.

"The wolves. The wolves will save me," Cheyenne screamed as she jumped on top of the bed and crouched low by the wall.

Andrea grabbed her poster and pulled it open. "This is what the wolves have done to your eagle, and this is what they'll do to you! I'm here to help you! I won't hurt you!"

Cheyenne stared at the poster in horror, as Andrea used her elbow to turn off the tape. After a long silence, Andrea ripped the poster into pieces and brought the painting down from the wall to place in front of Cheyenne.

"This is you, Cheyenne. This is you accepting God's world as a place of beauty, and yes, a place worth saving." Andrea picked up the mother and child statue. "And this is why we want to save the earth—for the children and their children and their children. We need you Cheyenne. God needs you to tenderly help Him."

THE END

About the Author

Teresa Millias was born in Cooperstown, NY and lives in Worcester, NY. She attended the K-12 Central School in Worcester and graduated with eighteen others in her Senior Class.

Continuing her education, she received her degree in Elementary Education from SUNY at Oneonta, New York.

Teresa taught Kindergarten and First Grade at Worcester CS for twenty-five years developing the love of reading and writing.

She has always had a fondness for the arts and has delved into painting, piano education, creativity, garden sculpting, quilting, and writing.

She says rural life has a kindness and goodness with a touch of mystique which she tries to describe in her stories.

Teresa has three children and nine grandchildren.

CPSIA information can be obtained at www.ICGtesting.com
Printed in the USA
BVOW04s2024071016

464499BV00001B/2/P